THE DOCTOR FROM MADRAS

by
Chandru Murthi

Flexible Press
Minneapolis, Minnesota, 2025

Print ISBN: 979-8-9914928-0-5
eBook ISBN: 979-8-9914928-1-2

Flexible Press LLC
Minneapolis, Minnesota
www.flexiblepub.com
Editors William E Burleson
Vicki Adang, Mark My Words Editorial Services, LLC

What people are saying about *The Doctor From Madras*:

In this multi-generational saga, Chandru Murthi weaves together a patchwork quilt of stories involving agonizing family secrets, the birth pangs of a modern nation, and the emergence of a new diaspora into the 21st century. This is a stunningly well-crafted story, and a debut novel to celebrate!
—Raza Mir, author of *Murder at the Mushaira*

Suspenseful, loving, lyrical, historical, and often heartbreaking, this journey of discovery by a grown man yearning to know the secrets of his childhood in Madras is a page-turning odyssey. You need not ever have ventured to India to consume this. It is a delicious and revealing tour de force.
—Ken Carlton, Author of *Food for Marriage*

Emotionally resonant, richly detailed, and often gently humorous, The Doctor from Madras explores the tension between old and new, tradition and liberation, fate and ambition, duty and love. Filled with memorable characters and surprising twists, it's a compulsively-readable story that brings to life a significant chapter in India's complex history.
—Siobhan Adcock, author of *The Completionist* and *The Barter*

India

New Delhi / Delhi
Calcutta / Kolkata
Bombay / Mumbai
Venpuri
Madras / Chennai
Bangalore

The Characters

Venpuri:

The Janappans

Mohan—The patriarch

Jyothi—The matriarch

Narin—Their youngest son

Sheela—Their youngest daughter

The Vasans

Subbu—The father

Mina—Subbu's daughter, Narin's wife

Jaggie—Subbu's son

Sara & Saran—The twin cousins

San Francisco:

Vishram—Narin's son

Elena—Vishram's wife

Madras Medical College:

Laxman—Narin's close friend

Ambika—Laxman's partner

Neeta—Ambika's friend

Part I

Marriage can wait, education cannot.
—Khaled Hosseini

I

San Francisco, 2001

Late one midsummer evening, the multicolored Victorian houses along tree-lined Haight Street watched a blue Lancia convertible speeding along. The shreds of a shimmering purple-yellow twilight graced the western skies and reflected off the interior of the car. From within it, the voices of Vishram and Elena rose in an off-key rendition of the Beatles song—*Do you want to know a secret.* The song ended, and the singers dissolved in giggles. Elena brushed Vishram's ear with her lips and whispered, "Next stop, Carnegie Hall."

Vishram steered the car onto a narrow uphill street and parked at their house.

Elena stepped out and pulled her jacket tight around her. A cool, drippy evening had replaced dense morning cloud cover and afternoon warmth, tricking those unaccustomed to San Francisco's idiosyncratic weather patterns. She noticed two figures scurrying along the opposite pavement, smiled, and said, "You can always tell the tourists by their shorts and goose bumps."

They went upstairs, an inebriated Vishram skimming the stair railing as Elena kept a firm hand on his back.

"Wonderful dinner, wasn't it?" he said.

"Yeah, inspired, Vish. Let's hope Cocotte is there for a while. Restaurants in that location don't seem to last long. It's what, the third in seven years? Maybe they should call the next one The Graveyard."

"Guaranteed to bring in gawkers."

"Dead sure thing for hipsters."

They entered their apartment, and the babysitter, a symphony in black, raised her multi-studded head from her Game Boy and rose from the dark couch.

"Hey. All quiet. Neel went to sleep at eight-thirty, no fuss," she said.

"Oh, good, Erin. Thanks." Elena took out her wallet and paid the sitter, who collected her things and left with a wave and a cheery "Ciao," her steel-heeled clogs beating a staccato farewell down the wooden stairs.

Vishram peeked into Neel's bedroom. He'd run his son ragged around the house before leaving, playing one of Neel's self-designed games, and he was now sound asleep. Vishram's memory flashed to his own father, Narin. Had he ever gazed at him as fondly? Had Narin ever had the affectionate and boisterous manner toward him that he displayed toward Neel? He couldn't remember a time.

As Vishram and Elena entered their bedroom, they bumped into each other. The bottle of Châteauneuf-du-Pape '95, the cool night air, and memories of their meal worked their magic. The silence was unbroken as they turned toward each other. Holding one another close, they moved farther into the room. It had been too long. Quickly, facilely, they undressed each other and tumbled onto the bed, slid together in practiced rhythms, slowly at first, then increasing in speed and intensity until an exquisitely satisfying crescendo. They collapsed against each other, breast to breast, body to body, a totality of contact, a welcome exhaustion.

They were soon asleep.

THE TELEPHONE SHRILLED.

Vishram shook himself awake and glanced at the clock. Half past midnight.

"Hello. Hello? Vish, hello?" His cousin Carla's voice echoed, calling from Madras.

"Yes, hi. How are you, Carla?"

"Listen, I'm sorry to tell you. Your mother just died," she stated in her usual direct way. "Died." No preliminaries. Not "passed away" or some other euphemism.

"Dead? How?"

"In her sleep. It must have been peaceful."

"Oh."

He almost said, "Finally."

His mother had been hinting at her demise for the last ten years or more, so it didn't come as a surprise. No grief, no sorrow descended.

Memories of his childhood flooded in. It had been a lonely one, reinforced by his mother's attitude toward child-rearing. The fabric of love and regard was present, but threadbare. He tried to think of a time when she hugged him but could not. For that matter, could he remember a time she'd hugged his father, Narin? Did this make her a cold or unfeeling person, or just withholding? He re-examined his feelings as if they belonged to another. Did the painful memories of his stunted childhood suppress grief over his mother's death?

He found words. "How did it happen? Who found her?"

"When her maid came in this morning, your mother hadn't yet come down. She went upstairs to see why. She said she was quite sure your mother was still sleeping, as that's how she looked, and was terrified to find her dead. It's all been taken care of. Dr. Hansa rushed over and said it was quite natural. She just stopped breathing in her sleep." Pause. "I suppose you will not be coming right away?"

"Can't now, but will come soon," he muttered.

He was relieved. Funerals in India were held in short order, sometimes even on the same day, unless the law required an autopsy. He had no desire to hop on a plane to get to Madras twenty-three exhausting hours later, only to be an appendage as other more worldly men—but no women—took care of the cremation. As the only son, he would have been expected to light the funeral pyre. He hated the thought of being an active participant in that rite. He would go later to take care of the necessary business. Distance, in this case, lent comfort.

He extricated himself from the sheets and sat on the edge of the bed. He needed a strong drink. He heard an impatient click on the line. Carla.

"Do you need any help from me?" he asked, as if that were possible from thousands of miles away. Seemed the right thing to say.

"Don't worry about a thing."

Vishram felt sorry that his mother's maid, Bela, had suffered the shock of her death. She'd been with his mother for decades, and over the years they'd settled into a relationship more companionable than master-servant. It had been tenuous, though. His mother's cantankerousness could show itself in unexpected flashes of temper. Bela would ignore it with a double shake of her head, no doubt knowing the real balance of power lay in her hands—more so as his mother had gotten older and needed more care.

"The house," Vishram said. "Would you handle the rent and utility payments? I wouldn't want to get back to no water or electricity. And please pay Bela, too." Then remembering how little she got—his mother being generous to her in many ways except her salary—"Oh, would you double her pay for now until I get there?"

"Double? She doesn't need that."

"Mother paid her way too little. You know how I used to fight with her, trying to get her to raise her pay. Just do it. As a favor to me."

"Okay, if you think that's right."

"Thank you very much. And how are you? How are the kids … daughters?"

"Well, getting along. The usual. Both doing well. One married, the other to go. And you? How are Elena and the baby?"

"Baby no more, he's six now. In first gra— … ah … standard at a nearby school. Elena is painting away and does some awesome but gloomy things. All these heads glaring down at us around the house." Elena kicked him under the blankets. "She's been in several shows, and I hope she gets to sell some soon." Pause. To Carla's silence, he said, "Thanks again."

They said their goodbyes.

Elena got up and hugged him tightly. "Oh, Vish. I'm so sorry. How do you feel?"

"Empty. Shouldn't I feel something?"

"You've always had mixed feelings about her. It's time you remember the good things."

Elena looked stricken, her eyes gleaming with tears. She had met his mother twice, and they'd become close, writing to each other more frequently than he did. Vishram resented her ability to feel the grief he could not. He walked over to the bar and poured himself a double scotch, waving the bottle at Elena, who shook her head.

"What are you going to do with her house?"

"I'll have to settle her things, finance and all that. Soon. Want to come with me to India next month? Neel would love it."

"No, he wouldn't. It'll be hot and miserable and so will you."

"Misery loves company."

"Please. Besides, I don't think I'll be of any use to you. From what you've told me of the system, it's going to be a nightmare.

You can deal with it. You know your way around, and Carla will help."

"Me? I don't even speak Tamil, or not very well, anyway. I have no idea what I need to deal with the bank and other places. This is India. It's impossible to get information or do stuff on the phone. And bureaucracy and paperwork everywhere. I don't know if my mother left a will. I'll have to bribe everyone, and I've never done that."

"You must have some other relatives or friends you can call on."

Vishram struggled to think of friends he knew who might make his visit more pleasant, but none came to mind except Carla. "Not many. My mother discouraged me from having friends over or going to visit others." His face tightened, and he closed his eyes. "You know, I never asked why? I once invited this kid over, his name was Trevor—yes, a Christian, they were called Anglo-Indians. I'd gotten to know him pretty well. He hated sports, like me, so we didn't fit in with the others.

"My mother wasn't happy about Trevor—he wasn't 'one of us,' you see, he came from a lower-class background, she said. She told me I wasn't to visit his house, as if it were infected or something. He never came over again, I don't think. So, much of my free time, I hung out with her at home, reading, playing cards, or solving puzzles. God, going away to Anna Architecture School was a gush of relief—new friends, not being watched, alone to think."

He gulped down the drink and poured another. He fixed his look on Elena. "Come with me. Maybe a smile from a sexy American woman would work better than money."

"Fat chance." But she smiled nonetheless.

Vishram's mother had met his son, Neel, only once, as a baby, and they did not bond. She was a little unnerved by his preverbal intensity, and he was put off by her lack of maternal warmth.

Vishram thought she would have liked him better now that Neel was assertive and opinionated.

Last year, when he was almost six, Neel had announced to his parents that he was a pessimist. This bothered Elena. Vishram's reaction was that's him "talking adult," not knowing what being a pessimist meant. Hers was that Vishram was responsible and he should stop indoctrinating Neel.

"I don't want him to be like your mother," she'd said.

"Meaning?"

"You know I love—sorry—loved your mother. But she's so negative. She's had a good life, nice stable family and helpful friends around her. I never met your father, but you say he was an accomplished and honest man, and he earned a good living. She's traveled the world—"

"She had me."

"Well, yes … she's done well, wouldn't you say? And yet so negative. Talks a lot about dying. You have that in you, too, and I sure don't want Neel to be that way."

"When's the last time I talked about dying?"

"You're being deliberately obtuse. I meant being negative."

"Maybe she was unfulfilled."

"How?"

"Oh, I don't know. Something about not doing as well as she could or should."

"We all feel that way."

"Not everyone. Not Bush. Look at him. *He's* doing much better than he could, should, whatever. Third-rate scholar. Ran that oil company into the ground. Mediocre governor. And you guys elected him president. Father, then son, too."

"'We' elected him," Elena said, quotes hanging in the air.

"Huh?"

"Not 'you guys.' You're an American now, too, you know."

"Not by choice though. And I didn't vote for him."

"Neither did I. And you had more choice than I had. I was born here. You chose to live here and become a citizen."

"Yes, you always love the good ol' U.S. of A."

"See what I mean? You talk to Neel like this all the time. No wonder he's bleak and a pessimist."

"It's not all bad, being a pessimist. Gives you something to look forward to."

"What are you talking about?"

"You know, there's always another half-full glass hidden away somewhere."

"Stop being asinine."

Now, Vishram wondered why she wouldn't want to visit India with him.

They—or at least she—had been through hell with Neel's pregnancy. She had always wanted a second child but couldn't have another. For a while they had talked about adoption, maybe from India, as his connections there would smooth the way for a couple over the age of forty. They had never acted on it. The daunting process of adoption soon overwhelmed his sputtering desire, and he'd changed his mind, but Elena stayed firm. He'd balked for three years and didn't see any reason to change his decision now.

As if she'd read his mind, Elena said, "And when you go to India, it would be a good opportunity to talk to your cousin about—"

"Not that again. I thought we'd settled it."

"No, we have not. You *have* to contact the agency, Vish."

"No. They might want to meet the mother," he said.

"This would be a preliminary meeting. We can go over later."

"Neel doesn't want a sibling."

Elena made an exasperated face. "That is the most ridiculous argument you've ever made. Besides, I am not running my life on a six-year-old's wish, even if he understood what he was talking about."

"And we can't afford it."

"Are you nuts? It's not *Cheaper by the Dozen* territory. We have more than enough to support two children."

"And didn't you say you weren't sure if you could take care of a second child? You wanted to devote more time to your painting?"

"That was years ago. I've had a studio now for—what?—three, almost four years, and I'm fine with the time constraints." Her eyes narrowed. "You just want Neel to duplicate your only-child upbringing. What's that you said … misery loves company?"

Vishram raised his hands to ward off more. "*Please.* Can we talk about this later? I can't deal with it right now." He gulped the rest of the scotch and reached for the bottle.

"*Don't.* You've had enough."

His hand stopped mid-grasp.

Elena's expression changed as she noticed his distress. She dropped her voice, "Oh, Vish, I'm so sorry … I got carried away. Of course we should wait until later." She came to him and held him close.

He lost himself in her silky auburn hair. Not quite the ending he would have wanted. Discretion being the better part of valor and all that, he said nothing as she comforted him. But he knew she would not forget the issue.

II
Venpuri, in the Province of
Madras, India, 1936

Two ladies of a "certain age" stepped with trepidation over the puddles that threatened their otherwise stately passage. The monsoon had inundated their village of Venpuri and reduced the roadway to a vestigial blacktop in the middle of the right-of-way. The rains had ceased two days before, bringing the welcome respite of sunny, clear days and an ephemeral clean smell, soon to be replaced by the ever-present stink of mud, decay, and rubbish.

The euphoniously named twins Saraswathi and Saranmathi, informally Sara and Saran, moved like battleships among lesser vessels, thrusting through a throng of people who shuffled slower and yet with the same deliberation. This steady minuet ensured never a collision, bodies sidling from each other's paths, punctuated by the numerous cattle-pulled carts, cycle rickshaws, the occasional truck or, surprise, a private car.

Sara and Saran, née Vasan, had married the brothers Janappan on the same day many years ago. Comfortably married, comfortably vested with several children each, comfortably dressed in their flowing colored silk saris, they were a well-known sight as they traveled together through their village. Today they were on their weekly twenty-minute walk to the home of their cousin, Mohankumar Janappan. Mohan was younger than they were by more than a decade, and this advantage of age allowed the sisters to exert a considerable influence over many details of his life.

"Almost there," said Sara, now sweating in the full sun.

"Maybe we should've taken a rickshaw," Saran offered.

"Rickshaw? Saran, that's a waste of money."

"We can afford it. I'm hot, and so are you."

"Mohan will have some cold lemonade."

As they negotiated the last of many puddles, Mohan's house came into view, a two-storied structure typical of the middle-class houses in the village. Once whitewashed with a lime-based finish, it was now a nondescript muddy brown with streaks of indeterminate color. Cracks small and large festooned its façade, and the bars on its many windows were rusting inexorably into non-existence. Nevertheless, its brick-and-concrete construction exuded an air of permanence in contrast with the many thatched huts of the poor.

A gap-toothed wall, decrepit and of little use from a security standpoint, marked the perimeter of Mohan's small plot of land, much of it now a muddy swamp in the aftermath of the recent downpours. The few brave plantings that survived no longer resembled a garden. On one side of the front yard, a large banyan tree with its magnificent exposed roots towered over the house and provided welcome shade.

Sara and Saran had neither the time nor the inclination to examine the remnant greens, and they made their steady way to the front door, which stood open, as was the custom outside the cities. One could look straight through the house through this welcoming aperture to the similarly open back door. This transparency was the mark of good design, and the rumored harbinger of good luck. Lesser houses had only the one front opening and were lucky to have a usable door at all.

Mohan's resident servant, Mari, a dark-complexioned woman with a face lined beyond her early-thirties age, appeared just as the sisters reached the threshold, drawn by that mysterious instinct of good servants to fulfill their many obligations without being called. She waved the sisters in with a sideways tilt of her head, a gesture they did not acknowledge. Their welcome assured, they sailed past the tiny front room—part hall, part office—into the larger room on its left and sank onto a protesting sofa.

"Where is cousin Janappan?" Saraswathi, or maybe it was Saranmathi, barked at the servant, who made a vague gesture of acquiescence and walked away. She returned a moment later and muttered something that could have meant the master of the house was on his way, thereby satisfying the sisters.

Mohan soon appeared, a man in his early fifties with a slight stoop, which made him seem shorter than his medium height. The shock of streaked gray hair covering his head contrasted with his still-black mustache. He pushed up the center of his straying eyeglasses as he greeted his cousins with a slight smile on his calm face.

"Can't you see my elder cousins are here?" he shouted at the servant behind him. "Get some lemonade and snacks."

NARINDER JANAPPAN—NARIN—was walking back to his father's house from Venpuri college when he noticed the sisters on their way there. This was not unusual, as their visits were frequent, regular, and longish. But he always reacted with a slight start, as if it might reduce their visits if he were surprised to see them. Not that he had anything against the redoubtable pair, but in their presence the conversation always circled around the subject uppermost on their minds—him. Or more accurately, his impending departure to the wilds of Madras.

Narin's father, Mohan, was an engineer, and like all men of his generation, he preferred to steer his son toward his own profession. Two years before, he had made his son apply to the Madras College of Science and Engineering, but Narin had been denied admission despite his acceptable academic status. Devastated that his second son would not be an engineer like his first, Mohan had a heartfelt talk with Narin. They were members of the top Hindu caste, Mohan emphasized.

"Middle-class Brahmins like us, you know," he said, "must become engineers, doctors, or lawyers. I suggest you join our local college for a B.A. while you think about what to do next. You should think about applying to medical college."

His father's pushing him toward a medical degree was a serendipitous fit with Narin's own desires, but a thought occurred, and he asked, "Is the rumor true that the engineering college entrance board is controlled by non-Brahmins, so we don't stand a chance there anymore?"

His father had made a noncommittal reply.

Brahmins had more or less been in charge since the British formed a natural alliance with this elite and educated group. The stratifications of the Indian caste system meshed well with the British concept of class. The situation had changed in the last few years as other castes jockeyed for power and extracted paybacks. Non-Brahmins on the Madras Engineering College entrance board now had total authority over the selection of entrants, with no means of appeal.

To his surprise, Narin obtained admission two years later to Madras Medical College.

Narin knew that the prestigious college was the oldest medical institution in India, and it had originated as a hospital in the mid-1600s, soon to become a training institution for British medical personnel. The British administration formalized it as a college in 1850. They considered it important to train the "natives" in Western medicine and began admitting Indian students. Most Indian women were not allowed to see a male physician, so the college started admitting female students to improve women's access to health care. English women first attended in 1878. With time, progressive Indian families sent their daughters to study at MMC, and the first Indian woman doctor graduated in 1912.

Narin's elder brother, Gopal, had studied at the engineering college in Madras that Narin had applied to, and he hoped his brother's relocation would smooth the way for his own move. No such luck. The family had the same discussions as eight years before: the dangers of sending a son—no, a child—all alone to that vast metropolis, the temptations that would befall him. He never heard specifics, even though the conversations were conducted in the presence of the "children," who, in typical Indian fashion, were seen, but assumed to be unable to hear.

So his irritation at seeing the sisters hove into view as he neared home had a hopeful counterpoint—maybe this time they would mention a danger lurking in the distant city. He avoided the pair by ducking behind the roots of the banyan tree and leaning against its scabrous bark, savoring the pungent smell. After a few moments, he dodged around the crumbling walls to the back of the house.

Sheela, the youngest of his three sisters, was on a makeshift swing set up for the younger members of the family. It was tied to two convenient *neem* trees flaunting sporadic flowers whose honey fragrance permeated far around them. The tall trees dipped in polite nods to each other with each arc of the swing.

"Hey, Narin," Sheela called out in her lilting, cheery voice. Her pretty oval face and large eyes were framed by a mass of cascading raven hair not quite tamed by oil grooming. Her light brown complexion contrasted with Narin's darker skin, but they shared much in common, wide-set eyes and an almost-too-prominent nose.

"Hello, Sheel, good to see you working hard."

Her eyes crinkled. "Better than you, slaving away at a desk all day. I'm free to do what I want."

"Right." Buoyed by her smile, he skipped closer to her and said in a lower voice, "You know, you'd better behave. The Aunties S are here."

Sheela clapped her forehead in comic dismay, stopped the swing, jumped off with a mouthed "thanks," and darted into the house on her way to a more girl-appropriate activity such as mending her sari. She was eighteen years old, and by all rights, should have been married, as most girls in Venpuri were by that age. Married girls—or those who should have been married by now—did not engage in frivolous pastimes like the swing. Had their aunts seen her, it would have meant many minutes of berating. In addition, their father would have been harangued for not bringing up his youngest daughter properly.

Narin took over the swing and strained his muscles as he pushed off. He emptied his mind of all that was ahead: Madras, the college, the nose-to-the-grindstone studies he'd heard were required, the unknown status of friends, the distance from his beloved Sheela, and the comfortable habits of the only place he'd ever known. To swing as high as possible, all the way to a true horizontal, was his goal, though he knew the laws of physics made that impossible. Still, he felt a step away from flying. He was free.

Not for long, though. Mari came out the back door a few minutes later and looked up at him without saying a word, but her expression was eloquent enough. He stared far into the distance and took his time slowing down in smaller and smaller arcs, doing nothing to brake the swing, until the servant's patience was exhausted and she broke her silence.

"They want you inside. Sister-Aunties are waiting to talk to you."

A patent exaggeration. Narin was never included in the conversation, but Sister-Aunties would have noticed his absence and commented on it, and that made the servant shiver.

WELL BEFORE HE entered the living room, Narin heard Aunt Saraswathi say, "You will be getting him married off before he goes, I'm sure." Or maybe it was Saranmathi.

"Of course you will," her sister concurred.

Nobody acknowledged his entry, and his father, who seemed to be unfazed by the statement, nodded in acquiescence. This was the first Narin had heard of his impending marriage, even though Aunt Saranmathi, or maybe it was Saraswathi, spoke in a tone suggesting it was a fait accompli, so they must have already discussed it in detail. When? He'd been present, willy-nilly, for most of the conversations that took place between the sisters and his parents.

Narin's feelings changed from an initial thrill regarding the mystery to concern as he absorbed the enormity of the issue. The word he associated with marriage was "settled," and he thought himself too young to be so. Could he be settled before going through the trials of unsettlement? What had his friend Sivan said when he had brought up the topic of experimentation and exploring the unknown? "Why are you worrying your head about such things, Narin? *Chalta-hai*—life goes on. Don't tempt fate." Other friends had been equally dismissive when he tried to discuss their futures. He felt differently.

He refocused when his father made a sound—what?—not an unequivocal yes, but not a no, either. This meant the issue was unresolved, regardless of the sisters' certainty. Interesting. Sure enough, the sisters called in reinforcements.

"And what has *she* said about this since last week?"

That "she" was, of course, Narin's mother, Jyothi. Names were little used in conversation when referring to those younger than the speaker.

His father's eyes were distant, and his face wore a small smile, a state he often assumed when faced with his formidable cousins. He waved his hands around disarmingly. "We talked about it a bit since last week, and she agrees it may be a good idea."

A good idea? Narin didn't think it unusual that his mother would agree with the sisters and his father, she not being one to rock the boat. What surprised him was that she had not found a way to inform him of such an important matter.

"Good," said the sisters. They tended to step on each other's words and even speak in lockstep when they got their way. "And have we settled on the girl? Do we agree about Mina?" The smile Aunt Sara flashed at Narin did not extend to her eyes and reassured him not at all.

Shock. This was real. The mention of Mina, a nickname for Minalakshmi, brought a real person, a real girl, into focus. Until now, he'd been following the conversation as if removed from its intimate connection to himself, like an interesting, but not compelling, snippet of news about a mutual acquaintance.

Mina was a distant cousin of some sort. Families tended to use the word "cousin" for relations of similar age, regardless of intervening marriages and generations, just as "auntie" or "uncle" were used when referring to anyone significantly older. Mina lived an inconvenient distance from his home—farther than a thirty-minute walk—so the families didn't meet often. He'd see her only at festivals, birthdays, and marriages. Now she was just under thirteen years old to his nineteen-and-a-half. Boys and girls were discouraged from socializing after about the age of ten, so he knew little of her personality or interests. He did know that she had been out of school for a while. Once her parents considered her close to marriageable age, they saw no need for further formal education. Narin doubted she read much. He recalled her face, pretty but vacant. Did she have the burning curiosity about the world he'd had at her age?

Two of his sisters had been married by the age of seventeen, and the continued single status of his younger sister was beginning to cause a host of head shaking among the clan and the village. What were their parents thinking? But many believed Sheela had a stubborn streak, and while the rumor far outweighed the reality, it was enough to make conservative parents wary. She had not yet received any marriage offers, and as far as their mother, Jyothi, was concerned, that was fine. She preferred to have her youngest child at home with her as long as possible. For boys, the age of marriage tended to vary more, though being married at twenty was common among those who did not continue to college. His brother, eight years older, had only recently married, so Narin didn't think he would be next in line for a while. Certainly, Sheela should marry before him.

Perhaps those conversations about the temptations of the big, bad city made a little more sense. The change in his marital status would ward off those demon girl students at Madras Medical College.

Casting aside the image of Mina, Narin pondered the situation. What did it mean to be married before he went away to college? He was sure there were no facilities for married students. In any event, Mina was well under the age when man and wife stayed together. At thirteen, she was still far from her *ritu kala* ceremony celebrating her entry to womanhood. While her parents might entertain a proposal, she would remain at home after the wedding.

Sheela's ceremony had been celebrated a little more than two years earlier. She'd been kept in seclusion for days before the *ritu kala*, which had been conducted, unusually, by a female cast and followed by the typical boisterous celebration with much food and many guests. In addition to marking a girl's readiness for marriage, the ceremony was supposed to urge her toward a higher level of spirituality. Narin associated such an enlightenment with the older and duller members of his acquaintance, so to his relief, it had not taken root in his sister, who'd retained her vivacious and rebellious nature.

He settled on the bench under the window shaded by the soaring banyan tree, the coolest seat in the sun-flooded living room. As he did so, his mother, Jyothi, who had been away on an errand, came in and greeted her cousins with a quiet nod. The sisters nodded in return and adjusted their bodies away from Jyothi as she sat next to them, an unspoken disapproval that she had not been there to receive them when they arrived. Narin expected his mother's usual welcoming smile but got only a brief glance and an unreadable expression. Conversation ceased as the servant brought in and distributed the drinks, savory fried *vadais*, chutney, and sweets.

Narin was not offered any.

III
Venpuri, 1936

Within two weeks or so—too short a time in Narin's view—the marriage proposal reached its expected culmination. His aunts encouraged his parents to formally approach Mina's parents, so they sent advance word of their visit—a social call did not require such notice. They took a rickshaw, wearing their wedding best, his mother in a bright green silk sari with lavish gold trim and his father sporting a suit. Narin's mother later told him Mina's parents had happily received and accepted the proposal.

Under the deadline of Narin's impending departure, the elaborate arrangements of the wedding had to be completed in short order. The next step was to consult an astrologer to ensure the couple's horoscopes were compatible. Narin himself disdained astrology, as his rational side deemed it so much hocus-pocus. The random movement of stars and planets millions of miles away could not determine the future. He listened to his aunts discuss the subject with his parents one evening and wondered how much of a formality the astrological matching process was. Clearly it was in the best interests of all parties for the marriage to go forward.

As if she'd heard Narin's thoughts, Jyothi said, "Is Mina's horoscope problem of the seventh house settled? The *Mangalya Bhava* showed a short length of marriage, no?"

The twins turned on her as attack dogs on a lamb.

"Rubbish. The planets won't give us any guff," Aunt Saranmathi snapped.

"Of course not," Saraswathi barked.

Narin felt a pang of pity for the recalcitrant astrologer who might give them unwelcome news. Could astrologers be bribed?

However, all went well, and Minalakshmi Vasan of Chettapur was told she was to marry Narinder Janappan of Venpuri, her third cousin once removed.

A few days later, Narin was present when his twin aunts arrived in a gushing mood.

"So," said Saran, a smile lighting up her face as she greeted his parents who were at the door to receive them, "everything is settled?"

"Yes," his father replied.

"How about the dowry? Did you get what we talked about?"

"You know, they are not that well-off and——"

"So, they did not agree?" Sara asked. "What did they not agree to?"

The bride's side bore the major cost of the wedding and paid the dowry, which was a common sticking point in marriage arrangements. Mohan was a senior engineer for the county government, and his status, coupled with his son's as a would-be doctor, would have raised Narin's dowry potential considerably. But as his father was not traditional and had a comfortable income, Narin hadn't expected him to be contentious about the dowry. No doubt, the Sara-Saran combo were pushing this. In families like theirs, it would be a matter of expensive clothes for the bride and other female family members, perhaps household effects, and a cash gift "to allow the couple to be settled."

Narin was not interested in details. He had little access to money except for the small sums he would ask his mother for occasionally. Apart from his cherished books, he had no notion of what it meant to have his own possessions. So he tuned out and watched a gray-brown gecko on the wall with its bulgy eyes glued on a tasty fly. He bet himself the number of seconds it would take before it pounced. He lost.

He paid attention when the usual argument between his parents and the S&S duo subsided. With an air of finality, his father said, "I think it's all fine."

A moment's silence while the sisters weighed the pushback.

"Okay, if you say so, though we think you should've stayed strong. It's not good to start the marriage off by backing down like that," Sara said, then turned to Jyothi. "And you'll have to be firm with Mina as well."

His mother nodded. "Yes, don't worry. You know Mina's a very nice girl."

"Nice." Of course, nothing better to say? Damning with faint praise. And what was with the "be firm?" Would the reprieve from the full dowry embolden the girl to do something she shouldn't?

More such discussion followed.

Soon Narin was informed that the marriage date was set for July 25, just weeks before he had to pack his bags to move to Madras. Never during this process had anyone asked him what he wanted to do, what he felt about marrying Mina. What would this mean to him? Would he be happy? Could he live with her? He was unused to examining his own desires, let alone acting on them. To be fair, this was the first time anything so important had come up, and seeing no way to influence the matter, he decided to let it wash over him without leaving a mark.

NARIN TRUDGED HOME on the last day of college, a week after he first learned of his marriage. Instead of contemplating the happy release of summer, he obsessed over the coming event. By the time he reached home, a cloying loneliness had settled on him, and he wandered toward the backyard in a foul mood. He did not want to be married. The more he fixated on this Mina person, the greater his aversion to her grew. He tried to remember the few times he'd seen her and the fewer times they'd exchanged anything but cursory greetings. What was she like, anyway? What were *girls* like? He thought of those he knew best: his mother and sisters. His much older sisters were more like his mother. Quiet overall, not assertive and dogmatic like many of the men he knew. Which made him reflect how unfortunate it was that his father was not more assertive with the Aunties S.

Entering the backyard, his irritation increased on seeing Sheela on the swing.

"Can you get off?"

"Hello to you, too, Narin. Glad to be finished with college?"

"No."

"I wish *I* had continued at school, you know. Maybe I could've gone to college."

"Get off the swing. I want it."

Sheela frowned and opened her mouth as if to say something but did not. She seemed puzzled by his unaccustomed rudeness. She slowed the swing to get off. "What's the matter? Something happen at college? Your marks okay? Exams?"

"My marks are fine, thanks," he said, shutting out the drumbeat of parental reminders that he could do better.

"Well?"

Why was she pretending everything should be all right with him? A momentous event in his life was nearing, one that he had no desire to participate in, and she's asking about his stupid college? And his exam results? Why had they not talked about this before? Since the marriage had been settled, he'd been in such a fog of irritation that he hadn't even taken the time to chat much with his favorite sister. He stared hard at her, and quite without warning, Mina's face superimposed itself on Sheela's. She was there, on Sheela's swing, with that calm, simplistic expression of hers. How could Mina sit there and look at—no, through—him like that? Did she have none of the doubts he had? Did she not wonder who he was, as he wondered about her?

"I can't stand it," he shouted at her and jerked his head around, expecting a reprimand from the house. Mina morphed back into Sheela.

"Narin, what is it?" Sheela said, her brows furrowed with concern.

"You know. I'm being married off."

Sheela's eyes opened wide. "Married? Why? Why now? To whom? When?"

Narin returned her stare as he took in what she'd said. She *didn't know*. So she was not the unfeeling, unconcerned sister. She had been oblivious to his moodiness the last week.

"Because I'm going to college in Madras. It's too far away. It's too dangerous. No, too tempting. Don't know what exactly. It's what our Aunties S want. They are always the ones pushing it. Don't they always get what they want? To Mina in four weeks. July 25. Before I go, of course."

"Mina? What Mina? You mean Minalakshmi from Chettapur?"

"Yes. How many Minas do we know?"

"Oh, Narin … but … she's fair. And she's nice, isn't she? Nice family. We've known them a long time."

"Nice? *That's* all you have to say about this? And you didn't know about it? You said nothing all this time? Are you lying?"

"But I didn't, Narin, I really didn't. How long has this been going on? Why did no one tell me? Why didn't you?"

Sheela was on the verge of tears.

Yes, why hadn't he told her, his only confidante, weeks ago? He forced himself to see Sheela as the friend she'd always been, a friend who happened to be a girl. She was different. The unmarried-at-eighteen oddity. She could help him unravel the secrets of girlhood. And why hadn't she heard of it? Perhaps the family thought she might be offended or slighted if she knew her last sibling was to be married while she was still single? That meant they didn't know her well. She often said being unmarried was the best part of her prosaic life. No responsibilities. No dealing with the inevitable demands of a mother-in-law and other in-laws. Staying in the house she loved, where she'd been born and grown up. Being playful. Being able to use the swing.

In a softer voice, he said, "I don't know why you haven't been told. I thought you knew why I'm like this. Sorry. You probably keep away from the gossip as well, no?"

"Yes." Sheela still looked stricken.

He felt a surge of sympathy and protectiveness toward her. How could he have been so nasty? "I'll tell you all about it. This was after I got into medical college, that's when *they*," he waved his right hand toward the house as Sheela nodded, "decided it had to be done before I went to Madras."

"When did you know they settled on Mina? Did they ask you?"

"All of it happened in such a rush, I can't quite remember, and no, they didn't ask me. I learned of it only after the decision, though Amma did ask me later how I felt about marrying Mina. I just went along and said 'fine.' Don't think I had a choice by then, though."

"No."

"What do you think of this, Sheel?"

"I … I don't know what to say."

"I don't either. Maybe there's nothing to say."

He hadn't known Sheela to be so reticent. Her face was not easy to read, but she was frowning, looking disappointed, as if she'd expected him to stand up for himself. Was he projecting his ambivalence about his passive behavior onto her? In all the time they spent together, nothing this important had ever occurred.

What did they talk about, anyway? Simple things. Food. Friends. School, until Sheela left, but she often asked him for details of his experience, sometimes expressing her regret at not being there. They never spoke of serious matters like politics. Or shared their emotions.

They sat a while in contemplative peace.

"Narin, this could be for the best, after all. You know how everybody is going on and on about me not being married off. I sometimes wish I were. But then I think how much more I can do because I'm not, and I'm glad. But it's different for you. You have medical college to go to, you'll be a doctor, you'll have to work hard after that. Being married is normal."

She paused to look into the distance, swinging her legs to keep moving in short arcs. "Do you know, I think about a job sometimes, and wonder what it would be like to be a boy and study and work and be able to wander free. Auntie Kala in Madras has a job. Sometimes I can't believe it—a woman from our family going out to work? Maybe things are changing. Maybe if I don't get married after all, I'll join you in Madras and work. Wouldn't that be fun?"

Could work be fun? He'd never thought of it that way. Their father and his male friends never discussed their work in his presence, so he had nothing to go on. Sheela working in Madras was a happy idea, but he had no way of judging how probable it was. Sheela must have given this more consideration than he was aware. Where was she getting her insights? She hadn't been in the habit of reading much, but for a year or so now, he'd suggested books for her to read. He smiled as he took credit for her knowledge.

"Sheel, I never considered that. Of course it would be wonderful if you could work." A different thought arose. "Do you know, Madras Medical College has lots of girls ... one-fifth of the students, I hear."

"No. Oh. Is that why they're marrying you off? Because there are girls in your class?"

"I suppose."

"Oh."

They settled into quiet again. Sheela swung higher. Narin reflected on Mina and marriage but pushed it aside. For now, Madras was the reality and the excitement. Being at a challenging college in a real city instead of this provincial village. New people to meet from distant parts of India with fresh perspectives and attitudes. The goal of becoming a doctor came into sharp focus. He looked forward to helping people after his graduation, writing for journals, making a mark in medical circles.

The outer world, seemingly fallen silent when he first saw Sheela, came roaring back. Carts on the side road rattled and creaked as they passed. The raucous complaints of crows filled the air. The clink of pots and pans and the sharp voices of Mari and the cook floated by from the kitchen a few dozen feet away.

Narin's angst quieted. He looked at Sheela. They would carry on.

IV
Venpuri & Madras, 1936

"There it is at last," Narin said as he sighted the approaching train, which was late as usual.

Six weeks after the conversation with Sheela that had cleared the air between them, and two weeks after his wedding, he stood on the Venpuri Station platform. His parents, three sisters, brother, and assorted in-laws and cousins had come to see him off, not to mention the Aunts Saraswathi and Saranmathi. The twins' portly husbands were standing apart from the rest, ignoring the hubbub of conversation in their customary Tweedledum-Tweedledee complacency.

Mina was not present.

"Good luck, son. You must study hard, you understand?" his mother said.

"Of course he will," the Aunties S said in unison.

"You must write at least once a month," his mother said.

"At least twice a month to me, no?" Sheela whispered, not quite low enough.

"He won't have any time to write to you with his studies," one of the twins said.

"Of course not. So don't let your silly letters distract him from what's important," said the other.

"Of course, Sheel. I'll do that," Narin said in a low voice. He didn't care about defying the aunties now that he'd be far from their weekly scrutiny.

"Remember what I told you about food," his mother said.

She had given him a list of foods to find, convinced he would suffer without the comfort of home ingredients. He had pointed out that he'd have no choice of food at the hostel, and he'd have no facilities to cook for himself.

His brother Gopal winked at him and mouthed, "Eight years ago," referring to the identical instructions he'd received when he left for Madras. "You can just toddle over and raid Moore Market every day." He struggled to suppress a smile.

"Yes," Narin said to his mother, ignoring Gopal.

"And be sure to make good friends. I'm sure you'll meet many Brahmin boys there. Brahmin boys are always nice."

That word "nice" again. "Okay."

"Jaggie will be looking after you as well," one of the Aunties S said. "Remember, he has promised to come to see you often."

Narin had met Mina's elder brother Jaggie, his new brother-in-law, at his wedding. Jaggie was in his late twenties and worked in Madras as a junior lawyer in a major law office. Narin had disliked him at first sight, as he'd inherited the unfortunate officious manners of his distant relatives Saraswathi and Saranmathi. An old man in a youngster's clothing.

"I'm sure he's much too busy to worry about me," Narin said.

"What are you talking about? Busy? His young brother-in-law? When he is only twenty minutes away? Of course he will come over. He promised, and so did your *Mamanaar*, Subbu, when he visits Jaggie also."

That was Mina's father, his father-in-law, Subramaniam. He wondered if the whole damn family planned to camp out at his college.

"And don't worry about anything," Saraswathi continued. "We will give you plenty of notice of *that event*."

Oh yes, another thing to look forward to. Or not. Mina's *ritu kala* ceremony, which remained a delicate topic, though mentionable now that Narin was her husband. How would his life change besides consummating his marriage to Mina? Oh well, plenty of time before it happened.

The approaching train drowned out their conversation and came to a stop with a self-satisfied thunk of heavy machinery put to rest, the locomotive enveloped in surreal clouds of steam belching from its various orifices. The crowd pushed closer. Gopal had grabbed the smaller of Narin's trunks and placed himself at the door of the closest compartment, waiting as it disgorged its passengers. Narin had never been on a train, so he watched with interest as his brother, familiar with the routine, rushed to jump in and save a seat.

Narin recalled Gopal saying, "Lucky Venpuri is a somewhat major railway junction where many people get off, so it's much easier to get a seat here than at other stations."

He turned to give his mother a hug. Sheela gave him a warm and extended one and teared up, earning a passing stern look from the Aunties S. He extended his hands to his father, the man who was responsible for what he had come to realize was his flight to freedom. Would his father miss him? He held his father's hands for a few moments, stammering, "Thank you for everything, Appa. I will do my best."

"Yes, of course you will. Your amma and I are wishing you all success. God bless you."

He gave a general *namaskaar* greeting and waved goodbyes to his friends.

"Got everything?" someone shouted as he turned away.

"Yes."

The locomotive geared up for departure. Everyone began shouting to compete with the increasing noise. As Narin climbed into the compartment, someone handed him his other luggage box and a *tiffin carrier* stuffed with food. He found room to jam his trunk on the saggy overhead luggage rack, took the seat Gopal had been saving for him, and shook his hand.

As Gopal left, he said, "You'll have a good time. Madras is enjoyable. Take a tram to nowhere. Go see some pictures before classes start; there are more theaters now than when I was there. Good luck."

The engine shrieked its whistle, let out another huge belch of steam, and drowned all conversation with a staccato chuffing as it started its journey to Madras.

"GOING TO COLLEGE, are you?" barked the older man seated opposite Narin. The man's face was round, and his intent eyes were shadowed by bushy brows. Startled out of his trance watching the countryside roll by, Narin tried to keep from squirming under that penetrating scrutiny. He was not surprised at the interruption. Train journeys were long and boring and brought out the best, or worst, of people's innate chattiness.

"Yes, Madras Medical College."

"Oh, MMC. Very good place. You will be a good doctor."

"Thank you." Good to have a vote of confidence.

"And you're from Venpuri? What is your father doing?"

"He's a senior engineer with the Venpuri Public Works Department."

"And he makes you want to be a doctor? How very strange." The eyebrows shot up, and he clucked his tongue several times in disbelief at the state the world was coming to.

Narin gritted his teeth. The man merely glanced at personal boundaries as he overstepped them.

"Yes, my older brother is also an engineer. So he thought I should do something different. And you, sir? Are you also going to Madras? On work?" A daring attempt to change the subject.

"Oh, yes, yes, of course," the man said with a dismissive wave of his hand. "And how many other brothers and sisters do you have?"

"Only one brother and three sisters. One is younger, Sheela." Narin missed her already and resolved to write to her as soon as he got to Madras.

"Good. Nice family, is it?"

Was it? What about the new addition to his family?

Narin recalled his wedding two weeks ago. It had been the end of a long and tiring day, religious ceremonies being his least favorite activity. During a break in the goodbyes to the departing guests, his father had turned to him and said, "Happy marriage, Narin. I know you and Mina are well matched."

"Yes."

Actually, no. During the two days the shortened wedding ceremony had lasted, Narin had garnered a better picture of Mina. He was not surprised that she was reserved with him and his family, but he noticed she spoke as little to her mother and other relatives. She was even quieter than he had previously noticed, her eyes incurious as he tried various conversational gambits. He told himself to be less harsh with her—she was thirteen, a child pulled out of school and thrown into a strange and scary situation. A wave of pity overcame him. Was that a good way to begin a marriage, to be sorry for your spouse?

He tried to elicit information from his brother, Gopal, who was eight years his senior and now married for four years.

"What is it like being married?" he asked.

"Oh, you know, nothing much different," Gopal replied.

"Appa and Amma don't talk together much. What do you and your wife talk about?"

"Oh, not a lot. She's busy with her own things, and I like other things. It's not like talking with friends, you know."

"Not even about your son? Or about household matters?"

Gopal gave a bark of a laugh. "She's in charge, no? So what's there to talk about? I sometimes tell her off if the child's being bad."

"Do you have disagreements?" Narin didn't use the word "arguments" as he'd never heard his parents arguing and was unsure if husbands and wives argued in the boisterous but amicable manner he often did with his friends.

Gopal didn't reply.

"But we … you and I do … no?"

"She wouldn't disagree with me, would she?" Gopal said with another bark.

He also dismissed Narin's curiosity regarding the wedding ceremony. "You don't have to worry about a thing, Narin. Mina's family will take care of everything. You only have to show up and nod whenever the priests look at you. Just don't burn yourself on the *vivaah homa*"—the ceremonial fire. "You're lucky that the short notice makes for a short ceremony. And thank God, you don't have to ride in on a horse or anything like they do up north. You'd probably fall off and break your skull." He burst out laughing.

After the ceremonies ended, Narin watched Mina and Sheela talking softly a little apart from the crowd. For once, Mina's mother and aunts weren't hovering over her. The petite Mina wore a resplendent green sari, and Sheela, who stood a head taller, was dressed in an equally startling red one. Both garments' profusely gold embellished *pallus* draped over their left shoulders and trailed gaily to the ground. Sheela was animated with an easy smile. Already Narin could see her burgeoning self-confidence in the way she held herself, her shoulders upright and firm, a characteristic right tilt of her head. He knew Sheela would be kind to Mina and hoped she could draw her out of her shell. But because Mina was to remain at her parents' house for three years or more, they wouldn't see much of each other. After that, what? After the *ritu kala*, as was the custom, she'd go back to her family's house to live. And Sheela may have left home by then, perhaps married.

Narin snapped back to the present. His over-eyebrowed companion in the seat across from him had his gaze still fixed on him, waiting for a reply so he could continue probing. Ignoring him was not an option, and Narin couldn't think of a change of topic that might divert his focus. What had he said last? Something about his family.

"It's a nice family, thanks."

"Your mother, she will miss you when you are not there."

"Yes."

"She is how old, your mother? She is in good health, is she?"

Narin squirmed and settled into his seat for the long haul.

THE TRAIN CAME to a slow, shuddering halt at Madras Central Station. It had been an interminable seven hours since Venpuri, including the wait to get into the Madras area, where heavy local traffic often caused delays. The platform was crowded with passengers, porters, food carts, and hangers-on. Wooden crates, broken and abandoned, were scattered everywhere. A few defiant rats perched on top of the crates, whiskers a-quiver, acutely aware but disdainful of the wandering hollow-eyed, hungry stray dogs. Crows and sparrows sat in uneasy alliance on the exposed metal girders of the platform roof, waiting to pounce on stray morsels. Several small boys had jumped on the train's running boards as it slowed to a stop, trying to get a head start on the red-shirted *coolies* by offering to carry the passengers' luggage for less than the porters' official charge. Boys careless enough to be close to an unsmiling *coolie* were unceremoniously yanked off with a shout and a swat.

Narin stood, shaking his limbs to reanimate them before pulling his two trunks from the upper luggage rack. Outside, he glimpsed Jaggie—short, plump, and dripping with sweat—as he scanned the compartments.

As Narin heaved his luggage down, a baggage boy, who could not have been older than eleven, sized him up before dismissing him for more promising passengers. Narin sighed and maneu-vered one trunk to the platform while a helpful stranger handed him the other. He left the trunks unattended while he walked the short distance to where Jaggie stood.

"Hello."

Jaggie started and turned. "Oh, there you are. I was looking for you everywhere."

"I'm here."

"I have been waiting here a long time. Your train was quite late."

"Sorry. Thanks for staying."

"Got everything? Where is your luggage?" Narin gestured back along the platform. "You left it where? That's stupid of you, any-body could have pinched it, get it immediately." They strode the dozen yards back, Jaggie's bulk an impediment to matching Narin's fast pace. Jaggie uttered a cry of satisfaction on seeing the luggage safe, and his face softened. He asked Narin, "Are you hungry?"

"I ate some okra curry and rice on the platform a couple of hours ago."

Among the newfound delights of Narin's journey, once his forced acquaintance had tired of questioning him and fallen asleep, were the many food carts on the platforms, some with for-bidding, blazing coal kettles with hot food. Vendors jumped onto the train, shouting wares and prices, a miracle that their precarious trays of snacks didn't topple from their hands. He'd eaten many small items during the long journey, and food was the last thing on his mind.

Narin and his brother-in-law continued their casual conversa-tion as they walked the length of the platform toward the exit. Madras Central was vast compared to Venpuri Station. Dozens of people scurrying around, and almost as many just lounging—not a common sight in Venpuri. Narin had an uneasy sense of being watched by a horde of hard-eyed men looking for an easy mark.

He'd often heard his father's disdain for the city's noise and abrasive manners, and now resolved not to let it influence his own impressions. He absorbed the sensations of Madras—the air of excitement, the smells, the people, the sounds—and let a tide of euphoria invigorate him. This was Madras. His new home.

Already Venpuri seemed a faraway, fading ghost.

Outside the station enclosure, Narin was surprised by the brutal noise level. The street swarmed with all sorts of vehicles, from handcarts and horse and cattle carts to pedaled vehicles and the constantly honking motor-driven lorries, buses, and cars. As they continued through the small open yard to the street, he saw the fabled tram, which his brother, Gopal, had mentioned, arrive in front.

The colorful vehicle was a multi-wheeled contraption of wood and steel with a long row of wood-slatted seats set lengthwise, facing out on each side, with running boards for the passengers' feet. The open passage between the seats provided additional standing room. The front-mounted destination board proclaimed "Egmore" in bright white letters with the number "19" below it. His age. He drank in its beauty as it screeched to a stop. He noticed that many of the passengers were girls.

Enchanted, he asked Jaggie, "Can we take that?"

"Of course not. It doesn't go by your hostel. Also they're always full of Anglo-Indian girls." He made it sound like a plague.

"What's wrong with Anglo-Indian girls?"

"You don't want to know. Half-breeds, they are all loose."

Loose? He knew that Anglo-Indians—the offspring of British fathers and Indian women, some legitimate, but most not—were often looked down upon by Indians, but the level of disdain in Jaggie's voice still surprised him. He had not expected such prejudice from a well-educated lawyer living in a large city. The tram restarted with a loud clunk, and Narin watched it disappear along with the animated, laughing group of girls.

He was enrolled in a hostel over a half-mile away, too far to walk saddled with luggage. Jaggie hailed a cycle rickshaw, and they loaded Narin's things. The scrawny driver strained on the pedals under the weight of the luggage and Jaggie's portliness during the few minutes it took to reach the hostel.

Narin was fascinated by the four-story yellow brick hostel, built by the British like many other majestic buildings in Madras. It had bright red corner quoins, and fluted columns every ten or twelve feet apart supported a series of balconies on all visible sides. A broad flight of steps led up to the open doors of the main entrance. On the keystone above the door, Narin read the chiseled inscription: "Lord Malcolm Hopewaithe, 1849." In Venpuri, the buildings were predominantly one or two stories, and the taller ones were on a smaller scale.

The driver helped carry Narin's trunks inside and left grumbling at the fare Jaggie paid him. Narin, curious to learn the ins and outs of such matters, asked his brother–in-law how much he'd given the man, but Jaggie only snapped, "Enough for that scoundrel. Let's go sign in."

A bored clerk at the front desk pointed out the administrative office where Narin spent the next half-hour filling out forms. At last, the clerk assigned him a room and the all-important student number, "M. N. Janappan, Roll Number 36-173N," and handed him a sheet of smudged mimeograph paper with information of dubious worth.

Jaggie accompanied Narin to his room, looked around, and stretched his arms out as if to get a precise measurement. "Fine. It's larger than I expected. So, I'll come to see how you are next week. If you want, you can come over for food on Sunday afternoon."

"Thanks, maybe … I'll see how much stuff I have to do. You really don't have to come. I'll be fine."

"Of course not. Your appa told me to see you every week."

Narin sighed and walked him out. He drank in the relative quiet and realized he was lucky. His room was in the rear of the building, overlooking an interior courtyard. In spite of the open window to the balcony, it was peaceful compared to the street-side cacophony.

He examined the courtyard, which was dirt paved with concrete walkways. Coconut trees were scattered along its perimeter, reaching well above his balcony. He stretched out a hand to reach a nearby tree and stroked its glossy leaves, wondering if he could grab a nut when in season. He watched a worker shouldering a large earthen pot pour a stream of water into one of the circular depressions dug around each tree. It cheered him to note the hostel was serious about its horticultural duties. There was a small patch of grass in the middle of the courtyard, in the center of which stood a pedestalled statue of a man holding a large book in his hands, his head turned to one side and upward in a heroic gaze. Several well-faded garlands encircled his neck. Narin wondered if this was the Lord Malcolm Hopewaithe of the front door's inscription.

When he'd first entered the building, he'd sniffed a faint decay, so he looked around his room. It was clean except for the ubiquitous dust that blew through the open windows. Jaggie had considered the room large, but it shrank as Narin envisioned it with three roommates and their belongings. Painted white from walls to ceiling, the only color in the room was the dull maroon of the concrete floor—which had a series of hairline cracks resembling a crazed map—and a pair of twisted black-and-yellow wires tacked haphazardly to the wall and leading from the brass light switch to the single overhead light. He clicked the switch. Nothing. He reached up and tapped the bulb, noting the broken filament. Would the sheet with "useful information" tell him where to find a replacement? No. Beside each of the four narrow cots sat a table with an empty inkwell and a simple wooden stool. No chairs? Then he noticed a few folded metal ones stored under one of the beds. No place for storage. This would be his home for the next four years, and he would be living out of his trunks.

He lay down on one of the bare mattresses, closed his eyes, and savored the solitude.

V

Selected Letters, 1936–1939

Venpuri

October 1936

Dear Brother Narin,

I hope you had a good journey to Madras and have settled into your hostel by now. You must tell me all about it. Your letters to me and Amma didn't have many details. Did you tell Appa and others more? How big is your room? How many boys do you share it with? Do you get along with them? Have you made many friends?

I have done nothing since you left. Well, not really nothing, just not much. I won't bore you with family gossip. I'm sure Amma keeps you up on that.

Elder-Brother Gopal had his second child last week, and he's so overly proud it's another son. He goes around boasting to everyone on how he has kept his duty as a husband, as if a daughter wouldn't be welcome. Maybe not. I tried to get him to explain, pointing out that I'm a girl and why should he think his child was better for being unlike his own sister (does that make sense?), and he did that look-down-your-nose thing he's so good at. He's got enough bulk there to make that meaningful. Oops, is that mean? I'm wishing him at least three girls next.

The swing broke last week, and no one wanted to mend it as I am the only one who uses it. I tried to tie up the rope to the seat myself, but it slipped the first time and I fell hard, but luckily the bruise did not show. Can you imagine what the Aunties S would say? I finally pinched a few *anna* coins from Ma's money store (what do you think she'd do if she found out?) and gave it to this fellow who delivers goods from Narseem's Store who agreed to repair it. I asked him to come back when most of the servants were out, but I'm surprised no one noticed. Maybe they assumed I'd done it. I wish I knew how. Anyway, I can swing again.

Regards, Sheel

Madras
November 1936
Dear Sheel:
I'm sorry I've been a bad writer. I'm not even writing to Amma every week as I promised. Every Sunday I swear to myself that I will write to both of you, but somehow the day goes by, and suddenly it's evening, and I have to study in preparation for my classes on Monday.

To catch you up: The room is small, and I have three others staying with me. We have to walk around each other sometimes, as it's pretty crowded. We each have a cot, a table, and a chair. There's a single light in the room, so if one of us has to study late (that happens often), others have to sleep with the light on, but we're pretty tired at the end of the day, so it's easy enough to fall asleep.

The food is pretty bad. I don't tell Amma that, and you shouldn't worry her either. She might get Jaggie or Auntie Kala to bring something over, and that would be embarrassing. We all complain about the food and say it's a good thing there's a good hospital nearby (ha ha).

Since we have class weekdays and Saturday mornings, Sunday is our only day off, and we try to relax then. After visiting once,

I've managed to avoid Jaggie's invitation to eat at his house for several weeks, always claiming studies. He doesn't seem to mind. I have to go and see Auntie Kala again. She's so calm and nice in contrast with Jaggie, and her husband just sits around and doesn't say much. Quiet and relaxing. Mostly I go out with some of the friends I've made. Laxman is becoming a good friend.

We have seen several pictures over the months. I'd never seen a *talking* picture before. You won't believe the difference between "talkies" and non-talking movies. You must try and go to Chettapur Picture House and see one. I hear they started to show talkies also. Maybe you could ask the Aunties S to take you as a treat for your birthday (joke)? It's quite indescribable. It was all images before. Now you have to pay much more attention as there's the whole new thing of sound, music, conversation.

I saw *The Big Trail*. It was a "Western," which means it's about cowboys and sometimes Red Indians (isn't that funny?), and it starred this huge American actor, John Wayne, who has the squarest face you can imagine. Laxman loved it, but I was not so sure if I liked the story (Wayne is out to get revenge when his good friend, a fur trapper, is killed. He suspects who the killer is and follows him out West). The American West is so wide open and beautiful, it makes me want to visit. I think everyone should see other countries (don't you?), and America would be high on my list.

Your loving brother, Narin

Venpuri

April 1937

Brother Narin,

I'm jealous of your descriptions of life in Madras, and it makes me sad sometimes. My life is so dull by comparison. Thank you again for the list of books I should read. I am reading faster now, and it's much more enjoyable. The idea of a "mystery" was surprising to me, and I found these books hard to read at first. I almost said, "a mystery to me," ha ha. I found I had to read them at a more simple level (is the correct word "superficial?") than what I think of as heavier books. But thank you for opening up a new area of reading. I do think, though, we are reading so much English fiction that it's time I (and maybe you) started reading some of the great Indian authors. Don't you agree?

But you'll never guess what happened last week, maybe you've heard from others? Amma told me that we'd received a marriage proposal for me from the family of—you'll never guess—V. K. Badrinath from down the street. Of all people. You and I have talked a lot about him over the years. I'm sure you have as bad an opinion of him as I do (at least I hope you do). So I refused, of course. Appa was furious. Amma tried for a while to change my mind, but she didn't get angry. I was thinking that she felt she had to say what she said, and she really didn't mean it. Our Aunties S said I was "willful and obstinate." They said refusing a proposal was dangerous, and how many times did I think I could do so? I pointed out that it was my first. That made them angrier, and they told me not to argue with them. How is it an argument to point out a fact? They say the strangest things sometimes.

Appa said it would be a complete shame to the family. I told him I was really, really sorry, but Badri was just not the sort of boy I could marry because he is stupid. I suppose that was not a good use of words because Appa got angrier. Amma said Badri had failed his SSC exams twice, so he couldn't be too clever, could he? Which caused another round of shouting by all until Amma finally calmed everybody down. What I wonder is why they gave me a choice at all. I remember you were only told of what was to happen. Lucky me, I guess.

Anyway, I'm happy. Can I really stay unmarried forever? Do tell me what you think, Narin. I'm okay about Badri, of course, but what should I do next time, if there's one?

Regards, Sheel

Madras

April 1937

Dear Sheel,

I'm both glad and sorry to hear the proposal fell through. Glad that you decided to follow your instincts and sorry for all the anger and pain in the family (and the effect on you). I really admire your strength, Sheel, particularly as I wonder about my own situation and why I agreed to my marriage without thinking what it meant. Talking about that, have you seen Mina? Does she come visit us, or do you visit her? I had hoped you and she would become friends over time.

I've been thinking why exactly Appa wouldn't want you to be more independent (a word I hear a lot from the girl students here). Maybe our family is too traditional. Auntie Kala is the only woman among our relatives who's working. It's risky, perhaps, but if you refuse a few more proposals, would Appa suggest you find a job?

Your fond brother, Narin

Venpuri

May 1937

Dear Brother Narin,

You mentioned me working? That's not very likely. What can I do? I'm good with my hands, of course, but can you imagine the family letting me work, say, at stitching? I wish I'd stayed on in school. Maybe I could be a steno or something.

You asked about Mina, but I've only seen her once this year, by coincidence, last week. She and her parents came to visit and were with Amma and Appa a while. Probably something to do with the marriage? I didn't hear anything, and she and I didn't speak much as her parents were around all the time. She did slip me the enclosed letter for you. I wondered why she didn't post it to you, and then I remembered when I was her age, it would have been difficult without Amma knowing. If I had to do something like that now, I'd just pinch a couple of *annas* from Amma's purse (wink). So treat her letter with this in mind.

Do send me more suggestions of books to read, though I couldn't find at least half the books that you last suggested at the library. Poor Mrs. Shetty (she's the new librarian, you know old Mr. Appurathnam died?) looked at me strangely as I asked her for books like *Gone with the Wind* and *The Painted Veil*, which she had to order from the Main Library. I'm sure she'll complain to Amma about my strange tastes the next time she sees her.

Oh, and I just thought of something: There's a job I'd love, working in a library. I wish they'd let me wander along the book-shelves, as you say it's possible at the MMC library. I'd love that. I could take my own time deciding what to read, breathing in the musty smell of books, touching them, running my hands along them. Do you do that often?

Elder-Brother Gopal and his two sons send their regards (he says). I asked if I should include his dear wife in the greetings, and he smirked but didn't say anything. I notice she seems to be fading into the background more and more as she has more children. Maybe it's too much work for her. I try to help her out by offering to watch the children for a while if she wants to do something, but she only smiles and says, "What would I do by myself?" The last time she said that, I was ready to burst. I wanted to scream at her, "Being with yourself is so important. It's what makes you hu-man." But she might have thought I was crazy. I sometimes wonder if I am.

Regards, Sheel

Mina's letter to Narin was written in Tamil:

May 1937

Dear Husband,

I thought I should write to you to see how you are doing. I hope your studies are going well. I don't have a lot to say about myself. I continue to do the same things I did before our marriage.

I have noticed, though, that my friends are not coming over as much as before, and I am not invited to their houses as much. Amma says I should be more serious with them now, whatever that means.

Do you see Elder-Brother Jaggie often? Amma says his wife makes very good curries. Do you think so?

Please write to me sometime. I would really like to hear from you directly. Of course, whenever I see Elder-Sister-in-Law Sheela, she is very kind to me and tells me many details of your life. She has brought me some books lately, which I find slow going. I have to ask Appa for the meaning of many words, and he is not very patient with me. Elder-Sister-in-Law Sheela told me the last time that she would bring me a Tamil dictionary, which she said was written by a woman called Neelambikai. Imagine a woman being able to do that.

I cannot think what a big city like Madras must be like compared to our village. How do "trams" work? Are they faster than motorcars?

Amma and Appa send you their best wishes.

Minalakshmi

From Narin to Mina, in Tamil:

July 1937

Dear Mina,

Thank you very much for writing to me. It was a pleasant surprise. I am glad that you and Sheela have met and she is helpful to you. Please do try to read more. I've found books very important in understanding life, and the world in general. Perhaps your parents could find you a tutor to help you? I might write to *Mamanaar* Subbu to urge him to do so.

As for me, I am studying very hard and not doing much else. Of course, I have made friends here, and I do go out sometimes with them. Other times we just meet in the common room of the dormitory to talk or play cards.

I expect I will see you this summer at our family's next *Guru Purnima* festival, just like last year.

My regards to your parents.

Narin

Madras

August 1938

Dear Sheel,

Seeing the family just once a year is hard. I particularly miss you. I miss our talking and friendship. I now have quite a few friends here, but I find myself not as open with them as I am with you. I hang out with Laxman's groups (he has more than one) a lot, and somehow they all read books and magazines in addition to classwork. Laxman has given me many good books to read, so I will have to send you yet another list. I hope you are reading more than ever. Here's the odd thing, though: I'm looking forward to coming there soon. But—and this is the worrying part—I also am beginning to really miss Madras while I'm at home.

As I tell Amma and Appa, studies are hard, but I'm doing fine. The two years at Venpuri College was a help to me. It taught me study habits, which I'd have had to learn from the start otherwise.

I don't know whether to write to Mina or not. Strange, no, considering? But what am I to say to her? I can't write much of what I write to you. Her mother will probably read it first, and then what? So maybe the next time you see her, tell her I'm swamped (that convenient excuse) and give her a condensed version of my life here. Thanks.

Your loving brother, Narin

Venpuri

June 1939

Dear Brother Narin,

It's been a while since I wrote to you, so please forgive me. You must know what's been happening here after that second proposal. I couldn't. Just couldn't. He was worse than Badri the First (as I think of him), if that's possible. Seems like the parents of every strange boy in town want their sons to marry me. I suppose I'm not exactly first-class goods.

I've been giving a lot of thought to what it means to be married or, in my case, not married. I see that most women give up a lot, and for what? A sense of stability? But that's only because our society says it's so, no? I mean, why can't I live by myself without everyone assuming I need to be with a husband? Whenever you mention all the girls at MMC, I feel so envious. I'm sure all of them will get married, too, but in the meanwhile, they will have studied and learned to become doctors. I read *Gone with the Wind* and think Scarlett is just deluded. Sorry, I am being maudlin, but I wish Appa would've let me do something, become somebody.

Everyone is now going on about how I will never be married. I hear rumors that people think I'm "too big" to marry anyone in Venpuri. Apparently refusing two boys is enough to destroy my chances. Is that a bad thing? I remember you once told me the story in some old American novel of a woman with a strange name—Prim?—who had a red A for "Adultery" stitched on her clothes. I feel I have a U on mine for "Unmarriageable." Amma and Appa have been worrying about me for months, and now they're really in a state.

The Aunties S have also been giving all of us a really bad time. They said they blame themselves for this whole problem, as if Amma and Appa were not the ones who brought me up. And as if finally it wasn't my own decision to not accept the proposals.

Narin, I put this letter aside for a few days while I decided whether to inflict all this on you. Good thing. Our aunties came over last week and had a new suggestion. I have no idea where it came from. I walked into the living room just as one of them—you know I can never tell them apart at first—said "Why don't you send her to Kala? She will sort her out."

I didn't know what they were talking about. Never heard of this before. Turns out that they were saying Amma and Appa should send me to stay in Madras for a few months with Auntie Kala who may be able to "talk sense" into me. Now, I don't see how they could think this. Auntie Kala, as you know, works, so she won't be home all that much, and I'd have thought that my being by myself much of the day would not be good from their viewpoint. (I think it will be fun.) Perhaps it's because Auntie Kala has always said I'm her favorite niece. But I'd love to go to Madras for a while, especially to be at her house. I pretended I thought this was a terrible idea and hated it, so of course the Aunties S were all for it. They soon persuaded Amma and Appa.

So I'm coming to stay in Madras. I'll be twenty minutes from you. There's even a tram stop somewhere near Auntie Kala's house. I remember her talking about the noises at night when it goes by. I don't think she'll allow me to take it. Or even go any-where alone, so you'll just have to come to visit me.

And our dear sister-in-law is pregnant again. You heard this news first from me. I'm praying (no longer just wishing) for a girl this time.

Regards, Sheel

P.S. Did you recommend *Painted Veil* because the heroine re-fuses "dozens" of suitors?

Madras

June 1939

Dear Sheel:

That is great news. (The coming-to-Madras bit, I mean, though I'm happy that Elder-Brother Gopal and his wife are adding to the population.) So you will be here just after my third year ends. I will ask Auntie Kala if I can stay maybe a week after term so we can have some time together. We must go see a talking picture. They're all talking (ha ha) about *King Kong,* which arrives next month—a story about a monkey so big that it can easily climb onto large buildings. It's set in New York, where there are hundreds of skyscrapers, and the monkey is jumping from one to another, carrying a pretty girl for some reason.

Okay, what else is happening … Remember I told you about our worst prof, Megarathnam? The one who's so hard on us in class and yells at us when we dare to ask questions? One girl in particular asks a lot, which makes her stand out. The prof doesn't like her much. Well, she made some drawings of Megarathnam, very funny ones (she calls them "caricatures," I had to look that up in the Oxford) and handed them around to friends. She nearly got caught twice in class. I will send you one I got from a friend of hers if you promise not to show it to anyone and send it back. I wish I could put it up in my room, but of course I can't. Can you imagine how much trouble I'd get in?

Laxman and I are close friends now, as I'm sure I've told you many times. I find myself studying his manner a lot. He fascinates me with his sense of looseness, an air of self-certainty, which I don't have. I think it makes him more able to handle problems in life than, say, someone like me. I think about things endlessly. I worry and look at every possibility, while Laxman will just charge ahead, making a decision as he does so. I do think he's also prone to making more mistakes with this attitude, and sometimes I worry (that word again) about the effect it may have on his ability as a doctor. But I suppose there's a middle way between his impetuosity and my—what?—plodding along while I consider every possibility. Oh hell, I'm thinking too much again. Anyway, dear sister, remember that moderation seems to be the key (as I learn from watching Laxman's excesses).

More later. Must study.

A hug from your brother, Narin

Part II

There could have been no two hearts so open, no tastes so similar, no feelings so in unison.
—Jane Austen, *Persuasion*

VI
Chennai (formerly Madras), 2001

Vishram shook himself awake from his nap, still fatigued after his long flight from San Francisco. He left his lodgings in the luxurious Vivanta by Taj Hotel, previously known, and still referred to by most, as the Connemara. Ironically, the hotel's beige-concrete stolidity had no trace of the traits of "vivanta," an Esperanto word redolent of life and joy.

Names persist as memories do. This city would always be Madras to him, not the new-fangled—well, quite old-fangled—"Chennai."

Binny Street, outside the hotel, was definitely vivant-ish, in a way that only the teeming energy of an overcrowded country like India can muster. Negotiating the chaotic, aggressive traffic was like walking through a Dodgem Car facility, but Vishram minded neither the danger nor the street urchins who clamored for money from a middle-aged "foreign-returned" guy wearing jeans.

Vishram's parents' house was a flat-roofed, stuccoed, brick two-story building set in a medium-sized yard with a tiny separate garage set in the back corner. Remembering the unbearable summer heat on the upper floor, Vishram's architectural training rebelled at how most houses were built exactly as they had been for decades, ignoring many techniques that could've been used for improved cooling. He envisioned a large dome over the roof—a signature passive cooling feature of the famous Indian architect B. Doshi.

Though worn, its appearance was pristine compared to its siblings—his parents had maintained it themselves because of their neglectful landlord. A sunny yellow wash covered the walls of the house and the inside of the yard walls, and it was not flaking off like the neighbors'. The yard was lush with several large trees and plenty of bushes. The wooden frames of the double entrance gate were kept square by a network of ropes tied in random directions. *Chalta-hai*—so it goes. His father's white metal nameplate, drizzled with rust but still readable, was secured to the left supporting column of the gates.

Dr. M. Narinder Janappan, M.D., M.R.C.P., F.R.C.P.
(Edinburgh)
Director, Government Victoria Hospital, Madras
Visiting Hours: Mon–Fri 7–9 p.m., Sat 11 a.m.–2 p.m.

Vishram flipped the metal latch on the gate, remembering the sounds that attracted attention when a visitor arrived: the squeak of the hasp, the slap of metal on wood, the harsh screeching of the gate's support wheel against the metal strip set in the dry, hardened ground.

He entered the yard and paused to admire a tall gulmohar tree dotted with remnants of red flowers. He remembered when his father had ordered it as a small sapling many decades ago; it had sparked Narin's interest in gardening. His mother disdained his fledgling pastime and mocked him for "trying to imitate the lower classes." Narin persisted until his Brahmin upbringing reasserted itself, and he considered dirtying his hands distasteful. So he took on a supervisory role, overseeing the early-morning tending and watering before he left for his hospital. Vishram could see him standing beside one plant after the next, willing its growth with the force of his spirit.

The house had been empty since his mother's death the previous month, and Vishram was apprehensive as he entered, though he knew her maid, Bela, had been keeping it in order. Would there be a smell of death, and does it linger? No, only a trace odor of the detergent—Dettol?—used to clean the cement floors, the lingering scent of spices from the kitchen, and the musty smell of dust. Geckos everywhere. They'd had the walls to themselves for a month and now gazed at the interloper through dull, orange-flecked eyes, clicking their displeasure.

As he went upstairs, he paused at the fifth step, imagining their dog, Alfa, splayed like a frog as he watched the outside world through a window inexplicably placed at stair level. His mother had pampered that dog, preparing his meals on a separate Primus stove with dedicated pots because their Brahmin cook wouldn't touch meat. On her last visit, Elena had noticed the cooking paraphernalia gathering dust in a corner (Alfa was long gone), and he'd explained its significance.

"A kosher dog," she exclaimed, inaccurately but with delight. "Your mother must've really loved him."

Loved Alfa? Vishram remembered the time he'd brought home his ninth-grade report card and watched his mother read it with pursed lips, disappointment clouding her face.

"*Third* in class? Vish, you should … can do better than that. How could Shreeti's son—what's his name—have beaten you?"

"Just happened, Amma."

"You *must* do better. You're not that stupid."

Alfa, alarmed at her tone, started pawing at her sari for attention. She picked up the dog and made cooing noises.

He watched. "You like that dog more than me," he shouted.

His mother stopped petting Alfa. Her expression neutralized.

"No, stop being ridiculous," she said, then dropped Alfa to the floor and turned away.

The air in the room at the top of the stairs was hot and humid. Vishram turned on the forty-year-old ceiling fan, which spun noiselessly, its air drying the sweat on his face and bare arms and lending a welcome coolness. A faded and torn curtain that divided the space in two flapped against him as the breeze picked up.

When he was in his teens, Vishram's father had been the chief county medical officer in a nearby town, a prestigious position in the government medical hierarchy. They had lived in one of the perks of his father's status, a palatial ex-British mansion, which had devolved to the government after Indian independence, where he had one of the sizable bedrooms to himself. His father had rented this house in 1962 when he returned as a director at the Victoria Hospital in Madras. Vishram's desire for solitude had boiled over, and he'd balked at moving into this confine from his previous abundance.

"Is this my room?" he'd asked his mother, perplexed by its odd layout, *L*-shaped and attached to a smaller room, but with only one door to the hallway.

"Yes. Your father and I will take the other one over there."

"But you have to walk through my room to get to yours."

"So?"

"I think I want more privacy."

She'd looked at him, mystified. Privacy was not a strong point in India, where entire families could be housed in two or three adjacent rooms. Children having their own space was quite rare at their income level. But Vishram spent much free time by himself. For the previous few years, he hadn't hung out much with friends outside school. He cherished being alone.

"What can we do?"

He looked around the room and realized its potential as two areas. "Can I put up a curtain?"

"What curtain? How?"

"Get a pipe to attach between these walls and hang cloth on it. I'll take the space behind it."

"No. That's too much trouble." She turned away to other duties.

"I'll do it, Amma. Please. I know I can if you get me the stuff."

"Don't be ridiculous, Vish. It's a stupid idea. No."

He appealed to his father. After a lot of back and forth with his mother, Narin had orchestrated the installation of the curtain.

Vishram's mother kept a little shrine in his parents' bedroom with her deities, Ganesh, Parvati, Shiva, and the Goddess Lakshmi holding oil receptacles, a small book of prayers, and another of religious extracts. His parents were nominally Hindu, but for decades they'd seldom gone to temple and never performed religious ceremonies themselves. They began to practice low-level Hindu observances when they grew older. They'd brought him up in a non-theistic manner while trying to ingrain the concept of Karma in him. The idea that one's actions have inevitable repercussions is entrenched in Hindu philosophy and leads to a sense of fatalism and pessimism, which he still felt resonant in the room where his parents had lived and died. Why were two such successful, accomplished, world-traveled people so fatalistic? Did they have a secret sorrow in their lives? This was not the sort of thing an Indian teen could ask his parents.

Vishram went downstairs and examined the kitchen. He could still see his father using a battered metal spatula to flip his Sunday breakfast omelet, a rare ritual for a man of his generation; the kitchen would be foreign territory to others of his cohort. Narin would suffuse the eggs with green chilies, a treat because food cooked in their house was extremely bland to suit his mother's delicate palate. His father would call Vishram when he'd finished, and they'd have breakfast without his mother, a staunch vegetarian who'd say she preferred her breakfast untainted by the stink of hen embryos.

Those moments might have been ripe for father-son bonding, but they never fulfilled their promise. They talked mostly about politics. But Vishram missed his father's comfortable presence, his low voice, and his gentle smile, which often threatened but never broke into a full laugh.

BELA WOULD KNOW where to donate appliances, lamps, knick-knacks, clothes—in India, everything not completely decrepit is worth something to someone. "Reuse, recycle, and redo" could be the national slogan.

She showed up an hour later with her teenage daughter. Bela was almost a foot shorter than Vishram, and he felt a twinge of awkwardness, towering over her. Surely she couldn't have grown shorter in the last few years? Her large eyes rimmed with kohl were a startling counterpoint to her dark face, and her gold nose ring matched her daughter's smaller version. He was uneasy talking to them since his Tamil was marginal at best, and while she understood English moderately well, she did not speak it fluently. He smiled at them and was thankful it wasn't customary to use names in greeting, as he had quite forgotten her daughter's. He managed to dredge a few opening statements from his reluctant memory.

"How are you? Thank you very much for taking care of my mother." Though he suspected he'd said "managing" rather than "taking care." Perhaps more accurate.

She smiled, nodded, and said something that he translated as, "No problem."

He hadn't gotten many details of his mother's death and wondered if it had been a lingering one. Bela would know more. Were his language skills up to the questioning? "Was she ill the last ... in the end ... the final days?"

"No. She took her medicines as usual. She ate well. She went to her club two days before she died. And the day before that, also, I think."

His mother, the mad bridge player, had to have her fix twice a week.

"Your cousin Carla-Amma came to visit her a few days before, and I'm sure she would have noticed if anything had been wrong."

He was relieved to hear that, and the regularity of her visits to her club showed her strength of spirit. Tamil was failing him. He continued in English. "It must have been a shock to find my mother's body."

"*Ah-ma,*" she agreed, then continued in her improved English, "I am surprised. Not to expect. Upstairs she looked only … sleepy. At first, I was afraid."

"Asleep," he corrected automatically. "Thank you for everything. And how is your husband doing?" Another forgotten name.

"Well. Now he is high garden … er at Mainath Museum compound. Better money."

Good, a stable union job at last. They could now afford to marry off their youngest daughter, who had uttered not a word since they'd arrived. The marriage expenses for their two older daughters had been a severe burden. His mother had helped by giving Bela clothes and money, along with a strong lecture on the evils and illegality of the dowry system. He could imagine Bela, perforce a good listener, nodding in agreement and marveling at his mother's naiveté.

"Do you know a furniture dealer for all this stuff?"

"Oh, yes," she said with a definitive nod-shake of her head, the classic Indian affirmation. She turned to her daughter and asked her to fetch a man she knew.

They continued in a mixture of Tamil and English as he went over the list he'd made, and he admired her organizational ability. In other circumstances, in another country, she might have climbed a corporate ladder. In India, her education and lower caste status were insuperable barriers. He mentally totted up the money his mother had left and considered giving the entire amount to her. Would that make a difference? In the meantime, he pulled out the couple hundred dollars he'd changed to rupees at the airport and gave them to Bela.

"Thank you so much again. You've been with my mother for, what, eighteen years?"

"Twenty."

Vishram's Tamil evaporated. Bela appeared overwhelmed by the gift. Was that a hint of tears in her eyes? To her, it represented much, much more than its value in dollars. Her life was unimaginably hardscrabble. His mother gave her one week off a year, and that was uncommon. Otherwise, she was at the house seven days a week. Plus, she had to do what all women in her position did— feed and care for her family of five. He felt an even stronger desire to help her out somehow, and now, not later.

Squeak. Slap. Screech. The furniture guy.

Bela conducted most of the negotiation, bargaining with the dealer, pointing out when the man was shorting him. Another skill underutilized. The furniture guy loaded his items on a wooden cart, handed him a wad of well-used notes, and left. He'd come back for the *almirahs*, the heavy wardrobes.

Bela sent her daughter out for a cycle rickshaw to take the items she'd picked for herself.

"So, I will see you after?" she asked in English.

"Yes, of course. Maybe the day after tomorrow. Definitely before I leave. Thank you again."

"I will keep house key then? Do not forget to get."

She continued in Tamil with a hint of a smile. "You don't know how to bargain well. *Suh-ree. Po-ittu vuhrén."*—*Okay, I leave and will be back.*—So much more elegant than "goodbye." He smiled in return as she left.

He could now relax. Anything left? He did a walk-through of the house, then double-checked the three rosewood wardrobes and realized he'd forgotten about one small locked drawer in one of them because he didn't have its key. He rattled the drawer hard, but it didn't open. Having sold the *almirah*, he didn't want to damage it. He found a screwdriver and jiggled the lock, which soon abandoned its resistance and clicked open. He found a tan envelope squished into the confines of the space and added it to the stash of documents he'd previously collected, now piled on the floor. He should have gone through them while a table was still available, he realized, as he sank to the floor in a yoga pose with a sigh.

He spent a few minutes examining faded photos, some dating decades back, but without many markers of place or time. Images of one parent with various relatives predominated, and he wondered why so many subjects were unsmiling. He grinned at one of his mother holding a chubby kid, him. Keep 'em all.

There were some letters. He noted a few with the salutation "Dear Madam," signed by his father. For a moment he wondered why they'd be there, as if unsent, then remembered that in those pre-copy-machine days, his father would save a hand copy of important letters. Keep, read later. Bills—his mother had kept them for decades—toss. Canceled checks, toss—oh, maybe keep the most recent ones. Stock certificates and bank statements, keep. He glanced at a recent statement to memorize the name of his mother's bank officer; always useful to have a name when you call the uncooperative bank receptionist.

The tan envelope caught his eye. It was legal sized, which was unusual. On opening it, he found a yellowing sheaf of papers, many of them legal documents. Why on earth would his mother have sequestered these ancient papers in a locked drawer? He peeled off a few pages and flattened the curling edges. The faded words on the top page stared at him:

In the Subordinate Court of Madras
Friday, the 21st day of March, One Thousand Nine Hundred
and Fifty-Three.
100 Mangalchetty Road, George Town, Madras
Present: Learned Justice R. K. Karthikan
In the matter of:
Minalakshmi alias Mrs. M. M. Janappan, Plaintiff
vs.
Dr. M. Narinder Janappan, Defendant

What? Who? Vishram collapsed on the sagging bed, ignoring its indignant protest.

VII
Madras, 1939

"Well, that was a relief. Three years gone awry, and only one yet to go," Laxman said as he and Narin walked out of the hall after the final examination. "And how did you do, my good friend, Shri Narinder Janappan?"

"Pretty damn well," Narin said. "I think I'll meet the expectations of my father and family, or so I hope."

"Still hard on you, are they?"

"Yes. Aren't yours?"

"Sometimes. But I ignore them when they get too pushy."

"I can't … haven't learned to do that yet."

"Told you, you should. You will, finally. Smoke?" He extracted two cigarettes from a pack of One Elevens and lit both using his silver Ronson lighter.

Laxman Saidu was not quite what Narin's mother had in mind when she suggested he make friends with nice Brahmin boys, as he was a *Kshatriya*, a non-Brahmin. His family was from the large city of Bangalore, two hundred miles northwest of Madras, which served as the head of the principality of Mysore. He had wanted to study away from his parents' influence and persuaded his father, a doctor with a successful private practice in Bangalore, to let him enroll at Madras Medical College on the grounds that it was the most prestigious institution nearby.

He smoked too much, drank too much, and flirted aggressively with every girl student he could talk to. Narin was fascinated.

Laxman enjoyed a level of autonomy at home that young adults in Venpuri lacked. He would visit his father's private club to swim in the pool or play tennis. He'd also mentioned that he would meet girls at the club's monthly dance.

"How did you learn to dance?" Narin asked.

"It's easy, Narin. If you can walk, you can dance."

Which made Narin feel no better.

With a wink, Laxman added, "And I could more than dance with some of them, if you know what I mean."

Laxman had invited Narin to visit him in Bangalore the previous summer. The idea thrilled Narin as he had never ventured beyond Madras, and a visit to another large city was intriguing. He imagined Bangalore as a beguiling city populated with easygoing creatures like his friend, whose families watched as they flitted on their unquestioned ways. But he knew his father would never allow it. And he could imagine his mother and aunts, after hearing Laxman's full name, being uneasy at his intimate association with one of *them*—a non-Brahmin. Visiting them? Impossible. Too expensive. Too far. Too different from us.

A month before, Laxman had noticed a fellow classmate, Ambika, walking ahead of them as he and Narin were walking to their lecture hall.

"There's an eminently shaggable one," he said, snapping his fingers.

"God, Lax, can you be a little more crude?"

"I know as a married virgin, you may be envious, Narin, but you should go for it sometime. Yer a handsome chap."

"I wouldn't know how, and I'm not sure I want to."

"Confidence, m'boy, confidence. Girls can smell fear or uncertainty. Puts them off."

Narin soon noticed that Laxman had, indeed, charmed Ambika. First, he had brought her along to their group outings; then he began spending more of his free time alone with her.

"Have you fallen for her or something?" Narin asked a few weeks later as he noticed Laxman's eyes lingering on her retreating figure after they'd said farewell.

Laxman's face flushed. "Don't be silly, m'boy," he said, fumbling in his shirt pocket for his cigarettes.

Like Laxman, Ambika was from Bangalore, and she shared his easy air of assurance. The three began to explore the city. Male and female students were discouraged from mingling, so this took some subterfuge. If they were going to a theater near the college, it was simpler to go there separately and meet up inside the hall. This arrangement suited Ambika. Narin admired her independence, as he had never seen a woman student so at ease when traveling alone. He wondered how her upbringing had encouraged her self-sufficiency. After the show, they'd decide where to have snacks or dinner, forgoing, in Laxman's words, the swill that the hostel provided.

Laxman, Ambika, and Narin began to meet at one of the many nondescript coffee shops far enough from the college that censorious eyes were unlikely to see them together. The first time Ambika had joined Laxman and him, the attention they elicited from the exclusively male clientele made Narin squirm.

"Maybe we should go somewhere else," he muttered.

Laxman glanced around the shop with a slight smirk on his devilish face. "Oh worry not, Narin. Sticks and stones may break our bones, but stares will never harm us. Anyway, it's my treat so you won't refuse. Now, how about an order of those delicious mutton samosas?"

"Not for me, thanks."

"Time to get over your vegetarian Brahmin habits, Narin."

"Next time, maybe."

"Which is what you said last time. And the time before that. Etcetera. Etcetera. We'll make a meat-eater of you in the end. Expand your horizons. Got you to smoke, didn't I? Right, Ambika?"

Ambika shook her head. "I'm going to ignore that … and all the riff-raff. You shouldn't look so uncomfortable, Narin. The best defense is a good offense—stare back at them." She looked around at the circle of men, who dropped their heads as she did so.

She had reminded Narin of a more-poised Sheela. He wondered how his sister would have fared if she'd had the same opportunities and a more supportive family. Would she have been a successful student at some prestigious college?

Standing outside the examination hall, Narin, still not at ease with smoking, fumbled with the lit cigarette that Laxman pushed between his lips.

"Well, Narin," said Laxman, "how about visiting us in Bangalore this summer?"

Us, Narin noted. He envied Laxman and Ambika for being able to spend unfettered time together in their hometown in summer, while he was confined to his stifling hot house in Venpuri, occasionally seeing the few contemporaries he still called friends. Then he remembered that Sheela would be there, and life seemed bearable again. Selfishly, Narin thanked the Shiva—whom he didn't believe in—that she had refused the marriage offers as they came her way.

"Thanks much, Lax, but my family—"

"I know, I know," Laxman said, offering a wry smile. "Can't pollute your saintly being hanging out with us lowlifes."

They puffed in silence for a few moments. Laxman suddenly perked up and tapped Narin on the shoulder. "Now you and I *must* celebrate the end of this brutal year before we go home and die of boredom. What shall we do? It will have to be a small group, as most of the others are leaving by tomorrow. Shanti, Rajan, Carla, Rohit, all ridden away into the sunset."

"You've been seeing Westerns too much. Oh, maybe we could see a picture?"

"We do that a lot. And besides, Ambika and I have seen both the good ones playing. Wonder where she is. We could ask her opinion." He watched a smoke ring float away. He tapped Narin on the shoulder. "Hey, I have an idea. Ambika has a friend she wants to meet before we all leave, so I'll suggest she invite her friend along, and all four of us can do something."

"A friend? Someone I don't know, you mean? What's his name?"

"It's a girl."

"Uh … who? I'm not sure about this."

"Oh, don't be silly. I know you're supposed to be married and all that. But it's not really real yet, is it? Or is it?" He chuckled at the look on Narin's face. "Are you hiding something from me? Has she been ritually prepared?"

"No. It'll be in a few months, I suppose. Maybe during vacation."

"Oh, she's finally coming through, is she? Lucky dog."

"Don't be crass."

"Well, we are soon-to-be doctors after all. If we can't call a shag a shag, who can?"

"Well, you certainly can, considering the girls you've—"

"Shh. Ambika may be around," Laxman said, swiveling his head.

Narin laughed. "If I ever need money, I know how to blackmail you. But about this friend. Who is she?"

"Ah, now you're interested."

"Just changing the subject."

"Sure. It's our excellent friend Neeta—you know, the girl who draws caricatures."

"Neeta Pai? The one from some place near Bombay … Konkan, isn't it?"

Narin well remembered the time a month or so ago when Neeta had joined them as he was walking from one class to another with Laxman and Ambika. She was a striking girl with an olive-toned, almost southern European complexion, high cheekbones, and large, liquid eyes capped by strong, shapely eyebrows. She wore her raven hair down to her shoulders, uncommon compared to the prevailing severely-tied-in-a-bun style. And she sported jasmine flowers in her hair, a Tamil custom considered the province of the lower classes. As she joined them, she had begun speaking in Tamil, unsettling Laxman and Ambika, as it was not their native tongue.

"Why are we speaking Tamil?" Narin asked, delighting in her fluency.

"Practice makes perfect," she said. "I'm from Konkan, and since my mother tongue is not very … umm … general, and"—Narin forgave her the error—"I decided I must speak other languages."

"She speaks lots of them," Laxman said. "Marathi, Hindi, her own dialect—"

"Dialect? Konkani is a real language. It's the language of the gods."

Narin thought that pretentious, but forgave her for her impassioned manner, a refreshing contrast to the timidity of other girls he knew.

Laxman said with a sly smile, "Of course, sorry. And, as you say, you blokes are the chosen people, no?"

Neeta flashed him a disdainful look.

"What's that paper you're carrying so carefully?" Ambika asked.

Neeta's face glowed. "It's the prof. Here, look." She unrolled the paper, displaying a caricature of their anatomy professor, Dr. Megarathnam. As the others admired it, she turned to Narin. "Here, Narin, you can have this one. I must make better sketches. I'll give you two a copy later."

Narin had accepted it with mild protestation, secretly glad she'd given it to him. He later sent it to Venpuri for Sheela's amusement.

The recollection of that first encounter with Neeta brought a smile to Narin's lips, and he turned away for a moment, hoping Laxman hadn't noticed his expression. He didn't need one of Laxman's trademark snide comments. But when he turned back, Laxman just winked.

"Ah, you remember the god's chosen one. Quite the pretty one, isn't she?"

"Hadn't thought of it. But yes, she's fair and … yes, pretty. Uh, wonder how she's getting along with the profs now? Her asking too many questions created all that to-do, didn't it? What a *tamasha.*"

"All the fuss has blown over, I expect. She probably smiled sweetly at them before inserting the shiv. You know how she is."

"Okay, enough, don't be nasty. What should we do?"

"I suggest we take a picnic lunch tomorrow to Fairlands Grounds. And we can walk on the beach after."

Narin squirmed at the thought of the four of them being in such a public space on a holiday. "What? There'll be plenty of people there."

"Ah, but no one who knows us. The unwashed mass of students will have dissipated by then, and I'm not sure I care what the general public thinks. And do you really think our profs will be sunning themselves on Fairlands Grounds?"

"Guess not. Maybe you're right. So what should I do?"

Laxman paused a moment before deciding. "Ambika is good with details, and she will carry Neeta along. Leave it to the girls to settle the food. You will bring something to drink. Let's not use drab ol' bottles this time. Let's make a show of it. Grab a beaker or two from the lab and get some ice. And of course, some glass tumblers."

"You're joking, right? Steal beakers from the lab?"

"Borrow. There'll be nobody there in the morning. It'll be easy as cake."

"What will you do?"

"I will arrange the transport."

"What, get tickets for the tram?"

"No, silly. We will take two rickshaws."

"Separately?"

"Naturally."

Narin nodded goodbye and turned to leave.

Laxman called after him, "Oh, Narin, do you want to join Ambika and me for a spot of dinner at six?"

Narin stopped. "Ah, no, thanks. Just want to hang around tonight. Must pack."

"What, you'd rather dine on the last meal of term at the mess?" He winked. "Remember, it's a hash of whatever the masses wouldn't eat last night."

"Lax, stop. I'll see you tomorrow," Narin said as he waved and left.

In Reality, Narin had a plan, one that he didn't want his friend to know.

Although he'd never been overtly political, Narin had recently developed a burning curiosity about events happening in his backyard. The Indian National Congress had come to power in eight provinces a few years earlier, a sure indicator of the strength of India's desire for independence from British rule. Consequential changes were happening in the country, but he and his friends were isolated in their MMC bubble, not always reading the newspapers or following the radio news. Narin wondered if that was because they'd been so indoctrinated in their "duty" to study hard and be assured of a respectable future.

The INC had replaced English with Hindi as the lingua franca, a major policy point that was fraught with dissension. Hindi, or a kindred language, was spoken throughout the North, but Tamilians in the southern Madras Presidency did not take kindly to the imposition of an unfamiliar language. An anti-Hindi agitation in Madras began, and Narin had been keenly following its actions in the news. Tonight he had decided to attend a planning meeting of the organizers of the protest movement. He had no idea what to expect, and wished he could've been more candid with Laxman, but wanted to avoid his friend's almost-certain scorn.

The meeting was held at a large community hall in the center of the city. As Narin approached the ornate building housing the hall, he was joined by several dozen others, mostly men, but a smattering of women as well. Several hard-eyed men in khaki uniforms stood on the front steps of the hall, but they did not interrupt anyone's progress. Narin was late enough to the meeting that the hall was almost full, and just as he entered and found a chair at the back, several men and one woman appeared from the wings and seated themselves at the podium. The group clapped loudly. Narin recognized a couple of the men as leaders of the protest; he'd seen them featured prominently in news articles. The sole woman sat a little apart from the men on the extreme left. He could see both from her confident demeanor and the deference paid her by the men who passed and greeted her that she was not a mere auxiliary figure. He wondered who she was. He considered asking a neighbor, but he would have had to shout over the ambient noise, and he felt just a little uneasy about drawing attention to himself. Most of the crowd was dressed in the ubiquitous paisley shirt and white *dhoti* of the working class—also worn by the men on the podium. Dressed as he was, more formally—he wished he'd worn his sandals instead of polished black shoes—would they think he was some kind of government official or reporter, ignoring his obvious youthful appearance?

The meeting commenced after the briefest of introductions, but he did hear the mystery woman's name—Neelambikai—

which he recognized as that of a well-known scholar, writer, and activist.

The location of future protests was foremost on the agenda. One speaker made an impassioned rant about how Hindi was being taught at an increasing number of schools in Madras—indoctrination of our children!—and made a motion to organize in the grounds of the larger schools. The committee caucused, then selected the Hindu Theosophical School, a large co-educational school incorporating classes from elementary to high, as the next venue. Narin thought the choice appropriate, given that the school's founder, the well-known British educationist Annie Besant, had been a prominent activist for Indian nationalist rights and an avid supporter of the INC until her death recently.

Narin left the meeting having absorbed the group's energy and enthusiasm, his ears ringing. He'd stood up with all of them and raised his fist when the speaker demanded attention. He'd shouted out the INC slogans when urged to. He was exhilarated.

When he got back to his hostel, a figure detached itself from the shadows as he climbed the main steps. Surprisingly it was Laxman, complete with lit cigarette, who accosted him.

"Well, well, Narin, what clandestine activity have you been up to?" he asked with a wide smile.

Narin saw no point in lying; he was too excited from his adventure, and he was glad to share the moment with his friend. He accepted Laxman's offer of a cigarette and commenced his story.

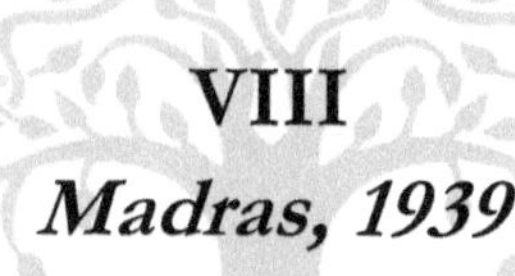

VIII
Madras, 1939

The group had arranged to meet the following afternoon at the main hospital gate. When Narin arrived clutching a cloth bag with the beakers of lemonade, the other three were already there, Laxman smoking a One Eleven as usual. As he neared the group, the scent of jasmine tickled his nostrils. Neeta appeared to be wearing a beehive of the white flowers on her head. Ambika's hair was unadorned but for two Bakelite combs, a new fad she'd determinedly latched onto. Neeta wore a brightly colored cotton sari, Ambika a more subdued one, but both were far from the ubiquitous white or beige preferred by others. The girls were similar in height and build, and Narin thought he'd be hard-pressed to say who was the more attractive.

"There you are, Narin. You know the lovely Neeta, of course," Laxman said.

"Oh, yes. Hello, Neeta," Narin said, quieting his nervousness.

"Hi, Narinder," she replied, her face lighting up.

He found a smile in return. "Narin … Narin is fine."

He turned toward Ambika in mild discomfort from Neeta's steady gaze. Ambika's familiar presence reduced his anxiety. He noted her colorful rhinestone-studded sandals, which, as usual, complemented her sari, as did the combs in her hair. He marveled at the number of accessories she must have. He wished he'd worn sandals newer than the ratty ones he had on.

"Hey, Ambika, how did your exams go?"

"Very well," Ambika replied. "What a relief it's over. That anatomy paper was a tough one, wasn't it? Trust Prof. Megarathnam to set something extra hard."

"He'll probably come back as a beetle in his next life for the way he abuses his students," interjected Neeta.

Narin noted that for all Ambika's self-assuredness, Neeta assumed the dominant role.

"Mmm, yes. I did okay, but you know who's the real wiz here. Neeta claims she'll top it, get cent percent."

"Not one to hide her light under a bushel, our Neeta," Laxman put in.

"That's great. I hear you always do very well," Narin said.

"Yes, thanks. And I hear you always do just well enough to keep your family off your back. I wish I could slack off like that."

Narin glared at Laxman as he realized the extent to which his confidences had been broadcast, but Laxman ignored him, turning to Ambika to share a private moment.

Narin asked Neeta, "Going back to Konkan tomorrow?"

"No, but soon enough. I have a sister in Madras, and I'll stay with her for a while. It's much more fun being here than going home."

"Don't you miss your parents? And your family in Konkan?"

"Of course I do, but it's only my mother now. And not as much as you do your younger sister, I suppose. You keep in touch often, don't you? What's her name again … Shilpa?"

"It's Sheel … her name's Sheela."

Had the three of them discussed his entire life? A sudden fear gripped him—Laxman of course knew he was married, and he assumed Ambika also knew. But did Neeta? He thought it unlikely she'd be acting so free toward him if she did. On the other hand, if she did not, was he not being deceitful? What was he doing, anyway? He pushed these reluctant thoughts away.

Neeta smiled. "What a pretty name. Is she much like you? I'd like to see a photograph of her."

Photograph? Did anyone in his family even own a camera? He said nothing, realizing how primitive it might make them appear.

Neeta continued after a moment. "I know she had to leave school a couple of years ago, which I can't understand nowadays. My family encourages all us girls who want to study. I guess I'm lucky they're that way."

"How did they send you so far away from home? As a girl—"

"You know, MMC is one of the few places that allows us lesser creatures to join."

"You note us lesser creatures seem to head the rolls," Ambika added, sharing a grin with Neeta.

Laxman turned back to them. "Well, enough chit-chat, creatures all. Let's get going. Girls, you're on your own." His left arm windmilled at a passing cycle rickshaw. "Narin and I will take that rickshaw there, you can follow," he shouted over his shoulder to the girls. "You know where to meet on Fairlands Grounds, right? Okay, then."

So much for Laxman "arranging transport," Narin thought as they settled into the rickshaw.

"*Suh-ree, Fairlands Poh-lam*," Laxman told the driver in his atrocious Tamil accent, then continued with more exact directions. The rickshaw merged into traffic in its trademark aggressive and heart-stopping maneuver, its rubber horn emitting loud, plaintive bleats.

Laxman turned to Narin and said, pointing toward the driver, "We can never do that."

"Huh?"

"Blow that horn-thing, Narin. We're doctors, and we think we're high on the manual dexterity scale, but operating that instrument would beat us. Too soft, and it sighs. Too fast and hard, and it squeaks like a sparrow. Needs precise pumping."

"Rubbish, Lax. When have you tried it, anyway?"

"I stole one once. My pals and I were … hmm … high. We considered taking the whole rickshaw, but none of us knew how to drive it. And none of us in our, shall I say, compromised state were able to get a bleat out of the horn." He let out a short guffaw. "I still have it at home." Tossing his stub out of the open side of the vehicle, he leant back into the lurching seat. He didn't reach for another cigarette but continued with a smirk, "Well, how is she?"

"Who?"

"How do you like Neeta, you dummy? I think she likes you."

"Laxman, what are you up to? Of course there's no such thing."

"Up to? Nothing. Just want all my friends to get along famously."

Narin cringed inwardly and wished he'd worn more of a poker face during his conversation with Neeta; clearly his attraction for her had been obvious to Laxman. He didn't want Laxman's jokiness to spoil his mood. "Sure. How come you've never brought her along to our group before?"

"She's not much for group activities. But she's become great friends with Ambika, so I thought we all should get together. She has that serious air about her, but she's funny, also." He leaned over and tapped Narin's knee. "She must like you. I've seen her be quite cutting with boys she has no use for. Which is most of them. Must like your disheveled hairdo—when's the last time you visited a barber, anyway? You can make a move, but tread carefully, m'boy."

Laxman's affirmation that Neeta was flirting with him buoyed Narin. In his three years at MMC, no other girl had been as open with him, and he liked—no, basked—in the warmth of her presence. But what did that signify? He was glad Laxman and Ambika were with them.

FAIRLANDS GROUNDS WAS a narrow park of several acres in northeast Madras, bounded by a branch of the river Couvam on one side and Flag Staff Road on the other. A small beach bordered the eastern edge where the Couvam emptied into the ocean. Public events and fairs were held there in cooler months, but in this heat, it was just a spotty green place with a few trees providing shelter from the midday sun. Narin realized he didn't have to be concerned about the number of people at the park—there were few.

Neeta had brought a bed sheet, which they spread out in the shade of a large tree. The girls laid out the metal *tiffin* carriers containing the food, and as they split them apart, Narin was glad to see no sign of chicken or mutton. Neeta was a Brahmin and a vegetarian like him, so the omission was in deference to both of them. His meat-eating initiation had been postponed again. Neeta and Ambika ladled the food onto stainless-steel plates, and Narin set the tumblers down, adjusting them just so on the uneven ground, then pulled out the glass beakers from his bag.

"What on earth is that? Looks like a lab beaker," Neeta said.

"Ah, yes," Narin replied.

"You stole them from the lab?"

"Not exactly. Borrowed," he said with a baleful glance at Laxman.

"The pyramidal shape enhances the flavor of the contents," Laxman said.

"What do the chemical dregs do?" Neeta asked, her gaze still fixed on Narin.

He tried to smile as he poured out the juice, embarrassed by her disapproval.

They settled in to eat, and the conversation turned to the events of the day: what the Indian National Congress was up to.

Laxman said with a sly grin, "So, about the event of the month. Who among us thinks ol' Stalin is faking it?" referring to an activist with the language protests who had started a fast almost four weeks ago. His words surprised the others, who would've been hard-pressed to remember the faster's memorable name of Stalin Jagadeesan.

"Faking it, faking what?" asked Neeta.

"There are many rumors that he's faking his fast and he's being fed late at night when only his supporters are around. No one is allowed to visit him in the wee hours of the night, you know." Amid general sounds of dissension, he drawled, "Well, you should know, Narin. What did you hear from the horse's mouth?"

"What?" said both girls.

Neeta turned to Narin. "What on earth does he mean?"

Startled by Laxman's disclosure, Narin took a moment to consider his response.

Laxman stepped in. "Well, Narin infiltrated a protest meeting yesterday. I wondered if you knew of it, but maybe it was very hush-hush. A Brahmin sallying forth among the heathens." Laxman winked at Neeta, herself a Brahmin, and she returned a frown.

Narin found his voice. "Don't be stupid, Laxman. I told you it was just one of the meetings organized by the boycott committee. Nothing mentioned about Jagadeesan's fast. It was completely open to all, and I'm sure Brahmins were welcome." His face shone with elation as he recalled the collective energy at the meeting.

With the pedantic look he wore when he was digressing, Laxman said, "Hmm, yes, of course. Interesting word, that, 'boycott.' Actually, comes from a chap—Irish, I think—called Boycott. Oddly enough, he was the bad chap, the boycott-ee, so to speak, not the boycott-er, when he tried to collect taxes or something. Finally, the riff-raff had had it with their lord's impositions and revolted against him. So we've reversed the connotation. Hmm

… now that girls are also protesting, maybe we should change the name to—"

"Oh, stop showing off and shut it, Lax," Ambika said. "I want to hear from Narin what happened there."

Laxman sighed. "Just a little etymology lesson. Well, Narinder, take it away. The stage is all yours."

As the three of them faced Narin, he was struck by the anticipation on Neeta's face. He didn't know what her stance was on the language issue—her own language was akin to Hindi, so she might support its proselytization. And how did she feel about the protests? Her expression indicated more than a passing interest in the matter. Or in him?

"It was … interesting," he said, flushing. "No, fascinating. Over three hundred people there. The main purpose appeared to be to rouse the troops. And it did that. Lots of energy. And screaming. Hard to understand what the speakers were saying much of the time. But it wasn't intimidating. Fact is, in a way I was happy there were people of various classes and educational levels. You know we …" Narin made a collective gesture, "… we're used to socializing with only our own types. If all of you weren't so disdainful of the 'lower classes' and of these events, I'd have invited you."

"Ouch. So what was decided?" Ambika asked.

"Not much discussion; this was the public face of the organization. We were only informed of the decisions the bigwigs had made in private. They issued a list of protest dates, times, and places. You know they're targeting schools where Hindi is now being taught?" Bravado overtook him, and he continued, "Maybe I'll take a picket board to the Hindu Theosophical School on Sunday. It's in Triplicane, no? Not too far."

Narin had thought about it after he'd left the meeting the previous evening but hadn't decided whether to go. The possibility of jeopardizing his status at MMC by participating in such a demonstration, however legitimate it might be, was a strong deterrent. Why had he blurted it out now? To register Neeta's reaction? She appeared attentive but was silent.

"Narin, you can't do that." Ambika's voice rose sharply. "There might be some police action. In fact, it's more likely than not. What will happen to you if you get arrested or beaten up?"

Laxman's words overlapped Ambika's, and for once, he held back his sarcastic side. "Well, Narin, bully for you. I didn't know you had it in you. Where do you get this newfound conviction? Be careful, my friend."

Narin consulted his internal auditor, that invisible being he had grown up with who seemed to throttle his actions—and thoughts. Why had he thrown out this intention so facilely without thinking it through? His upbringing had trained him to toe the line, to consider consequences, to think about repercussions. Not like him to join a screaming line of pickets, waving a crude, hand-lettered sign for a cause he felt marginal about. Tamil? Yes, of course, Tamil was his mother tongue, but he'd been fluent in English for years and used it almost exclusively when speaking or writing. Why would the sudden imposition of Hindi bother him in any way? *He* wasn't being forced to learn it, though if it became the standard in the administration, he might have to if he worked beyond Madras province.

Laxman, Neeta, and Ambika were still focused on him as he returned from his reverie.

"Narin," Neeta said, "I find your resolve admirable. Lax and Ambika are right. You'd have a lot to lose if things go wrong, but sometimes you just have to do what your heart tells you and not listen to the naysayers."

He looked at her with affection. "Thanks, Neeta … chaps. I'll try not to get in too much trouble."

"Don't expect me to bail you out, Narin. Way too bothersome. And expensive," Laxman said.

The girls shouted, "Stop it, Lax," and "Be serious for once."

"Well, as you wish. What's serious is that we've finished our food and now need to work it off by walking on yonder beach."

Laxman got up with an unabashed smile and moved away, leaving the cleanup and repacking of the dishes to the others, not surprising Narin. After they'd finished, he turned back with a congratulatory look on his face and shepherded them the short distance to the beach.

The heat of the sun had driven away the few stragglers, and the beach was deserted. They walked on the scorching sand for a while, though the heat penetrated the soles of their sandals. The girls folded up their saris, and Laxman and Narin rolled up their trousers so they could wade through the cooling waters, sandals in hand, reveling as fluid sand percolated through warm toes with each receding wave. After walking through the surf for about fifteen minutes, they paused. They sat on the grass under the shade of a tree and watched the gulls swoop precipitously down to them, then fly away squawking when they realized there was no food.

"So, to change the subject, what about P and P?" Ambika asked after a few moments. She had become quite the Jane Austen fan during the last year and suggested everyone read *Pride and Prejudice* and discuss it at the end of the year. She and Laxman had read the book in the last weeks of the term, even with exams looming, but Narin had only managed to squeeze in a few hurried scans, so he hoped the discussion would stay on a general level.

"Great. I'll start," Laxman said unsurprisingly. "Greatest love story I've ever read. There. Argue the point if you will."

They pondered his opening gambit.

"Well, I *loved* the Elizabeth Bennet character," Neeta said. "She's so strong and straightforward."

"And lucky," Laxman added.

"Lucky? How so?"

"The whole thing could've blown up. She rejected Darcy in that go-to-the-devil way. And yet he came back."

"Well, men don't take no for an answer," said Ambika.

"That's ridiculous," Neeta said. "Of course you should accept it when someone says no."

"Not when you're in love," Laxman said.

"I'm not sure what that means," Narin said.

"It means you really want to be with someone so badly it hurts, and it distorts your perspective."

Narin wondered if that was from personal experience.

"I suppose if I *really* want something, I'll make sure I go for it," Neeta said.

"And you'll get it, too," Laxman said with that grin.

"Being snide, again, Lax," Ambika said.

Narin chipped in. "You know, I think the whole story is contrived. I find it quite unbelievable. Don't you see how carefully plotted it is, so we're sucked into it?"

His friends looked at each other in surprise.

"Narin, that's cynical," Neeta said. "I agree that Austen had her own ideas to push along, but the writing is not contrived. It's genius. You feel for those people. You want Elizabeth to marry Darcy, even with all their problems."

"And you have to consider the time," Ambika added. "Women had no choice but to marry someone who'd take care of them. We don't have to do that nowadays."

"Really?" Laxman said. "Why don't you ask Narin about that?"

Narin shot Laxman a warning look. He didn't want his family, his sister, or his marriage subject to dissection. Laxman raised his eyebrows, which Narin took as consenting to his unspoken request.

Neeta had picked up on the exchange. "Why, Narin? What do you know that's special?"

"Oh, well, Laxman just means that my family is … maybe more conservative and traditional than yours. So women in my family don't have the same opportunities."

"Like your sister?"

"Maybe. But back to the book, people. Greatest love story you said, Laxman? No, I think *Romeo and Juliet* is."

"Dying, unrequited lovers being your preference?" asked Laxman.

"Of course not. But there's more at stake in that story. Romeo and Juliet obviously had more to lose. Their family connections. Their friends, who hated the other clan. They were pretty sure to be ostracized. And they went ahead in spite of all that."

"True. That *is* so much more romantic than ol' Elizabeth Bennet."

Narin looked at Neeta. "I said I didn't know what love is. Well, Romeo says, 'Love is a smoke made from a fume of sighs. A choking gall and a preserving sweet.'"

She laughed. "That's beautiful, Narin. You must like the play a lot."

"You can't compare the writings of Austen to Shakespeare," Ambika said. "I read somewhere he wrote, what, in a 'heightened emotional state?' So it wasn't realistic writing, was it? And Austen's is. She actually lived through some of the stuff she wrote about. Did any of you read the Austen biography by E. Jenkins? We know she was jilted, or at least broke off an engagement and never married."

"Okay," Narin conceded, "there are parallels to her life. Authors do put a lot of themselves in their work, you know. So, agreed the characters are real. But they're trivial."

Silence ensued. The girls stared at each other. Ambika said, "Trivial?" and Neeta said, "What? How?" simultaneously. Laxman lit the One Eleven he had been twirling in his fingers. He sat back, smirked, and narrowed his eyes, as if watching a specimen about to be dissected.

"Yes, trivial," Narin repeated. "They all loll around the house and eat, drink, and be merry—"

"As we're doing now," said Laxman.

"No, not like us. This is a sometime thing. We don't do picnics in the park every day. They do, metaphorically. They spend all day deciding where to go the next day, and then they spend all the next day going there. They're like parasites, ah—"

"Feeding on the body politic?"

"Maybe."

"Well, Narin, I didn't know you were so the Marxist," Ambika said.

Neeta's face flushed with passion. "And Narin, you're ignoring the context. So that's the life they led, but they didn't know any different. It's not as if they were the French nobility with peasants starving around them. They were decent sorts. They did no real harm. I think you're ignoring the poetry in the writing and the depth of the characters because you're caught up in the humdrum physical details. *That's* the trivial part to me."

Laxman blew two smoke rings and watched them float languidly away. "Bull by the horns, Narin."

Narin turned away from Neeta. He'd been distracted paying too much attention to her and now wanted to defend his position, to point out that Austen's prose was quite idiosyncratic, hardly describable as poetic. "Well, you can read it from different angles, I suppose, and I chose to concentrate on their actions and their effect on society. It's as if nothing outside their world existed. Did they ever think about events beyond their immediate surroundings? Of politics? Or how much injustice their country was inflicting on others? Wasn't England violently colonizing the whole world then?"

"Narin bats a sixer!" Laxman said, sweeping his hand through the air as if following the cricket ball's spectacular flight out of bounds.

Neeta exchanged a pained look with Ambika.

"Narin, I think it's great you read it that way. You have more of a social conscience than we do."

"Or the soul of a bureaucrat," Laxman said.

"Stop it, Laxman," Ambika said, an admonishment she used often. He grinned. She returned the grin. "I predict you're going to be a mega-bureaucrat yourself one day, ordering all the peons around." She reached over and patted him on the shoulder, her hand sliding close to his face as she withdrew it. Laxman turned his head and ostentatiously kissed her moving fingers.

Narin looked over at Neeta, who was also watching the couple. Her face was animated and lively, flushed from exposure to the sun. She was beautiful.

It seemed a good breaking point, as it was now late afternoon. They got up more or less simultaneously. Narin reached out to help Neeta up and thrilled as their hands met. The four retraced their steps across the park, over the decrepit fencing at the perimeter of Fairlands Grounds to Flag Staff Road, where they would look for rickshaws to take them back to their hostels. Laxman and Ambika were a few steps ahead of the others.

"I had a wonderful time, Neeta," Narin said.

"Likewise." Her eyes sparkled.

"I hope you have fun during your stay with your sister. And back home. I'll see you next term."

"You're staying a few days with your aunt, no? Kala? And your sister, Sheela, is there also?"

Did the girl keep a diary on him? "Yes, Auntie Kala. I didn't know you⸺"

"Knew? Of course. No secrets between Ambika and me."

Maybe there should be, Narin thought with a glimmer of annoyance at the unaccustomed transparency of his family life. This was soon replaced by relief as he realized that, although she knew much of his family history, she still wanted to further their relationship. But did she know he was married?

"Why don't you come see me at my sister Deepa's? She's at 24 Thembu Chetty Road. Maybe the day after tomorrow?" She made a move toward her purse but didn't open it. "At four? I don't have a pencil. Can you remember?"

Could he remember? "Yes … that would be … nice."

That smile flashed. She moved closer to him, and he put out his hand tentatively to take hers, but she made no further move, and neither did he. For a moment, their eyes locked on each other. Then she turned and walked to the waiting rickshaw, gracefully stepped in, and waved goodbye through its open side. Narin waved back and started walking toward Laxman, who had flagged down another rickshaw.

"Narinder!"

He turned toward the shout.

Improbably, impossibly, across the dusty street stood a large, sweaty presence glaring at him. His brother-in-law, Jaggie. As the shock wore off, the voice repeated, "Narin."

Laxman chuckled. Narin glared at him, then strolled across the street—almost too slowly, as a tonga cart rushed inches from him, and he had to jump out of its way.

He tamped his emotion and said, "Hello, Brother-in-law Jaggie. What are you doing here?"

"What are *you* doing here? Who are those people?" Jaggie was using that aggrieved tone he often favored, now sharpened by irritation.

"They're all students from my class. You remember Laxman, he came by your house once to pick me up? He's a good friend of mine."

"But the girls?"

"Uh … students also. There are many girls at MMC."

"What were you doing? Do you know them?"

Ignoring the urge to say, no, they'd just collected them from the street, Narin replied, "They're Laxman's friends. We had some food on Fairlands Grounds. A picnic. We finished exams yesterday, and it seemed like a good idea. Here, want some lemonade?" He opened the cloth bag and took out one of the beakers containing dregs of juice. "Maybe it's still cold."

"What? No."

"Okay."

Jaggie was now staring across the road, his eyes wide. "That Laxman … he's smoking."

Damn Laxman and his inability to keep away from cigarettes for more than a few minutes. "Yes, he does, sometimes. Many of the students smoke, you know."

"Do you?"

"No. Look, I really must go. Have to pack. You know I'm off to Auntie Kala's tomorrow. I'll meet you before I go. Bye."

As Narin turned and walked back, the street noise did not drown Jaggie's shout. "This is not right. We have to talk about this."

He shouted back, "Why don't you come to Auntie Kala's at *tiffin* time? We'll have *chaat* and lemonade." Narin beamed at his pun.

Jaggie opened and closed his mouth several times but didn't answer.

Laxman stood grinning with his hand on the stopped rickshaw, no sympathy showing in his eyes. "You look wrecked. Cigarette? It will calm your nerves."

"No! Can't you see he's still watching?"

Laxman turned to look across Flag Staff Road at Jaggie, who was still staring at them, took a deliberate drag off his cigarette, and blew a smoke ring. "Really bad luck him being there, no? Are you going to be in much trouble?"

"I don't know yet. Maybe I don't care."

"That's the spirit. You'll learn to make your own way, m'boy. Let's take a walk back. A pleasant saunter is as good for your nerves as a smoke." Laxman dismissed the rickshaw driver with a well-tossed coin, who rode off grumbling. "You can fill me in on the latest on Jaggie. What's he doing so far from his office, anyway? Isn't he stouter than the last time I saw him at his house? His wife must be a good cook. Can you get him to invite us all over for a good Brahmin vegetarian meal? I miss it so."

Laxman's steady chatter eased Narin's jangled state of mind as they walked back to the hostel. They bid each other goodbye with a hearty hug, promising to write. Narin went down to the lab to return the beakers. The door was inexplicably locked. He took the beakers back to his room and placed them on his study table, adjusting them until centered. He sat down and gazed at their shining crystalline symmetry, immersed in his thoughts.

IX
Madras, 1939

Aunt Kalakshetra—Kala to the family—was Narinder's mother's younger sister and lived with her husband, Maruti, a few miles east of Narin's hostel.

The day after the picnic, Narin lugged the smaller of his two trunks to the tram stop en route to his aunt's house. He'd left the other behind in the care of the college porter. He'd learned the ways of the world and dropped a *baksheesh* of a quarter rupee into the porter's willing hand to ensure its safety, in addition to the official amount charged by the college. He clambered aboard the tram and stood in its open center passage, his long hair blowing askew. He would need a haircut before confronting his twin aunts in Venpuri. He alighted and walked a short distance along the main road before turning down a narrow side street. The muffled roar of traffic from the busy main road quieted as he reached his aunt's house. The many trees that dotted the street and Aunt Kala's yard lent a pleasant dappled note to the full sun. This would be a sanctuary after his last hectic weeks at college.

Within seconds of his ringing the doorbell, Sheela opened the door and gave him a warm embrace. He examined her at arms length and was happy to see Madras suited her. Her face glowed, showing no ill effects from the family brouhaha over her recent rejection of a proposal.

"You look great, Sheel."

"Good to see you too, Narin. You're in time."

"In time for what?"

"I only meant I'm glad you came before Auntie Kala. You should hear this from me first."

"What? Good news?"

"No, well … you decide. Jaggie came over here last night to talk to Auntie Kala. Of course I listened in. He doesn't exactly whisper, does he? So he was going on about seeing you with some really bad company and what was to be done about it? Auntie and Uncle took a while to calm him down. I guess he saw you with Laxman and … two girls? And everyone was laughing and smoking and carrying on? Is this all true?" Sheela appeared more excited than worried.

Damn Jaggie, Narin thought; he's nothing if not prompt to stir up trouble. "He's exaggerating. But yes, there were four of us, and we'd gone for a picnic in Fairlands Grounds. And of course Laxman smokes like a chimney, though I guess Jaggie didn't know that, even though they've met before."

He recalled the time when Laxman came to collect him from Jaggie's house. The unlikely pair did not hit it off—Laxman, suave, youthful, with an air of ease, and Jaggie, older, insecure, and struggling to make it in the big city. Laxman had striven to keep his snide side at bay, and Jaggie had overcompensated with his hearty, loud manner. Later, Jaggie had warned Narin against "getting mixed up with the wrong sort." When Narin asked what the matter with Laxman was, Jaggie only sputtered. After that, Narin made sure they didn't meet. Until the previous day's encounter. No doubt Jaggie now had the ammunition to prove the wrongness of Laxman's sort.

"Oh, Fairlands … that's near your college, isn't it? A picnic sounds like great fun. But who were the girls?"

"I know them through Laxman. I must've mentioned Ambika. She hangs out with Laxman a lot." Abandoning the euphemism, he said, "Actually, she and Laxman are a pair, have been for almost a year. I wouldn't be surprised if they announced they're going to get married soon. And the other was Neeta, Ambika's best friend."

Sheela laughed. "Yes, you wrote to me about her once. She drew that wonderful picture—caricature—of Prof. M-something. That's clever. I remember you said she asks lots of questions in class and is quite argumentative, no? Is she pleasant or sort of nasty?"

Narin was elated both at her remembering the details he'd written months ago and her evident pleasure in Neeta's mocking a professor. It should have made his answer easier, but he still equivocated. "Pleasant ... well, mostly." Why so bland a word? He might've said "wonderful" or "exciting." His feelings toward Neeta were new to him, and his cautious nature prevented him from opening up even to his sister. He wasn't sure how Sheela would react if he revealed his true feelings.

Sheela intuited much from the change in his manner and pounced. "Oh, Narin. You must really like her."

"I ... don't know." Sheela's tone and eager manner reassured him she would be supportive. "Well, yes, I do. I do like her a lot. She was easy to talk to from the first. She asked me about you and said you had a pretty name. We discussed books. She also invited me to visit her at her sister's house tomorrow."

"Really? Of course you're going. I wish I could come with you to meet her, but I'm sure she meant that you should come by yourself. What are you going to tell Auntie?"

"I won't lie. I'll just say I'm going to meet a friend and will be back for dinner. She probably won't ask who."

"Of course."

Narin marveled that the conversation about a married man visiting another woman flowed so easily. Why was Sheela so undisturbed by the implications? Why was he? How easy it was for him to forget Mina after another year of separation with only one short letter exchanged. Having a quiet "wife" waiting for him in Venpuri was unreal. Better to think about the vivacious and intelligent Neeta who might—delicious thought—also be thinking of him.

"I'll get us some snacks," Sheela said and left.

Narin was impressed that she hadn't summoned the servant to cater to them. He put away his trunk in a bedroom and returned to the living room. It was the largest room in the house with windows on two sides ensuring plenty of light. These had the obligatory bars in an elaborate filigree style, less oppressive than the plain iron rods of Narin's Venpuri house. A comfortable sofa and several wooden armchairs, the latter with puffy bright red cushions, filled the room. Narin had always admired his aunt's taste. He now noticed newly framed decorated pages from ancient Indian books among the wall hangings, a recent fad. He sat down and thought about his forthcoming meeting with Neeta in pleasant anticipation.

Sheela returned with the snacks.

"Tell me what you've been doing the last few weeks," he said.

She had begun to explore the neighborhood. "Those three houses on the next road, with the lovely flower boxes? There's always someone tending them. I like that. And that hidden garden in the middle of Jacobs Street, so nice and quiet? Those tallish buildings around it make it hard to see the entrance."

Narin had never known Sheela to pay much attention to her surroundings before, so her observations surprised him.

"I even walked into a nearby coffee shop and ordered tea. That was an adventure. They all stared at me as if I was a *rakshasa* or something." Narin gave a snort of laughter, imagining his little sister as a demon. "Not too comfortable, but I stayed and finished the tea anyway. Later I found a bookstore nearby. Bet you don't know it, do you?" Narin shook his head. "With a decent selection of English language books, no less. It was so exciting to see and touch the books on the shelves. I'd hoped to find some of your many suggestions. I found two books I was going to buy, then realized I didn't have anywhere near the money I needed." She shrugged. "I only take a rupee or two with me when I go out, and even that feels strange as I never carried money with me in Venpuri. Luckily, they knew Auntie and Uncle, and trusted me to come back to pay them.

"Do you know, that's what I find surprising about being here in Madras. Even though it's a huge city, so much bigger than Venpuri, in many ways it's still like a village. People know each other."

"Do they look out for each other? Do you feel as safe as at home?"

"Yes ... mostly. Auntie Kala doesn't like me to go too far. She's warned me of some places I should avoid. And always watch out for groups of men, she said."

"You know, you're very lucky. Auntie Kala is quite loose with you."

"Well, I'm glad I'm free here."

They continued their conversation until their aunt came home. A plump woman of pleasant demeanor, almost fifty, she had moved to Madras some twenty-eight years ago after she married her husband, Maruthi, and they'd lived in this house ever since. As they had no children, they devoted their attention to various nieces and nephews, sent to visit them on occasion. The perfect aunt, they called her. Sheela was Kala's favorite, no doubt recognizing in her a kindred spirit.

Kala greeted Narin, then draped an arm around Sheela's shoulders and said, "Look. Isn't Sheel happy? I'm so glad she didn't agree to marry that strange son of those horrible neighbors." Sheela and Narin burst out laughing at this description, which would have been unimaginable from any of their family.

"Yes," Narin said, "she doesn't act like someone who's had a narrow escape."

"You weren't there, Narin. It was awful. I felt like hiding every time our relatives came over, particularly those … our twin aunties."

"Sheel, you must be respectful of them," Aunt Kala said. "They have all our best interests at heart. Well, it's over now." She turned to Narin. "And you? Exams I'm sure went well. I'm so glad you decided to come and stay with us for a while. What do you plan to do these two weeks before you go to Venpuri?"

"Well, Sheel and I will see at least one picture, *King Kong,* at the Elphinstone on Monday. And I have some friends to visit."

"Oh, do you have classmates in Madras? I don't remember you talking about them before. You can invite them over for dinner soon."

"Uh, yes, Auntie. Well, one or two, you don't know them. And thanks for the invitation. I should tell you I'm meeting one friend tomorrow afternoon, but I'll be back for dinner."

"Sure. Maybe you could take Sheela with you. She hasn't seen much of Madras beyond this area."

"I suppose you and Uncle haven't had the time to take her around yet. I'll show her around Madras, but not tomorrow. Sheel doesn't know … uh, him, my friend," Narin said as Sheela shook her head and winked at him.

Aunt Kala probed no further about the visit, and Narin volunteered no more. She didn't mention Jaggie, but Narin assumed that his revelations would spark a conversation later. Perhaps she was waiting for her husband so they could confront him together. After further conversation, his aunt left to talk to her cook about dinner. The siblings decided to walk around the neighborhood, Sheela promising to show Narin the garden on Jacobs Street. They went out into the bustle and wandered for a while, soon dropping into the silence that marked their friendship.

When they returned, their Uncle Maruthi was home, and dinner was ready. Aunt Kala had an exceptional cook, and Narin ate the food with pleasure, contrasting it with his mediocre hostel fare. He braced himself for a discussion of Jaggie's visit, but it wasn't mentioned. After dinner, when Sheela excused herself to write to her mother, Maruthi exchanged a significant look with his wife.

Kala sighed and said, "Narin, your brother-in-law, Jaggie, came here yesterday. He had a story about you."

Narin looked wide-eyed at them. "Yes. He saw me outside the Fairlands Grounds Park."

"And he says you were there smoking and in the company of some strange people."

Narin chuckled. "Are those his words? I'm surprised he didn't use 'loose.' He likes that word a lot. Well, the 'strange people' were close friends of mine, fellow students, all of them. Nothing strange there. And only Laxman, he only saw Laxman smoking."

Aunt Kala seemed amused at his description of Jaggie. "That's what I thought too. But it took a while to calm him down, and I think he's writing to your father and your *Mamanaar* Subbu right now. He's upset about your being in the company of these girls. Do you see them much?"

Narin didn't care what his father-in-law thought of his conduct, but his father? He hoped he would have the chance to put things in perspective.

"Auntie, at college lots of students hang out together," he said. "Girls and boys. Laxman and his friend Ambika are … often together, and they invited another friend, a girl, and we all went on a picnic. That's all."

His aunt and uncle exchanged a look. Maruthi shrugged.

Kala smiled. "Well, I'm sure no harm was done, Narin, but Jaggie will be blowing it up to something much bigger in his letters. I'd be prepared for a blast from your *Mamanaar* and maybe also from your father. But let's leave it at that."

Narin had been covertly watching his uncle during this exchange, and although he found it hard to read his uncle's poker face, he was happy that he appeared unperturbed.

"Maybe you should take your picnics in farther-away places," Maruthi said as he rose. "Now let's move to the living room, and you can tell us more about the last month or so since your aunt and I saw you."

Narin exhaled silently and followed his uncle, relieved to chat about life at MMC.

THE NEXT DAY Narin stood before 24 Thembu Chetty Road, Neeta's sister Deepa's house, a detached whitish brick-and-stucco building set in a small compound. Two squat stories devoid of any architectural adornment, its stippled walls were dotted with small windows with ornate iron bars, each window with a small sunshade of dubious utility set above. The flat roof had a continuous parapet that provided some shade. Atop the roof perched a partially hidden concrete cistern, a recent feature that provided running water indoors.

A male servant, stripped to the waist in deference to the heat, bobbed at the pump, which filled the tank. Narin stood unmoving in the street for a few minutes, watching the rhythmic motion of the man's body, sweat draining down his face. He wondered if this visit was a good idea. His experience with the opposite sex at college was quite at variance with Laxman's and far from what was expected in his family life, where boys and girls had minimal socialization after the age of ten. At MMC, though the sexes lived separately in hostels on opposite sides of the campus, and interaction was not encouraged, mixed-sex groups existed.

Narin admired the beauty and symmetry of a *kolam*, elaborate colored rice-powder lines that decorated the width of the stone path leading from the gate to the front door. Rainbow motes from its blowing particles spiraled into the sunshine. It was a religious symbol thought to bring prosperity, and he worried that it might portend a traditional household. What if Neeta's sister Deepa were like his Aunts Saraswathi and Saranmathi, who would have been appalled at a lone boy daring to visit one of their daughters? He could imagine the ensuing ruckus, the sisters rudely shooing the visitor away, perhaps even threatening him.

This is silly, he thought, shaking off his doubts. Neeta had invited him to visit at a time when her sister would presumably be home, which argued that her family was much more accepting than his was. He could no longer hesitate. Still anxious, he walked up to the front door. His hand trembled a bit as he rang the doorbell.

Neeta opened the door with a broad smile. "Narin. Perfect timing. Are you hungry? We're about to have our *tiffin*. You can join us. Come in."

His apprehension dissolved. She could not have been more welcoming, and, obviously, he was to meet her sister immediately. No jasmine in Neeta's hair today, he noted. Her face was unadorned, without even a red *bindi* mark on her forehead, and he drank in the freshness of her features. He mumbled, "Thanks," as he entered and stammered, "Nice house," as he glanced around at the tasteful furnishings.

"Thanks. Did you have any problem getting here?"

"No. The tram's only two or three streets away, so it was easy."

"Not too many loose Anglo-Indian girls infesting it, I hope?" she asked with a glint of amusement in her eyes.

"Oh, how did you … when did I … mention Jaggie's comment to you?"

"Well, at the park, of course. You don't remember? You were making fun of his stuffiness."

He was? He'd been circumspect about his family members, even to Laxman and Ambika. Ridiculing any of them, even the busybody Jaggie, was a new phase. Now he was happy he had felt free enough to do so. Along with a pang of concern—had he mentioned his exact relationship to Jaggie?

"Oh, yes, speaking of Jaggie, he saw the four of us together as we were leaving. He's written something nasty to my father and to my ... to others."

"God, he's quite the tattletale, isn't he? Guess the 'others' include his father? Well, they'll just have to get used to life in the big city."

So Neeta knew he was married but could brush it off. A surprising but welcome revelation. "He's been here seven years. I doubt he ever will. Anyway, it's not his life he has to get used to, it's mine. He's like a spy set to report my every move."

"Enough. Stop worrying. Here's my sister."

Narin rose to greet her, and he had little doubt Deepa was related to Neeta. She was a few years older but shared the same complexion and facial features. Her easy and open demeanor put him at ease. Like her sister, she wore a bright but simple cotton sari and a slightly high-cut blouse, a style less favored by married women. She looked cool and elegant.

"Hello, Narin. Glad to meet you," Deepa said as she extended her hand.

He shook it lightly, unused to such a modern greeting from his older female relatives, but then she was closer to his generation and from a more progressive family. They moved to the living room where snacks had been laid out. Deepa set a plate and a tumbler for him and asked if he preferred tea or buttermilk, *mohhr.*

"Neeta mentioned that you and her friends had a very nice picnic two days ago. I wish I had the time to do something like that. Reminds me of my own college days."

"Of course you have the time," Neeta said. "You can go anytime on Sundays when Uncle Shyam doesn't work. You just have to persuade him to go along with you."

"Oh, your *Chitthappa* Shyam's an old stick-in-the-mud. Claims it's too hot to go out during the day when he's off work. He prefers to hang around reading boring law journals." Deepa shared a grin with Neeta.

Narin started in surprise—for a wife to mock her husband in front of a stranger would've been unthinkable in his family. He was beginning to appreciate the advantages of having a family such as hers.

"Can't be worse than boring old medical journals. I can't wait until we finish," Neeta said. "Narin, what are you going to do tomorrow? Still planning on going to the protest?"

"Yes, of course. Do you want to come?" He noticed Deepa's look of surprise.

"Oh, I'd love to," Neeta replied.

"Really? Well, we'll have to decide where to meet, or better yet, I could come by."

"Great. It's just a short walk from here."

Deepa found her voice. "Wait a minute, hold on. What protest?"

Narin mentioned the anti-Hindi boycott meeting he'd attended and told her about the planned demonstration at the Theosophical School.

Deepa shook her head. "Narin, I don't think that's a good idea at all. Not even for you and certainly not for a girl like—"

Neeta interrupted. "Deep, there are plenty of women and girls at these protests. Haven't you been reading the papers? Or listening to the radio? I think it will be a learning experience."

"Neeta, you can't go. What would Amma say if she knew?"

"And how would she find out? Only from you. I doubt Narin is thinking of writing to our mother."

"Well, you still can't go."

Neeta had a rebellious look, and Narin expected her to reject her sister's stricture. They looked at each other, and he could see where the balance of power lay. He didn't want to push the issue at the risk of antagonizing Deepa.

Attempting a compromise, he said, "I agree with your sister, Neeta. I'll give you a first-hand report after I go, and maybe we'll have a better idea of how safe it is. Maybe you can attend the next one."

Neeta sighed and, as her sister maintained her gaze, mouthed an "Okay, Elder-Sister Deepa" and attacked a fried *vadai* with gusto. "Narin," she said, "you'll have to come over after the protest and let me know what happened."

"Okay." Another chance to see her before he left for Venpuri.

Deepa appeared appeased. To Narin's surprise, she continued discussing the topic. "Narin, tell me what's actually happening with the language issue. I'm not in favor of anything being forced on anyone, but I think the India of the future needs a common language, and it shouldn't be English."

Glad of a chance to show his familiarity with the movement, Narin went over the ground he had discussed with his friends at the picnic.

Deepa paid rapt attention. "And what do you think will happen? After the protests, I mean?"

Narin shook his head. "I … don't really know."

"Did you get a feeling that the leaders had a long-term plan? After all, the National Congress-*wallahs* really control Madras Presidency—look how they appointed a non-Tamil, Rajaji, as our chief minister. As if we didn't have any qualified people in our state."

At a loss, Narin resolved to be better informed.

"No matter. Besides the radio news, I haven't paid too much attention to all this, so it's nice to hear first-hand from you, Narin. And now that the protest issue is settled …" Deepa gave an affectionate, yet elder-sisterly authoritative glance at Neeta. "Let's change the subject. Tell me about your family. Neeta's told me you have a favorite sister and aunt, both in Madras. How about in Venpuri?"

Narin made desultory conversation about his family members for a while, revealing little. He wondered at his own reticence. He was in no way ashamed of his family, but they seemed so … dull

… in comparison with the present company. He would have loved to relate that his brother had designed an important dam on the River Shakti or that his father had been praised for his beneficial work in the neglected areas of Venpuri County, but no such events existed.

"Do you have other brothers or sisters?" he asked.

"No, only us," Deepa said. "Our father passed away when Neeta was a child. Amma had difficulty raising us two by herself. It's a good thing our extended family was willing to help her. She took small jobs to supplement their donations. Amma was convinced we needed a good education. God knows how she saved enough to send me to college." Deepa smiled. "Yes, lucky I went to a good college. Doubly lucky as I met my husband there, you know. Shyam helped with Neeta's education."

"Did you work after passing out from college?"

"Yes, but I waited until after Shyam got his graduate degree in law, and we had our children then."

She turned to the snacks. "Now, are you still hungry?"

Deepa left after they had finished eating to attend to household chores, leaving Narin alone with Neeta. He thought this might be awkward, but Neeta was just as open, relaxed, and friendly as she'd been with her sister present, putting him at ease. They had much to talk about besides rundowns on college life, overbearing professors, and unreasonable study schedules. They both read a lot, and they had mutual friends in addition to Ambika and Laxman.

An hour later, Narin glanced at his watch. "Oh, it's getting late. I really have to go. Auntie Kala is expecting me for dinner."

"This early? And you just stuffed yourself with all that *tiffin*."

"Ah, yes, they do eat earlier on the weekends, not sure why. I may have to disguise my lack of appetite somewhat."

"No matter. Well, you've promised to come back after the protest. Your only excuse for not coming will be that you were beaten up so badly you couldn't even take a rickshaw over."

"God forbid. I don't expect any danger. I'll be extra careful."

Neeta stood up, brushing crumbs from her sari with a graceful sweep, and Narin was lost in admiration. She saw Narin out to the hall, opened the door, and extended her hand as he said goodbye. Narin touched it, then held it. After a moment, he let go, turned, and walked away.

The tram back was empty of Anglo-Indian girls, but he didn't miss their peals of silvery laughter. His own thoughts were sustenance enough. The memory of Neeta's smooth, light skin, the warmth of her touch, and her enigmatic smile stayed with him until he returned to his aunt's house.

NARIN FOUND BOTH "familial blasts" had arrived by post. He sighed and picked up his father's letter first.

> Dear Narin,
>
> If what Jaggie says is true, I'm very disappointed in you. And angry that you have not been able to conduct yourself responsibly. I understand there are many temptations in a big city, but you should have been able to resist. Firstly, you are not alone there. Jaggie has extended himself far beyond the call of duty to visit you, invite you over to his house, and in general, act *in loco parentis*.
>
> Secondly, you should've thought how this will affect our family. We are well respected in Venpuri, and that's due to our always watching our behavior. Reputation is critical and, once lost, difficult to regain. Third, you should be thinking about how your actions will affect your poor sister, Sheela. She is already having difficulty in marriage (I won't say it's not somewhat due to her own stubbornness), and if news of your conduct is

widely known in Venpuri, she will have even less of a chance.

That was a low blow, given his extreme fondness for Sheela. Perhaps his father thought he was a bad influence on her. He read on:

> Finally, remember you are married. The family and I thought that having you get married before you left would leave you less vulnerable to this sort of thing. You may not feel the power of the married state yet, as you and your wife have not been as one together.
>
> I am assured by your *Mamanaar* Subbu that your wife will be ready for the ceremony soon, which will probably be before the next term starts. Maybe you will take marriage and its responsibilities more seriously then. Your Aunts Saraswathi and Saranmathi are insisting that you come home immediately rather than next week. But I don't see any reason for that since you are with your Uncle Maruthi and your Aunt Kala, and I'm sure you will listen to them and act in an appropriate manner. I've written to say that they should meet any of your friends you might be seeing while there. You must obey them in every respect.

Narin was impressed by his father's "you and your wife have not been as one together" comment, which seemed a stretch beyond his father's usual cut-and-dried style. Euphemism, the mother of poetry? He noticed that his father didn't mention his exact transgression. What had Jaggie written, and how much of it was exaggeration?

And what phrase had his father used to describe Jaggie—*in loco parentis*? "Loco" being the key word. Narin grinned. Why his father thought he would welcome Jaggie's officious meddling in his life was beyond him. The times Narin had visited Jaggie, he'd sat in glum quiet while Jaggie went on about his work in excruciating detail, only to segue to no more interesting reminiscences about life in Venpuri. The only question he asked Narin was whether his studies were going well, which he did several times, as if Narin's repetitious, "Yes, it's fine," would raise his standing in the academic lineup. Jaggie's wife, a dutiful woman with little education, was as unspoken as Narin was. She prepared excellent South Indian Brahmin fare. They were well-off enough to afford a cook, but Narin suspected Jaggie preferred his wife to cater to him as much as possible. The one saving grace in the tedious visits was the gratifying meal he wolfed down.

His father-in-law Subbu's letter was short and echoed similar sentiments as Narin's father—the disappointment, the anger, the reminder of that magic word, responsibility. They might as well have been a single missive. Subbu also used the phrase "your wife." Damn it, Mina's your daughter, Narin fumed. She does have a name. Someone should mention it.

He tossed the letters aside. There seemed little reason to reply.

That Night After dinner, Narin told Sheela of his plan to go to the protest meeting and of Neeta's enthusiasm. "Neeta is quite independent, Sheel, and she immediately wanted to go with me."

Sheela's face lit up. "What a great idea, Narin. She and I could both come with you."

Narin raised his eyebrows. To his knowledge, Sheela had never focused on politics.

"Didn't think you'd be interested. What do you know of the movement?"

"What? You think I'm ignorant? I used to sneak and turn on the radio in Venpuri to hear all this. You know Appa never shares the newspaper, and it's impossible to find it after he finishes. Here I switch on the radio whenever I want."

Narin took a moment to digest this new information.

Sheela appeared annoyed at his silence. "Well?"

"Okay, I think. If you're sure."

"Of course I'm sure. What could be a problem?"

"Uh, many things. Also, we'd have to hide it from Auntie Kala, no?"

"A secret? From Auntie?"

"There's no way she'd allow you to go, Sheel. In fact, if you tell her, it's quite likely she'd forbid me to go as well."

"Aha. You weren't going to tell her about it either, were you? So it's no different her not knowing if we both go. Your friend Neeta and I can look out for each other. I can't wait to meet her."

"Well, strictly speaking, Neeta isn't allowed to go either. Her sister vetoed it. But I saw Neeta's look. She'll be glad to join me if she can sneak out."

"Narin, this is a great opportunity. I hear Neelambikai is speaking at the school."

Sheela was a string of surprises. He didn't recall noticing the activist's name in the sparse news reports. "I didn't know you knew of Neelambikai, but yes, she was at the meeting I went to recently."

Sheela rolled her eyes. "She's the first *woman* scholar to write on the importance of Tamil, right? She's also published a Tamil dictionary. Can you believe it, she has eight children? And she still goes around the state giving speeches and rousing up people. Now we have to go to it. Do you know if Neeta has a telephone? No?" She grabbed a notepad and a pencil and thrust them at Narin. "Here, write a note to your Neeta and give her the details. I'll get the servant's son to take it over. Do you have an *anna*? That should keep him quiet. You said Thembu Chetty Road, no? We can go by and pick her up on the way. Say two o'clock tomorrow. I'll make up an excuse for Auntie."

Narin gaped at her, taking charge like this, with so much more self-confidence than he'd noticed before. Comes from rejecting suitors and defying the family, he thought. The Aunties S would not approve, but he admired Sheela's new resoluteness, which would prove useful if she decided to continue her studies or look for a job.

And so it went. They sent the note and soon received a short and gushing response from Neeta: "YES. Love to. Looking forward to meeting your sister. I'll be outside the house at two."

Sheela jumped for joy and hugged Narin. "Wonderful. We'll have such an adventure tomorrow."

She and Narin discussed the details late into the night.

Narin went to bed that night full of trepidation. And anticipation.

X
Madras, 1939

Narin came out of a deep sleep in the early morning, flinging his bed covers aside. The magnitude of his folly came into stark focus. He was going to a demonstration with the potential for violence, taking two sheltered girls with him, using subterfuge if not an outright lie to deceive their guardians. Was he crazy? The rest of his night's sleep was restless as his doubts blossomed. He waited, throttling his impatience, until his aunt and uncle finished their leisurely breakfast and left for work, then pulled Sheela into the backyard.

"I'm having second thoughts," he said. "What on earth was I thinking when I agreed to let the two of you come?"

Sheela was in a state of high excitement. She gaped at him, her initial surprise turning to disappointment. "Narin, *we* made the decision to join you, not the other way around. It's our decision and our responsibility."

"That's not the way it works. If anything happens, you know I'll get blamed."

"Well, if anything happens, and it won't, I'll make sure that everyone knows I went of my own free will. I'll say you tried to stop me, but I insisted. They'll believe me," she said with a grin. "They're always calling me stubborn, you know? And I'm sure

Neeta will say something similar." She reached out and put a hand on his arm. "You know, Narin, the reason you like Neeta is that she's independent and decisive. Like me. So accept the fact that we girls don't need you to be too protective of us."

Narin admired Sheela for her conviction but was still dubious. Theirs was a strongly paternalistic society, where women had little freedom except in urban settings, although his Aunts Saraswathi and Saranmathi could run roughshod over anyone. The assumption would be that Narin had somehow induced Sheela and Neeta to join him on a dangerous adventure. He looked at his sister. He couldn't disappoint her. Or Neeta. He made up his mind.

"Okay, let's go. It's time we did something outside our normal, boring routine."

Relieved, Sheela laughed and gave him a hug.

THEY LEFT THEIR aunt Kala's house just after one o'clock. Sheela called their aunt at work to tell her they were going out for a few hours to explore the city. She didn't have to resort to a lie about their destination, as Kala asked only when they would be back.

"We'll take the tram to Neeta's house," Narin said as they walked a few streets over.

Seeing the tram at their stop, Sheela's eyes lit up. "I've never taken it before. It's marvelous. It looks so … modern." She insisted on standing with the male passengers in the center aisle instead of choosing the sideways benches where women usually sat. Her long hair spread in tendrils as the tram gathered speed, and she made no attempt to confine it.

They reached Thembu Chetty Road in good time after a short walk from the tram stop. For the second time in two days, Narin stood across the street from the white house, this time not with apprehension but familiarity and eagerness to see Neeta again. She must have been waiting and watching for them because she appeared outside within a few minutes, cheerfully waving goodbye to someone in the house. She crossed the street but, Narin noted with surprise and approval, not straight to where they were; in fact, not even looking in their direction. Sheela and Narin walked around the tree they'd been standing half-behind and caught up to her.

Narin said to her back, "Neeta, that was very clever. It's as if you didn't see us at all. Meet my sister Sheel … Sheela."

Neeta turned with a look of delight. "I'm so glad to meet you at last, Sheela. And so glad you and Narin invited me to this event. You're just as pretty as Narin said you were."

Somewhat overwhelmed by Neeta's manner, Sheela's "Pleased to meet you" was almost a whisper.

"Good timing, Narin. I didn't have to stand around watching out the window for more than a few minutes. Onward, lead the way to the meeting."

She took Sheela's arm, and they dropped a step or two behind Narin. He slowed down to join them, but Neeta gave him a slight push on the back. "We girls need to talk. And besides, we must follow meekly behind our man at the appropriate distance prescribed in the *Vedas*." Sheela giggled. "But be assured we will come to your defense if trouble arises. Right, Sheela?"

Sheela murmured an assent. She seemed in awe of Neeta.

"I don't think you should joke about it so," Narin said.

"Why not? I don't believe that talking about something is likely to make it happen, do you? Or you, Sheela? That's an old Hindu superstition anyway."

"You don't believe in fate?" Sheela asked.

"Not really. I think we're in complete control of our own lives."

Narin raised his voice so the girls behind him would hear. "Isn't that a Christian thing? Free will and all that? Definitely not Hindu."

"Well, then, I'll convert," he heard Neeta reply with a giggle. "I hear they give you twenty rupees at Mount Cathedral to do so. I could use a little extra pocket money."

He heard Sheela stifle a snort of surprise. He would've liked to see the look on her face. "Your family must be very, aah, forgiving," he said.

"Forgiving? You mean the way I talk about religion and all that? Not quite. My mother sometimes scolds me for being too … cheeky, I think she calls it. Actually, most of my family is quite irreverent."

"Lucky you," Sheela said, biting her lip as she looked away from Neeta.

Narin had had enough of being excluded and slowed to walk alongside Sheela. "You're lucky as well, Sheel. Auntie Kala doesn't keep you on a tight leash."

The streets of Madras could not have appeared more normal as the three of them walked along Mount Road, the major thoroughfare, then turned toward Triplicane, a large central neighborhood and one of the oldest in the city. Within a quarter of a mile, as they turned east on Wallajah Road, they noticed groups of people, mostly men with scattered pockets of women, marching in the same direction. Many carried signs written on canvas or wooden boards.

Along the way, they attracted many stares, as much for the two lively and well-dressed girls walking arm in arm as for their loud and animated conversation. Narin suggested they tone it down. Neeta disagreed and said she thought they should "tone it up," as the noise level was increasing, and they had to shout to hear each other. They laughed, a welcome relief from their anxiety.

But by the time they'd reached Triplicane High Road, Neeta, Narin, and Sheela were no longer bantering, affected by the mood of the marchers, which was not grim but purposeful. The narrower streets were nearly filled with protestors blocking traffic. Rickshaws and carts parked haphazardly added to the difficulty of passage. Policemen stationed every few yards at the edges of the street stared stonily at the throng.

Trying to avoid the crush of the crowd, the three ducked down a narrow, twisted side lane intersecting their destination, Jammi Road. The imposing brick three-story Hindu High School building loomed at the end of the lane on the right. It was set on large grounds whose gates were locked, with several policemen standing guard, their hands hard on the wooden *lathis* at their waists. The three moved as close as they could—fifty yards from the school—and settled into a narrow doorway that shielded them from the crush of the crowd.

Neeta said, "Isn't this exciting?" then repeated it, raising her voice several decibels in order to be heard.

Sheela put her lips close to Neeta's ears. "Yes. Wonderful."

Now in the heart of the protest, Narin glanced around and was overwhelmed by the crowd's brute energy and distracted behavior. The weight of his responsibility was crashing down on him. He'd agreed to this adventure more as a dare than out of conviction. He wondered if they should leave before the crowd became dangerous or unruly. He looked over at his companions, who seemed still at ease, calm but watchful, absorbing the noise and bustle.

A makeshift wooden stage had been set up a dozen feet outside the schoolyard walls to one side of the entrance. The P.A. system awoke and crackled with unrecognizable noises and loud pops, then morphed into voices as the system was wrestled into compliance. Soon they heard loud chanting, replaced after a minute or so by some kind of invocation, standard fare for most occasions, but it appeared out of place in this political spectrum.

"Shouldn't we pray along?" Neeta said and giggled.

A muted roar arose from the crowd as several men climbed onto the stage. Narin recognized one of them as the leader of the session he'd attended the week before. The man grabbed the microphone and began to shout at the crowd, struggling to control their clamor. After many attempts, the noise dropped to a manageable level. He proceeded to state the goals of the movement in a soporific mantra: Stop the takeover, stop the destruction of their beloved mother tongue, attack the cursed Northerners. Narin had heard it before, but this level of invective was surely new to Neeta and Sheela, who paid rapt attention.

The man at the microphone raised his arm to full stretch and paused. The crowd, sensing something important, quieted a bit. "And now, here's our dear Neelambikai herself."

The crowd went berserk. Narin wondered how Neelambikai had managed to sneak backstage without being recognized. A stroke of genius on the part of the organizers, as it would have taken her forever to make her way through the throng of well-wishers. She was a small figure, not much above five feet tall, and had to be helped onto the stage. She shook off her helpers, looked around confidently, waiting for the noise to settle, and grabbed the microphone. She first thanked the crowd for attending, then expressed the obligatory appreciation to the organizers and other heavies in the movement, which earned her another raucous round of screams and applause.

Good move, Narin thought; makes her seem one with the people rather than above them.

Neelambikai continued for a while, reiterating what Narin had heard many times before but with more intensity: the efforts to suppress the teaching of Tamil in the years ahead, the appeals to jingoism. She was articulate and confident, even as the only woman surrounded by men. After fifteen minutes, when the crowd was completely under her control, she delivered her punch line, excoriating the "Aryans"—Northern Indians, so called because of their Indo-Aryan origin—and the hated appointment of a non-Tamil as chief minister of the Madras Presidency.

"Remember Chief Minister Rajaji's cynical dismissal of Thalamuthu Nadar's death," she thundered and paused dramatically, milking the moment. "The Aryans were laughing while we Tamils shed tears for our hero. We must never forget this travesty. Never!"

The crowd roared its approval.

The hero in question was a protester whose death in police custody Rajaji had dismissed as accidental, and he further thwarted efforts by local party leaders to initiate an investigation. Since then, they had used the incident to drum up antagonism toward the national leaders.

The noise increased exponentially, and Narin could hear only an occasional word or two. Neelambikai was pointing at the school behind her, saying, "And that's *our* school, not theirs, taken over by the damned Northerners. Every one of our children who enters that school is being indoctrinated against you, against me, against our beloved land and language, and—"

A loud crash reverberated over the crowd's noise. Narin and the girls looked around, trying to pinpoint it, and saw a large group of men scaling the ten-foot high schoolyard walls. The police rushed over from the gate to stop them, yelling and unlatching their *lathis*. This left the gate unprotected, and several dozen men took the opportunity to run up to it and push against it in concert. Within a few seconds, it burst open, and the crowd spilled inside. The police regrouped for a moment, debating which action to pursue. Police sirens rang out as four vans forced their way through the crowd, people scattering to avoid being hit. The vans stopped, their back doors opened, and a mob of police rushed into the melee, using their wooden *lathis* freely. Most people ran from the assault, but a small group stood their ground and picked up what they could throw at the police.

Narin, Neeta, and Sheela were caught midway between the rock-throwers and the approaching police. Though they were sheltered by the overhang of a building, they realized it would be foolish to stay, but moving was impossible except with the mass of people around them. That mass started moving slowly away from the school, then faster and more incoherently as if propelled by an invisible force.

The police had cleared a large area in front of the school and appeared to be standing their ground. A half-dozen men a few yards ahead of Narin charged toward the front line of police directly ahead of them, screaming obscenities and throwing rocks. Two policemen fell, one bleeding profusely. A white-clad sergeant turned toward the men who had thrown the rocks, pointed with his *lathi*, and sped toward them, accompanied by a dozen policemen. The crowd parted frantically, and the rock-throwers stood mute and frozen as the police beat them with abandon. As a protestor turned and ran, he pitched a final stone at the sergeant, who raised his baton like a cricket bat to ward it aside, connecting solidly with it. Narin watched in horrified fascination as the rock changed trajectory and crashed into Neeta's shoulder. She screamed and fell to the ground. Sheela, her face ashen, dropped to her knees to help her.

Narin stared into the livid face of the sergeant who had batted the rock aside. For a moment they glared at each other, and Narin started to say something but thought better of it. The officer paused, unsure about taking on what appeared to be a well-dressed young man and two women. He glanced at Neeta but made no move to help her, turned back to Narin, and shouted, "For God's sake, what the hell are you stupid fools doing here? Get out!"

He stepped away to pursue easier prey.

The three stayed huddled in the relative protection of the doorway while the confrontation between police and protestors played itself out. Neeta, bloodied but not badly injured, refused offers to take her to a doctor or a hospital. Narin tore a portion off the end of her ruined sari to use as a makeshift bandage, which helped to contain the bleeding, and Neeta declared it "perfect." They continued to watch, horrified, as the crowd thinned and the police rushed among them, beating anyone in range. A few scattered diehards remained in the area, which had held close to a thousand minutes ago.

Neelambikai and the other speakers, watching from the stage, were not assailed by the violence but were helpless to intervene. Her face was a rictus of horror, and she was close to tears.

FIFTEEN MINUTES AFTER the incident, Narin and the girls walked slowly past watchful policemen, and they retraced their steps via Wallajah Road and Mount Road. Everything appeared different now. People scurried. More debris than the usual roadside rubbish was strewn around. An unnatural quiet blanketed the streets, and the street-side windows of the houses were slammed shut. No traffic moved except for the occasional police vehicle.

Sheela and Narin lightly supported Neeta, their heads inclined together as they spoke.

"Will any of this be reported in the newspapers?" asked Sheela.

"I've never seen details," Narin replied. "God, I'd heard of the overreaction of the police, but there's never photo evidence, so it's difficult to grasp the reality of it. Where the hell are the press? I wish we'd had a camera."

"That would've made you more of a target," Neeta said, jerking the words out through her hard breathing.

"Damn them. Damn the police. How dare they act so violently?" Sheela was sobbing.

"But we got off, didn't we?" Narin said. "It was because we were who we are, clearly of our class."

"Narin. Would you rather have been beaten up?"

"No. But do we ever think of that? Do we ever thank God that because of the way we look, the way we dress and behave, we're not likely to be treated like dirt? The police are after the rank-and-file supporters. I'm sure going after the leaders without due cause would result in too much recrimination later."

"Maybe next time you could dress down as a *coolie* and get beaten up," Neeta snapped.

Her angry tone caused Narin to lapse into surprised silence.

As they neared Neeta's house, the imminent problem loomed. What would Neeta say to Deepa? How were any of them to explain? They would have to invent a convincing lie, but could they pull it off?

Narin looked over at Sheela, whose face was steeped in concentration. Was she thinking the same thing? A surprising smile lit up her face as she turned to him.

"What's so funny?" he said.

"Nothing. Not funny. But I think you're wondering the same thing I am—how to find an explanation for this mess—and I have an idea."

Narin frowned, and Neeta muttered something unintelligible.

"Well, Deepa knows the three of us went out, but not where. So we have to keep the protest a secret. All we have to do is invent an accident that explains Neeta's injuries, no? She could've tripped and fallen. A rickshaw or something could've hit her. I think being attacked by a dog would be too melodramatic, don't you?"

Narin gaped at Sheela's audacity. And decisiveness. Lying to their family wasn't in his repertoire. But, he conceded, hadn't he lied by omission about life at college? Perhaps not so different.

"You don't have to lie for me," Neeta said. "I'll take the consequences."

Sheela waved that aside. "But there'll be consequences for all of us if we tell the truth. Look, it's not so bad what we did. In fact it's not bad at all, is it? Except that Auntie Kala and your Elder-Sister Deepa wouldn't agree. They'd think it was being stupid and dangerous. Which it may have been, but it was worth it. For me at least."

Neeta's mood had improved. "Okay, let's settle on a story."

"A cycle rickshaw accident. Everyone knows there are so many crazy drivers. We were crossing the street, and you, Neeta, were ahead, and you turned around to say something to us and didn't see the rickshaw coming, and it ran into you. Didn't stop either."

And so it went. They settled on the phantom rickshaw's color and size. The driver was given a suitably sinister demeanor, and they hashed over his irresponsible driving in meticulous detail. They rehearsed the details as if for a play until they neared Neeta's house.

Narin said with a sigh of relief, "Not bad for our first conspiracy, don't you think?"

Neeta had recovered from her shock and, aside from her visible injuries, appeared to be her old self. She took Narin's arm from her shoulder to hug his sister. "Thank you so much, Sheela."

"Don't mention it."

Neeta put her uninjured arm on Narin's shoulder. "And thank you, too, of course, Narin. I don't know what would've happened to me if you hadn't been there. Oh, and sorry about my—" She stopped as Narin put up his hand.

He drew closer to her, but their bodies didn't touch. The scent of the jasmine flowers in her hair was as sweet as any perfume, and the nearness of her soft body was intoxicating. He thought back to three days earlier—so long ago—when he'd said something to Laxman about not knowing what it was to be in love. Did he know now?

Neeta broke away, waving aside Sheela's proffered arm. "I should walk by myself. Looks better. Come in with me, and let's get the show on the road." She shuffled through the open gate toward the house, scattering clouds of *kolam* dust in her wake. Sheela and Narin gave each other a conspiratorial glance and followed her in to tell their tale of the reckless rickshaw.

Neeta's histrionics convinced Deepa, who was relieved, after her initial shock had worn off, that her sister's injury was superficial. She washed and rebound Neeta's wound and agreed with her that it needed no further attention. She asked, "You didn't get any identification on the rickshaw, did you?"

No, they did not, said all three, happy to not have to lie.

NARIN AND SHEELA decided to walk back to their aunt's house, unsure if the trams were running.

"Do you think we can ever go again?" Sheela asked, her eyes shining and her face glowing in the afternoon sun.

"Are you crazy?" Narin burst out laughing. "It's not funny, I know. I'm just amazed at your fearlessness. We were so lucky not to be hurt. Or arrested."

"I don't believe in luck. We can control our fate—I agree with Neeta on that. We can attend these protests without fear, as long as we're not too close and have a way to escape."

"And dress well. I'll have to consider attending another one, too." He paused. "Sheel, didn't you think it was terrible to see Neelambikai and the others helpless in the face of the police? Shows who has the real power there. Let's see what the papers have to say."

"It's all a matter of time. When India is independent, the people will take power. We don't have to follow the British pattern."

"Well, maybe. I think those with power will continue to wield it as they wish. They won't take the people's desires into account. That's what power does—it corrupts you."

"That's a pessimistic view, Narin. We have examples right here in Madras of politicians and others in power who listen to and work with their followers."

"Like Neelambikai?"

"Yes. Like her. I know many people dismiss her because she's a woman, but she will be a star."

"If the men at the top let her."

"Narin, that's a terrible thing to say. Don't you think women can be independent in politics?"

"Yes, but they will have to be special. A woman who doesn't care about convention and is willing to push off the insults and snide remarks. With a strong ambition. Neelambikai isn't quite like that. She's more of a scholar who speaks well."

"Rubbish. You heard her. She took complete charge of the meeting from the men. The protest is in good hands. It will be successful."

"Look, Sheel, the language disagreement is only going to get worse as we disengage from British rule. Every province will want its own language supreme within its area. We have, what, sixteen or more languages? So how do we all communicate? Everyone we know speaks English to some degree or other. Why not English? Why Hindi when only half our people are conversant with it?"

"Narin, you're looking at it through a narrow lens. You're educated, as I was, in English. But that's not true for the majority of us. English will forever be associated with the Colonial Era. Politicians will milk that discontent. Maybe it could be a second sort of unofficial official language. But India must have its own national language."

"Maybe we can select a completely different one. Esperanto?"

They continued bickering until they reached Aunt Kala's house, when Sheela shushed Narin.

He was glad to stop talking. He'd rather think of Neeta. He wouldn't see her again for almost three months, and his insides ached at their separation. When he thought of their next meeting, he felt an explosive anticipation. He ignored Sheela's stare. He would reveal his feelings for Neeta later.

XI
Madras, 1939–40

Narin was bored and restless in Venpuri during the summer break. Most of his school friends had moved away, and he missed Sheela, who had remained in Madras with their aunt. She'd arrived home late the night before, in time for the family's annual *Guru Purnima* festival, celebrating the Guru's spiritual life and teachings. All of Narin's in-laws, relatives, and many friends had been invited.

He had not yet met Mina.

He woke late that day, the sheets damp from the cloying humidity, with a twitching pain behind his left eye. Trying to blink away the tension, he closed that eye and turned toward the shadeless window to take in the clear sky. Outside, the air shimmered with invisible heat waves even at eight in the morning. The usually raucous crows and flittering sparrows rested under the cover of leaves, lending an unnatural calm. He would have liked to take a walk to clear his head, but it would only result in further sweaty discomfort. A bath would be better.

He staggered up and headed for the bathroom, where he squatted a long time, pouring lukewarm water over his grateful body with a brass pitcher. He walked out without drying his hair, letting the wetness cool his face, drawing a disapproving look from his mother as he dripped his way back to his room.

Later, he stood inches inside the front door waiting for Mina and her family to arrive. His mother glimpsed him and gestured for him to join the others outside. "Too hot," he mimed and stepped farther back. He watched from his almost-hidden position as his parents and elder siblings greeted his in-laws. Mina wore a pale green silk sari and hugged her mother's protective shadow, and he noted that her transition to early womanhood at sixteen hadn't changed her. She was a little taller, a little fuller, but still as shy and quiet as she had been. With little contact between them for almost three years, Narin found it hard to accept the reality that she was his wife. She was like a memory unremembered.

He greeted the group formally as they entered. As they continued into the main room, Mina's mother raised her hand to signal her to stay with Narin in the entrance hall.

Mina stopped, uncertain.

"How are you, Mina?" Narin said, his face blank of emotion.

"I'm fine, thank you, Husband. And you?" She paused. "You seem ... I was hoping to read more about ..." She paused again and looked around her in confusion, as if words might magically appear on the walls to help her. "But you don't write too often."

"Oh, too much work at college to write regularly," he replied, consoling himself that this was mostly true. "And you? Have your parents allowed you to continue your studies? Did you like the books Sheela sent you?"

"Oh." She turned red. "I haven't yet ... not had time to ..."

"Read? Too bad. We picked books we were sure you'd like."

"Amma says I don't need to continue." Mina attempted a smile. "She says it's enough that one person in my family is, um, educated."

"Me, you mean."

She looked stricken.

Her use of the word "family" grated on Narin's already jangled nerves. His twitch was reasserting itself, and he shook his head as if to dislodge it. He wondered if he'd been too brusque and, trying to mollify her, said, "How's the rest of your family?" He waited for her response, and when none came, continued. "I see your brother, Jaggie, a lot, eat at his house often." A slight exaggeration couldn't hurt.

"Oh? Yes, that's nice. And everyone's quite well." She looked down at her feet.

Further attempts at conversation did not go far. Narin had hoped for more. He was surprised that Mina still seemed unused to talking to male members of the species. He tried to be accommodating but couldn't conjure up his easy Madras self. He and Mina were like formal characters in a Victorian novel, although those would have engaged in cleverer and more amusing repartee.

"Mina," called her mother as she came back into the hall, "come inside. We need your help." Mina mouthed an assent and turned away from Narin without another word.

Narin turned on a vague smile for his mother-in-law, who only gave the smallest of nods in return as she took Mina by the hand and left. Narin wondered what she would have said if he'd said something like, "Surely you wouldn't want to drag my dear wife away from our charming conversation?" No, that was the Madras side of him. He doubted Mina or her mother would have understood. Besides, he was relieved that the stuttering conversation was over.

There was sudden commotion as servants materialized, running around with trays and cushions. Soon everyone was called to the main room, which had been decorated with dozens of flower garlands and *kolams*. Flickering oil lamps cast eerie shadows on the walls.

Narin seated himself cross-legged on cushions in a back corner of the room, squirming as he tried to extract some comfort from the thin cotton batting. Seating was sex-separated at these functions. When younger, he and Sheela had managed to sit together in a sort of no-(wo)man's zone between the two sides, but this had been curtailed when they reached their late teens. Now Sheela, joining the women's side, noticed his demeanor, grinned, and mouthed a discreet, "Cheer up."

Two priests wearing bright saffron robes, their faces and bodies smeared with ash, started the ceremony in full voice. Narin knew that not many of those attending understood the Sanskrit prayers, so they were merely nodding to the beat of the chanting. Were the priests actually saying what they were supposed to? Maybe we're all being cursed at, he thought with amusement. No, surely the priests were humorless, as he'd found when his younger self had argued the more tedious points of his own coming-of-age ceremony. They had shut him down, shouting at him for insulting them.

He had a fellow nonbeliever in Sheela. Both had decided to ignore the rituals as much as possible without incurring the wrath of the ever-observant Aunts Saranmathi and Saraswathi, who were sitting in the front row. He watched the twins nodding their heads in enthusiastic unison, uncannily like a synchronized pair of *Thalayatti Bommai*, nodding-head dolls. He glanced at Sheela, who had an observant air, but he knew better. She was in her own world.

Narin settled in to endure the long ceremony, tuning out the priests' haunting drone, the insistent jangle of the bells, and the swirls of scented smoke that permeated the room, and fell into a deep trance, thinking of Neeta. With joy he summoned her light-skinned face, her soft brown eyes, and her candescent smile. He recalled that she did not always wear the red *bindi* mark on her forehead, customary for Hindu women—only young girls were exempt—and wondered how she endured the inevitable disapproval from busybodies. Presumably she had no aunts like Saraswathi and Saranmathi to torment her.

The ceremony ended, and the room emptied in preparation for the dinner service. Narin stayed to avoid another painful interaction with his in-laws. He watched as a servant with a pile of large plantain leaves, which served as plates, laid each down in a graceful swoosh, followed by another servant who positioned metal drinking cups and tumblers. He found himself an early seat and called out to Sheela to sit next to him when he saw her enter. Before she could respond, his mother-in-law swept in with Mina in tow and called to him.

"Narin, come over here. You must sit next to your wife."

He ambled over to the place she'd reserved for him between Mina and a cousin-in-law in his fifties whom he'd rarely met, but now hoped would have more to say than Mina. The man had the demeanor of an older bore who would monopolize the conversation, and he would welcome that. He saw Sheela grinning at his discomfort, and he scowled at her in return.

NARIN WALKED THROUGH the peaceful house the day after the *Guru Purnima* and stepped out the back door, where he found Sheela on the swing.

"Sheel, you're brave. You'll get into more trouble than you did before."

"Because I'm older now? Or because the swing is practically rotten?" An ominous creak punctuated her words, and she glanced up at the creaky ropes holding the swing with unconcern.

"Both. Glad we have time to talk. How have you been in Madras the last few weeks?"

"Good. Auntie Kala's decided that I need to find some work to do, so she's going to tutor me." Sheela's voice undulated as she swung back and forth. "Maybe I can get my secondary school pass by taking a test or something. Learn to type? I'm not sure exactly."

"That would be great for you," Narin said. "What kind of work is she thinking of?"

Sheela slowed the swing, put a finger to her lips, and jumped off, then came closer to him and whispered, "Oh, I just remembered. Auntie Kala wanted to keep this quiet for a while, so don't tell anyone, will you? She thinks if I get through the school thing, maybe I could use my knowledge of books and literature somehow. Uncle will help. Auntie says he has connections everywhere."

Sheela apparently noticed the excitement on Narin's face be replaced by a quizzical look.

"Well, nobody here in Venpuri will be for it," she said. "Especially the you-know-whos."

Narin grinned. "Yes, they'll have a fit. And when they realize it was their idea to send you to Madras to become a better girl. Hmm, maybe they'll assign Jaggie to keep an eye on you as well. Wonder how he gets any work done, what with worrying about all his flighty relations."

Sheela smiled. "I'd be so glad of that. I'd feel important, having a spy follow me around."

"Well, you can have him all to yourself."

She arched an eyebrow. "So you and Neeta can be alone more?" She burst out laughing as Narin's face turned bright red. "Come, let's go in and get some tea. You can tell me all about her."

NARIN WAS INDECISIVE about his relationship with Neeta after he returned to college after the summer break. When they first met again after returning to Madras in August, they had been friendly but restrained, as if they had never written the letters they exchanged during the summer. In the three months since then, he hadn't been alone with her much. On social occasions, Laxman, Ambika, and other members of their group had been present, which limited their intimacy. That rush of emotion he'd felt after the dustup at the protest rally five months ago—how real was that? Since then, his desire for Neeta had increased, and he obsessed about her more than ever, her oval face hovering nightly in his dreams. He loved how animated she was during their conversations with friends and how calm and relaxed she appeared at other times, both equally attractive. She had an inner strength he admired and a sense of humor gentler than Laxman's often abrasive sarcasm. With time, he found himself relaxed and comfortable around her, less guarded than he was with Laxman or Ambika.

Their distant waltz continued for much of the term.

Toward the end of the year, Jaggie made another of his unannounced visits. He seemed to have an uncanny ability to sense when Narin would be in his hostel room, which was not all that often. Narin had returned to his room in the late afternoon from an arduous round at the infectious disease ward and thrown himself on the bed. He was contemplating seeing Neeta the next day when the semblance of a knock on the door interrupted his pleasant musing, and Jaggie's imposing presence intruded into the small room.

"Narin. So nice to see you." Jaggie planted his bulk on a squeaky chair.

Narin pulled himself up to sit on the edge of the bed, his apprehension growing, and responded with a nod. Jaggie's politeness was a sure indicator of unpleasantness ahead.

Wiping his face with his ever-present oversized handkerchief, Jaggie continued. "I have something that's serious. Guess where I was last Saturday?"

"At home eating too much of your wife's food?"

"Ha ha. No. I was out walking along Mount Road near Jamshedji Park." He paused, flashed a meaningful look at Narin, and added incongruously, "It was not hot at all, breezy, not at all like today, no."

"Thank you for the weather report. And …?"

Jaggie leaned forward toward Narin, jabbing at him with his finger. "And I saw you. With that girl. Neeta, isn't it? We talked about her before. My father has written to you about her, and I'm sure your father has also. Not to keep company with girls of that sort."

"She's a fellow student and a friend. We were going to meet Laxman and Ambika."

"You're lying. You were holding hands with her."

"What? When did you see—?" Narin thought back to the moment. He and Neeta had indeed walked for a while on Mount Road toward the park, but they had not held hands, then or ever. Trust Jaggie to exaggerate for effect. But he seemed to have been inside the park to observe them.

He glared at Jaggie. "So you were *in* the park? Why?" Getting no response from Jaggie except an increasing sneer, Narin reassessed. "You were following us?" This realization came as a shock. Even the minimal privacy he and Neeta expected had been an illusion. How could he have missed seeing Jaggie follow them? An unsettling image of his portly in-law shuffling from tree to tree came to mind, raising an inward chuckle.

Jaggie didn't deny the accusation. "I saw you two, that is all that matters. You must stop keeping company with her."

"I will not. It's none of your business anyway."

"Not my business when my poor sister's husband is gallivanting with loose girls?"

Resisting the urge to say that Neeta was not Anglo-Indian, the group that Jaggie detested and characterized as loose, Narin said, "I won't stop socializing with my friends. And there's nothing you can do about it." His voice was defiant, even as he felt a pang of apprehension about confronting Jaggie.

Jaggie's face relaxed into a mocking smile. "Oh, and here's a letter for you."

"What? Now you're sneaking my post?"

"Just picked it up from the post-*wallah* downstairs. It is from your father."

Narin was now uneasy. As far as he could recall, his father had written only one letter in all the time he'd been in college. He accepted the letter from Jaggie, read it, and sat still, staring at the fateful words, his stomach knotted. He was sure Jaggie knew the letter's contents.

> My dear son Narin,
>
> The happy matter of the final ceremony of your marriage, which you've been waiting for, has finally arrived. I apologize for the short notice, but we've decided to hold the *ritu kala* in three weeks.
>
> I have already written to the vice chancellor of Madras Medical College (reminding him of our mutual acquaintance, Mr. Shetty, the chairman of the board of Petra Iron Works) requesting that you be excused from college for four days, giving you five with a Sunday. That should be enough time, as the ceremony is on a Monday.
>
> I'm sure the astrologer your Aunt Saraswathi knows will find good augurs for that day. I am glad this is finally happening, particularly in view of the events that Jaggie wrote to us about last year, which troubled all of us greatly. I am also relieved that you have shown good judgment since then.
>
> Your father

Jaggie's gaze hadn't left Narin. "I suppose you should start packing. Don't you?"

"I'm not going."

"Not going? Don't start being ridiculous, Narin. You had better go, and you'd better never see your 'friend' again. If you do, I can make life difficult for you."

Narin was taken aback by this threat. He was not poised to do anything illegal or underhanded, though it was a betrayal of his wife. He pushed the thought aside. Jaggie could do nothing more than write home for reinforcements, and Narin had grown used to missives from Venpuri, which he read with little affect. He would have to find an excuse for his refusal to go now, or at least delay the trip.

Jaggie had a calculating look and appeared to be waiting for Narin to say something. Silence stretched out. Narin did not break it.

Jaggie got up and said as he walked out the door, "I can make life *so* difficult."

Narin watched the retreating bulk of Jaggie's figure and exhaled noisily as he realized he had been holding his breath. He had never been as angry with Jaggie as he was now, but a glimmer of apprehension remained. It seemed uncharacteristic for Jaggie to make idle threats. He mulled over what Jaggie had said but could find nothing. He doubted Jaggie could get his father to cut off or reduce his allowance, which would be disastrous. Could Jaggie affect his future career in any way? No, he was not high enough up the status ladder. Yet.

His letter to his father was a model of diplomacy and suggested postponing the ceremony until summer, but it had little mollifying effect. His father was furious and let Narin know in no uncertain terms how disappointed he was. Narin wrote a second letter explaining that he would have to study hard for the next few weeks to do well in the upcoming midterm exam. He put aside his father's reply, which arrived by return post.

DAYS LATER ON a harsh sunny day, Narin was slumped on a bench outside his hostel as a strong wind swirled dust, leaves, and debris around him. He had sent an urgent note to Neeta via a messenger boy and was waiting for her.

He looked up and shouted out to Neeta as he heard her approaching. "I failed the exam."

"You failed? Impossible. How? I remember you saying that you did quite well."

"I know, but there it is in black and white. What on earth can I tell my parents?"

Nothing like this had ever happened to him before. He'd studied hard and never entertained the possibility of failure. And in this particular phase, too, where he'd left the examination hall brimming with confidence. He yearned to be closer to Neeta, to absorb her warmth and sympathy, but that was impossible where they were, visible from the men's hostels.

"Can you talk to the chief examiner? Or your profs? Maybe they made a mistake in your roll number or something."

"I don't know." He had never cultivated any of his professors who might have put in a good word for him, and directly asking the chief examiner to review his case was daunting. He wasn't even sure how to get in touch with the man.

"Narinder."

The insolent voice sounded close behind him, a voice he knew well, the last one he wanted to hear. Since it was the middle of the afternoon, he wondered if Jaggie had been passing by on his way elsewhere or had come over on a break from work. Narin turned to face him and noted Jaggie wasn't carrying his usual bulging brown leather briefcase. A bad omen.

"Jaggie," he said, forcing a semblance of calm, "what are you doing here?"

Jaggie didn't reply.

"This is my friend, Neeta Pai," Narin said, though that should've been obvious.

Jaggie did not acknowledge her but continued to stare at Narin with the slightest of sneers on his lips. The two locked eyes, as if daring the other to speak first. After what seemed to be minutes, Jaggie said in that peculiar syntax he affected, "I am hearing your last examiner did not like your performance all that much." The sneer was more obvious now.

"How … how did you know?" asked Narin. "I just found out."

"I have my ways."

Jaggie's gaze was still fixed on Narin, and another silence descended. A realization dawned on Narin. Jaggie couldn't possibly have discovered the result so soon. Even if he had visited the main hall of the college where student scores were posted, the scores were identified by student number, not name. Jaggie could not know his number, nor could he have overheard his conversation with Neeta minutes before, as they had been in a well-exposed area. So eliminate the impossible. What's left? Jaggie had prior knowledge, and he could only have obtained it in one way.

"You know Chief Examiner Raja?"

A smile replaced the sneer. "Oh, you're the clever one, aren't you? Yes, I know him."

"And you bothered him just to get my result? And came here especially to crow? Why? You'd have found out soon enough."

Jaggie's smile did not waver. Narin, his temper on edge, moved back a little to put distance between him and his gloating relative. Now a second, more shocking realization intruded. Jaggie's contemptuous manner went well beyond mere pleasure in Narin's troubles. He hadn't just obtained his results from the chief examiner; he'd somehow manipulated the situation to fail him.

"What did you do? What did you tell him?" Narin shouted.

"I warned you the last time we met, Narin. I told you not to go on with your … friendship … with this girl." He jerked his thumb at Neeta. "And to not ignore your responsibility to my sister, to go to the *ritu kala* immediately. And you did not listen to me."

"And the scores?"

"Let's just say Chief Examiner Raja owes me a favor or two."

"You told him to fail Narin?" Neeta snapped. "How could you do such a despicable thing? My god. And you're a lawyer, too."

Jaggie didn't glance at her. Still addressing Narin, he replied, "I did no such thing. And I am being very aware of the ethical issues present in my profession. I merely was suggesting that you should be held to a very high standard. I think your father may have something interesting to say about this, don't you, Narin? Do let me know what he says. But you can still be reasonable. Things have a way of managing themselves when people are seeing the correct way." On that enigmatic note, he smiled again, a contemptuous smile that stretched across his face, then stumped away.

Narin clenched his fists and started to follow him, but Neeta put a hand on his arm, and he stopped, uncertain. They watched Jaggie disappear beyond the walls of the hostel compound.

Neeta had tears in her eyes. "That bastard!" she spit out. "How could he? Narin, what can you do?"

Narin hadn't heard that rage in her voice before. He controlled his own anger. "I'm going to see Lax," he said. "He always knows some way out. He's probably in his room by now. Sorry you can't come, Neeta, but if you wait here, maybe I can drag him out here."

Neeta nodded and sat down, wrapped in her thoughts.

Narin raced to Laxman's room in the next building. Luckily, his friend was there. He hadn't mentioned his father's letter to him when he had received it two weeks ago. Now he placed it wordlessly in his friend's hands and waited for him to read it. Laxman glanced it over and looked up.

Sensing that a snide comment was imminent, Narin held up his hand. "Lax, I refused to go. I wrote to my father, and he wrote back an angry letter. But I decided to wait it out. The thing is, on the same day I got that letter, my brother-in-law, Jaggie, came to see me, and he threatened me if I didn't go." Narin closed his eyes in frustration. "Then today ..."

"What happened today?"

Narin filled him in, and Laxman crushed the letter.

"I didn't take Jaggie's threat seriously. I didn't know what he would ... what he could do. What on earth could he have over the examiner? Jaggie came back just now to gloat, and he went on something strong about 'seeing the right way.'"

"Umm …" Laxman gazed into the distance for a while. "Well, this infamous ceremony has to happen sometime, Narin. I'm sure you'll be all right if you go to it. You'll be back here in no time, and life will be the same." He added, beginning a crude gesture, "And, if you want to, you can—"

"No! I don't want to have sex with her. Hell, Lax, that wouldn't be right, would it? How damned unfeeling are you anyway?"

Laxman stepped back. He scratched his brow and took a few rapid puffs on his cigarette, avoiding his friend's glare.

Narin consulted his feelings. "When I met Mina last summer, I had almost nothing to say to her. I don't know her. I wrote to her, I think, three times in four years. And her letters to me were … prosaic. I asked her once what she was reading, and you know what she replied? That she still has difficulty reading good books. Actually, why am I surprised? She stopped going to her school in seventh standard, I think. Her father ignores me when I suggest she get a tutor. What will we talk about? Or do? What will you and your gang think of her when you meet her?"

Laxman waved his cigarette. "Narin, that's still in the future. She's not going to come back with you next week or even while we're still in college. Maybe we'll never meet her because we'll all have spread far and away after passing out and will only communicate by letter. You'll stay here in Madras, have a wonderful career, and write tons of papers for *Lancet*."

"Yeah, Lax, so I'm just more of a homebody than you and your group, right? Thanks a lot. And I suppose you're saying you'll avoid my wife?" He tamped down his anger to focus on his future. "And me? I'll watch while Mina cooks and cleans for me and quietly flits around the house like her brother Jaggie's wife? You've met her. Could you have a real life with a woman like that?"

Narin stopped, thinking how snobbish he sounded. Was he so critical of Mina because she was not as erudite and well read as his friends? Or was that a convenient fiction he used to not think about the consequences of his romance with Neeta?

Laxman moved to Narin's side, put one arm over his shoulder, and patted it. "Maybe you'll marry again," he said with a grin.

"What? What do you mean?"

"You can have more than one wife here. I hear bigamy is a non-cognizable offense, whatever that exactly means—cognizable, meaning recognizable by the law, I suppose, so it sounds not quite criminal, no?" He appeared ready to delve into the etymological labyrinths of the word but thought better of it when he saw Narin's face. "You do need the first wife's consent to remarry, I believe." Narin did not react, so he continued. "Hey, better yet, you could have an entire harem if you convert to the Muslim faith. Or is it limited to four women even if you do? Needs looking up, m'boy. Oh, but then you'll have to get circumcised. Ouch!" He covered his crotch and executed a melodramatic hop.

Narin burst out laughing, and Laxman joined him.

Narin's laughter ceased. "And my exam results?"

"Well, you change your mind and go to Venpuri, and Jaggie will no doubt do something to correct it. He said as much," he drawled with a broad wink. "Now it's time for a shot of whiskey."

Narin didn't share Laxman's certainty, but he calmed down and was glad of the distraction of a drink. Sounded good. Though the state of Madras had introduced prohibition the year before in accordance with the austerity preached by Gandhi, Laxman had found ways to obtain liquor. Inviting trouble, he kept it in his room in a trunk under the bed, which he now pulled open to produce a bottle. He didn't mention finding a secluded spot to drink as they usually did. He closed the door of the room and clanked its bolt shut, unearthed two glasses from the trunk, and poured them each a stiff shot. He picked up his water jug, found it empty, and flourished it upside-down. "Well, too bad. Neat it is. Here." They clinked glasses, mouthed, "Cheers," and drank.

Narin recalled Neeta would still be sitting on the bench outside.

"Let's go join her and take her a sherry. Have to be sneaky about all this though," said Laxman. He picked up a second bottle from the trunk and wrapped both in newspaper. He placed a guiding hand on Narin's arm as they walked out of the room, a gesture Narin much appreciated. When they approached Neeta, Laxman winked and motioned them to the convenient cover of some bushes near the building. He handed Neeta her glass, and they toasted each other.

Neeta raised her eyebrows. "Well, has the genius come up with a plan?"

They looked at Laxman. "Yes," he said and spread his hands to give a soft clap. "We have concluded that the fat one has given us the key. He as much as told Narin that all would be well if he went to Venpuri pronto."

Narin thought this diverged from their actual conversation but said nothing.

Neeta half-closed her eyes. "But—"

"No buts, my dear," Laxman said. "It's not in Jaggie's interests to see Narin do badly. He has too much family pride for that. So this was just a warning shot across the bow. He'll yank in the examiner when Narin comes around."

Narin's spirits had been buoyed by Laxman's words—and the drink. He didn't notice Neeta's distress as she turned away and held out her glass, which Laxman refilled. Now he could reconsider the matter. His return to Venpuri would be short and endurable. He would sail though the ceremony unscathed, shut down emotionally. He would think of Neeta as he saw her now, a beautiful girl with a furtive glass of sherry in her hand. He resolved to write to his father immediately and to send a note to Jaggie about his decision.

Jaggie responded the next day with the news from the chief examiner that he, Raja, had urgently requested the registrar of the college to correct an unexplainable mistake. Raja had apparently mixed up some papers, and "M. N. Janappan, Roll Number 36-173" had not failed but had instead "passed his exam with honors."

Ten days later, Narin stood with his one slim bag on the platform of Madras Central, a vise of apprehension crushing his stomach, dreading the ritual ahead of him, waiting and waiting for the departure of the Southern Express to be announced. Late as usual.

AT THE RITU Kala, he stared at Mina standing opposite him, the priests at their side muttering their mantras, the heat of the flickering oil lamps adding to the oppressive atmosphere, the mass of people around them maintaining respectful silence, and he was appalled. Appalled at his shortsightedness in agreeing to marry her almost four years before. What could he have been thinking? Of course, that was it. He hadn't been thinking at all.

XII
Madras, 1940

Back at college after the ceremony, Narin isolated himself, hurrying from classes to the library or back to his hostel room with apologies about having "too much work to catch up on." Laxman and Ambika were puzzled but supportive, and Neeta stayed out of his way. After three weeks of this, apparently Laxman had had enough. He confronted Narin one evening as they were leaving the hostel mess after dinner.

"We're all worried about you and your newfound status as Hermit of the Year, Narin. You're not even talking to Neeta, for Christ's sake. Okay, my good man, what transpired in the wilds of Venpuri?"

Narin had never been comfortable discussing his private life, except in brief snippets, and it was hard to do so now. Could he disclose his unavowed feelings for Neeta? Could he say that he'd imagined being with her when he and Mina lay down on their connubial bed? It had been a clear and startling image, an insuperable impediment to any latent desire he might have had for Mina.

"We had the ceremony," Narin said. "There were many people there. We ate a lot. What else is there to say? You know, it must've been one of the few times my Aunties Saraswathi and Saranmathi had nothing much to say to me. They just beamed. I don't want to talk any more about it."

He started to walk away, but Laxman put out a hand and stopped him. Narin looked at Laxman, who shook his head, locking his eyes on Narin's.

"Okay, *yes*, I do want to talk about it," Narin said, his voice shaking. "Mina's sixteen now. She's a woman and much the same person as before. But me? I've changed since then, much thanks to you, Lax. I'm more confident now. I know more, I read more, and I'm better informed about the world around me.

"Mina's not like the girls I know here in Madras." *So unlike Neeta.* "It's not her fault, of course, but that's the same excuse I made four years ago. It rings hollow now. I married her. I should be responsible for my actions."

From the corner of his eye, Narin noticed Ambika and Neeta walking toward them. He was glad Laxman hadn't asked the obvious question: Did you consummate the marriage? Better to say nothing. How he wished he'd talked more to Sheela when they'd been in Venpuri for those two days. She would have understood. She would have been supportive. He resolved to go to Auntie Kala's house the next day, then remembered that his sister's return to Madras had been delayed. Had their Aunties S, arbiters of all things Sheela, reconsidered the beneficial effects of her stay in Madras? He put the thought away. That would be a disaster for her—as well as for him.

Neeta and Ambika joined them a moment later, and they exchanged subdued greetings.

Narin saw the concern evident in Laxman's and Ambika's faces and Neeta's lips set in a tight smile. He considered resurrecting the study excuse to make a hasty exit but rejected it as cowardly. Laxman's comment about him "not talking to Neeta" had been correct, but it was not by choice. He'd tried to get in touch with her a couple of times, but she'd always given an excuse. And he was sure he knew why. It couldn't be easy, if she felt about him the way he did about her, to contemplate his intimacy with another woman, however dutiful it might have been. He was overcome with an intense desire to unburden himself.

"Nothing much happened, that's it …" As he trailed away, Narin noticed a sardonic smile crossing Laxman's lips, which he suppressed as Narin raised a hand. "I don't see myself as a married man at all—that's my state over there. I'm *here* now, with friends, all of you, my other family. I don't look forward to staying in Venpuri over breaks anymore, especially now that Sheela's here. It's like Venpuri's a dream world with this phantom family—Mina's—that I don't care about and wish weren't part of my life."

His friends exchanged glances, each willing another to respond first.

Ambika patted his hand. "Narin, it is a little unreal. We all know of boys being married to a child and waiting for her to grow up, but that isn't usual in your family, is it? And to people like us," she continued with an inclusive gesture to the other two, "it's almost … foreign."

"It happened to me, though. And I don't know why I didn't refuse it."

"Look, don't beat yourself up over it. For now, we want you to be the person you were before you went to Venpuri. I—we—liked that person, not the mope you've become."

Neeta and Laxman joined in a chorus of agreement. Narin's tension reduced fractionally, but when he glanced at Neeta and smiled, he received no smile in return. Her face was still grave and closed. Would she have been more understanding if he had confided in her in private? He could only guess at how conflicted she must be, but her presence suggested that she had feelings for him still.

After a moment, Laxman reverted to his usual panacea for all things uncomfortable, saying, "Hey, let's go have a drink. When's the last time you had a whiskey? Bet they didn't serve any at your tribulation."

Narin grinned at the absurd image of having alcohol at a Hindu *puja* and agreed with relief. He and Laxman fetched the bottles from the hostel, then met the girls at their usual rendezvous. Laxman poured three glasses of whiskey for Narin, Ambika, and himself, and sherry for Neeta. "Sorry, no soda," he said as he raised his glass. "Cheers." Four glasses clinked.

Narin took a large gulp of whiskey and basked in its enveloping warmth. He felt better already. He was with friends who loved him. He would graduate as a doctor soon and throw himself into work at Egmore Medical Center where he had obtained an internship. He would stay in Madras forever. He would be free to ... what? Do as he wished? He glanced at Neeta, whose face was now flushed. Inky strands of hair streamed against her tight blouse and the wind drew her delicate sari snug against her lower body. He felt an urgent stirring in his loins, a feeling he'd never had while in Venpuri.

IT WAS LATE the next evening, and the setting sun painted the clouds in vivid streaks of red and orange. Narin and Neeta had ducked away from their friends and walked to one of their favorite places, Jamshedji Park, a small, walled area immediately off the busy Mount Road. Its entrances were on side streets, so it was shielded from excessive noise and bustle, and it was less crowded than other parks. The usual contingent of street people camped inside its entrances, but few food hawkers, child beggars, or shady characters wandered in, and no stray dogs. After they'd found this sanctuary, they'd visited it every few weeks, sometimes bringing food and drink. They'd kept this place secret, even from Ambika and Laxman, sharing a guilty pleasure in keeping it so. It was their private space in a society that did not prioritize privacy. Narin and Neeta headed for the concrete-and-wood benches positioned under the cover of a banyan tree at the northern end of the park, brushed the detritus off one, and sat down.

"So what really happened at Venpuri?" Neeta asked.

Narin paused, wondering how to reveal his feelings. The day before, when the four of them had been talking, he'd only touched the surface. They'd been sympathetic and understanding, which had been enough for him at the time. Now he wanted more from Neeta. He examined the turmoil that churned within him: his relief that the consummation ceremony had passed, the knowledge that he wouldn't have to deal with Mina's family for several months, and above all, his unabashed desire for Neeta. Where to start?

Equivocating, he said, "Well, not much to say about the visit, actually. It all went by in a bloody flash." God, he sounded like Laxman.

Neeta wore a look of complete disbelief.

He looked down. "No, it didn't. I dreaded going from the moment I realized I had to. It was painful. I know we've never spoken about my marriage. As Ambika put it yesterday, it's not real to me. But being there for the *ritu kala* made it all too real. Everyone had a smiling face on, even Mina, as if we were coming to the end of some painful period and happy days were ahead. I was glad the ceremony itself was short. Sheela later joked that it was so I wouldn't have time to change my mind."

Neeta grinned.

"Well, after the dinner we went ..."

He recalled how discreetly most of the guests had withdrawn, leaving only the closest family members with Mina and him. No conversation ensued. Nothing more had to be said. The priests came back after a while to perform some final ritual involving the usual Sanskrit chants and scattering of ash. His frame of mind at that moment had been grim. A fitting mood for the happy couple, indeed. Then they were escorted to their marriage bedroom. The door was closed. For the first time, Mina looked directly into Narin's eyes.

Returning from his thoughts, Narin said, "Why don't priests ever smile? I sometimes wonder if they can."

The apprehension on Neeta's face stopped him.

"And then?"

Narin paused for a moment. "I was angry. Very. I couldn't tell if it was anger against myself, at my family, or at my twin aunties who forced the issue on my parents. Probably the most at myself for not refusing to marry."

As he sat on the bed with Mina, anger had crystallized Narin's focus on his emotions, not for the woman who was with him, but for the woman who was not. It had been a revelation.

He needed to convey that passion, that desire now. The words rushed out.

"And then I thought about *you* and all the great times we've had. Your liveliness when you talk. You have a gorgeous smile. Do you know that? I've never told you before, have I? We went to that protest last year ... and I was so attracted to you there."

Through his jumble of thoughts, he continued. "We like the same things. Picture shows. And books. You understand what a myocardial infarction is." He stopped with a sheepish grin. "Damn, that's stupid. I'm so ... I feel so attached to you now and ... *nothing*, nothing happened in that room. Nothing at all."

He looked away, tears welling in his eyes.

When he turned back, Neeta reached out, not caring that they were in public, not checking for a lurking Jaggie, and folded the willing Narin in her arms. They sat embracing, Narin drinking in the closeness of her presence, savoring the touch and smell of her, their faces buried in each other's shoulders.

As they drew apart, he said, "I love you. I think ... I know I have loved you from the moment we first met, when you gave me that caricature of the professor. I loved being in your aunt's quiet house with you, just talking about nothing. I loved you when you shrugged off being hit by that rock in the protest march. And every moment since. My love was what stopped me from talking about Venpuri and the … ceremony … my fear of what you might say—"

She shushed him with a finger to his lips. He stopped. She dropped her hand, and slowly, gently, they moved back together, noses initially bumping as they tested their way to their first kiss.

YOU MUST TAKE hold of love where you find it.

Back in his hostel, Narin was lying on his thin cotton mattress staring at the whitewashed ceiling and the wavy glass lightshade swaying in the mild breeze. Two years ago, he couldn't have dreamed there could be a woman like Neeta, so sharing, so kind, so beautiful. He had never felt this way about anyone. Marriage. He'd never given the word the import it deserved. What was it Laxman jokingly said about many wives? That in India you could lawfully marry more than once? If he married Neeta, the law would wink at him, and he'd only have an unlikely civil complaint to watch out for.

He felt a strong sexual urge again. He could marry Neeta, take her to wife, to that blissful carnal state he couldn't have with Mina. As one his favorite novelists Somerset Maugham had said, he should grasp the nettle. It would be a fleeting pain with glorious joy to follow.

"NO! REALLY?" SHEELA cried out when Narin brought her up to date about his feelings for Neeta.

They were sitting in the back compound of their Aunt Kala's house, where Narin had arrived two hours earlier than usual to be sure of catching Sheela alone.

Sheela had met Neeta a few times since their pivotal rally outing many months ago. The three had visited the Elphinstone Picture house a few times and restaurants from time to time. She and Neeta were on their way to becoming good friends, and Narin's news delighted her. She remembered when Narin had boldly invited Neeta to their Aunt Kala's house. Much to their relief, Kala had been relaxed, though a little distant when she had met Narin's "friend." Later, Sheela and Narin amused themselves about how the encounter might have gone if their Aunties S had been present.

"Yes, I'm sure I'm in love," Narin said, "and she's sure too."

Wide-eyed, Sheela asked, "What will you do?"

"We want to be together …"

"And?"

"We want to get married."

"Oh, Narin. What about your … what about Mina?"

He explained the legal situation to her as if he weren't involved.

Her brow furrowed. "You're going to be in a lot of trouble at home."

"Most of my life I've wanted to please them—Appa and the others—but I'm not sure I want to anymore. I think there's a moment in your life when you realize that you're important, too. And you have to take care of yourself. I've never felt as strongly about anyone as I do about Neeta."

"Do you think you'll ever see Mina after this? What will happen to her?"

"You know, I'm sorry for her." He shut his eyes tightly for a moment. "But I have to focus on the present, not the past."

He looked at his sister, his friend, his confidante, hoping she'd understand and sympathize with him, but she looked troubled, and he braced himself for a rebuke. The silence stretched a long while. Then Sheela reached over and patted his hand, and they sat side by side, looking at the golden sun as it disappeared below the rooftops.

LIMBS NAKED AND entwined, Narin and Neeta lay on the scrappy cotton mattress in the hotel room.

They had arrived separately at the hotel and had entered with a feigned confidence, Neeta submissively walking behind Narin, who'd brought a book-laden brown suitcase as a prop. When he had signed them in as Mr. and Mrs. R. Balakrishnan, the bored clerk animated himself from the register to say, "Oh, sir, are you any chance relation to R. Balakrishnan, the big advocate?" Narin cursed the coincidence of name choice as he muttered, "No," and heard Neeta stifle a laugh behind him.

They climbed the three flights of stairs to room number twenty-three, entered, and latched the door behind them. They did not comment on the decrepit condition of the room. White-wash peeled in strips from the grimy walls. The room was devoid of furnishings other than the metal-framed cot and a streakily painted wooden table with a three-legged stool in front. No matter. It was their space, their haven, their private boudoir, and it couldn't have been any more luxurious had it been a top-floor suite at the Taj Hotel.

Much tentative movement, touching, and feeling followed. This can't be so difficult, Narin thought. Eventually, clothes stripped away, they sprawled on the bed, their desire overriding their shyness, their movements becoming more confident, their connection more vital, and they were sure. At the moment he entered her, she gasped with pain-joy.

After they reached the sweet apex of release, they disengaged their bodies with the reluctance of sticky sweat-coated flesh. They lay back on the unyielding mattress and reveled in the happiness of the sacred and profane act of love.

Narin looked at Neeta's light olive body with a sense of wonder. He had never so much as seen a blue movie or depictions of the erotic sculptures at the Khajuraho Temples or read the *Kama Sutra*. Barring medical images, his ignorance of the female body had been complete, and the pleasures of touch, of stimulation, of sex, astonished him. He resolved to be a quick learner. He smiled.

Neeta lay back, seemingly exhausted, but soon reached out an eager hand to his taut waist and forcefully pulled him toward her.

They explored each other's bodies for more than three hours. Sated, they got up and dressed without conversation. They walked down the stairs and passed the clerk without looking at him. In the privacy of the vestibule, Narin and Neeta exchanged a long goodbye kiss. They went their separate ways, each concentrating on pleasant erotic thoughts.

NEETA PROWLED THE length of Deepa's living room, running her hand along the well-arranged books set in a polished teak bookcase, pausing frequently as if to select one. She rearranged a group of carved Rajput terra-cotta figurines, then picked up the newspaper and glanced at its headline:

"Another Protest Planned for Sunday! Neelambikai Expected to Speak!"

She thought of that other protest, months ago, when she'd been injured. Had she fallen in love with him then, her knight in shining armor as she now thought of him? Maybe it was before then? Was it the first time she had met him while walking to class with Ambika and Laxman, when she'd flaunted her knowledge of Tamil on a sudden, whimsical impulse to impress the handsome stranger? Or during the second long meeting when they had verbally sparred over—of all things—Jane Austen? Or when he had visited her at her sister's house and made such an impression of steadiness and likeability on them? No matter. She only knew with crystalline clarity that she wanted this man. Only the present counted. And in the present, she was in love.

Deepa entered. "So, sister, what brings you early? Want a better meal than your hostel grub?"

Neeta could contain herself no more and burst out, "Oh, Deepa. It's Narin. I ... we ..." The memory of that passionate evening in the hotel three days before came flooding back to her, and as her voice faltered, she blushed and turned her head away to cover her discomfort.

Deepa's concern dissipated momentarily when she realized that her sister's emotion stemmed from embarrassment, not trouble. "What is it, dear? I know you've been seeing him by yourself. What's been happening?"

It came out in a rush. "It's so confusing. But it's great. I … we … feel so strongly about each other. There. I've said it. I'd like to say we love each other, but I've nothing to compare it to. I just want to be with him. That's all. And I know … I'm sure he feels the same way. Oh, Deepa, what are we going to do?"

Deepa was not shocked. Months ago she'd been surprised when Neeta invited a male friend to the house but had said nothing. She'd been quite taken with Narin, finding his reticent manner combined with quiet confidence quite endearing.

"What do you want to do?" she asked in a gentle tone.

"I want to be with him. I want to marry him. I know he's married. And I don't care. He's never been with Mi … his wife. I know he only married her as a way of not fighting with his family. He doesn't think of himself as *married*; he's said it to all of us often enough. Those twin aunts of his forced the issue."

"Neeta, this is very serious. You and Narin must decide how you will deal with his family, as I'm sure there will be difficulties. You may have problems when applying for work, for example. And his brother-in-law, Jaggie—isn't he a lawyer? Let's hope he won't create any trouble."

"Uncle's a lawyer, too. He can deal with him."

"Neeta, this is not a joking matter. You know that we, and our family, will support you, but we have to be sure. It's a family matter as well as your personal decision."

"I know." Neeta was distraught.

Deepa reached over to her sister to envelop her in a hug. "Cheer up, sister. I'm sure it will work itself out. I trust you enough to believe you've thought this through. And I've liked

Narin whenever we've met. Not arrogant like many other boys. He's the handsome one, too."

Deepa noticed the effort Neeta had made to keep her voice calm. "I want you to invite Narin here this weekend for a family grilling." Deepa smiled as she said so. She took Neeta by the arm. "Now, come see my fabulous *anthi mandhaarai* plant. It's all blooming." She led Neeta into the garden to enjoy the hordes of multicolored flowers.

NARIN AND NEETA married on the twentieth of December 1940.

They had submitted the Request for Marriage Service to the Marriage Bureau in September and endured the mandatory three-month wait. The affair itself was a small one, as only Laxman and Ambika joined them at Madras City Hall that morning. They'd considered inviting Sheela and the others, but decided against it in order to keep the party as inconspicuous as possible. All would celebrate later.

The four friends climbed the majestic stairway outside the Municipal Head Office building, picking their way through the always-present groups sitting haphazardly on the steps who were unfazed by the "No Sitting on Steps" signs and occasional threats from the guards.

A khaki-clad clerk escorted them into the office of the Registrar of Marriage. The two windows in the room were partially covered with government-issue beige curtains, darkening it and shielding some of the heat. The overhead fan, also beige, spun fast and efficiently. On the registrar's desk, stacks of paper fluttered like demented birds, held down by a varied selection of paperweights, including the common Ganesh figures. The clerk lingered until they were all seated on a long wooden bench, as if to be sure they didn't intrude on the mysteries of the desk.

Laxman looked around the empty room and remarked, "No other couples here, m'boys. Hope this wallah remembers what to say." Ambika unleashed her usual eye roll at him. Narin was too nervous and focused on Neeta to hear him.

Twenty minutes later, the registrar, a stooped man in his sixties, entered. He took Narin and Neeta's papers, straightened his back, and pointed to where they were to stand. He rummaged through several of his pockets for his reading glasses before he found them. He checked the papers with a thoroughness that tested Narin's patience, calling for his clerk a couple of times for additional documents from the inner offices. He paid particular attention to their MMC student cards, the only identification they possessed. "Medical students" he muttered to no one in particular. It did not seem to warrant a response.

Finally, he looked up at them. "Let us start. You, M. Narinder Janappan, son of K. M. Janappan of Venpuri, province of Madras, and you, V. Neetambai Pai, daughter of the late V. K. Pai of Konkan, province of Maharashtra, are here before me in my capacity as registrar of marriage in the province of Madras to enter the sacred state of marriage."

He proceeded to go through the legal requirements of the marriage ceremony, which took a short ten minutes. After he declared the process complete, he had them sign the marriage certificate with Laxman and Ambika as witnesses. Laxman made an elaborate show of hesitation until Ambika kicked his leg under the table, then signed his name. The registrar took his time sheathing the documents into one pile, caressed the edges just so, patted them down, and handed them to his aide, who scurried away.

"You can come back in two weeks to pick up the official marriage certificate," he said.

Narin struggled between two conflicting emotions—joy at being married to his beloved Neeta and an almost crushing disquiet about how to deal with the repercussions. During the short ceremony, he'd conjured vivid visions of the latter, and Laxman had to nudge him alert once or twice. At the end, he calmed himself with deep breaths.

Narin noticed that the registrar appeared to have sunk into his own world for a moment. He and the others shuffled around, wondering if there was more. Then the registrar shook himself awake. He wore the ghost of a smile for the first time.

"Now, before you leave …" He pulled out a stack of foolscap paper from somewhere under his desk and continued. "If you would indulge an old man's whim, I would like to read you this poetry that I have grown fond of. Quite relevant for marriages. I have made a copy for you." He handed Neeta and Narin a sheet of paper each, glanced over his own copy, his eyes alight, looked up at the couple, and quoted:

Love one another, but make not a bond of love.
Let it rather be a moving sea between the shores of your souls.
Fill each other's cup, but drink not from one cup.
Give one another of your bread, but eat not from the same loaf.
Sing and dance together and be joyous, but let each one of you be alone.
Even as the strings of a lute are alone, though they quiver with the same music.
Give your hearts, but not into each other's keeping,
For only the hand of Life can contain your hearts.
And stand together, yet not too near together;
For the pillars of the temple stand apart,
And the oak tree and the cypress grow not in each other's shadow.
Let there be spaces in your togetherness,
And let the winds of the heavens dance between you.
Love one another, but make not a bond of love.
—*On Marriage* by Kahlil Gibran

The registrar examined the sheet of paper another moment, put it down, and looked at the newly married couple. "Enjoy yourselves. After all, you only ever get married once," he said, now smiling more widely.

Narin, about to thank the registrar, stopped in confusion and heard a suppressed giggle from Neeta.

Laxman, always up to the challenge, responded with a smirk. "Sir, of course. But not everybody follows the same beat, no?"

The registrar's brows dipped in puzzlement, but he said nothing. Narin pushed Laxman away and thanked the registrar profusely. Neeta added her own thanks to his. The registrar smiled again, perhaps a little uncertainly this time. He stood up and ushered them from his office.

Laxman waited until they were outside on the steps of City Hall before he burst into prolonged laughter, saying, "Was he a psychic? Did he read your thoughts, Neeta? Or did Narin's face give away the truth?"

"One of these days you'll get in deep trouble," Ambika said. "Or get us all in trouble."

Neeta shushed them. "I'm so happy," she said. "Let's focus on his wonderful poem, not his last words." She had tears in her eyes. "I particularly liked the emphasis on being together but as two individuals."

Narin reached over and hugged her as Ambika did the same.

Laxman, standing a few feet apart, pulled an ever-present One-Eleven from his pocket.

Part III

Fate chooses our relatives, we choose our friends.
—Jacques Delille

XIII
Chennai (formerly Madras), 2001

Vishram stared at the court documents in bewilderment, not continuing beyond the opening lines:

In the Subordinate Court of Madras
Friday, the 21st day of March, One Thousand Nine Hundred
and Fifty-Three.
100 Mangalchetty Road, George Town, Madras
Present: Learned Justice R. K. Karthikan
In the matter of:
Minalakshmi alias Mrs. M. M. Janappan, Plaintiff
vs.
Dr. M. Narinder Janappan, Defendant

Who was this mysterious "Minalakshmi alias Mrs. M. M. Janappan," and why was she suing his father? Same last name, so a female relative? He probed for a childhood memory. Nothing. This had happened when he was a child, but surely he'd have heard something of this over the years? Surely his parents would've told him?

He turned the page and saw, with further surprise, the stark word "Divorce." *Divorcing his father?* In 1953? How could he have been married to this Minalakshmi, a woman he'd never heard of? Not his mother, referred to formally as Dr. Mrs. Neeta Janappan.

He had to make sense of this. He tried to recall the date of his parents' wedding anniversary. They had never celebrated it, and with the lines of communication on personal matters being so limited between his parents and him, Vishram couldn't even remember the year of their wedding. He'd deduced that the month was December because he noted that his father, arriving home on—was it the twenty-second?—had some small gift, which he'd give his mother almost offhandedly. She would accept it with simple thanks and open it in private. He'd questioned his father about this low-key ritual until Narin had tired of his badgering and, in Neeta's absence, admitted it was their anniversary. Vishram thought it sad they didn't appear to value their wedding anniversary, yet he never asked for an explanation. Now he regretted his lack of curiosity.

He read on. Stacks of organized yellowed papers, reluctant to stay open and reveal their contents after decades of secrecy. He marveled to see so many documents in an ersatz print style—no easy Xeroxing facilities in those days. He imagined the tedious work of a clerk using a Dexigraph reflex copier, each original faced with a sheet of photosensitive paper before being exposed to light to transfer the image. Lucky labor costs were minuscule in those days.

A major section of the papers dealt with the divorce judgment, including actual court transcripts, and the judge's summary. It was fascinating and unlike any legal document he'd read. The judge wrote in an easy but florid style with many colloquialisms and much informal language. This seemed out of place to Vishram, but then, he knew nothing of the Indian legal system of half a century ago. After the usual preliminaries on names, standing, and dates, the judge displayed his stylistic form:

This is the pathetic and unfortunate case of a marriage arranged by the parents and broken by the parties or, more correctly, by the husband. It is all the more a matter of regret as the parties are educated and belong to what may be called an official class. They are Tamilian Brahmins of the Aiyar sect. The defendant is now an assistant surgeon and head of a department in the Victoria Hospital. Plaintiff's father is a retired civil engineer. The marriage was celebrated in Venpuri on …

Many details followed. A blur of sentences floated by:

It is obvious from the subsequent history that the defendant had no real liking for the plaintiff, though he may not actually have disliked her …

The subsequent history is of a sad tale of a young, neglected wife attempting to contact her husband through the authorities …

It is possible that the marriage was arranged without his free consent and out of deference to his father's wishes. The defendant appears to have felt that [the plaintiff] and her father may have been persecuting him by their entreaties …

Justice Karthikan's rhetorical flourishes amplified:

How pitiable her case was, and with what anxiety she was trying to induce him to take her to live with him, in spite of children having been born to him through his second wife, is apparent from a most pitiable letter she wrote to him in her faltering English vide Ex. B-12 …

He was writing to the plaintiff's brother, advising him to get her educated so she may be able to earn a living for herself. If the poor old father and brother felt that this was insult added to injury and did not help to relieve the girl's misery, it would not be an exaggeration …

Vishram needed to talk to someone—his cousin Carla.

He was shocked that neither Carla nor anyone else had ever mentioned his father's first marriage and subsequent divorce to him, particularly because Carla, her husband, and he had been close friends. And the couple were also close to his parents. Carla, his mother's niece, was a Konkan, and her husband was a Tamil Brahmin like Vishram's father. They had fallen in love in college and had married against disapproval from his family. The serendipitous parallel had brought the four of them closer in spite of the generational distance. Perhaps Carla did not know about the events—no, that was not likely.

Vishram picked up the heavy black receiver of the phone in the hallway, circa 1960, raising motes of dust that spiraled away in the bright afternoon sunlight. Unsurprisingly, the phone was dead. He unearthed the cellphone he'd bought for the trip, clicked it on, and stared at the unresponsive screen as he jabbed at various icons. Damn, he needed a local SIM card. His hands shook as he coaxed the legal papers back into their folder. He went out of the house into the dusty street, the clang of the gate's hasp echoing behind him.

There were several tiny storefronts at the end of the road, a two-minute walk away, and Vishram was sure he'd find one that sold phone cards. Each store consisted of a single room, open at the front with a counter behind which sat the proprietor. Ubiquitous preteen boys lounged around two of the stores, gofers who should have been in school but were no doubt important contributors to their family's survival. The third store sold cigarettes, *bidis*, sodas, and a variety of odds and ends, and had a sign proclaiming: *Mobil Phone SIN Cards.*

Hoping their service was better than their spelling, Vishram asked the rail-thin proprietor for a card. The man sized him up in that disconcertingly direct way he had grown unused to while abroad and said in English, "Foreign returned, no? You will have to bring person with Madras address."

"What for?"

"Security instruction. We can't sell card to just everyone. You blow up something with phone."

He ignored the impulse to say that if he were a potential terrorist, he would simply have brought a working phone with him. Pointing down the road, he said, "My mother's address is 4C St. Peter's Road, you know, that house over there." Maybe that would do, even without an actual person.

"Oh, you're Doctor Madam's son, are you? We are waiting for you to be here." With an accepting double-shake of his head, he stubbed out his cigarette, and his eyes darted around as if to be sure no security inspectors were lurking. "Then no problem. Very sad to hear Doctor Madam going. Her *Velaikkar* Bela told us all, no pain, she said. Like she was asleep. Okay, give me the phone. I can set up. Five hundred phone time, okay?" Vishram nodded. It took the proprietor a few minutes to find the right card, insert it in the phone, and check if it worked. "Here, eight hundred twenty," he said as he handed Vishram the phone and a scrap of paper with the phone number scribbled on it.

"And a pack of filter Gold Flakes," Vishram said. He accepted the cigarettes and a matchbook, handed the man two five-hundred-rupee notes, nodded his thanks, and didn't bother with the change.

As he walked away, he glanced back. The proprietor had not taken his eyes from him, as if to ensure he was headed for Doctor Madam's house. He gave him a reassuring wave as he dislodged a cigarette from the golden ten-pack, which was embellished with the words *Tobacco Causes Cancer!* and a decorously clothed image of a presumably cancerous torso. He inhaled delicately, but the unaccustomed strength of the tobacco burned his throat, and he burst into a coughing fit. What he craved was a drink, a strong one, stronger than the bottle of sherry he'd found at his mother's house. A large shot of good single-malt scotch, splash of water, no ice. The sumptuous Vivanta Hotel had an always-open bar, and he considered walking back to it. Or he could throw himself open to his cousin's hospitality.

It would be early morning in San Francisco, but he needed to talk to Elena. To escape the incessant clamor of the street, he crossed to enter his parents' house, playing the usual dodgem with unyielding cars, trucks, rickshaws, and carts. He dialed Elena, taking three attempts to get the number right. She answered on the fifth ring, her voice groggy.

"Elena, it's me."

"Vish. Great to hear from you. I got your email earlier. How are you, dear? Are you super jet-lagged?" When he didn't reply, she continued. "Everything okay with the house? No squatters or dogs or anything like that?"

"No, the house is fine. I'll tell you the details later. But—" He began a short coughing fit as he took a surreptitious puff.

"You okay? You sound a little on edge."

"Just tired. But I discovered something."

"What?"

"I'm a bastard."

"So tell me something new." He imagined her smiling. "What is it really?"

"No, really. In the old-fashioned British sense. I'm a bastard child, born free of wedlock."

"Oh, Vish, stop being so melodramatic. And it's 'out of wedlock,' not 'free of.' What on earth do you mean? What did you find out?" He sensed a hint of irritation in her voice.

"Okay, here's the scoop." He calmed his breathing. "I found some legal papers hidden away. My father apparently got married quite young to a thirteen-year-old girl in his hometown. Soon after the marriage, he went to medical college in Madras where he met my mother, whom he married four years later. So that was a big-amous marriage, yeah? And I was born of it. I'd never heard of all this. Isn't it unreal?"

"Oh, my god … that's wild. I can't believe you're saying this. By the way, much as I dig the idea, what you found doesn't make you a bastard. Didn't you once tell me that a second or even third marriage is sort of legal in India? Particularly in those times?"

"Oh. One minor claim to fame gone." He trailed off and took a couple of more-vigorous puffs off the well-squished cigarette, trying not to cough again.

"How do you feel about this?"

"Crazy. Do you realize how completely screwed up this is? My parents, who I always thought of as boringly conventional." He gave Elena the gist of the story. "There's a lot of back-and-forth with his first wife's family. They threatened legal action if he did not live with … ah … Mina, which he refused to do. Don't see how they could've expected him to live with both of his wives. Finally, in 1953, Mina filed for divorce. The testimony is weird. Later there's a series of letters between my father and her. She wanted more maintenance. He pleaded poverty."

"What are you going to do?"

"Do? Have a strong drink, or three, for starters." He shook his head to clear it. "I can ask various relatives what they remember. Maybe Mina-what's-her-name's still around. She was six years younger than my dad and would be, like, close to eighty now."

Another pause, a final drag, and he tossed the butt into the open sewage ditch running outside the yard wall. "The whole thing reminds me of Ved Metha's dad's secret mistress in his book *Red* something."

"You must try to meet her. Grab a tape recorder if you do. It'll be useful to get her reminiscences if she'll talk. And hold off on the scotch, will you?"

"Hope she speaks English. I can only imagine how it'd go if I tried interviewing her in Tamil. Too bad my dad's siblings are all dead now. He and his sibs didn't have much contact, you know. I used to wonder about that, and now I guess I know why. His family probably went ballistic when he married my mother." He looked at the Gold Flake pack, which seemed to demand more attention.

"How about the other stuff—furniture, money, maid. Did you get much done with all that?"

"Yeah. Mostly the bureaucratic crap left. Wish you were here. Told ya. You would've been in on the breaking story."

"Well, in this case, you were right. But it's sixty-four and foggy here, and I'm snuggled in a warm bed under a comforter while you are ... what? Sweaty and bad-tempered and shooing away tons of flies with that cigarette?"

"I'm getting a tan. You should try it sometime, white girl." She burst out laughing. He didn't join her. "Miss you. And the little Neel, of course. Has he been talking your ear off?"

"Neel's been great. Yes, he misses you a lot. Call again tomorrow. I want more details. Say hello to your cuz when you see her later today. By the way, you may've met this first wife many times thinking she's an aunt, just like Metha described in his book. And it's called *Red Letters*. Love you. Bye."

"Love you too. Bye. I'm off to quiz Carla."

"BUT OF COURSE you knew," Carla protested.

Vishram had rattled over to her place in a three-wheeled auto-rickshaw, a sputtering and smoky replacement for the pedaled version. He was calming his nerves with a double shot of Bagpiper whiskey, an Indian brand not quite up to his regular scotch, but spicily palatable. Carla cradled a cup of sweet Darjeeling tea, having declined to join him by citing the drinks-only-after-dusk convention.

"No, I did not know," he repeated, annoyed at her turn of phrase, so Indian, the declarative "of course you knew" replacing a more reasonable "you must've known." Something about dealing from a position of strength when you're challenged. "Why on earth did you never tell me?"

"Because everyone in the family knew about it, I naturally expected you would, too. And how would I have brought it up, anyway? It's hardly casual conversation, is it? 'How's your mother doing today? And, by the way, is she still fuming about that divorce settlement from 1953?'"

"I'm sure there were other opportunities." But were there? Close as he and Carla were, there wasn't much emotional intimacy between them. Reticence must be in the DNA of the damned family, he thought sourly.

"Did what's-her-name ever visit us? Would you have known?"

"I think Mina came to your house a few times. You know, she held some kind of torch for your father and never gave up the idea of living with him. And with Auntie Neeta there as well, what a thought. Tragic, actually. Obviously she couldn't remarry in those times, but she could've had a more independent life if she'd given up on Uncle Narin."

Yes, Vishram thought, a divorced woman in 1953 would have been vanishingly rare, and someone like Mina had three strikes against her: being divorced, her advanced age of twenty-nine, and her poor education. All marriages were arranged, so she would have hit rock bottom on the marriageability scale. An already-married woman—who wants rejected goods? His Western side rebelled against the connotation, and he consoled himself that it's the way they think there.

Carla told him that Mina lived in Madras, within a mile or two of his parent's house on St. Peter's Road, from the late fifties until her death in 1996, a few years after his father had died. Carla knew little of her circumstances. Vishram wanted details and asked for Carla's help.

"How can I get in touch with my father's relatives? Do you know any of them?"

But the schism had lasted too long. Carla didn't know any of their addresses or telephone numbers, and she said she doubted any of them would want to talk about the matter. "You don't realize how traumatic this was when it happened. Your mother used to tell me horror tales of how badly Uncle Narin's father and his older sisters treated him the few times they met. Of the Venpuri group, only his brother Gopal was willing to visit Uncle sometimes. And since his sister Sheela had declared her loyalty to him, she bore a lot of resentment from others in the family. But you must remember that from before—"

"My mother … they must have hated her. How did they treat her?"

"As far as I know, she only met his family twice over the years. Poor Auntie Neeta, I'm sure it was so difficult for her, the way she was treated, but she was devoted to your father. Uncle's family wouldn't come near them for over twelve years. Then there was one famous meeting, I believe. You must've been six or so."

"I don't remember it."

"Really? Of course, your memory for names and events is terrible, isn't it? Anyway, your grandparents came to your parent's flat here, though they didn't stay there. Guess that would've been too much togetherness. They came to discuss the divorce, and also your father wanted them to reconcile with Auntie and meet you, their grandson."

"And how did it go?"

"I only have Auntie's side of it. She was … well, let's say she wasn't exactly the most forgiving person herself, no? So she wasn't inclined to look kindly on the whole event. Auntie said her father-in-law was polite to you but didn't talk much to her. Your grandmother was apparently much nicer. Uncle Narin's two aunts were also there, the twins, who drove everyone batty. Your mother had prepared an elaborate meal for their first lunch together, and the aunts complained it wasn't 'Tamil' enough. Oh, and of course that's when your Auntie Sheela—"

Vishram drowned out Carla's last words with a burst of laughter as he remembered his mother's out-of-the-norm food taste. "No way could she have made it as bland as the food she usually prepared. I guess I didn't make much of an impression, either. My grandparents didn't keep in touch, did they?"

Carla paused, thinking back. "No. They never came back to Madras to see Auntie and Uncle. Your father went to Venpuri a few times after that visit, but I don't recall your mother going with him."

When he moved to the U.S., Vishram had been surprised to meet many Americans who had indifferent relationships with even close family members. Now he thought his reaction was ironic, considering how estranged his own father's family was from his father—and from him. It hadn't made much of an impression when he was growing up, perhaps because his mother's family was so effusively present.

Vishram examined the liquid surface of the whiskey, then downed the rest of the glass. He walked over to the sideboard and poured himself another, ignoring Carla's sharp look. He slumped down in the soft chair and gulped half the second drink, the welcoming warmth replaced by a not-so-subtle stinging. His eyes drooped as the alcohol began to affect his jet-lagged body, and he heard Carla's voice echoing from afar.

"Why don't you ask Auntie Neeta's close friend, Dr. Hansa? I'm sure he could give you more details than me. And perhaps you should move to the bedroom to take a nap?"

XIV
Venpuri, 1940

Winter was not a memorable season in Venpuri, being a short not-so-hot respite sandwiched between months of heat and humidity. This day, however, the sky was clear with cottony clouds forming fantastical shapes, and the dappled sunlight had set the drab surroundings of the village aglow. Even the straw huts had come to shimmering life, and strong breezes fluttered the fronds of their brown thatched roofs. The always-present throngs were gliding along the streets with a lilt in their measured steps, exuding a feeling that this was a great day to be alive.

This euphoria did not extend to all. Two figures were wending their way without acknowledging the beauty of the day. Heads down, firm hands keeping their saris from total dishevelment, the twins Saraswathi and Saranmathi were on their way to their cousin Mohan's house on an unscheduled visit. They moved in their usual purposeful manner, but now never exchanging words. Their tight lips and narrowed eyes underscored their bad mood. They ignored a cheery *namaskaar* from a close neighbor as he passed them, and he stared in irritation at their retreating figures. They crossed the street to their cousin's house, defying the bleating horn of a mere car, which had to brake hard to avoid them, emitting a squeal of rubber. The chauffeur, without his master to curb him, hung his head out of the car's window to yell a few choice words before continuing, swerving to avoid other road-users whose meticulous progress had been ruined by his maneuvers. Sara and Saran paid no attention to his expletives. They were on a mission.

Narin's letter to his father had arrived the day before.

> Dear Father,
>
> I have to tell you how I have been feeling for a very long time. Until this point, I haven't had the courage to do so. It's easy to hide one's cowardice behind the pretense that silence is better, that not saying anything might lead to a solution. I can no longer take comfort in that pretense.
>
> As you well know, there has been another person in my life now for over a year. I remember the first letter you wrote to me when my dear Elder-Brother-in-law Jaggie sent you a no-doubt overblown account of an innocent meeting between friends. As I gathered from your response, as well as others' responses, Jaggie assumed the worst. He abandoned his lawyerly training and leapt from one to ten with little evidence. But he also objected to my friends' behavior, innocent or not, even that boys and girls were meeting together.
>
> At the time, of course, nothing inappropriate was happening. Laxman and Ambika were my close friends, and we had been socializing a lot. I first met their friend Neeta that day. I did not know then (how could I have known) the effect she was to have on me. You could not know, as I have never told anyone in Venpuri, of how Neeta and I connected immediately. It was quite mutual, I assure you. Do not believe that she was some sort of femme fatale who seduced me with her charms.

She was charming, of course, but I was also pushy in getting her to like me.

Let me explain that my marriage to Mina, which Neeta has always known of, was not an impediment to our attachment. I am sure you are shocked. But I was married at eighteen, over four years ago, which seems a lifetime to me now. I entered that marriage with eyes shut, so to speak. I did not know what I was doing or what being married really meant. You may think this is naïve or selfish, but it was so. I wanted to leave Venpuri (not to leave you, Amma, and the family, just to experience other places and people), and going to medical college was my way out. I'm sorry I treated my marriage to Mina as a necessary step for me to do so. Looking back, I can see that I should have objected, though I don't know if it would have changed anything. My twin aunties are not easy to push back against, as I'm sure you will agree. And you and Amma would have been disappointed in me had I refused.

I thought long and hard about this before I made my decision, and I thought it best if I informed you after the event. Neeta and I are married. We have been closely attached for a long while now. We have much in common. We are both doctors, and we both want to work toward bringing the best medical care to the masses. Maybe we're naïve in thinking we can make a difference. Our needs and personalities are much alike, and we are very happy.

I realize this will bring up a major issue regarding Mina. I often wonder if things would have been different if I had not met Neeta, but I think neither Mina nor I would have been happy. I because she was not the wife I wanted, and she because she could not (or her parents wouldn't let her) change to match my needs.

Harsh, but there it is. It is now too late for regrets. I have to deal with the reality. I cannot live with Mina now. Perhaps she can continue living with her parents, as she appears happy there, and I know she has never tried to live at your house. As for the future, I don't know. She will have to decide along with her parents.

Yours,

Narinder

Mohan had dropped the letter from his shaking hands. Although the whole Neeta affair was an ongoing dilemma for him, he had no idea that it was more than a casual—even, in his darker thoughts, sexual—relationship between his son and the girl.

When he showed the letter to his wife, she collapsed in her chair, weeping. "No, it can't be. How could he? Not my son."

Mohan tried to engage her in discussing the matter, to no avail. He realized the crisis was too much for them to deal with on their own. Jyothi would be of no help. He called for the obvious reinforcements. He sent the letter over to his twin cousins, lamenting the impossible situation and begging them for their help and advice.

Mohan greeted the newly cognizant sisters with a hopeful smile as they sailed up to his door, noting their black mood and lack of sympathetic words.

He cringed as Sara burst out, "He must be crazy," as she entered the house, sweeping past him and ignoring Jyothi, who was cowering behind her husband. The couch squawked as both sisters plopped down on it.

"I always knew he was different than us," Saran said. "He's too selfish. Now see what's happened."

"Cousin Subbu will hit the roof when he hears," her sister said.

"He probably knows already. You know how Jaggie snoops around. He'll have written to his father by now."

"Have you found out if this ... marriage ... was conducted properly? Perhaps it's not correct and legal."

"A woman called Neeta. What's her family name anyway?"

"Pai."

"Pai! What kind of a name is that?"

"It's Konkan."

"Oh my god. On top of everything, she's not even from Madras."

"She *is* a Brahmin and, I think, an *Aiyer* like us," Mohan interjected.

"Rubbish. No one in that godforsaken area up north can be a real Brahmin like us—"

"Like us? You know she's not one of us. What will the neighbors say?"

"And their children. They'll be what? Half ... *Konkanis*. How will they manage?"

"This is the end of Sheela's chances; you know now she can never get married."

The mention of Sheela's name triggered a violent reaction in Saran.

"I'm certain Sheela egged him on. She was always conspiring with Narin. And you know how stubborn she can be. We'll have to find out from Cousin Kala. I told you we had to keep a watch on her. Cousin Kala is too easy-going. Have you written to her to find out the facts?"

She directed this last question at Mohan, who was overwhelmed by the sisters' wrath.

He sputtered "No," and Saran continued, "And why not? What are you thinking of, to not get the real information? How could you not have known before this?"

Sara added, "Of course he knew," as if Mohan were not present. "He was just too cowardly to tell us about it." She turned her glare on Mohan. "Isn't that so?"

Mohan's feeble, "No, I didn't," did not interrupt the rant.

He waited until their anger abated and they sat eyeing each other, exhaling noisily. He offered them hot tea, which they accepted with an emphatic eye roll, an unspoken criticism for not having been offered it earlier. No one spoke for a few moments before and after the tea arrived. Mohan shooed the servant Mari away as soon as she laid the trays down and poured his cousins' tea himself. Saran ladled in an unaccustomed three spoonfuls of sugar. Her sister did not miss this excessive indulgence, shooting her a sharp look but saying nothing, and added a single, sparse half-spoonful into her own tea in response. They raised their cups in unison, looked meaningfully at each other, perfectly attuned to the moment, and took deep gulps.

Mohan cherished the temporary quiet. He reflected on all the sisters had said, much of which he considered bluster, but a couple of important points demanded attention. He sipped his tea.

"Let's be calm. I'm sure the marriage is valid and cannot be contested. So there are two things we need to talk about." He held up a hand to forestall Saran's challenge. "Firstly, what can we do about Mina? And—"

"Do?" Saran snapped. "Subbu will make us responsible for her keep. You, cousin, will have to take her in and support her for the rest of her life. How do you like that?"

Mohan did not see it that way at all. "Not necessarily. If Narin takes his marriage to Mina seriously, he will have to support her. Maybe she can still live with him."

While rare in their social circle, he knew that men who remarried while having the inconvenience of a first wife often made living arrangements for her.

"We know Narin. He won't do that, cousin," Saran said.

"And that devil Neeta will never agree either." Sara added.

They sat back and looked at each other, nodding in agreement.

Mohan knew better than to argue with that certainty. He doubted Mina would want to come and live in his house, empty of anyone close to her age. His older son and his family lived with him, of course, but Mina didn't know them well, and his daughter-in-law would have little time to spare for a wronged and uncommunicative eighteen-year-old, what with having to care for her three small boys.

As he thought about these possibilities, he heard the slight click of a toe-ring and turned to see Mari gliding up to him holding an envelope, her bare feet otherwise soundless on the red concrete floor. He was surprised, as the regular post was not due for several hours. He noticed the lack of a stamp. The letter had been hand-sent. He looked questioningly at Mari, who stood her ground, wordless as ever. He asked, "Where is that from?"

"Shri Subbu's servant came," she said in a low voice, as if to conceal the name from the others. She shook the letter, eager to be rid of it, looking with apprehension at the twins, who were staring daggers at her.

Mohan took the letter without any further acknowledgment. Mari turned and flitted out. He tore the letter open and held up his hand to stem further assaults from his cousins as he digested its contents. He crushed the letter. "Well, that was quick. It's from Subbu, of course. You were right, cousins. Efficient Jaggie has already written to him about Narin, and Subbu wants to know what we intend to do about this terrible situation." He stopped and picked up his cup of tea and blew on it, not drinking any, staring at it as if an answer to this mess would be written on its rippling brown surface.

The sisters looked at each other for a long moment, and Mohan prepared for the oncoming tirade.

"He'll ask for the dowry back."

"Mohan, don't you dare return a thing."

"Even if Mina comes to live with us."

Live with us, Mohan thought. Us?

"You must cut off Narin's allowance immediately."

"Yes, let's see how he does with no money. Maybe that floozy wife of his can support him."

He's a doctor, Mohan thought, and so is she. They can earn a decent living. Have you forgotten?

"She might leave him if you take a hard line. She must feel entitled to your family money. Maybe that's why she made this play for him."

"What family money?" Mohan asked.

Ignoring him, one cousin said, "Maybe you can pay her off. Girls like that have only money in mind."

"Bring him back here. We can settle this," the other said.

Mohan wondered how they expected him to force a grown man to do what he may not want to do. Didn't they realize he was no longer a child?

"Write to Kala, as well. Make her send Sheela back."

And what did his daughter have to do with her brother's actions? Why punish her?

"We have to get her out of Narin's influence."

"Yes. It's time she learned her duty to the family, cousin."

Mohan tuned out the continuing wail and looked out the window, listening to the harsh sound of a dog barking in sharp counterpoint to the steady rumble of traffic. This cacophony would have irritated him at other times, but now it was a respite that helped him concentrate. He knew he would have to write to his son himself. It was his problem alone, his responsibility. And he would have to find a way to defuse Subbu's justifiable outrage. He did not look forward to either. Half-listening to his cousins' ongoing wrathful harangue, he wondered why he didn't share their extreme anger. He was angry too, but Narin was his son, and he owed him at least a modicum of loyalty and support. Narin would need it, judging from his in-laws' reactions.

XV
Madras, 1941–42

Neeta and Narin moved into a flat six months after their wedding. Private accommodations for a young couple were not easy to find in Madras, so when a mutual acquaintance sent word to Narin about the availability of a flat, he suspected that Laxman had called in a favor. He would have to thank him.

The recently built flat hadn't yet acquired the overlay of grime so common with age. It was on the second floor, three flights of slippery-when-wet steps with no railing leading to a narrow, exposed corridor, which in turn led to eight apartments. The building's outside walls and the corridor were a deep and not-unpleasant maroon, contrasting with the dingy green front doors. Neeta's artistic color sense cringed at the clash.

Narin thought the interior confining, with only two rooms and a bath. A minimal kitchen area with a stone sink and counter was in a corner of the larger room. Better than nothing, Neeta declared as she turned on the sink's tap, which paused a moment before spitting a trickle of rusty water. At least she wouldn't have to squat on the floor—many so-called kitchens were mere empty rooms.

They'd discussed at length whether they could afford even this meager space, as Narin was concerned that his father might cut off his small allowance at any moment. But they could manage with some help from Neeta's family and their stipends from the training hospitals, which were due to start soon. Narin was tired of living with his aunt Kala while his beloved Neeta stayed twenty long minutes away at her sister's place. Sexual encounters, he'd grumbled, were frustrating and infrequent.

On the day they moved in, Laxman arrived with a sheesham wood Jodhpuri dining table and four chairs with filigree backs and arms.

"That's beautiful," exclaimed Neeta, caressing the polished rosewood, "but Laxman, it must have been so expensive. We can't accept this from you."

Laxman waved her protests aside. "No problem. My good ol' father's effectively paying. It came out of my allowance, and, you know," he said with a wink, "how big that is."

"Without his knowledge?" asked Narin.

"Not to worry, darlings. He won't notice a thing. And even if he knows, he'll agree it's for a good cause when I explain that it's for a deserving but impoverished couple of my friends."

He turned to the two men who had brought the furniture in and, indicating exactly where to set the objects, said in his now almost intelligible Tamil, "*Audhu ellah inguh pohd-lam*," observing the placement with a satisfied smile as they complied. After getting the men to make minor adjustments, he slipped them a few rupees, shooing away Narin who was belatedly reaching for his wallet. He grabbed a convenient rag and brushed away some smudges on the tabletop, pulled out a medical journal from his pocket like a magician extracting a rabbit, and positioned it squarely in the center.

"Now you have a place to spread out your *Lancets* while you *inhale* their contents, Neeta." He pirouetted slowly, looking askance at the expanse of plain whitewashed walls. "Must brighten this place up. Hmm, you could get some good paste to put up Neeta's daubs."

Narin nodded in agreement as he picked up an unopened box and took it into the bedroom. Laxman followed him into the smaller room, shooing Neeta ahead of him. He found a pile of her drawings in an open box and riffled through them. He uttered a happy cry as he brandished one and said, "I recommend you put up this lovely image of Professor Megarathnam here, right above your cot, where his gaze can reproach you forever. That will make you grateful to be here after those years of hell at MMC."

"We'd never get any sleep if we did that," Neeta said.

This earned a broad leer from Laxman and a sigh from Neeta as she grabbed the drawing from him and replaced it in the box, then took a moment to select and hand him a more pleasant composition. She gestured to Narin, who paused his unpacking for a moment to glance at it and nod approval.

Laxman took his time, moving the drawing back and forth in critical appraisal. "Soothing colors."

Neeta propped the drawing on the bed, and all three enjoyed a contemplative moment.

Narin interrupted Laxman as he resumed his discourse on wall decoration. "Listen, you and Ambika are invited this Saturday for our first dinner party. And we can christen that beautiful table you've given us."

"Dinner shay, my friends? Marvelous. Who's … ah … going to cook?"

"Me, of course," Neeta said with a smile.

"My felicitations. I didn't know you could. I hope we're not the guinea pigs for your first culinary experimentation, Neeta. My dear Ambika, you know, has never been seen in the confines of a kitchen. I doubt she'd know how to light a Primus stove or which end of a *kirpan* knife to hold when slaughtering a chicken."

Neeta made an exasperated sound. "Laxman, that's stupid. Who on earth uses a *kirpan* in the kitchen? It's ceremonial. Or kills chickens indoors?"

"Ambika might to impress the stray onlooker. Or to repel all boarders." He struck an exaggerated pose with upraised arm mimicking a brandished weapon. "Hmm ... but she has an unreasonable dread of fire."

"Well, maybe that will control your smoking around her," Neeta said. "Anyway, when you and Ambika establish a home, I'm sure she'll have a cook from the start. Unlike us."

"Oh, I'm sure you'll find one soon. Are you having difficulty? I hear finding good servants can be so trying. Maybe I can put out feelers. Are you particular about her being a Brahmin, or can you accept one of a lesser tribe?"

"We can't afford one. You know that," said Neeta with a tight look.

"Oops, Neeta, please forgive me. I'm sorry. I abase myself. I'm so looking forward to your fantastic banquet. I'll bring that bottle of Jerez-Xeres sherry. Lovely name, that, isn't it? Spanish, even if I have no idea how it's pronounced. You'll like it. Won't she, Narin?" Laxman continued in a manner so conciliatory that he earned Neeta's trademark radiant smile in return, and even Narin had to admire his ability to defuse a situation.

NARIN AND NEETA spent the next few months in their cocoon of happiness. Their nemesis, Jaggie, had not appeared at their door. Neeta's family sent sincere letters of congratulations, and her mother wrote to Narin separately to invite them to visit her at her home in Konkan at any time. Narin rejoiced in the ample support and friendship of Neeta's family but was heartsick at the cold condemnation from his own, Sheela's enthusiastic support being the exception. His aunt Kala and her husband were less disapproving than his Venpuri family, but he hadn't visited his aunt and uncle since moving out of their house to this flat. He tried to not let it affect him, but the continued pressure of letters from his first in-laws was chipping away at his confidence and contentment.

Neeta managed to eke out time from her schedule as an intern to continue drawing. She pasted her images on the walls of their flat and wondered what she'd do when she'd used up all the space. Whenever she asked Narin what he thought of her latest effort, he would be positive but noncommittal. She attributed the paucity of his comments to his not having been exposed to art growing up. When she asked him to describe his home in Venpuri, he noted that the only decorations on its walls were large portraits of his grandparents, their stern countenances monitoring the integrity of the household, and one overbearing image of a blue Shiva, a staple of many Hindu houses.

"And it's the one where he's clutching a trident instead of cuddling up to his buxom wife," Narin said, laughing irreverently one night as he held Neeta close in bed.

"Consort," she corrected. "You say 'consort' for the gods' partners."

"Still, shows he has his priorities quite wrong, or maybe the artists were too scared to show them embracing."

"Isn't that blasphemy? Or is that only a Western thing?" She reached down to stroke him.

"We need Laxman to explain the origin of the word and if it applies to Hindus, as well."

"We need you to be quiet and pay attention to me."

Which he then did.

NEETA OPENED THEIR door in response to a knock to see Laxman standing there. She waved him in, but he didn't come striding in as he usually did. He shuffled his feet and looked past her at Narin, who was sitting on the sofa in the living room.

"Where's Ambika?" Neeta asked.

"Aaah … she's busy right now. And—"

"Come on in. I'll get us a drink. Are you hungry?"

"Actually, Neeta, I was going to take a walk to stretch my muscles. Long day at the hospital." He raised his voice. "Hey, Narin, let's take a jaunt, shall we?"

Narin shrugged and nodded, then slipped on his sandals. As they walked away, Narin glanced back at Neeta, who had a perplexed expression. He winked at her.

They walked for fifteen minutes with Laxman trailing Narin, who had to stop several times to let his friend catch up. Narin chitchatted about trivialities with little response from the uncharacteristically silent Laxman.

Laxman finally put out a hand to stop Narin. "I think I've messed up badly, Narin." He raised his other hand to his face and rubbed his eyes. He didn't look at his friend, and his face was tight with distress.

"Wow, Lax, you seem devastated. What's happened? Ambika? Is she okay?"

"She's not okay! Well, yes, she is, physically, I mean … It's just that—"

"What, you two have a fight? Don't you do that every week?" Narin smiled and punched Laxman's shoulder lightly; he still didn't look up. Narin, taking in his friend's misery, said, "Oh damn it, what is it, Lax? You can tell me."

"Narin, well, … let's say she's angry at something I did. With … it's not, I shouldn't have, she—"

"My god! You didn't … you couldn't have, Lax. Are you saying you shagged someone?" Laxman was concentrating on the parched earth at his feet. "And Ambika found out. How?" Laxman was silent. "Talk to me, Lax."

Laxman sat on a concrete embankment, adjusting his body to its rough contours, while Narin remained standing in front of him. "It was a stupid thing, Narin. She's a nurse at my hospital, and I knew she fancied me because … well, she was sort of coming on strong to me and—"

"Hope you didn't use that as an excuse."

"No! Not excusing, just explaining. Working very late several nights in a row. It just happened."

"And Ambika?"

"I told her."

"Why? *Why?*"

There was a long silence as Narin shook his head and looked up at the sky where a murder of crows was circling slowly. When he had exhausted his examination of the birds, he turned back to Laxman. "Why?" he repeated.

"Can't explain it. Guilt? Regret? Needing to tell someone, to confess, be purged?"

"You could've just jumped into the Couvam for the *Maha Kumbh*, Lax. I hear the Great Bath washes away all sins."

"Can you not be flip? What am I going to do? Ambika hasn't talked to me for three days; she won't even let me into her room."

"Has she threatened to stop being with you? Have you really tried to talk to her?"

Laxman's hands were shaking as he reached for his pack of One-Elevens. He pulled out a cigarette, not offering one to Narin, and took his time lighting it. He inhaled deeply.

"No. And yes. Many times."

Narin considered. He had never seen his friend in less than complete self-control. Laxman always knew how to proceed in any circumstance, always had ready advice on any subject. Had he ever asked Narin what to do about a problem? Or even *mentioned* a problem?

"Firstly, Lax, stop with the 'it just happened' rubbish. It didn't 'just;' *you* acted on your impulses." Narin summoned up his courage to tell Laxman what he had often berated himself for not doing. "You have to take responsibility, or you won't be able to stop it from happening again."

"No—"

Narin watched Laxman trying, and failing, to blow his trademark smoke rings. "Yes. Tell her now. Tell her how you feel about this." Laxman dropped the unfinished cigarette and ground it out under his shoe, taking longer than necessary. "Tell Ambika how sorry you are. When you were at our house a week ago, you used the word 'abased,' jokingly, I suppose, to Neeta. I had to look it up, I wasn't sure what it meant. Well, it's perfect. You have to abase yourself before her."

This brought a hint of a smile from Laxman, whose tightly wound body relaxed a bit.

"Yeah, I'm sure my extensive vocabulary is going to prove useful."

"Stop it, Laxman. You're not being serious about this. Ambika will throw you out if you're not sincere."

"Maybe I'll propose. Been long enough."

Narin threw up his hands in exasperation. "What the hell do you think she'll say to *that*?"

"Okay, okay, Narin. Sorry. It's the way I deal with strain—"

"Making stupid jokes?"

"Yes. Anyway ..." He pulled out another cigarette, tossed aside the empty pack, jammed it between his lips, but didn't light it. He tilted his head to look at Narin. "I've really been thinking about it, really. We have talked about it, more than once. Marriage. I know it sounds like a total excuse for what happened, but the finality ... of marriage ... scares the hell out of me. Even to Ambika, whom I really ... do ... love."

Narin sat on the embankment beside his friend. He put his arm over Laxman's shoulders and pulled him close. "Lax, I've known you for years now. I've watched you change. You've become more serious, and I think your connection with Ambika has much to do with it. You two are perfect for each other. One woman's love is enough. I can attest to that. Don't destroy it. Confide in her." He added with a grin, "And your father will love to have another doctor from the family working in his clinic."

They sat a while in silence. Then Laxman got up and took Narin's hands in his and shook them slowly, then walked away. Narin watched him until he was out of sight. In spite of his advice, he wasn't at all sure Laxman would stop straying. He'd admired the sureness of Laxman's manner, but it bordered on an arrogant conviction of his own invincibility. And his uncanny ability to attract women wouldn't help, either. He hoped Laxman would find a way to behave differently with—or without—Ambika's knowledge. Should he tell Neeta about Laxman's confession? They had no secrets from each other. But she was less forgiving than he was, and he could well imagine her critical nature condemning Laxman in no uncertain terms, perhaps influencing Ambika as well. Best to keep silent.

Two days later, as Narin was thinking of going over to Laxman's flat to see how he was faring, a servant delivered this note:

> Narin, you're a godsend. And a good friend. Thanks for the pep talk two days ago. I took your advice and practically fell at Ambika's feet asking for forgiveness. It worked after a (very long) while. She says she's going to keep me on a short leash from now on. And she's letting me visit her room again (wink). See you both soon.

XVI
Madras, 1942

After his initial retreat, Jaggie turned up unannounced one day at Narin and Neeta's flat. He barged in, ignored Neeta, dismissed Narin's reluctant gesture toward a chair, and said, "Well, Narin, you've made a pretty mess of things, haven't you?"

"Jaggie, good to see you, too. Have a seat," Narin said, glancing at Neeta's reddening face. He lowered himself into a chair and looked up at Jaggie.

"Don't prevaricate with me, Narin. Our family has been insulted, and we have to talk about this. Appa has told me to look into legal possibilities. He thinks I'm a magician or something. I know what's legal and not legal."

"Well, I'm glad you're thinking that way."

"What about my poor sister?"

"Jaggie, you know that marriage was between us as children … at least in her case and almost in mine. Nobody asked me whether I wanted to or not."

Jaggie sputtered something unintelligible, collected himself, and continued. "But you did it. And you have responsibilities to Mina."

"Which we can discuss, preferably calmly. Have a seat," Narin said.

"What do you think of Appa's proposal that you take Mina in to live with you and …?" Nodding at Neeta.

Neeta threw out an exasperated sigh. She told them she had errands and rushed out.

When she returned an hour later, Narin said, "He's gone, all clear," but didn't offer anything more on their conversation. He avoided her eyes until she started putting away her purchases and puttering around.

Just as Narin thought she had relaxed, Neeta asked abruptly, "So did you and he resolve these 'responsibilities' to … her?"

"We are still discussing it, and—"

"Don't you dare consider it, Narin."

"Okay, but—"

"No buts, Narin. What the hell else did he want?"

"Nothing special, just checking up on our well-being."

"Don't be funny, Narin. He's going to keep coming over. Can't you tell him not to?"

"I don't think I can, Neeta. Please try to understand." He gave her a pleading look.

"I understand that you don't have the guts to stand up to him."

"Difficult, considering the size of his belly."

"Narin! Stop it. Can't you see this is serious?"

Narin had smiled at his own repartee but backed down. "Just a joke." She was still glaring at him, so he continued. "Maybe you could talk to him when he comes here next."

"Talk? He doesn't even look at me. I'm not catering to his rudeness. Anyway, he's your responsibility."

"Ours."

"No. He's your nasty relation."

"Neeta, yes. But the reason he's so nasty is—"

"Because of me? Is that what you were going to say?"

"No, not exactly—"

"Yes. That's what you meant. You're trying to put the blame for that stupid man's behavior on me. No, I'm not having it."

"If we … If I'm too nasty to him, it will just make it harder for me to reconcile with my parents. There'll be repercussions from our extended family. It will be a complete break between me and my family. You must realize that, Neeta. Can't we present a united front on this?"

"No!" Her voice went up an octave. "As for your family, your parents must, will, come around, even if it takes a while. And damn Jaggie. I don't give a damn what he thinks or what he'll do if you throw him out the next time he barges in. And that's what you'd better do. Or … I'll …" Neeta's eyes were damp.

Narin was alarmed at how their first argument was developing. He looked at her in dismay, wondering whether to rush over and fold her in his arms or talk it out, hoping her anger would dissipate. For a while, he did neither, and she soon burst into tears, mumbling something.

Narin thought he heard her say, "… have to leave." Appalled, he rushed to her and held her close, despite her halfhearted attempts to push him away.

After a few moments, she quieted. "He's not worth fighting about."

Narin agreed.

"WE'LL MISS YOU terribly," said Narin one evening eight weeks later as he walked with Neeta, Laxman, and Ambika toward the recently opened Chola restaurant. This was both a celebratory and a poignant moment. Laxman and Ambika had decided to get married after more than four years together and were moving back to their home city of Bangalore. Neeta and Narin had tempered their disappointment at their friends' departure with their genuine happiness for their future. Laxman airily suggested that he and Ambika would visit often, but travel wasn't easy, even between cities as close as Madras and Bangalore, and they all knew there would be long periods between their meetings.

Laxman spread his arms as he shepherded the others inside. "We are in for a treat. Chola specializes in 'quasi-Indian food with a Chinese overbite.'"

Neeta rolled her eyes at the pretension, and he put up a hand in a disarming gesture. "Not my words, dears. It's from the *India Times'* critic from last week." He glanced at Ambika, who was shaking her head. "Well, close enough. Anyway, you'll love their chana daal 'layered' with tofu. Guaranteed vegetarian."

Chola's designers had spared no expense. Rich curtains separated the tables, and there was a slew of modernist wall hangings. White tablecloths were decorated along their edges with beaded mirror embellishments. The dull electric sconces that lined the restaurant's walls were cleverly disguised as temple oil lamps. Narin commented on how gloomy it looked.

"Gloomy? Best get with the times, boys and girls," Laxman said as the maître d' greeted him with familiarity. "It's called 'atmosphere,' and it's all the rage nowadays."

"Why? So you can't tell what you're being served?"

"Neeta, get your hubby to be less of a stick-in-the-mud, would you?"

Neeta gave Narin a not-so-subtle jab in the side.

"We can pretend we're in a Viennese nightclub. I hear it's considered gauche there to actually know who you're talking to across the table." He produced two liquor bottles from behind him with the flourish of a magic trick and handed them to one of the three white-garbed waiters who had surrounded them. He offered no instructions.

"One of the few civilized places where you can drink at the table," he noted as the waiter nodded and scurried away. "Now, if you'll put yourself in my able hands, I'll do the honors for all of us." No one objected, so he proceeded to order a variety of dishes, most of which neither Narin nor Neeta recognized.

Narin shook his head in incredulity when he heard "Kung Pao mutton *à la* jalfrezi."

"Time to shut the lights," he muttered to Neeta, who jabbed him a little harder.

The drinks arrived, and the waiter placed three generous shots of whiskey in front of the men and Ambika, a large bottle of cold soda water, and a sherry for Neeta.

"A toast," Laxman said, "to friendship and conjugal bliss." They clinked glasses and drank.

"And to thorny diagnoses," Neeta added, as Narin said simultaneously, "And a prosperous future."

Narin looked around. More than two-thirds of the restaurant's tables were occupied, and the insistent thrum of conversation filled the air. For a place as fancy as this, the obligatory British contingent was present, expat businessmen, high-level administrators, and others, seated with their wives, enveloped by a collective air of seriousness. The war, of course, was their primary concern, thousands of miles away though they were. Narin had read of the extreme privations Britain was enduring. Food was scarce, and fresh vegetables a luxury. Did they feel any guilt at living so far away in relative ease? And might things change?

The others noticed Narin's silence, and their banter stopped.

"A penny for your thoughts," said Ambika, nudging him.

"The war," he said, surprising himself.

"What about it?"

"Here we are, enjoying ourselves, and thousands of people are dying around the world. Is that right?"

"It's not directly our war, Narin," Ambika said.

"There will always be wars in the world," added Laxman.

"So we should ignore it?"

"No, but put it in perspective. If we had the Krauts ready to occupy Kashmir, we'd take it a lot more seriously. As it is, we're not likely to be affected."

"Unless the Japanese waltz over us from the East."

"Be serious. There are thousands of miles between us. And a country named China, not to mention Burma. Do you really think a tiny island country like Japan could pose a threat?"

"Don't you read the news, Lax?" Narin asked. "They had over one hundred thousand troops at Changsa way back when. And now they've attacked the Philippines and even bombed Australia. Singapore and the Dutch East Indies have surrendered. As you'd say, good ol' America is the only thing keeping them at bay."

Narin's raised voice had attracted the attention of other diners, who looked over at their table. Neeta muttered a "Quietly, Narin," and took his hand in hers. He picked up his whiskey and took a large gulp. Laxman silently refilled his glass, his natural lightness stifled by the severity of Narin's reaction.

"But we're not exactly dilettantes, right?" Neeta said. "I remember Narin's famous statement at the park years ago about the Jane Austen characters we were discussing being 'trivial' and not doing anything. Is that what's bothering you?" She looked at Narin. "That we're not involved?" He continued staring into his glass, and she continued. "Narin, we're all going to be doing good, we're going to be working hard, dealing with illnesses and dying babies and emergency procedures. We *will* be important in this world, and you shouldn't downplay it."

Narin looked up. "Yes, Neeta, we went to one protest meeting a year ago. Haven't been to any since. I know the language issue has cooled off since learning Hindi is no longer required in the South. That's satisfied those protesters. For now. But there are other issues. We're still privileged. We *are* dilettantes ignoring the war. There are over two hundred thousand Indian soldiers fighting abroad. Thousands are dying in support of our colonial overlords. I wonder if these white men and women"—with a wave toward the other tables—"are grateful for the enforced service. I don't think so. And yet our Indian army has grown to over two million. Volunteers are flocking to enlist. Why?"

"That's hardly fair. The soldiers didn't have any choice as the Brits unilaterally declared India was joining the war," Ambika said.

"Yes, they did that over the objections of our politicians. Don't you see the irony of our colonial masters braying for 'freedom' while denying democratic rights and liberties to us in India? You can't simultaneously say 'it's not our war' and accept the conscription of our people into the hostilities. *We're* not involved. We're safe from being drawn into the war.

"Look, I'm not blaming you all, right? It's just like we ignore poverty, the deprivation of so much of our population. We close our eyes to people sleeping on the street, to beggars deliberately maiming their children to make us pity them and give them money. We're a product of our upbringing, which is to toe the line and not make waves. I don't know about you, but I have this … thing … being … in me that stops me from wandering too far. Maybe you all have one, too?"

Neeta broke the uncomfortable silence. "I understand what Narin is saying, and I also agree with you, Ambika, that war isn't our primary concern. We must make the best of it unless we have an altruistic streak strong enough to join the army. Well, we girls can't do that anyway."

"Thank god for that," said Laxman with a wide grin.

Narin looked at the others. Would his diatribe change anything? Could he even convince Neeta? Tension tightened his face as he felt isolated even from his wife and friends. Only Sheela might've agreed. He realized his personal anguish wasn't appropriate to the moment. He forced the tightness to ease. They were there to celebrate his friends' move. His wife would be supportive of his career and their future.

He shook off his doldrums. "Well, let's talk about happier things."

Laxman had lit an inevitable cigarette. "How about Ted Williams and his point four-zero-six batting average?" He laughed at the utter mystification on his companions' faces. "Red Sox base-ball," he added to no one's clarification.

They finished their meal two hours later. Laxman and Ambika led the way out with Narin and Neeta following. Narin watched Laxman walking unsteadily with Ambika keeping a firm grip on his back as his hand caressed her waist. He thought it ironic that they seemed not to give a damn about displaying public affection, whereas he and Neeta, the married couple, were restrained. He looked at Neeta, contentment and pleasure written on her face. Would she reach out to him like that? Neeta made her love for him clear in less overt ways, but he wished she could be more direct. But then, he was not overly emotional, so perhaps they were a good match in that way.

The four stood wordlessly in the restaurant's portico. It was a seminal moment, a changing of the guard. Six years together, six formative years in their lives never to be replaced.

XVII
Madras, 1942–43

Neeta puttered around the house, procrastinating. She had been given some case notes to study and categorize and had gladly accepted the chance to work at home that day. But the creative itch warred with the need to fulfill her work. She hadn't drawn anything in several months. She wondered whether she had time to sketch the shops at the local market, which would be crowded and challenging at this time. But it was scorching outside. Best to stay in.

She searched for her sketching tools and drawing paper, still secreted in an unopened packing box. She set up her easel, which dominated the small room; she'd have to put it away after each session. She pinned up a smallish sheet of paper and, without much thought, began drawing a likeness of her least favorite character, Jaggie. The strokes flowed with abandon as she watched the image take coherent shape, annoyed features emerging, watchful eyes set deep into dark, fleshy folds. She pondered a background suitable for the figure. Perhaps a jungle? Too obvious. She tried to think of suitably bleak settings.

Her concentration was interrupted by a knock on the door. For a moment, she panicked at the thought that it might be Jaggie himself, drawn by mystical forces emanating from her incomplete caricature, though he had never come over during the day before. She drew aside the curtain with a shaky hand, peeked out the window, and was relieved to see the postman, a wizened man in his fifties who had already begun a conversation with her when she opened the door.

"How are you, Mrs. Narinder?" he said and continued without waiting for a reply. "And how is that nice doctor husband of yours? Keeping busy, I hear. And you? Not at your own hospital today?"

Neeta attempted a smile as he handed her a small parcel from Konkan. Pausing to tuck a few stray letters back into his threadbare brown satchel, he continued with what Neeta thought was close to a leer. "Nothing wrong, I hope? No news about …" he said as he patted his belly and waited for a reply.

Neeta suppressed a desire to scream. No point in antagonizing him or they might not get any more post. Which might not be a bad thing. "No. And I'm home today to do some work. Have a nice day." She turned away and put her hand on the door to nudge it closed, but he hadn't finished.

"Oh, yes, these two letters, almost missed them." He handed them over, and Neeta fumbled with them. "Yes, yes, I see more from Venpuri again. Lots of letters from Chettiar Road, no?"

"Yes. Sorry, would like to continue chatting, but I have to finish up inside." She closed the door with a decisive thud as the postman backed up with a half-opened mouth.

Neeta opened the parcel and put away the food items her mother sent her every month, convinced she would be deprived otherwise. She luxuriated in the smell of spicy *sambhar* powder, a staple of Tamil meals that was readily available in Madras, but her mother considered hers the best.

She turned to the letters and sighed, holding them at half-arm's length as if they might snap at her. Two more from Venpuri. One from Narin's first *Mamanaar*, Subbu, and the other from Narin's father. This had become a monthly ritual.

The contents of the letters had gone through a distinct transformation. She remembered those she and Narin had read during the last year. At first, they'd been full of blame and wrath. How could Narin treat his beloved and guiltless daughter so? How could he ignore his sacred responsibilities? What God was Narin listening to? Did he not know that a Hindu marriage was the highest state of union and could not be thrown aside lightly? Who was this woman Neeta, and how could she have so egregiously wormed her way into his life? Did he not know the fates were not to be taunted lightly?

The next stage was more conciliatory. Subbu appeared to have accepted Narin's second marriage and knew he would have to deal with its effects on his daughter. He claimed to be speaking for Mina, whose only desire was to live with her husband. He said Narin must accept his responsibility toward her and the moral thing was to bring her into his home. He didn't mention Neeta, as her acquiescence with this plan was not worthy of discussion. Narin, noncommittal as always in his response, asked if Subbu was sure that Mina shared this desire. Subbu always ignored that question, and though Narin had requested several times to hear from Mina herself, she never wrote to him.

Neeta had hoped that Narin's father, in the spirit of joining familial forces against a common enemy, would be more understanding of his second marriage, but Mohan was not accommodating enough to want to meet her, and explicitly refused to do so.

When Narin came home, Neeta pointed out the pair of letters, her face a mask of strain. She was used to Narin ignoring the Venpuri post for days, no doubt hoping the letters would mysteriously vanish. This time she saw him look at them, sigh, and pick one open with an ivory-handled letter opener—another of Laxman's generous gifts. After scanning a few paragraphs, he handed it to her with a look of resignation and pointed at a section. "He even refers to his daughter with the title Mrs. Minalakshmi."

If you had a daughter like *Sow.* Minalakshmi (a true incarnation of innocence) and God is pleased to bless you with a son-in-law like yourself but harsh enough to sacrifice a poor innocent girl in the prime of her life at the altar of Mammon without realizing the sanctity of the Hindu married Brahmin girl, you would try supremely, like me, to rectify the matter.

I am sure you will realize how my daughter would feel among societies, in the train, in the marriage halls and all other public places when she sees girls of her age going up and down with their consorts. Where she has none. My daughter, your dear, innocent wife, wants nothing more than to live with you as she has the right and the desire …

Neeta looked up at Narin, whose dark, handsome face had creased with frustration. She didn't know whether to laugh at Subbu's writing style or cry at the contents—altar of Mammon?—surely Subbu knew how frugally they lived. Doing neither, she handed the letter back to Narin, who folded it back into the envelope carefully, as if it were an important document. She often wondered why he kept the damned letters. She would've thrown them away, first tearing them ritually into tiny, satisfactory shreds.

Subbu tried a new tactic in his letter. He dwelt on the inequity of his family having turned over vast amounts of money, vessels, and goods (his words) as a dowry, which his daughter was not able to enjoy as all the largesse benefitted Narin's family (his words again). Neeta saw the look of growing disbelief on Narin's face as he read this charge.

"The damned dowry. My Aunties Saranmathi and Saraswathi carped about my father not getting the full amount they wanted. And I never saw these 'vessels and goods.'"

Neeta suggested he write to his father to ask what this signified.

In his reply, Mohan put aside his aggrieved tone and responded that if Subbu wanted any return from the dowry, he was welcome to it, but this was the first he had heard about the matter. Neeta was happy that Narin's father was more understanding at last, suggesting that Mohan was also tiring of Subbu's persistent barrage.

"You should go to Venpuri and talk to your parents," she told him.

"That'll do no good. My aunts absolutely will be there, and there's no talking sense to them. And I can't accept the fact that my parents never want to meet you."

"They're angry right now, Narin, and need someone to blame for this situation. I'm sure they will soften with time. But you should offer to go. Don't you miss your mother and father?"

"I do miss my mother. But she hasn't written a single letter to me as she used to regularly before, and I gather from what Appa writes that she's as angry with me as he is. I'm surprised. I thought she'd be the forgiving one. She just doesn't show her anger in the same way. She's quiet about it."

"A womanly thing to do."

"You show your anger quite well," he said with a grin.

"That's not funny."

"Maybe we could change our names so the postman won't be able to find us anymore."

Neeta struggled to find a smile. "Oh, Narin, stop being stupid. We can't go around hiding our heads in the sand forever. We have to take some action."

A knock on the door startled them. Neeta glanced out the kitchen window and grimaced. "Oh, god. It's Jaggie again."

"I noticed someone peeking in a moment ago, so he knows we're here. Action! Break out the tea and *vadais*."

"Damn him. I'm leaving," Neeta said, flinging open the front door and pushing past the chubby figure in her path.

IT WAS PAST time to make a decision. Neeta had been suggesting for a while that she could no longer deal with the letters and Jaggie's visits, during which he studiously ignored her and berated Narin.

"This has to stop. We have to leave Madras," Neeta said, sobbing, after she had endured yet another fraught encounter with Jaggie.

Narin's job prospects were excellent. His house surgeoncy, a preliminary to getting a full-time position, was due to end soon, and he would have to apply for a regular job. In college, he had done well, but not brilliantly. He considered himself somewhat a plodder, working his way toward success and having the tenacity to achieve it. But he'd worked hard at Egmore Medical Center, and his superior was well pleased, so the obvious choice would be to continue there as a junior staff doctor. Neeta, for her part, would also complete her training, but, unlike him, she had made no move toward looking for regular employment. With her excellent school credentials, she would have no difficulty in finding work, but she'd decided to bide her time.

"Why don't we move to Bangalore?" Neeta suggested. Laxman and Ambika were now working in his father's clinic. "You know how often they've written about being happy there? If we move there, Jaggie couldn't drop in at will."

Narin knew he had to confront reality. He had many options in Madras, but Bangalore? "I've never been outside Madras province, and I'm not sure I could live elsewhere," he said.

Neeta continued her tearful pleas. She finally persuaded Narin, and he wrote to Laxman.

My dear Laxman,

I am quite fed up with the harassment from my first in-laws. Neeta is practically in tears whenever Jaggie shows up. I suppose I could refuse to let him in, but I have not yet reached that point, and besides, he'd probably stand outside and give me his standard diatribe anyway, and the neighbors would have an earful. Neeta and I have decided we should leave Madras but are not sure where to go. She'd originally suggested Konkan, but that's too far and unfamiliar to me (not that I know much outside Madras and Venpuri).

So I'm wondering if you think Bangalore would be good for us. How is the medical service in your state, and would there be any problems if a Tamil like me from Madras applied? I won't even ask if being a Brahmin would be a problem.

Please let us know as soon as possible.

Hope this finds you and Ambika well and prospering.

Cheers, Narinder

Laxman responded immediately:

… This is a great time to apply to the Medical Service in Bangalore, as they appear to have obtained a substantial budget increase from our local government. I'm sure it's due to the recent cholera epidemic that has devastated this state. You blokes were lucky in Madras not to have been subject to it. Malaria is on the rise as well, and it's likely to be an on-going problem, especially with the slums and their nonexistent sewage system. So. Nothing like a good medical scare to make the accountant-*wallahs* loosen the purse strings. They're engaging lots of new medics right now, and you're right on time.

> Both Ambika and I think it'd be super to have you
> living in the same city or even nearby …

Neeta noted the relief on her husband's face as he showed her the letter. "What do you think? I can apply immediately if you agree."

"Yes," said Neeta and hugged him. She started planning the packing that day.

Six weeks later, he received an enthusiastic response from the Bangalore Medical Service.

But to Neeta's dismay, a postscript noted, "In additional response to your inquiry on lodging, the hospital housing stock is overbooked, and quarters are reserved only for new senior staff. A stipend is payable to you, but you will have to arrange your own accommodations."

"So we are on our own?" she said.

"Perhaps Laxman will know of something?"

He did. A week after sending a request to Laxman, they received a response:

> … Good thing my father has plenty of connections
> here. I've found the ideal place for you. It's only a mile
> or so from your Tripcone Hospital. Unfortunately, it is
> in a newly constructed outer area of the city, but it will
> be quieter there than in the older quarters where Am-
> bika and I live. Not to worry, m'boy. We'll visit you as
> often as possible. It's a quick jaunt by car.

NEETA LOOKED AROUND their tiny flat, now empty except for their last-minute belongings, the day they were scheduled to leave. She tried not to feel too downcast. It would forever be the first place where she and Narin had lived together, the place they'd furnished sparsely from their almost nonexistent savings, except for

Laxman's gift of the luxurious dining set. The place where warm, breezy nights and hot, sweaty days alternated to create a universe of fond remembrances. The place they were driven from by the unending harassment of Narin's first in-laws. The city to which they might never return.

Narin returned with a rickshaw and said, "Well, that's it, then. Let's start our adventure."

"We've had plenty of adventures here, I think. I'm looking forward to a little peace and quiet."

"Jaggie won't find our address for a while."

"He's probably already got it. He's nothing if not resourceful."

"Pessimist."

"No, realist. Let's go."

"Lax and Ambika will be at the station to pick us up in their spanking new car."

Neeta's face lit up in anticipation. "The Perfection he calls it," referring to Laxman's nickname for the Ford Prefect his father had given him as a wedding gift.

They padlocked the door, handing the key to their neighbors, exchanging *Po-ittu Vuhren* goodbyes. Another connection broken, Neeta thought. She had recently begun a better acquaintance with that neighbor and relished the chance of having a friend nearby. She had never found it easy to make friends and hadn't expanded her circle much after she finished her studies. She wondered whether Bangalore would be different and rejoiced at the thought of being near Ambika again. Narin, who had visited there for his interview, had been reticent in describing the city, merely saying that it was "very similar to Madras." Neeta had written several times to Ambika asking about the city, and her friend's detailed answers reassured her.

She was quiet during the ride to Madras Central Station, concentrating on the slowly moving streetscape. She had lived in three places—home in Konkan, at the college hostel, and most memorably, with her lover and husband Narin. She'd felt secure in each, perhaps for different reasons and in different ways, but secure nonetheless. Now, although she'd still be living with Narin and would have at least one set of close friends nearby, a looming disquiet settled within her. She was not an adventurous sort and preferred stability to change. She'd completed her house surgeoncy. Now she wasn't sure what she would do next and didn't know why she was so indecisive. Perhaps she might stay home and have a child, although she and Narin hadn't discussed starting a family. It was the normal thing to do, with overtones of stability and conventionality. She would take care of their house and make it a safe, cozy place for them both, filled with the noise of children, the drawings she still dabbled in, and the seductive smell of her beloved jasmine flowers.

Too bad the Madras postman would never know, she giggled to herself, but I could write him a letter.

At Madras Central Station, Narin and Neeta turned their bags over to the first of several small boys who offered to carry them. Their train was on time and resting alongside the crowded platform.

NARIN HAD SPLURGED on first-class tickets, so they expected the journey to be more pleasant than their usual jammed third-class student travel. As they stopped mid-platform and searched for their assigned compartment, they were greeted by several voices in chorus, including that of Sheela, Deepa, and others. They'd had a farewell party two days before, so they were surprised and glad to see them. A babble of conversation broke out with many professions of "How I'll miss you," "You will absolutely love Bangalore," and "Can't believe you're actually leaving." Neeta and Deepa teared up. Narin went around shaking hands and hugging as was appropriate, also struggling to maintain his composure.

When he hugged Sheela, she said with a grin, "Well, I won't remind you to write to me regularly this time, Narin."

"I promise I will, Sheel. I have better reasons to."

"What, you're more mature now?" With a wink.

"God, I hope so."

Minutes passed. Narin placed their belongings in their compartment. The stationmaster announced the train would leave in twenty minutes, only ten minutes past its scheduled departure time. The group surrounding the couple exhausted their goodbyes, questions, and exhortations, and settled into a ruminative quiet.

"Narinder."

That unctuous voice. Narin turned, his eyes wide in shock, to see Jaggie, accompanied by his father, Subbu, and two others he did not recognize. He looked at the man first, wondering at his scruffy clothes that did not quite fit in with the others, then at the smaller figure, hidden behind Subbu and the stranger. With further shock, he saw it was Mina, whom he hadn't seen in more than a year since his last visit home. She maintained a downward look and wore a dark green sari in the conservative style prevalent in Venpuri, unlike the women in Madras who appeared flamboyant by contrast. She seemed younger and more vulnerable than her eighteen years. The nightmare he and Neeta had dreaded for months had arrived.

Neeta's family and Narin's friends withdrew a few yards.

Jaggie exchanged nods with Narin. Subbu was silent. Neither bothered to introduce the strange man. Mina was fixated on her sandals. Narin waited for someone to speak.

"*Mamanaar.*" Narin finally greeted Subbu, and from the corner of his eye, he saw Neeta cringe and move away to stand beside her sister, who affected a protective air over her. "I didn't know you were coming to Madras. Do you have special business here?"

Subbu glared at him and raised his voice. "My business is with you. You have decided to run away from us. You have decided to abandon your wife. Do you think you can get away with this? Here she is in front of you now. What do you have to say to her?"

"I don't have any more to say than I wrote to you last month. I think that should've more or less settled the matter and—"

"No, it didn't," interjected Jaggie, his face florid. "We settled nothing."

"I mentioned that your sister could live with my father if she does not want to continue living at home, and Appa has agreed to that. I think that settles it from my point of view."

Jaggie spoke formally, as if he were in a courtroom. "You should know that my sister, *Sow.* Minalakshmi, has expressed a desire to live with her husband."

"And I wrote to both of you that it would be impossible given my pay and the living conditions where I am going."

"Where you are going? You can name it now. Bangalore, we know it. Don't think you will escape us by decamping like this."

"Narin, you have to be reasonable," Subbu said in a conciliatory tone. "Mina cannot live with your family if you are away. She wants to live with you."

Narin had had enough of this charade. Mina's improbable desire to live with them had always horrified Neeta. She had never confronted Narin or reproached him for not explicitly rejecting the idea. Perhaps it was time to clear the air in Neeta's presence.

He turned to Mina and asked her directly, "Do you? Is that what you really want to do?" Mina gasped and looked away. Jaggie moved closer to her. Narin ignored the provocation. "Please tell me in your own words," he said with less hostility.

Mina still did not say a word and kept her eyes down with a distraught look on her face.

Jaggie imposed his bulk between them. "Narin, do not harass my sister. You know what she wants."

"No, I don't. I know what *you* say she wants, and that's impossible. Since you seem to know everything about me, you know I'm a junior house surgeon in Bangalore, and you must know what I am paid. I cannot support Mina and certainly not there with us."

Jaggie's face turned sullen. Subbu appeared lost. Neither spoke.

A small voice broke the silence. "Please write to me, husband."

Narin turned to Mina in surprise and muttered, "Okay."

The train's whistle shrilled.

Narin threw a cursory goodbye to his in-laws, dashed by his friends with a last look, grabbed Neeta's hand, and jumped on board as the train began its noisy departure. He collapsed into the seat beside Neeta and covered his head in his hands.

Neeta, staring at the group outside, said, "Nice send-off, eh?"

He was conscious of the couple who shared their compartment. The scene with his first in-laws on the platform had played itself publicly and audibly. If his travel companions lived up to the nosiness of the average person, they would question them about the brouhaha. He yearned to lie in Neeta's comforting arms, but that would be impossible in public.

Neeta turned toward him and said in a voice that hid her edginess, "I didn't expect to see all our friends at the station, did you?"

"And some not our friends. Wonder how they found out?" He recalled the unacknowledged man who had not spoken a word. Narin had noticed him sizing up the group as they retreated and, for a long moment, staring at Neeta, who had turned her back to escape his scrutiny.

As if she'd read his mind, Neeta said, "And who was that man standing in front of—"

"I don't know. Nobody introduced him. And from his clothing style, I don't think he's some distant relative."

"Too not middle class?"

"Umm. A clerk type. He looked at all of us quite directly, out of character for a man like that."

"Maybe he works for Jaggie and was taking notes."

"I suppose we can expect more interference," Narin said with a sigh.

"Jaggie can't come to Bangalore every week."

"God forbid." Narin's mood lightened a bit. "I'll miss his plump face." He moved closer to Neeta and rested his hand on her arm. "We're starting fresh."

Neeta nodded.

The train gathered speed as it left the spaghetti-like configuration of tracks beyond Madras Station. The steady sound of the train wheels clacking over the rail joints, the creaking of the wooden cabin as it swayed, and the drone of voices all lulled her senses, and she soon fell into a restless sleep.

Narin looked at his wife and felt a surge of remorse for the trials he was putting her through. He puzzled over the mysterious figure at the station for a few moments, then let it go and looked out the window. He watched the telephone wires, strung in long arcs from one pole to the next, rhythmically rise and fall. Lines of sparrows sat motionless on the wires, like sentries monitoring the train's progress.

It was time to restart their lives, time to take charge of their fate.

XVIII
Bangalore, 1944

Narin and Neeta settled into their small flat on the outskirts of Bangalore. The streets, freshly paved and not yet pockmarked, were laid out in a grid pattern, unlike the more chaotic patterns prevalent in the older parts of the city. There were few trees and little greenery. The running sewer at the edge of the road was mostly covered with concrete slabs. Luckily, many one-room storefronts had sprung up at street corners to serve the population. And the main street linking the area to other parts of Bangalore had plenty of shops and a large produce-and-goods market.

The new four-story building contained sixteen apartments. Neeta was dismayed that their flat, only one flight up, was subject to street noise and dust. But running water was a pleasant amenity, with an electric pump to reliably carry water to the cistern on the roof. Narin had never seen such a device and was fascinated by its black industrial bulk and purposeful noisiness as it whirled. He said it represented to him all that was new and exciting about the modern world. Neeta appreciated his delight, but for herself, she was glad not to haul water to the kitchen and bathroom.

Their flat had three rooms in all, a decent-sized living room, a bedroom, and a kitchen, and their furniture from the Madras flat fit easily in the larger space. Life promised to be more comfortable than in their previous stifling apartment.

There were two electric ceiling fans, another novelty. Narin watched the bedroom fan wobble irregularly at higher speeds. "Wonder how long it'll stay up," he said, a flip comment that horrified Neeta, who had to be convinced that the heavy object wouldn't crash down on them in the night. She made Narin move their bed far to one side, amusing Narin. He observed that a falling fan might not drop straight down and could still mangle them. She told him to shut up.

NEETA DIDN'T MAKE many friends in their building or in those nearby. She kept to herself, even though she'd met several women with children who stayed at home much of the time, as she did. Narin suggested she try to socialize more with the neighbors—"It'll do you good to be with people more."—but she would plead the pressures of taking care of the house. She preferred to spend most of her time alone. She still read much and had recently discovered the Agatha Christie mysteries, which she loved so much she limited herself to one a month in the vain hope she'd never complete the canon.

Neeta was reluctant to admit that she felt superior to the other women near her, and maybe even to their husbands. Few of the women had attended college, and certainly none had a medical degree, which to her represented the epitome of educational achievement. None appeared to share her interest in reading, catching up on politics, or discussing art.

This was a lively and challenging time in India with the imminent transition of power from the British to the new Indian government. Bangalore had never been embroiled in the language issues that Madras experienced, and Neeta noted that Narin no longer mentioned his interest in the protest movement. His colleagues and their spouses, like the majority of their fellow MMC students, saw the coming changes as positive and natural, but not in any way requiring their involvement. They enjoyed the changes vicariously as they followed the Indian National Congress's push against British rule. Certainly the women in the building would not be interested in discussing those events.

What else could Neeta talk to them about? Whether the local *dhobi* was ruining their saris in the wash? Their children's frequent tantrums and inevitable problems? Or worse, how their husbands and in-laws mistreated them? How would the women react if she disclosed her unusual marital status or her fractured relationship with her husband's family? Would they be sympathetic, or would they shun her? She'd rather not find out. After the first few weeks of overtures, her neighbors kept their distance and considered her shy and withdrawn if they were charitable, and snooty if they were not.

NARIN LEFT EARLY every morning for the hospital. He usually walked the mile or so, but during the cooler autumn and winter months when it was only seventy-five degrees, he rode a bicycle. From the beginning, he liked his work there, though as a junior house physician, he was assigned to patients lower on the ubiquitous social status scale. "Makes for more interesting cases," he would tell Neeta, "and more challenging. The patients are less articulate, so less likely to remember all their symptoms." He was still learning Kannada, the local language, and added, "Besides, right now, my language barrier is an additional hurdle."

Neeta didn't see any of these as positives, but Narin spoke with such enthusiasm that she realized how much he relished a challenge. She kept up with medical issues, diligently reading the *British Medical Journal, The Lancet,* and other journals that Narin brought home from his work when he judged they would not be missed. Sometimes their conversation would turn toward a difficult diagnosis of one of Narin's patients. Neeta would ask for details, which he would solemnly recount as though presenting the case for peer review. And as often as not, Neeta would find the diagnosis, even dredging up a reference to an article she had read years before.

"So, what do you think? It's not a normal epileptic presentation, is it?" Narin once asked about a teenaged patient who was suffering seizures and oddly deteriorating mental abilities.

"Lafora disease," Neeta stated authoritatively, referring to the epileptic condition. "The twitching and ataxia are not definitive, but the dementia is a sure marker. It's an autosomal recessive disorder. I remember reading about it in *BMJ* long ago. I'm so sorry, Narin. I think the only treatment is palliative. She's so young to have to die, isn't she?"

Narin gave her a wry smile and nodded. His less faithful memory hadn't recalled the obscure disease.

THE NATURAL CAMARADERIE of young doctors working in stressful conditions made for easy acquaintances and many friendships. Narin mentioned one couple who'd invited them to dinner several times, but they hadn't reciprocated recently. "We should invite the Seths for dinner soon," he said one day as they sat down to eat. "I really enjoyed their company and their Gujarati meal last month, didn't you?"

"Their food was too hot. And it's too hard to cook so often," Neeta said, pouring herself a glass of lemonade.

"Maybe we could hire a cook."

"You bring this up all the time. We can't afford one."

"Maybe you could ... find some work?"

"I keep busy straightening you out."

"We could really use the money, you know."

"Narin, you're repeating yourself," she said, her jaw clenched.

"Neeta, you never explain why you won't. You were first-in-class at MMC. You have great diagnostic skills. Why wouldn't you want to use all that?"

"It would be too much pressure, all that routine of telling inarticulate patients the same things over and over again. You've mentioned that frustration yourself, how hard it is to pull information from them. I can't imagine I'd enjoy it."

"Neeta, that's my patient community. You can work at Laxman's father's Saidu clinic. He'll be happy to have you there. His patients are middle class and above." He added with a small smile, "You won't sully your hands."

"God, no. I'd be the only woman doctor in the practice, so I'd get all the neurotic wives with their nonthreatening but nagging ailments. I'd have to coddle them and be so, *so* polite. No thanks."

"Are you forgetting Ambika works there, too?"

She looked down at her plate, picked up her lemonade, and took a quick gulp.

"There are clinics for the poor that would love to have you. Won't pay anywhere as much as Saidu's clinic, but it would be something."

Neeta banged her glass down on the table. "No. And I'm not talking about this anymore."

Narin's body mirrored her tension "My friends will just stop inviting us over. I suppose that's all right with you."

"Meaning?"

"You don't need friends as much as I do, Neeta. You're not a natural people person."

"I do perfectly well by myself, thank you. And why don't you try cooking for a change?"

She slammed her utensils down and stamped out of the room.

NARIN PICKED UP the post when he came back from his hospital one day and tossed it on the dining table, then smiled as he spied one letter, which he opened first. He scanned it quickly and said in an excited voice, "Neeta, guess what? My little sister's on her way to finding a job."

Neeta grimaced as she tasted the hot stew from the pot of *sambhar* cooking on the stove and looked up. She wiped her mouth and said, "What?"

"It seems that Sheel has just obtained her high school leaving certificate and is going to apply for college."

"That's fantastic, Narin. Which one? How did she manage all the paperwork?"

Neeta knew it wasn't easy for someone who had stopped going to school to restart the process, particularly the way Sheela had managed, studying with a tutor and finessing the certificate. Then to apply to college? Quite a coup.

"I see the clear hand of our uncle," Narin said. "Must've pulled out the heavy guns. Lawyers like him, and Jaggie can make use of the dirt they discover about people."

"That's too cynical, Narin. Your uncle is much more ethical than your brother-in-law. No comparison there."

"However it happened, she's going to Women's Christian College."

"Oh, the 'Lighted for Lightning' or something-like-that place? Let's hope she doesn't convert to Christianity," said Neeta with a terse laugh.

"Don't be silly. And what's with the lightning motif?"

"Their motto. It's on their shield. It's something like that."

"You remember the strangest things. It doesn't make sense, anyway."

"It's my eidetic memory, and I have no control over it. Sometimes I think I'll 'drown in remembrances of things past.' Makes me wonder what I'm forgetting that's important."

"Like the pot boiling over?"

Neeta turned with a cry to check the stove where the pot of *sambhar* was indeed dribbling over. She tended to it and continued. "Got it. 'Lighted to Lighten.' Still doesn't ring quite right."

"Now it sounds like they're setting their students on fire."

"Well, I'm sure that's the correct one." She giggled. "And funny you should say 'fire.' The college's shield also has a weird image that looks like a sleeping cat on fire, but it's really just a terrible representation of an oil lamp." Noticing Narin's perplexed look, she continued. "Sorry, can't help it. It's the art critic in me." Her demeanor turned serious. "This won't go down too well with your battleax aunts, will it?"

"They'll be apoplectic. Particularly as they'd insisted on sending her away to Madras. But I think they know their influence over her has faded, so they're probably working on the next generation by now. Of which there's a new one, according to Sheel. My brother's fourth son, Aarjav. I wonder when he'd have told me."

"Aarjav, hmm, unusual name. It means 'steadfast' in Sanskrit, I think. Probably named him in reaction to a certain black sheep uncle." She laughed again.

MANY SUNDAYS THEIR friends would drive over in their beloved Ford Prefect, and all would pile in for a nearby trip or to see a motion picture. They also regularly visited Laxman's father's club, the Gymkhana, the principal venue where the middle-class elite socialized. Laxman's father was a member, so Laxman and Ambika could visit freely. Members were accepted to the club by invitation only, and Laxman was in the process of cultivating connections so he, too, could join. He'd promised Narin that when he did, he in turn would invite Narin. He brushed aside Narin's demurral that it was too expensive.

By inviting his friends, Laxman was subverting the letter of the club's guest rules, as it was his father, not he, who was allowed to invite guests. "Don't worry, old chap. The sign-in *wallah* will be more than happy to accept a small *baksheesh* while you and Neeta slip by," he'd say to Narin with a wink.

One evening as the two couples drank at the bar, Laxman raised his shot of Johnnie Walker. "A toast," he said, "to what? Let's skip the health and happiness blather, as they've been covered too many times over. I know, a toast to the wonderful times long ago when we had to skulk behind the MMC hostel bushes to drink."

"It wasn't that long ago," Narin said with a smile as they clinked glasses, "and it might not be long before it happens again when Gandhi gets his way."

Laxman waved his drink in small circles. "Not to worry, old friends, the lawyers will figure it out." He took a gulp of scotch and gave a thumbs-up. "In fact, I've found a way."

"A way to do what? What scheme are you cooking up now, Laxman?" Ambika asked.

"Ah, you would like to know, wouldn't you?"

"I'll bet it has something to do with drinking," divined Neeta, pointing at the half-empty glass in Laxman's hand.

"Perfectly right, m'dear," said Laxman. "You see, we all may soon be reduced to a state of law-breaking desperation in order to drink our life-sustaining nectar, otherwise known as alcohol."

"Because of prohibition?" asked Neeta. She remembered that one article in the soon-to-be-adopted Indian Constitution would require "Prohibition of the use, except for medicinal purposes, of intoxicating drinks and drugs, which are injurious to health," a clause complying with Gandhi's ascetic viewpoint.

"Yes, of course, the Presidency of Madras introduced prohibition years ago. It seems that the august cities of New Delhi and Bombay will suffer next, as their state governments implement the ban. We should be okay here for a while. Bangalore is not considered provincial for no reason." He waved another round from the bartender.

"And what's this 'way' you've found when it does happen?" asked his wife. "I hope it's not going to land you in jail."

"No, darling. Jail garb would not suit me at all. Any of you know the wording of Article 47, which implements prohibition? No, I thought not," he said with a smirk, ignoring Neeta's nod. He quoted it and continued. "See? It has an explicit exception for 'medicinal purposes.' Anything come to mind?" He accepted his scotch from the barman, palming a *two-anna* coin, which was smoothly accepted in blatant contravention of the club's ban on tipping employees.

Ambika had had enough. "Laxman, in about two seconds Neeta and I are going to the other corner to have an intelligent conversation. Put up or shut it."

Unabashed, Laxman laughed. "Well, my plan is that we docs certify those wanting to have a wee one," he said, tapping his glass, "or two as being unable to live without drinking. Their quality of life would be severely impaired in the absence of liquor. So drinking is *a certiorari* 'medicinal' for them. Genius, ain't it?"

A protracted silence ensued.

"Brilliant effort," Narin said, "whether or not it's practical. The thought of us doctors certifying people as alcoholics so they can legally obtain liquor is so bizarre, it might work. And of course, middle-class people who can afford to see a doctor about this mythical 'condition' are the most likely to be ignored by the authorities."

As they often did when exasperated with Laxman, Neeta and Ambika chorused, "Ridiculous" and "You're joking."

Laxman emptied half his second glass of scotch in one gulp and offered the women drinks, which they refused, as they were "teetotaling today," as Neeta put it. "No matter, m'dears. Time for a couple of rubbers before dinner, then?"

At their first meeting at the club, the four had started to play bridge, which Neeta had found compelling. Narin partnered her with good grace. He had never played cards before and never became comfortable with the intricacies and arcane conventions of this "king of card games," as Laxman called it. They settled down at a table and called an attendant for cards.

XIX
Bangalore, 1948

Neeta gazed down through the bedroom window at the bustling life in the street, with its constant throng of people, pushcart vendors laden with food and vegetables screaming their wares, rickshaws, carts, colorful flower-bedecked trucks, and meandering cows.

Four years after their move, Neeta and Narin had two boys: Vikrant, almost four years old, and Vishram, recently born. Narin's salary was now enough for them to afford a maid, but Neeta still confined herself to home.

A quick sketch followed. Sometimes when the children were napping and the maid was there to oversee them, she would leave the house to walk to the nearby park with her pad and pencils and draw from life. She considered whether she should buy one of the newfangled Kodak 35mm cameras so she could draw from photographs, but due to postwar restrictions, imported goods were still quite expensive. And the ongoing cost of buying the film and developing the prints would not be agreeable to Narin.

Their neighborhood was pleasant, verdant with many trees, with light traffic on the newer, wider roads around them, and Neeta enjoyed short walks nearby. On her way home one day, she took a wrong turn toward a vast area filled with a mass of mud huts. She was appalled to see their condition at close range, their sparsely thatched roofs and the open sewers running along the dirt paths. She had not lived so close to the poverty that was ubiquitous in India. People of her class did their best to avoid overwhelming their senses by ignoring it. As she hesitated, a swarm of poorly clothed children surrounded her, clutching her sari and begging for money, food, anything this well-dressed stranger might have.

She was carrying Vish in her arms, and the contrast between his life of ease and the impoverished lives of these little ones unnerved her. She blinked back her tears and held Vish tightly as she shook off the horde with verbal threats, then strode away, tripping on the uneven path, until she reached the comforting surroundings of her familiar middle-class neighborhood.

For days those liquid, hungry little eyes haunted her, and she incorporated them into some of her abstract drawings. She didn't mention the incident to Narin, thinking he might accuse her of putting herself and Vish at risk, or being so naïve as to be moved by the plight of the slum-dwellers who were an inescapable part of life everywhere. Narin's mention of clinics for the poor came back to mind. How would her family and friends react if she changed her mind and began working at a clinic devoted to the poor? Would they think it was beneath her, with her stellar past and gold medals? Should she discuss it with Narin?

NEETA SAT ON the front steps of their apartment building feeding the year-old Vishram while his brother Vikrant flew around the earthen courtyard. An advantage of living in a new building meant the surroundings were clean, at least when it wasn't raining, though in the five years they'd lived there, growing heaps of rubbish had collected like tumors within the low walls of the yard. She'd assumed that passers-by, too lazy to walk to the infrequent collection sites, had dumped their trash. It had piled up since the city's trash hauling was sporadic and unpredictable. But lately, she'd noticed her own neighbors surreptitiously tossing in a bag or two. Waste begets waste, she thought. For a while she wondered if she could dissuade the perpetrators, but Narin insisted it would further spoil her tenuous relationship with the neighbors.

Her neighbor Kantha appeared with her four-year-old and greeted her as she seated herself beside Neeta. After the usual exchanges about the children, Neeta strained to think of a promising subject of conversation that didn't involve husbands, in-laws, or household help. Ready to give up and discuss the weather, she heard Kantha say, "Did you hear another coconut fell yesterday?" gesturing to the tall palm trees that ringed the inside of the yard. "Almost hit our servant square on the head, got her shoulder instead."

Neeta was horrified. She was aware, of course, that this was the season when ripe nuts dropped, but she'd never thought of them hitting anyone in her vicinity. "My god," she said as she looked over at Vikrant playing with Kantha's son, "it could hit the children."

"Well, maybe."

"You're not worried?"

"It hardly ever happens, Neeta."

This *chalta-hai* attitude dismayed Neeta. She looked up. The palms swaying in the light breeze had taken on a menacing air. She tried to count the coconuts as if knowing how many there were would help her assess the chances of one falling. She heard a creaking sound amid the rustle of the large pinnate fronds, stared hard to identify the threatening tree, then turned to Vikrant and shouted, "Vik. Don't play under the trees. Don't! Play in the center of the yard."

"Calm down, Neeta. You're being too careful."

"No, you cannot be too careful with your children." Her throat tightened. She sprung up and called to her son, "Vik. Come on in, it's time to go inside." Vikrant first shook his head, then seeing the urgency on his mother's face, shook off his companion's arm and dashed over to her. Neeta threw a cursory goodbye to the befuddled Kantha, grabbed Vik's hand, and started back to her apartment. She glanced back at Kantha, whose look suggested that she thought her neighbor mad.

That evening she relayed the incident to Narin. "I'm never letting Vik run in the yard again."

"Neeta, that's silly. All the children have been playing there for years, and there's been no problem. You have to think of the very low probability."

"Don't flaunt your mathematics at me. It only takes one incident. How would you like it if Vik got brain damage from a concussion?"

Narin said no more. He hoped her excessive caution wouldn't extend to other events.

Neeta Enrolled Vikrant in a nursery school in his fourth year, but childhood maladies often kept him at home. "He'll have to miss school again today," Neeta said one day, looking at Vikrant's flushed face, which he'd developed the night before.

"Let it be, Neeta," Narin said. "It's probably only a bad cold."

"But he gets them so often. Now he's complaining about a headache. It could be something else."

He checked the child's eyes. "No other symptoms. Let's wait a day or two before you unleash your *Lancet* skills."

"That's not funny, Narin."

Narin threw up calming hands in response to her glare.

By the third day, when Vikrant's condition hadn't improved, she was not sanguine either.

"I'm fine, I am," Vikrant said as he pushed away Neeta's proffered medicine.

"You have to take this."

"Didn't take any this morning, and I got better, didn't I?" he said, folding his arms tightly.

"But of course you did. You were half-asleep and probably don't remember."

"If my body doesn't remember, how can the medicine work?"

"Silly, medicine is … well … it just works. It doesn't know anything about your body."

"Must know something or it's the same as water, no? Water doesn't cure anything."

He thinks too much, clever child, Neeta said to herself as he downed the medicine. She tucked him in and patted his feverish brow. Shortly after, she left Vikrant with the maid, giving her precise instructions if he were to wake while she was out shopping. When she returned an hour later, Vikrant was still asleep, but as she put away the purchases, he woke up and began to cry.

She examined his face as a clinician. It had been somewhat flushed since the day before, but was it now redder than when she'd left? He also appeared more irritable. He had a slight frown on his face, and he stared at her instead of smiling or talking. She picked him up and held him close, nestling his head on her shoulder. As she gently pulled it back to dry his damp face with a handkerchief, he cried out in pain. Alarmed, she turned his head slightly back and forth, ignoring his continuing protest, and considered. His neck was stiff. With growing apprehension, she moved to the window, where the bright noontime sun reflected off the window surround and sill. Vikrant, now exhibiting more unease, first half-closed his eyes, then shut them tightly against the light.

With a frisson of fear, she thought *photophobia*—light sensitivity. Put together with the fever, the redness in his face, and the stiff neck, he showed all the signs of *Neisseria meningitidis*, a bacterial affliction. How could she have missed it? And Narin, too? She told herself not to panic as she prepared to take Vikrant to the hospital and dumped a change of clothes for him into a bag. They didn't have a telephone, and she wondered if it would be worth going to the shop down the street to call Narin, then decided it would be a waste of time. He would tell her to get Vikrant to the hospital immediately, in any case.

The maid was due to leave soon. Neeta rushed to the apartment below and begged her neighbor Kantha to keep Vishram while she took his brother to the hospital. A moment later, she hailed a cycle rickshaw and urged the driver to hurry to Tripcone Hospital. Vikrant, whom she'd swaddled in clothes despite the warm weather, silently watched his mother through slitted eyes.

"I'M SUCH A fool," Neeta wailed to Narin, who had hurried to the emergency ward when he received her message. "How could I have missed it?"

After a quick examination, the young house physician on duty made Vikrant comfortable with a dose of sedative and an anti-pyretic drug. Now he lay sleeping, an IV drip in his arm. The physician's diagnosis concurred with Neeta's suspicion, so an immediate dose of sulfa antibiotic was indicated. He conferred with Narin, who suggested using the newly introduced penicillin instead. The imported drug was normally reserved exclusively for military hospitals, but Narin's civilian hospital had a supply as it was the backup for a nearby military base.

The physician asked Neeta whether Vikrant was allergic to penicillin.

"I don't know." She hadn't given it any thought, although six months earlier when penicillin had appeared as a magic bullet, Narin had mentioned the importance of that determination to her.

"We'll have to do an allergy test," the physician said.

"It'll take time. Can he wait?"

"It's a normal precautionary procedure, madam … uh, Doctor."

She was forced to agree, though the decision not to take immediate action was hard. Narin's agreement calmed her. The test was negative. She watched a nurse try three times before finding a vein in Vikrant's slack arm for the penicillin drip and struggled with her impulse to interfere.

She spent the next two days in seething agony. Adding to her motherly protectiveness was the knowledge that her mind had let her down at a crucial moment. How could she have missed the signs? She prided herself on the acuity of her diagnostic skills. She'd graduated first in a class of a hundred students at MMC, well above Narin. She thought back to those moments during the past five years when she would pluck the diagnosis of some obscure disease from Narin's descriptions. She'd done so well with secondhand information without even examining the patient, but when it came to her own son, she'd failed.

Vikrant was in a small private room in the overcrowded hospital, a privilege granted due to Narin's status. Neeta refused to leave the room, and she slept on a small cot with its meager mattress, which Narin had managed to get for her. He offered to bring her food from outside, but she insisted it would be too much trouble and managed with the mediocre hospital fare. At least the meals prepared for the sick weren't blazing hot, she consoled herself as she picked at them.

She spent the first night in feverish anxiety, waking up every hour or so and listening closely to her son's breathing, as if that alone would give solace about his progress. Her waking hours flew by as if in a dream. The hospital had its own rhythm of sounds, activity, smells, commotion. She grew acutely aware of these cadences, which washed over her disquiet like waves over a beach.

Neeta sent word to her neighbor Kantha, as she was concerned that taking care of the baby Vishram might be too much for her. Kantha sent back an effusive note saying it was absolutely no problem. She and another neighbor were sharing baby-sitting duties during the day, and Narin took Vishram back to their flat for the night. Neeta's maid had also altered her schedule to be at their home in the evening, helping Narin as needed. Neeta was somewhat overwhelmed by this outpouring of assistance and felt ashamed of herself for not cultivating stronger friendships with her neighbors.

The second day was much like the first. She tried to calm her mind by reading the last two days' newspapers and stared at the printed pages a long while, her mind so unfocused she found herself rereading the same articles. She threw the papers aside in disgust and pulled out a pack of cards to play solitaire.

On the third day, Vikrant was better, more animated and comfortable. Neeta was exhausted, and Narin mentioned he was worried she might fall ill.

"Ridiculous. No one falls ill from sheer tiredness," she said. "I'm sitting or lying down most of the day, anyway." Narin didn't agree, but he couldn't persuade her to go home to rest. In the evenings, he sat holding her hand when they were alone. She looked at him and was glad he was there, her rock of comfort in this unsteady time.

That evening Laxman and Ambika arrived at the hospital, as they had on each previous day. Narin greeted them in the corridor, a weary enthusiasm in his voice. "I'm so glad you're here," he said, bringing them up to date on Vikrant's progress. "Much better," was his prognosis, "only a low-grade fever today."

"And Neeta?" Ambika asked.

"Today's the first time she looks relieved. She's been here constantly for three days," Narin said with a wave to his wife as they entered the room. "I think you need a break, Neeta."

"Yes, you do," Ambika agreed. "Maybe we can drag you out for a while." Neeta smiled wanly. She exchanged greetings with Laxman, who was still standing in the doorway. Ambika surreptitiously motioned the men away and turned to Neeta with a grave look. "You look all-in, Neeta. I think the both of you need a break.

Is Vish being taken care of by your neighbors? Do they need any help? Our *ayah* could easily manage another."

"Thanks a lot. It's okay for now, and I think Narin enjoys having Vish at home at night."

"Why don't we all go to the Gymkhana Club for a spot of dinner? Nothing like some of their famous masala to perk us up."

Neeta demurred, though the idea seemed attractive. "I'm not so fond of the club food."

"Well, at this point, you must prefer it to hospital swill," Ambika said with a smile.

Neeta managed to return the smile. Ambika continued her inducement and succeeded in persuading her reluctant friend. Neeta got up, brushing off her sari to cleanse it of hospital detritus, and they walked out to join the men.

"I don't know how she talked me into it," she said, "but Ambika suggested we go to the club for an early dinner. I can be back here by eight, and Vik's fast asleep now, so ..." She squeezed Ambika's arm. Narin gave her a thumbs-up.

"Spic and span as usual," Neeta said, admiring the polished black metal sheen of Laxman's Ford Perfection as the four approached the car, which was parked in the hospital's portico. "How do you do it? Do your minions follow you around with cleaning bits?"

"Oh, didn't I tell you? I've invented a concoction that repels dirt," said Laxman as he opened the back door for her. "I intend to parcel and sell it, and you and Narin shall be the first to benefit from the thousands I make."

"Well, you might use it on the seats," said Ambika, scraping a lump of dubious substance off the back seat. "More important than the outside."

Laxman grinned as he jumped into the driver's seat, and they sped away.

Neeta assumed a cheerful demeanor, thankful that Laxman didn't interrupt her low-toned conversation with Ambika as he often did. His sensitivity reinforced her gratitude for having such good friends.

The early evening sky had turned an inky blue-black with threatening drops of rain. By the time they reached the Gymkhana Club, what promised to be a torrential downpour began. They opened their car doors to a flood of water. As they jumped out, three men rushed out and greeted them with open umbrellas to usher them the short distance to the shelter of the club's portico.

"Damn it," Laxman said, shaking drops of water from his hair. "Nothing like a little rain to clear the air, no?"

They were soon seated in the sparsely occupied dining room, little changed since the club had been built in the previous century as a meeting place for the British elite. The beige-painted walls contrasted with dark wood panels. A bank of tall glass-paned doors graced the end wall and were now mostly closed in deference to the rain. Neeta had always found the room gloomy, and now the air was sultry as well. She wished it didn't match her mood so well. The others were talking among themselves, and she resented their overly polite demeanor toward her. She grabbed her drink and half-emptied it in one gulp, noting Ambika eyeing her.

"Well, no medical talk, you all," she said. Their conversation ceased, and they darted glances at each other. Her features relaxed into a small smile. "Is it up to me? Well, then, Ambika, have you bought your tickets to Bombay yet?"

"Yes. It's just three weeks away. Our first trip on an airplane." Ambika's eyes shone with anticipation. She and Laxman were flying to Bombay on the recently nationalized airline Air India, formerly the private Tata Airlines. "You know A.I. has been buying lots of modern planes and expanding its routes? They started flying internationally to Europe recently, and most passengers get on at Bombay, so we got a reduced fare from here to there."

"I can't imagine how interesting it will be to fly," Narin said. "Neeta, we should go take an air ride sometime."

"We'll have to use your charm to pay for the passage."

"Well, maybe in a few years when we're doing better."

"Are you excited?" Neeta asked, gazing at her friends intently.

Laxman and Ambika said "Yes" simultaneously, glanced at each other, and laughed.

"I'm still a little afraid of it," Ambika said.

Laxman stepped in immediately. "It's as safe as a car trip."

"God forbid. Not if you fly the way you drive."

"Well, I'm not planning to, darling."

"With our luck we'll have your friend Srikanth as the pilot."

"He drives better than me—planes, anyway. And there's less than a one-in-a-ten-thousand chance of a crash." He ignored his wife's exasperation and continued. "Time to order, gang. I'll do the usual, I expect?" He got the standard South Indian vegetarian special for Neeta, who had never strayed from her culinary up-bringing, and mutton dishes for the rest of them.

Ambika handed a small photograph to Neeta. "We're going to stay with my brother. He's moved to a fancy new flat. Here, look at it. That Gothic frou-frou building is called Waterloo Mansion. Can you imagine?"

The food arrived. Neeta devoured hers, for once not complaining about its spiciness. She drank more than usual and cheered up as the evening wore on. She'd temporarily put aside her gnawing worry about Vik. She noticed that the tension had left Narin's face. Watching him relaxed and laughing with the others, she felt resentful at bearing an unfair burden of care for their son.

WHEN THEY LEFT the club an hour later, huddled under umbrellas on their way to the car, the rain was still pelting down, and the sky, black with clouds, cast an ominous gloom quite in contrast with their ebullient mood.

The unceasing sheets of rain presaged plenty of washed-out roads. The trip from Tripcone Hospital to the club, a little over three miles, had taken twenty minutes. In these conditions, the drive back would be longer, and Neeta fretted at the delay. As Laxman drove out of the club's parking area and sidled into traffic on the main road, he proceeded with unusual caution, swerving often to avoid deep puddles. When he had driven a third of the way, he made an abrupt right turn, causing Neeta's stomach to lurch.

"Why on earth Lazenby Street?" rebuked his wife.

He muttered something about flooding but maintained his concentration on driving.

Neeta had settled into an uneasy silence. Fatigue dropped over her like a cloak. Unsettling thoughts of Vikrant displaced the warmth of food and camaraderie. Suppose he had woken and cried out for her? She stared out the car window at the dark. The streetlights had not turned on. Broken as usual, she fumed. She looked ahead. She knew the illuminated headlights of oncoming vehicles could be misleading—a single light could be a two-wheeler but often morphed into a dark lorry with a burned-out second headlight. The ubiquitous smaller vehicles and carts had no lights at all. Neeta closed her eyes tightly and willed Laxman to go faster, ignoring the danger.

Ambika, alarmed at an inundated intersection ahead, said, "You can't drive through that."

"Not to worry, chaps," Laxman said with bravado. "This car is built for super-wet British conditions, you know. I hear they have sudden floods all the time there. This machine is guaranteed to sail through piddly stuff like this."

"Sail's the operative word. You'd better slow it," Ambika said.

Instead, Laxman increased his speed as they entered the inter-section, and the car created a wash of water on both sides.

"See? No problem." He laughed just as the car lurched to the right. "Oops, nasty rut," he said as he slowed and attempted to steer the car out of it, but instead he drove both wheels off the pavement, braked hard, and bumped into an obstacle that stopped the car.

"Damn," he said as a chorus of questions arose from his passengers. "Best check the front."

"I told you to slow down. How do you plan to get out of this?" shouted Ambika.

"We have this miraculous contraption called a reversing gear."

Laxman opened his door to step out, not looking behind him.

A large horse cart was moving close to the stalled car, its tall wheels churning the deep water. One wheel dropped into the rut in the road, and the axle engaged squarely with the edge of Laxman's open door. With a rending crash, the cart yanked the door out of his hands, the hinges snapped, and the door fell with a satisfactory splash into the water. The cart driver, who had turned when he heard the crash, turned back to lash at the horse and disappear into the gloom.

Ambika screamed as the car lurched and she was thrown against her door.

Narin shouted, "Bloody hell!"

Laxman shuddered. His hand was bleeding where the door handle had been yanked from his hold, and he still had one foot in the water. He stepped out, watching more carefully this time, and waded a few steps toward the front of the car where the door stuck up partially from the water.

Neeta had been quiet during the entire incident, absorbed in her own world. She tried to suppress the melee around her and refocus her thoughts on her son. Now, as Laxman picked up the door with some effort, she uttered a small scream. The others turned to her.

"What? What is it? Are you hurt?"

Neeta had a frozen, horrified look on her face. "Go! We have to go on."

"Of course, dear," Narin said.

"Yes, we will," Ambika said. "Don't worry—"

"We have to go now. It's terrible. What the hell are you waiting for?" Anger was etched on her face as she glared at the drenched Laxman, who was still standing outside holding the door.

Narin and Ambika glanced at each other.

Neeta felt like screaming again. Why were they ignoring her urgency?

Ambika opened her door and moved to the back, waving Narin to the front. She put her arms around the now-shivering Neeta. "We're going as soon as hubby over there …" she paused to glare at Laxman, "stops caressing his car parts."

Neeta continued to mutter, "Go. Let's go," but quieted as Ambika held her tight. Laxman stowed the door in the trunk, ignoring the unsolicited advice being showered on him by the dozen dripping men who had gathered to enjoy the spectacle.

"Well, looks like we need a good tinker," he said with a shrug to no one in particular as he squelched down in his seat.

The car balked when he tried to reverse it. After a few more tries, he waved to the group standing around and held out a few rupee notes through the convenient door opening, saying in Kannada, "*Nanage idannu puś sahāya.*" Several men enthusiastically splashed forward and pushed as Laxman continued to spin the wheels. The car groaned back. Laxman avoided the rut and crept across the intersection.

The delay only made Neeta more anxious. Sobbing, she said, "I know it's too late."

Laxman, driving at a cautious pace, made his way to higher ground where the roads were running wild with rivulets of water without flooding. After twenty minutes, he turned into Tripcone Hospital and had scarcely stopped under its sheltered entry when Neeta, shrugging off Ambika's protective arm, jerked open her door, jumped out, and flew inside.

Neeta rushed to the second-floor ward, glancing behind her as she turned the corner of the main stairs, seeing Narin and Ambika way behind. As she reached the nurse's station, two nurses spun around to her with stricken looks. Impossible, she thought, it's impossible. About to question them, she changed her mind and rushed into Vikrant's room, shaking. Her fears realized, she let out a wail that tore from the depths of her heart, a shriek of pain, a mother's heartbroken scream. She heard Ambika's gasp as she came in behind her. She half-saw Narin, frozen at the door, his face an anguish of indecision, turning to look behind him.

Metal heels clicked on the red concrete floor as the house physician came up to Narin.

"Sir. Dr. Janappan ... I ... we ... trying to phone you at the Gymkhana Club ... line was down ... only twenty minutes ago ..."

Forcing himself to control his shock, Narin said in a calm voice, "What was the etiology?"

"Your son appeared to be progressing normally ..." He paused a moment to gather his scattered wits. "... until the nurse tried to wake him for his evening meal. He appeared groggy but exhibited no other alarming symptoms. She started to feed him and soon realized he was breathing badly. She immediately called for me. I came within minutes, but he had aspirated already. He exhibited increasing difficulty in breathing and was asphyxiating. We tried to resuscitate, but we were too late. I phoned Dr. Sunder, and he is on his way. I'm so sorry. We tried ..."

Narin listened, struggling to control his emotions. A sudden relapse then, probably resulting from an incomplete treatment. Or perhaps a rare and unpredictable patient resistance to penicillin, which was still an experimental drug here. Hard to gauge for a child. Nothing concrete to pin any blame on.

A chance occurrence, a tiny probability in the universe of possible outcomes, and yet it loomed as a malign act of fate.

Fate forever entwined in the lives of Hindus, observant or lapsed. Fate that watches you carefully, meting out its rewards and punishments as it deems fit. Fate that you had to embrace, however reluctant you were. Fate that you could never outmaneuver.

Neeta had collapsed in Ambika's arms sobbing and didn't see Narin walk silently into the room where their son's lifeless body lay.

229

Part IV

Secrets, silent, stony sit in the dark palaces of both our hearts:
secrets weary of their tyranny: tyrants willing to be dethroned.
—James Joyce

XX

Chennai (formerly Madras), 2001

Vishram concluded the tedious business of winding up his mother's affairs. While he was eager to get more information on his father's marriage to Mina, he could not get in touch with any of his father's family outside Madras. And he couldn't extend his trip.

His cousin Carla had suggested he ask Dr. Hansa, his parents' long-time close friend, a fellow club member, and his mother's regular bridge partner. When Vishram called him, Hansa's effusive voice boomed.

"No arguments, Vish. You will come over this evening."

Hansa was a decade younger than his mother and still maintained his youthful appearance from when Vishram had last seen him. He walked over to Vishram with a springier step than usual in those of his age and greeted him with open arms. He offered Vishram a plentiful array of tea and snacks, an unrefusable aspect of Indian hospitality. He expressed his condolences several times in his characteristic staccato style, and he revisited many anecdotes of his friendship with Vishram's father and dissections of memorable bridge games with his mother. After half an hour, Hansa stopped reminiscing and asked about Elena, whom he had met on her last visit to India a few years before.

"And you have a son … Neelkanth. How old?"

"Neel. Six and a bit now."

"Wonderful. I was always telling your parents that it was about time you had children. And they grandchildren. Two are best, you know. No more planned, I suppose?" he asked, staring at Vishram. "No, you said six-plus years. And I seem to remember some problems with your wife having a baby? Were you not looking into adopting an Indian baby? Neeta was not being happy about that, I think. You know how important heritage is in India. Well, water under the bridge, does not matter now." He dismissed further thoughts with a wave of his hands. "You should have brought your son to see your mother last time. She was looking forward to seeing him again. She had met him only once when he was a baby, no? She said he was very clever. And Elena too, of course. I never got to meet them, sadly. I was out of station then."

Flailing at this thicket of statements, Vishram nodded and mumbled "Yes" at intervals.

It was time to change the subject. "Doc, I want to ask you about something I just found out, something I never knew. It's my father's first marriage. I'd like some firsthand information if you have it."

Hansa's easy and genial manner turned grave, and his smile faded. "No, you really didn't know about it? Surprising. I know Narin and your mother were secretive, but I assumed they would have told you of all people. Odd, that, very odd."

"We were never, you know, that close."

"What? No, no, they were always so kind to you."

"Yes, Doc, but I mean in the sense of talking honestly, you know, communicating—"

"Of course they talked, Vish. They were talking about you all the time to me. They always were having your welfare upfront in their minds."

Vishram realized this was not productive. The word "communication" in the sense of showing openness and intimacy had little meaning for Indian men of Hansa's generation who were used to *stating* rather than *asking,* lecturing rather than dialoging. He'd have to backtrack if he were to get any information from him.

"Yes, they did," he said. "I didn't mean they neglected me or anything like that, not at all, Doc. It's only that they kept secrets from me, you know, and this was one of them. I'm sure they confided in you, as you were such a good friend to them. And a wonderful bridge player, my mother always said." Flattery may get you everywhere.

Hansa appeared mollified and nodded his head several times. "Of course, of course, yes, yes, you're correct, Vish. It was a long time ago. I can tell you some things. Let me think."

Much of Dr. Hansa's recollections Vishram already knew from the court documents he'd found. Beyond that, he offered only bare-bones detail, which Vishram found surprising. Apparently his parents had maintained their secretiveness on this topic even from a most intimate associate. He tried to get Dr. Hansa to expand on his parents' feelings, focusing his questions on the early days of their meeting and marriage, but Hansa replied with either a lack of knowledge or standard clichés about it being a difficult situation: "What could they do?" "It was fate, after all." Déjà vu, as his parents spoke identically about life in general.

"Did Appa ever say how he felt regarding Mina?"

"Felt? Bad. Of course, Narin was feeling sorry for her because she was living in that two-room place in Triplicane nearby. Not sure exactly where."

So she *had* lived less than two miles from his parents' house on St. Peter's Road. He would have to find the address.

In one of the last of his father's letters to Mina (a copy of which he'd found in his mother's secret paper stash), his father's salutation was "Dear Madam," and he continued with statements like, "You have always hounded me about money, and now you must stop. I have tried desperately over the years to get you to stop this …" Hardly amicable.

"Was he always angry with her?"

"Angry? Oh no, no, no. Your father could never be angry at anyone. You know that."

Vishram pressed for more. After fielding a few more questions with noncommittal answers, Hansa imparted a new piece of information. "Late in the fifties, I think, she did get a job. It was in a factory or assembly shop for plastic fittings, I think. Yes, yes, definitely plastics. At that time it was just getting to be very popular, you know. Of course, everything is made of plastic nowadays."

Something concrete on the elusive Mina at last. "Do you know how she got it? And what the name of the place was?"

"I do not quite remember. Kilpathy-something … Works? I do not remember how it happened, either. Getting that job, I mean. I often wondered if your father was behind it. Somebody must have helped her. She was not the most industrious girl, you know."

Vishram cringed at this dismissal of Mina, who had weathered so much and lived so meagerly, misguided though she may have been in her desire to stay in touch with her ex-husband. However, this was an important point, given his father's antagonistic attitude toward her.

"Anything else you can remember, Doc?"

"Hmm, I do remember that she paid a visit to your father sometime after she got that job, maybe a few months or a year later. She was having problems with her hands. It was an allergic reaction to chemicals used in the manufacturing method. Your father sent her to me for some treatment. That was the one time I ever met her. He prescribed … ah … how can I remember? Misocortisone cream, yes, yes, that was it. Twice? No, three times a day."

"Anything else?"

"She went back to your father again. He gave her some sets of surgical gloves to protect her hands. From his hospital, I suppose.

Apparently, that caused a *tamasha* at her workplace, as her boss said it was unfair to the other workers and that he would dismiss her. Don't know what the entire outfall was. But I think she was continuing with the job for several years. I never met her again."

This was interesting indeed. Vishram was happy to find evidence of some solicitude on his father's part toward Mina. He knew him to be a calm, even-keeled person, a well-respected member of the medical community who never raised his voice in anger and, in general, appeared to be quite unemotional. His mother was quite the opposite—she was volatile, quick to judge, quick to form an opinion, with no qualms about forcefully expressing her opinion. He would not have picked either as being in the throes of passion, but that was the only explanation for their behavior. How had they fallen so in love in the 1940s, flouting its societal taboos to enter a bigamous marriage, with one family who had been horrified and unsupportive? How had they stayed together under all the pressure? Or was the pressure the glue that helped them do so?

They had finished the snacks by now, and Hansa stumped over to a liquor cabinet and poured two glasses of scotch, handing one to Vishram unasked.

Vishram took a gulp. "Doc, I admire my mother for enduring all the grief from my father's family."

"Grief? Of course. Your mother was always in a sort of depressive state, Vish. How could she ever forget the death of your brother?"

"*My brother?*" His eyes opened wide, and he spilled his drink. "What ... who?"

Hansa's brows drew together. "Your brother, Vikrant, of course. Who passed in 1948."

"Are you joking, Doc? I don't have a brother." Vishram instantly regretted his rudeness and said, "I'm sorry. Really, Dr. Hansa. Sorry." He collected his emotions. "Please, please, explain what you mean. My god. I always thought I was an only child. Honestly!"

Dr. Hansa took his time, looking down at his outstretched hand, palms down, while gently shaking his head. "This is even more shocking, Vish. I simply cannot believe you did not know of your brother. How can this possibly be?"

Vishram shook his head.

"Another secret between you and your parents, then. Most shocking."

Vishram gulped the rest of his drink. Hansa refilled it, watching him closely, as if to reassure himself that Vishram was really unaware of his brother's existence.

"Who … What was his name? What happened?"

"Vikrant. He passed from bacterial meningitis in Bangalore." Hansa, his face grave, explained as much as he knew of the event. "I suppose … I think your mother was always was blaming herself for not being at the hospital then."

And he talked of Neeta's never achieving closure, using "a sense of finality" instead.

"She always wanted another child, you know, after Vikrant. She was always saying having just one child was too difficult. She said she thought you were too lonely as a child, having no brothers or sisters. But she could never forget the effect of her first child's death. And it made her careful of becoming too involved with you."

They talked long about this shattering event.

Vishram thanked Dr. Hansa and took his leave. They made the obligatory promises to keep in touch now that email was so easy. He wondered if they would.

ELENA'S REACTION TO his news was explosive.

"Fuck, Vish, that is simply unbelievable! I don't know what to say. I mean, who the hell conceals the existence of a sibling from their child? Especially after they've grown up? And your cuz Carla never mentioned him either? Wow. Your family is so … so … never mind. If I ever meet your relatives again, I'm toting a lie detector." Pause. "Are you sure you haven't been overdoing the ganja?"

"I'm clean. A few too many scotches perhaps."

"Well, maybe you should consider hanging out there a while to get more information. Now you've unearthed two secrets. What if there's a third?"

"Yeah, maybe next I'll find I'm adopted."

"No way, you're the spitting image of your dad. And …" she chuckled, "the spitting emotional image of your mom. Sometimes."

"Ha ha."

"Speaking of adoption, Vish—"

"Gotta go, El. Taxi's here."

"Damn it, Vish, you put this off every time I try to talk about it. This is really pissing me off."

"Please. I'll get around to it."

"When? When will you? Think about it. You're there; it would be easy to contact the agency. Maybe I should jump on a plane and join you."

"No, don't do that, El—"

"Well?"

"I promise I'll give it some serious thought. Later. Love ya. Bye."

THE NEXT DAY Vishram remembered that when Dr. Hansa said he'd met Mina, he'd forgotten to ask Hansa what she looked like. He had no photographs, no description, and no solid image in his mind of this nebulous woman whose life was so entwined with that of his parents.

And he had a newfound brother.

No photographs of him either? He pored over his mother's extensive stash of photos. Had her unending grief prevented her from keeping such a memento? He examined the one framed photo he'd found, of his parents on their wedding day. His mother's love of mystery stories, and her obsession with secrets came to mind. He pried open the back of the frame. There were a dozen yellowing photographs, all with images of one child or two. One was dated 1948.

A four-year-old Vikrant and an infant Vishram.

He stared at the images a long time, and an overflowing sadness enveloped him. How could he miss having a brother he'd never known about? How did such a yearning for a sibling suddenly materialize? Memories, unintended, kept intruding. No, not so much memories as emotions—those related to his unique, lonely, friendless childhood. His brother-less childhood. His mother's impossibly unrelievable grief and the burden it had laid on him.

Vishram blinked away his tears. Hadn't he just promised Elena he'd give "serious thought" to her demand for adoption?

XXI
Bangalore & Madras, 1948–1949

The room unwraps like a flower opening on a warm spring day as Neeta enters. A trick of perspective, no doubt. She settles into the plump red sofa, unhooks Vish's sleepy arms from her shoulders, and places him beside her. She rests her purse on the back of the sofa and looks around. A pang of apprehension overtakes her unexpectedly—she has forgotten something. What is it? She goes over a mental checklist, but nothing comes to mind. She will ask Narin when he comes back home. Where is he, anyway? She was late and had expected him to meet her here, but there is no sign of him.

She enjoys the welcome silence after the bustle of the street, but in a few moments the flaccid silence begins to bother her. She turns to look behind her at the windows, which are wide open. Why is there no noise? And, welcome though it is, why is it so cool? The blank white walls shimmer and appear to ripple. A voice in her head nags: You *have* forgotten something, you *have*. Neeta stands up, willing the voice to be quiet, but it escapes her head like a freed bird, reverberating around the room, enveloping her, as if emanating from hidden speakers. Why doesn't the sound bother baby Vish? She notices he is muttering something too softly to hear. She bends lower and reads his lips as he repeats himself.

"Where is he?"

His arms reach out to hug her. She screams and turns away.

THE DREAMS CONTINUE.

Neeta notes Narin's concern as he leaves every morning. He tries to talk to her, uttering a few reassuring words, but she is taciturn, dismissing him with "I'm all right. You'll be late for work. Go." He goes hesitatingly.

They recently had a phone installed, and Narin calls Neeta from the hospital twice a day. She does not reliably answer, and when she does, she cuts the conversation short. She doesn't tell him that she is often lying in bed when he phones and listens to the harsh ringing without summoning the energy to get up and answer it. She stares straight up, willing the shrill noise to stop. The ceiling exerts a dread fascination as she studies its stark white palette, its myriad cracks, the geckos wandering in their syncopated dance, and the always wobbly fan, looping in its steady-unsteady arcs. Is Narin right about the fan? Could it come tumbling down on her? Would that be a bad thing? What would it do to her?

She shakes off these morbid thoughts and waits for Vish to wake and demand her undivided attention. The baby is her only source of happiness. Her apprehension grows. Vishram. Can she survive another tragedy like the death of Vikrant? Should she distance herself from Vish's affection, his love, his need for her (and hers for him) to lessen the pain of an inconceivable second loss? The pain grows like a living thing, gnawing at her, destroying her, defying her attempts to subdue it. This psychic malady that sweeps over her like an angry tide immobilizing her is beyond her diagnostic capacity. She breathes in harsh sobbing breaths and feels kinship with Edgar Allen Poe's words: *I felt that I breathed an atmosphere of sorrow.*

Seeking distraction, Neeta turns on the radio and spins the dial left and right searching for music. Between the bursts of static, she finds only one station with any pretense of audibility, and she twists the tuner in small increments until she homes in on it. All-India Radio, Bangalore.

Within minutes, the music stops. She hears the announcer say, "We now bring you the afternoon news. The latest count of refugees displaced in the Punjab has been estimated at over one-and-a-half million, with thousands, if not tens of thousands, of people still on the move …"

The heavy hand of communalism descended on the northern state of Punjab, where millions of Sikhs, Hindus, and Muslims had lived peaceably for centuries, when, two months before, the region was split between India and Pakistan by the Indian Independence Act 1947. Terrible violence had begun months before the official date of partition. A mass exodus of Sikhs and Hindus from the western regions of Punjab, seeking escape from unwelcome statehood in a Muslim country, mirrored the eastern Punjab Muslims moving to Pakistan. Wherever the groups met on their opposite journeys, clashes resulted in tens of thousands of deaths.

Neeta listens, horrified but unable to turn off the radio, as the announcer compiles the latest statistics of death. The sheer number is so overwhelming that she is incapable of fully comprehending it. What do three hundred thousand deaths signify? She waits out the entire announcement, the statistics of terror, the requests for charity, the names of the politicians and leaders—some who pledge to aid, others to avenge, the refugees.

What does such mass death mean? She has had one death in her life, and that one means all. She stirs, drained of emotion, as the broadcast concludes. Her eyes are wet with tears, and she dabs at them ineffectually with her sari. She silences the radio. She staggers to her feet and turns to the easel she set up earlier in the day. The blank paper draws her to it irresistibly. She picks up her charcoal pencil and begins to draw dark, heavy lines, slashing the paper.

The newly hired *ayah* comes in with Vishram, sets him on the couch, and takes her leave. Vishram, fussing, calls out to his mother. She ignores him and fixates on the somber image on her easel. He cries out for her again. She rips the drawing off the easel and tears it into fluttering strips. She picks Vishram up, touching but not soothing him. After a while, he soothes himself. She puts him back on the couch.

NARIN MEANDERED HOMEWARD from the hospital on his bicycle, sweat from the June heat clouding his eyes. He needed time to think. It has been more than nine months since Vikrant's death. He thought of Neeta, now less prone to fits of weeping and long spells of depression, but talking little to anyone, even him. Neither he nor their friends, Ambika and Laxman, could ease her anguish, but he was grateful for their attempts.

On a whim, he changed his route and headed for Ambika and Laxman's house. When he arrived, his muscles weary from the forty-minute ride, they were home, and he gladly endured a noisy welcome from their two children, who were happy to see their Uncle Narin after a long while.

He greeted his friends somberly. After a round of drinks, which cheered him up not at all, they asked why Neeta wasn't with him.

"She's tired, resting."

"We'd love to see her ... and Vish," Ambika said.

Narin paused, then took a moody gulp of his drink. "Yes."

"Narin, tell us what's on your mind."

"I need to find a way to get Neeta's mind off her obsession with Vik's death."

"It'll take time."

"I know. But she blames herself so much for what happened. I don't see it getting better. I need to find a solution, and soon."

"I don't suppose you and Neeta could go away for a week or so?" Laxman said. "You know we'd be happy to look after Vish."

"No. I don't think being with me will help her. Not that she blames me in any way, I'm sure, but being without Vish would, I think, remind her more of Vik. And she can't get enough of Vish. Haven't you noticed she hangs on to him like a limpet? She doesn't want to let him out of her sight. She takes him everywhere, shopping, walking, whatever."

"Maybe her sister can come and stay with her? Or she could go to Madras for a while?"

"I suggested both. Neeta won't hear of it … as if Deepa would hesitate or think it was a burden. You know she was here for a while after Vik … died … and I thought Neeta was glad to have her here. And when my sister Sheela came a few days later, she offered to stay for a month or so, even though she'd just been offered a job. But Neeta refused both. She just wants to be alone, she says."

He paused to accept the cigarette that Laxman pushed into his lips and took a few quick puffs. "There's more than that. You haven't seen the drawings she's done in the last few months. Scary. They're works of despair."

Narin remembered staring at Neeta's last drawing in amazement. He'd returned from work and found it mounted on the wall where she must have forgotten it. Wide, angry gashes of black on a field of white. Unlike her usual representational compositions, it was abstract except for a series of half-hidden, random, melancholic eyes. Malevolent and creepy. He decided not to ask her about it and went out to run an errand. When he came back, it had disappeared. He'd never mentioned it, nor had she. She never showed him any of her later drawings.

Ambika appeared at a loss.

"I hate to suggest this," Laxman said. "But maybe both of you need to go away. Move, that is. This town and your hospital will be forever in her mind as symbolic of your loss. You could ask for a transfer somewhere nearby."

"My god, I can't even contemplate a move. And staying near Bangalore won't help, I don't think. And I'd have to find another job. I've become comfortable here."

"You can do it."

With rising irritation, Narin said, "Easy for you to say. You've never had to look for a job or to settle in with a bunch of blowhards." He stopped, and when his friends didn't reply, he continued. "Sorry. I didn't mean to sound so harsh. But it's hard for me to work with most people. They seem so … slow to me. And the whole process of making friends, it's so complex because Neeta seems to disapprove of most of my colleagues." He snickered. "Listen to me. A second ago, I said most of them were slow and blowhards. Maybe Neeta and I are birds of a feather."

Ambika and Laxman shared a nervous laugh.

"But yes, I will have to think about it. Where would I go, though? How will I ever find friends like you?"

Neeta Perked Up and shook off her recent taciturnity when Narin suggested moving from Bangalore. Where would they go? Wanting to be near her relatives, she suggested Bombay, the capital of the newly formed state of Maharashtra, but Narin dug in his heels and pointed out that her relatives didn't really live in the city— most of them were over a hundred miles away in Konkan. And he characterized Bombay as having a reputation for fast pace and ultra-competitiveness, which meshed with its status as a major financial center as well as the epicenter of the Indian Nationalist movement. It was not his ideal.

Neeta conceded Narin's apprehension of Bombay. She knew he was aware of his own abilities and employability, but he wasn't naturally competitive. His bridge playing was an apt metaphor. He was a good player, but he didn't possess the killer instinct necessary to be a great one.

Narin insisted that moving back to Madras made more sense. "It's the one place I know well," he said, "and I'd rather not have too many more changes in my life right now. And the service will be a good place to work." The Madras Medical Service was considered a model of its kind and served the entire state with a system of regional and local hospitals, as well as several hundred clinics. Narin would have no difficulty getting a job there with his previous service and several published papers behind him.

"I don't understand," countered Neeta. "Your family caused you nothing but pain before we left Madras and in all the years since we moved. You'd be reopening raw wounds. And your first wife,"—Neeta never mentioned her name—"will be close by."

"We'll have to deal with that issue sooner or later. It would be good to be close to our college friends who are still in Madras. And Sheela. You have your sister, Deepa, in Madras, too."

"Yes. And you will have Jaggie."

"*We* will have Jaggie."

"No! He's *yours*. You have to promise me that he won't come dropping by any time he pleases. You can meet him somewhere outside of our house if he insists."

Narin wasn't sure this would be a workable plan, given Jaggie's blatant disregard of social niceties, but he nodded.

"Look, Jaggie or no, Madras would be better. Bombay is much more expensive. Plus, you know how hard it is for me to learn languages. I hate the thought of having to learn Hindi or Marathi in Bombay. I've been here in Bangalore for five years, and I'm almost fluent in Kannada, but they still laugh at my Madrasi accent at the hospital."

"You don't try hard enough. I picked up Kannada in two months."

"Well, you're good at languages. But Bombay? Speaking Hindi?"

"What, are you still fulminating about the language imposition by 'those Northerners'?"

"Not quite. I do ask myself why I only went to one protest, though. Guess my conviction wasn't strong enough." He smiled at Neeta and opened his arms to embrace her. "But you know, that's when I first fell in love with you."

Neeta was silent, her body unresponsive even as Narin held her. Why couldn't she reciprocate? She sensed Narin's dismay at her unresponsiveness.

"We can continue later," he said. "How about the club and a game of bridge?"

Neeta declined. Seeing a twinge of disappointment on Narin's face, she closed her arms around him. "I'm glad we're moving," she whispered.

WITHIN A COUPLE of weeks, Neeta had agreed to move to Madras. "Anything to get out of here," she said, gratified to see how joyful Narin became.

Days later, he told her he'd handed a short and direct letter of resignation to his superior, effective in three months.

"He was quite shocked," Narin said. "He said I was his most promising doctor. He tried hard to change my decision, but I told him my mind was set."

"Is it? Really set, I mean?" Neeta watched him for any sign of indecision.

He paused for a long moment, his expression seemingly unsettled. "Yes. It's the best thing for both of us, and it will be great to have Sheela near us again."

Neeta, reenergized, poured herself into the details of the move. Narin was happy to let her do most of the arrangements, and it suited her well to be kept busy.

A few days later, Narin interrupted her packing. He moved to his desk, sat down, opened the drawer, and extracted a letter. He held it in front of him but didn't say anything.

Neeta stopped, surprised at his silence. "What's up, Narin?" she asked.

"I got another letter from Subbu today."

"What? You didn't tell me. What does he want?"

"What else? Same as before. But here, look at this part."

She took the letter and read: "And I hear you are now resigning from the B.M.S."

"What? How could he possibly know of our decision so soon?"

"I think he must have a spy somewhere. Maybe we should be looking under our cot every night. Note that he goes on as usual about 'Mrs. Minalakshmi' wanting to live with me, or us, and how that would 'rectify' the matter. But go on."

Neeta continued reading.

> We have also been aware that your (heavy worker that you are) responsibility of work has been more important than family matters until now. But your moving should make your life more settled and you more willing to consider again your real family. We have given you more than enough chances to rectify your action toward my poor, wronged daughter *Sow.* Minalakshmi. But if we will not reach a fitting resolution, I should tell you that she is considering a divorce, despite the mortal shame it will bring forever on her and our family. If this is the fate you wish to wash over your saintly wife …

The unexpected concept of a divorce galvanized Neeta, though she doubted that Mina had suggested it. "A divorce? Narin. That may be the best solution."

"Maybe, but it's difficult. We'll have to find a lawyer. They're expensive. And have you heard of maintenance?" Neeta shook her head, as divorce in India was extremely rare and she knew nothing about it. Narin continued. "It's the money that a man is forced—asked—to pay his wife every month after the divorce for her living expenses."

"Why? She can live with her parents, can't she?"

"It's just the law."

"But, Narin, how much will this 'maintenance' be?"

"I suppose the judge decides that. And knowing Subbu and his clan, he will get a pushy lawyer to get as much as possible from us."

"My god. Bloody Jaggie will be advising their lawyer. And you mentioned 'our' lawyer? How will we afford a lawyer?"

"We'll have to use up what we've saved and borrow money, if we have to. Since I had a steady salary at the time we married, and will probably have a better one after we move to Madras, the maintenance will be a proportion of that."

Neeta considered that if she started to work, it would ease their financial straits, and they could easily afford the cook they'd long wanted. But would that increase the maintenance? Was it based on individual or family income? She sighed. So much to learn. Could she ever make a decision?

XXII
Madras, 1949–1953

Narin left the Bangalore Medical Service in late 1949.

Neeta compared her somber apprehension of the move with the relief and eagerness she'd felt during the opposite journey six years before. She tried to look on the positive side—Narin's good job and their being near their sisters again. Against that was certain harassment from Jaggie. On balance, would it be tolerable?

As the train pulled into Madras Central Station and clanked to a stop, Neeta looked out over the platform and noticed an attractive woman in a colorful sari waving vigorously *Oh, that's Sheela!* She and Narin had not seen her in the year and a half since she'd visited them after Vikrant's death. Neeta admired her sister-in-law's dress, more fashionable and colorful than she remembered, and her more confident demeanor. She had changed, and for the better. Narin saw Sheela and jumped out to hurry to where she stood. They enveloped one another in a heartfelt embrace, then he returned to the compartment with a *coolie* to help get their effects off the train.

Neeta placed Vishram in the carrier slung over her shoulders, collected her personal belongings, and stepped off the train behind Narin. She was thinking how much she and Sheela had changed since that memorable moment they'd first met almost nine years before. Both had matured over those years, but only she had endured a life-changing loss. As she embraced her sister-in-law, she noted that Sheela was restraining her bubbly personality in deference to her subdued mood. Neeta hoped she'd manage to match Sheela's joy soon enough.

Neeta occupied herself fussing over Vishram, to the point that when Sheela reached out to hold him, Neeta drew back and ignored her. The walk along the length of the platform occupied several minutes, and by its end, Neeta strove to make amends. She turned and said, "Sheela, I'm really glad to see you after all this time. I missed you. And you look so fashionable, too." She handed Vishram to Narin and tucked her arm in Sheela's as they departed the station.

"WANT TO GO get some *tiffin?*" Sheela asked later that afternoon as Narin softly closed the door of the bedroom where the exhausted Neeta was taking a nap with Vishram.

"You mean not here? Go out?"

"Yes, silly, there's lots more places to get snacks now. Let's not scrounge around here. We'll be back soon."

He agreed, glad to stretch his legs after sitting in place for so many hours. They left their aunt's house, walked to the main road, and traveled a short way down to the newly opened Swami's Chaat Shop, its bright and colorful neon sign blinking "Eat."

"Madras has changed," Sheela said as they entered the space, which was freshly painted in a garish purple hue and equipped with vivid red-topped tables and chairs. She saw Narin wince, and she laughed. "Guess we'll have to keep our sunglasses on in here." She led him to a table in the back of the room. "You know, Narin, I can come here by myself and not get stared at. Of course, it helps that Mr. Swami knows Uncle Maruti." She exchanged a brief wave with the stout, bearded man behind the counter, who smiled and waved back. "Because," she dropped her voice, "Uncle helped him out in getting his restaurant permit."

Narin knew from the proprietor's looks and manner of dress that he was a Northerner and wondered if that had created the permitting problem. He settled in across from his sister, and a khaki-clad waiter rushed over to take their orders.

"Who goes first?" she asked after they had ordered *bhel puri* and lemonade. "Our letters haven't been enough. Details."

"You, of course, Sheel. Tell me all about your job."

True to her word, Sheela had graduated from the Women's Christian College with a B.A. in literature two years ago. Their uncle initially got her a job as a secretary at a law firm he was connected to. "That was not interesting at all, Narin. I was always slow at typing, and I'd make lots of mistakes, so I'd have to catch up by staying late. And my boss was always yelling at us girls when he thought they did something wrong. Not as much at me, though. I guess he had to think about how Uncle Maruti might've not liked that. I tried not to complain, but Uncle is quite intuitive. So after a year or so, he found me another job, at the Adyar Library and Research Centre.

"So far it's quite enjoyable. The walk is short, and the work is interesting. I'm sure I wouldn't have found anything like this without Uncle's help. It's a private specialized library, you know. The building is set far back in its compound, enough so the quiet makes me actually enjoy the noise in the streets when I go back outside. Mostly scholars visit. Quiet old men, shuffling around and never talking. I started out as before, doing secretarial and filing work, but I'm doing some lookups for the clients now. I don't know enough yet to be at the desk to answer questions but may soon. Besides books and paper documents, there're also thousands of palm-leaf manuscripts, can you believe, kept in locked rooms. I so want to be inside that room one day. But ..." her eyes opened wide, "it's so wonderful to be among *books*. The *smells*. Touching their backs ... spines. Do you remember, I once wrote to you about how lucky I thought you were, Narin, being able to walk through the book stacks at medical college? Now I do it every day."

Narin was happy at the unexpected chance that allowed her to indulge her tactile pleasure of books. "Does it pay much?"

"Oh, I don't care," Sheela said with a wave. "It's only pocket money to me right now, as long as I am at Auntie's house."

Something in the way she said it made him ask, "Do you mean you might want to move out of her house?"

"Oh, not for a while. But finally, I think I will. It'd be good to be independent, don't you think?" Her eyes sparkled with anticipation. "I'll be a free woman of the world."

Narin contemplated the implications of an independent Sheela. With her clear inner strength, she radiated confidence, and he was proud of this new incarnation. "Have you mentioned this to Amma and Appa? How will they react?"

"No, but I hope not all that bad. I suppose having one child who's been a 'major disappointment'—their words, of course— takes the strain off me." She winked at him, and he frowned. "Amma has been writing to me frequently, nice letters, too. Appa, of course, never writes, but I hear about him from Amma. You should try to meet them, Narin. They're not getting any younger, you know. And Gopal's having more and more children. I expect to be a grand-aunt in five years as I'm sure Auntie Saraswathi is working on an early marriage for his first son. He's almost twelve, you know. Old enough for them to start looking." She winked again, and her brother joined in her laugh.

Narin noted she'd dropped the "elder-brother" honorific for Gopal, using only his name. Another sign of her break with tradition. He felt a pang of longing, and a frisson of envy, as he compared her frequent correspondence with their family to the silence he'd endured. He forced himself to concentrate on his sister's happiness and wondered whether she had any doubts about her current trajectory, which was unlikely to result in the conventional marriage-and-children scenario. He resolved to ask her about it another time, not wanting to cause her any discomfort.

As if reading his mind—she was good at that—Sheela said, "They ask me sometimes when I'm getting married." She smiled, but her eyes were distant. "Not 'if,' but 'when,' as if it's my choice and I could do that at any time."

"Do you think about it?"

"Of course. It's hard not to. Don't you see how much I stand out? Auntie and Uncle are quite loose with me, but I can never go where I want to when I want to. I can never be completely free." She smiled tightly. "Unless I find a man-friend." She noted Narin's frown, looked down at her plate, and toyed with her food as if it had demanded her immediate attention.

Narin had déjà vu of Subbu's letter from years ago, bemoaning how his daughter would feel in society, traveling, or at public places when she sees women of her age with their consorts. Was even an independent, self-sufficient woman like Sheela incomplete without a "consort"? He reflected on his own life and how fulfilled he was because he had the comfort of Neeta's constant presence. Could he imagine life without her? He knew Sheela's chances of getting married were slim. She was nearly thirty years old, not living with her parents, and had an avowed stubborn streak and a regular job. He so wanted to help her but knew he could do nothing.

Seeing the expression on her brother's face, Sheela rallied. "Cheer up, Narin. I'm quite happy, really. I think about how it might have been, living in Manipur with one of my many charming suitors." She enjoyed Narin's surprise. "Yes, I'm being frivolous, but this is great. I have a job, a few friends—all married, you know, but they make allowances for me—and I don't have a nasty mother-in-law. Seems like a good balance.

"Okay, enough about me. Talking about work, has Neeta decided on anything? In your last letter, you said you were talking it over with her."

This was still a sore subject between Narin and Neeta. "She was considering working at one of those free dispensaries, but that was before … before … you know."

Sheela put a hand up to stop him. "You don't have to explain. But it's been well over a year. Is she managing okay?"

Was she? She'd come out of her severe withdrawal, but she was far from the animated woman he remembered and loved. Could he expect anything different? Does loss teach you something and help you grow? He considered his own reaction. He'd immersed himself in work and managed to ease his pain. But Neeta? He couldn't be sure.

"I don't know. She's become more adamant about not wanting to leave Vishram with an *ayah* when she goes out. She never goes anywhere without him. What on earth will she do when he's ready for nursery school? Her nightmares have stopped. That's good. But her playful side … I haven't seen that forever."

They settled into silence, finishing their snacks.

NARIN WALKED TO Victoria Hospital that morning, reporting for his first day on duty. He was looking forward to getting back to work. The clerk at the front desk said as Narin walked by, "The director wants to see you, sir," and motioned down the hall toward an office. He thanked the clerk and strode down the corridor to the director's office, knocked, and entered on hearing an acknowledgment.

"Director Sarathy, how are you?"

The director was unsmiling as she rose from her desk. She was a woman in her fifties, gray haired and distinguished looking, with a restrained manner. She shook his hand with a strong grip. He thought that was a good sign, asserting her authority. "Please sit down," she said and did so herself. "I'm very happy you're here, Dr. Janappan." Her face belied her words. "I'm sure our hospital will be proud to have such an accomplished doctor on our staff."

"Thank you."

"Your personal needs will be taken care of by my clerk at the end of the corridor. You've probably met him already. And of course you'll have to fill out the usual endless paperwork, but I'm sure you know all that." She continued to discuss Narin's ward assignments and immediate duties.

When she finished, she paused.

Narin had muttered a "thank you" and looked at her inquiringly. What else was on her mind? He'd noticed that she was fingering a sheet of paper that lay on her desk, having picked it up several times since he had entered. She now picked it up again and apparently came to a decision. "This is a letter I received yesterday. From a …" She glanced down. "Mr. J. Vasan, who bills himself, rather redundantly, as 'senior attorney-at-law' as well as 'chief counselor.'" She paused to register the shock on Narin's face. "So you know the gist of what he writes?" Not waiting for an answer, she continued. "It's quite a diatribe."

So Subbu had wasted no time rekindling his campaign of harassment on learning of Narin's return to Madras. Why now? Was it just a way of proving he could cause trouble for him at work? Or of pressuring him on the divorce issue? He collected his scattered wits and asked, "What does it say? I should tell you that he—"

"It is an accusation about your conduct," the director said. "Toward an unnamed person whom he says you married ten years ago and then abandoned. He claims to represent her interests and is shocked that, as he puts it, 'this august institution has descended to employing a person of such dubitable character.'" A ghost of a smile flitted across her face. "He must read a lot of Victorian fiction. Anyway, what's your side of this story?"

Narin feigned calmness. "Yes, the true part is my first marriage. To his sister. He left that out. And I am now married to my current wife, Dr. Neeta Pai, and have a child. I have never lived with his sister. We were married as children." He tried to read the play of emotions on the director's face, but as he didn't know her, he had to rely on his instincts. She was looking at him steadily, but not exhibiting anger or disapproval, maybe concern about her institution.

He decided it was best to be clear. "In fact, I had received a note from him a couple of months ago, saying that his sister intends to file for divorce soon. I naturally assumed that any issues would be settled in court during the case. Not that I intend to contest it," he said with a surety he did not feel. He knew divorce was a rare occurrence and was conscious of the stigma attached to it. But it could not have remained a secret.

The director tapped on the damning letter, moving it back and forth in small circles with her finger, lost in thought. Narin considered what the worst case could be. A few months later, his status as a midlevel doctor in the medical service would have protected him, but he had just joined, and his probationary state made him vulnerable to dismissal. That would be a major blot on his record, maybe even make him unemployable. The thought of so catastrophic a result left him in sick despair, which he struggled to conceal.

The director looked up at him with a benign face. "Obviously I have checked with your references and found nothing but praise. We have obtained the highest of recommendations on you and know of your excellent publications, so I have no doubt your work and your conduct are exemplary. I had already decided this is none of our business, but I have to respond when a person sends what looks like an official objection to your appointment. You see that, don't you?"

Narin relaxed, realizing he had dodged a bullet.

"I only hope he doesn't cause any real problems, like coming over here and disturbing the staff or patients."

"Oh, no, I'm sure he won't do that. His issue is only with me and Neeta," Narin said, again with a certainty he did not feel.

"Well, Dr. Janappan … Narinder? I'm sorry about all this and hope it settles out for you. As for the letter, I have already sent an acknowledgment of its receipt. I am going to leave it at that." She stood up to offer her hand. "Welcome to Victoria Hospital."

Narin took her hand with a sigh of relief and bade her good-bye. He stopped in the corridor, taking deep breaths. It had started. So soon. Had Neeta been right? Should they have moved farther north instead of back to Madras? It was too late now, of course. They would have to make the best of it. But what else Jaggie could toss at him?

SHEELA CAME BY several times a week to help Narin and Neeta establish their new home. This evolved into a weekly visit with Neeta. One day Sheela said, "Why don't you come to the library around lunchtime on Saturday? They're moving some new shelves in, and I have to take an hour or two off since I won't have much of a place to work while that's going on."

"Oh, that would be nice, Sheel, but I can't leave Vish, can I?"

"Well, of course you can bring him with you. He's old enough to take out to eat with us. So what do you say?"

Neeta agreed, her look uncertain.

On that Saturday, Sheela met Neeta and Vish at a small restaurant near the Adyar Library. Sheela apologized for its nondescript decor, as no better places existed nearby. Neeta, who'd rarely eaten in a restaurant since she moved back to Madras, hadn't noticed and didn't comment.

Vish greeted Sheela's hug with a cheery, "Hi, Auntie," took off his floppy straw hat, and gave it to her with the admonition, "Please keep it safe."

They ordered two Madras vegetarian plates, and Sheela added two bottles of the newly introduced Fanta orange soda, saying, "It's the latest fizzy drink." She winked at Vish, who was sitting on his mother's lap. "You can have a taste."

"What's 'fee-see' mean?" he demanded.

"It has gas in it to make bubbles."

"What kind of gas?"

"Oh, Vish, I don't know. It's carbon-something."

"Why do they put it?"

"Because it tastes good."

"How?"

"It tickles your nose, silly."

Wrinkling his nose, Vish said, "Smells good." He accepted a taste of the drink but giggled and sputtered out most of it.

From her bag, Neeta pulled out an elaborate wooden car transporter complete with many small vehicles and handed it to Vish, who was soon engrossed in its complexities. Noting Sheela's admiration of the colorful toy, she said, "Laxman's fifth birthday present. A world-famous Tillicum Toy, he said, from America, I think. I wonder how on earth he got it."

"Just like him. And how is Vish doing at nursery school? Didn't you have some problem there?"

"Yes, Saint Stephens Catholic requires all students to be in a catechism class first thing every morning. Can you imagine? I told them we were Hindus, and they said almost all of the children were, but it's a rule. So——"

"You put your foot down." With a smile at her sister-in-law's rising tone.

"Yes. I had to. I think I was screaming at the end. But I suppose they really didn't want me to leave without enrolling Vish, so they agreed to let him skip the class."

"I hate that," piped up Vish, looking up from motivating the car toys. "They make me sit outside the class in a chair until it's over."

"Well, at least you're not listening to Catholic teachings."

"I wish I did. All the others are angry at me. Some won't even talk to me now."

"Oh no, Vish. Should I talk to Sister Catherine?"

"No!"

"That'll probably make things worse, Neeta," Sheela said. "Best leave it alone."

"Maybe I shouldn't have him in school. I miss him terribly. I hope you're all right, Vish."

Vish rolled his eyes. He put his arms out to his mother, but she only patted them and turned away after a moment. Vish turned back to his cars.

"Of course Vish will be fine," Sheela said. "I mean, I know you're worried about being away from him, but you need to look after yourself as well."

"What do you mean?"

"Neeta, have you even been out of the house without—" gesturing toward Vish. "Just you and Narin in the last year? Or played bridge? You used to write to me that you enjoyed that."

"Well, yes, but I don't quite remember when—"

"Of course, you don't. I'm sure it's been forever. I know that sounds abrupt, and maybe it's none of my business, but you have to get a hold of yourself."

"I can't leave Vish alone."

"Neeta, you're being overprotective. Stop smothering him." Neeta gasped. "Well, sorry, but it's true." Sheela let the play of emotions on Neeta's face settle. "Neeta, do you remember when you were first married, and I'd come over for food? What did we talk about?"

"What?"

"Well, you and Narin talked about medicine most of the time."

"Oh no, was it? It must have been quite boring for you."

"Yes … no … I mean, I didn't get most of it, but it was so nice seeing the two of you so absorbed in your work. And in each other. Remember, that was when I was sitting at home in Auntie Kala's house every day, often reading and wondering what I would do for the rest of my life. I was so envious of Narin, both of you, working away, all those interesting cases—"

"All those strange patients," said Neeta with a giggle.

"Well, what I'm getting at is, I think it's time for you to get back to work."

Neeta's heart raced. She shook her head and said through pursed lips, "I don't know if I can."

"Of course you can. It's what you were trained for, and you're good at it. Now I know you had an idea about working at a poor people's clinic for a while. There are lots of them in Madras. Why, there's a new one quite near you, the Jayaraman Clinic."

Neeta forced herself to be calm. "Oh. I don't know, working for a religious institution—"

"The clinic is run by the Swami Jayaraman Ashram, which of course is religious, but it's independently managed. Uncle told me about it when it opened because he'd decided he needed a guru and thinks the Swami is it, so he started going over to their meetings. Auntie Kala says that's what happens as you get older, you need reassurance. Listen, you'd be working with poor people at the clinic, exactly what you've said you prefer. Most of them are women, so they need more women doctors. The religious-*wallahs* won't interfere with you. You don't have to go to *puja* ceremonies at the Ashram or anything."

"And listen to some fat swami go on about duty and humility."

"Or sit in the dreary women's section."

They burst out laughing. Neeta saw Vish look up, startled, then break into a wide smile himself. She realized he hadn't seen that side of her for a long time. Glad that Sheela had prodded her out of her doldrums, and seeing Vish's happiness, she resolved to be more lighthearted, at least in his presence.

Having Vish at nursery school had eliminated one barrier to her working. She would have to overcome the other internal ones.

A MONTH LATER, Neeta was meeting Sheela for lunch. She had taken a rickshaw over to Sheela's Aunt Kala's house but waited outside. Even after all these years, she was not comfortable in her aunt-in-law's house—the memory of their not exactly accepting response to Narin informing them of his impending marriage to her rankled. Sheela appeared momentarily and greeted Neeta. The two linked arms and walked to the main road, then settled at a table at the *chaat* shop.

"So," said Sheela after they had ordered snacks and chai, "you seemed quite excited on the telephone. What news?"

Neeta smiled and pressed Sheela's arm. "I decided to take your advice from a few weeks ago. I applied to the Jayaraman Ashram Clinic, and they accepted me."

"That's wonderful, Neet! Have you started yet?"

"Tomorrow. In the OB-gyn section. I'm actually quite nervous."

"I'm sure your diagnostic and medical skills haven't rusted away. Narin's told me all about you helping him along from time to time with tricky cases."

"Oh, yes. But now I have to deal with real patients—"

"You'll be fine! Neet, I'm happy for you. What prompted your decision?"

"A level of guilt, I suppose? When we were in Bangalore and struggling a bit without having servants and all, Narin would badger me about not working. At the time, I used to slough it off, but after moving here, Vish being in school, and also listening to your comments, I began to feel quite selfish about not helping out."

As Neeta continued with details of her new job, she noticed a change in Sheela's manner; she seemed to have lost her cheerfulness. Neeta stopped her gushing. "Sheel?" She placed a hand on Sheela's arm.

"You mentioned guilt. Yes, a powerful emotion, isn't it? I wish it were easier to deal with," said Sheela as she turned slightly away from Neeta and freed her arm.

Neeta waited a few moments for her sister-in-law to continue and, when she did not, said, "Sheel? Something the matter?"

"No."

"Yes! What is it? You can tell me anything, you know."

Sheela smiled tightly. "Not a good liar, am I?" Sheela looked out the window for a while, where the bustle of traffic in the street seemed to fascinate her. When she spoke again, her voice was soft and had a dreamy quality. "About two months ago, my boss told me that I had to complete, by day's end, some work he had given me that morning. I knew I couldn't finish it before the end of my usual workday. He wasn't happy." She paused again.

"Did your boss cause trouble? What happened?"

"Well, I said I'd stay late to finish, and I could take the typed papers over to the client when done, which placated my boss. He gave me the client's home address, and I took a rickshaw over. Mr. Ghosh—that's the client—was so relieved to have the papers and thanked me quite graciously. I must've looked a sight, dusty and cross and tired, because he invited me in for a cup of tea." Sheela stopped again, then continued. "He was alone in that huge house. I don't know why there were no servants around, but he mentioned his wife and children were having dinner with her mother across town." Sheela had picked up the end of her sari and was twisting it in tight curls. "Neeta, it was the books."

"Books?"

"Yes, he had shelves of them. Not that common, no, for most people we know? I started asking him about his books, and soon we were having all kinds of interesting conversations about novels we'd both read. I must've stayed there for over two hours. Got a shellacking from Auntie when I turned up past nine p.m."

Neeta reflected that Sheela had alluded to "guilt" at the start of the conversation but said nothing; she didn't want to break her sister-in-law's narrative, and she put aside any speculation on where this was going. Sheela dropped the sari tail and looked Neeta full in the eyes. Again, a faint smile crossed her lips.

"Well, Ghosh had said that he'd like to continue talking about books—apparently his wife wasn't at all a reader—so he asked if I'd like to come again the next week."

"Same time, same place?"

"Yes. I did … and … Neeta." Her words suddenly came out in a rush. "I never knew what being attracted to … a man was like! And it felt so natural. And the second time we met, he … we … well, you know." She looked up at Neeta.

Though Neeta's suspicions were confirmed, she was still shocked. Nothing that Sheela had mentioned before had prepared her for this revelation.

Sheela's face crumpled. "Oh god, you're appalled. You think I'm a horrible person."

"No, Sheela, no. It's just a huge surprise. I'm not judging you. Why should I?"

"He's married and a client, and it's all so … shabby! How could I not feel guilty? Three hours maybe every week or two. It's not as if we could ever go out together. And the constant fear of his family coming home early or a friend or servant dropping in or …" She shook her head. "But it's also so pleasant. I used to say I loved touching books and smelling them when I used to visit the library in Venpuri—god, that seems ages ago. Now, touching, feeling, smelling another human being so intimately. And being looked at differently by him. Differently, that is, from the way others—men—my friends' husbands, look at me."

"Is he … nice?"

Sheela composed herself. "Yes. I think he's a kind man."

There was a long silence as they both nibbled tentatively at their food. The sounds from the busy street ebbed and flowed, washed over their inattentive ears like water over a dam, leaving no mark behind.

Sheela continued. "I suppose it was a *sangam* of several things. Of loneliness. Of having these feelings, sexual, though I mightn't have known to call it that, of becoming tired of being what others wanted me to be, obedient and quiet. Because I wanted to be free. You know what Ghosh's response was when I said that? 'And are you? Free, I mean?' I said 'Yes.' And he replied, 'No, freedom is an illusion. Fate assigns us a role, and we either embrace it or reject it at our peril.'

"I may have screamed, 'I don't believe that! I don't believe in fate!' And he said, 'You will, you cannot escape fate.' At first I thought it was a mean thing to say. But he wasn't being mean. He believes that, as most of us do."

"I know you don't agree with that," Neeta said with a forced smile.

"No. But it was another thing we talked about. For quite a while. Oh, Neeta, you can't imagine how it was for me all those years you were away. I really didn't have anyone like you and Narin. Auntie Kala and Uncle … well they're a different generation, aren't they? I'm close to her, but not a 'friend.' Of course, I have my own-age friends, but all are married, so I don't get to see them all that often. And, definitely, no men I can *actually* talk to. This was a breath of fresh air. Purifying. Exhilarating."

Sheela's face had resumed its usual calm glow, and her voice, previously strident, had dropped to an excited cadence. She shook her head as if to clear it. "But it's still a bad thing, no? Sometimes after I get home, I lie awake wondering about his marriage, his wife, his children. What am I doing to all that? How do I live with all the guilt?"

Neeta absorbed the enormity of Sheela's revelation. She was no longer shocked. Clearly the whole affair had more of a positive than negative impact on her sister-in-law. She chose her words carefully. "Don't let guilt ruin what seems to be a good event in your life, Sheel. It was your decision to enter into this, and I won't second-guess that. From the way you describe Ghosh, he's not a run-of-the-mill seducer type. We don't have a society where you can correct early wrong decisions in your life—god, Narin and I should know—and it's clear he is not intellectually fulfilled by his wife. And you seem to get something good out of it, too. You know I'll support you whatever you do."

A trace of a smile appeared on Sheela's face. She sighed and said, "Thanks a lot, Neet. I get down like this sometimes when the gravity of it hits me. But I feel happy about it at other times."

"Does Narin know?"

"Oh, god, no. This is the first time I've talked about it with anyone." She giggled a moment as she continued. "Can you imagine my telling my much-married friends?"

Neeta laughed in return. "Depending on the state of their marriages, maybe some will be envious." Her face adopted a serious air. "Of course I won't tell Narin. It's up to you."

Sheela agreed that, close as she was to Narin, she wasn't quite sure how he would take this news. Neeta patted her on the arm. They finished the last of their meals and went outside where the sun had hidden itself in dense cloud cover and the temperature had dropped a bit. They decided to walk back to Sheela's house in comfortable silence.

THE OFFICIAL LOOKING envelope arrived at Narin and Neeta's house a few months later. Narin held it a minute or so, reluctant to open it—he was sure what it was. He opened it, confirming his suspicions, and went inside to show Neeta.

"It's from Jaggie. He's started the divorce proceedings."

"Oh, Narin. In a way, that's good news, isn't it? We'll finally get a resolution. And Jaggie won't turn up to bother you again."

"You're being optimistic. Or naive! He'll find a way to torment us forever."

"I wish you weren't such a naysayer, Narin. Things are going well for you, aren't they? You seem to love working at Victoria.

I'm getting along … OK … at my clinic. And look at Sheela. She seems to be positively glowing of late."

"Yes, isn't she? She must have a special secret in her life."

Neeta's heart skipped a beat, and she paused, wondering if Narin was aware of Sheela's escapade, but he did not continue. Perhaps he did know and was keeping it a secret from her? No, too convoluted. If Sheela had told him, she'd surely have mentioned it to her.

Narin flicked the envelope onto the dining table. He smiled. "Yes. It's all going well."

SHEELA CALLED NEETA and suggested they meet, her voice strained and pitched high. She would not explain on the phone when Neeta asked her what was the matter, insisting they meet as soon as possible. Neeta suggested meeting at her house, and Sheela asked if Narin would be there, which surprised her. She wondered if Sheela had mentioned her affair to Narin and he had reacted badly.

Neeta and Sheela had rarely talked about Sheela's affair in the past months. Neeta would sometimes broach the subject casually, and Sheela would more often than not dismiss her inquiry with a short "Nothing to add, Neeta, it's all the same. *Chalta-hai.*" Neeta was reluctant to comment how Sheela seemed happier than she had ever been before, a contentment that seemed to have taken root within her and infused her demeanor.

When Sheela entered, Neeta was overwhelmed with concern at her appearance. Her face was drawn; she looked stricken. Besides a wan greeting, Sheela said nothing as she settled herself on the sofa. Neeta mimed "Tea?" and, receiving a nod, went to the kitchen where she had a pot of water already on the boil. As she brewed the tea, she looked out the kitchen door, through which she had a good view of the downcast Sheela. She stared intently. Something in Sheela's demeanor alighted a spark of alarm in her.

All those months of working in the Jayaraman Clinic with women in their most fecund years had sharply honed her instincts. Could Sheela be …? She resolved to let her sister-in-law talk for herself, brought over the tea service, and sat next to her.

Sheela sipped her tea, blowing on the surface between sips, still holding back. She made some preliminary enquiries about how Neeta's work was going and how her nephew was faring at school. She was working hard to maintain her composure, and the strain showed on her face. She could delay no longer.

"There's no point my trying to soft-pedal this, Neeta. I'm pregnant."

In spite of her premonition, shock rippled through Neeta. Hearing the word from Sheela destroyed any hopes she had that she was wrong, that Sheela's angst stemmed from a less awful source. She forced her voice to calmness. "How far along are you?"

"Two months and a bit. I thought the first menses I missed was just late or was an exception or something, but now of course I'm sure."

Neeta moved over to Sheela and enveloped her in a hug. "Oh, Sheela, I'm so sorry." She heard Sheela mutter, her voice muffled against her breast, "And I thought I was being so careful, too." Neeta continued to hold her, patting her shoulder lightly. Thoughts raced through her mind. Did her lover, Ghosh, know?

"No." Sheela cried out when asked. "Of course I can't tell him. I don't want to burden him. And besides, as well as I know him, I don't know how he will react."

"Well, we'll have to tell Narin," Neeta said and, noting the alarm on Sheela's face, continued. "I will help you in any way I can, but this requires more than one person to work out."

Sheela had started sobbing quietly. "I hate this. I hate myself. All the trouble I'm causing you—"

"Stop. I am completely here for you, Sheel. And so is Narin."

"But I feel so guilty." She looked up from her tears. "Do you … do you think I can have the baby?"

Neeta could hardly believe Sheela would even consider so rash an action. "Don't be ridiculous, Sheela! How on earth are you going to manage with a child?"

Sheela looked down again.

"There's no choice. You cannot have the child, can you? In our society, you would be shunned and shamed. And they'd fire you from your job the moment it became obvious. You've talked a lot about being independent, about living free, maybe even by yourself. Can you give all that up? Do you want to go back to being dependent on your aunt and uncle or others in your family? Maybe even being forced to leave Madras? We need to find a way … of termination. We'll bring Narin into the picture. I hope he has the resources."

She took Sheela's chin in her hand and lifted it so their eyes met. "And never feel guilty about the procedure. It's not a baby. It's a fetus. Just cells."

Sheela nodded miserably.

XXIII
Madras, 1953

Narin woke early on the day the divorce was due to be heard in court. Sheela and Neeta accompanied him in silence as they drove there in the little Ford Anglia he'd borrowed from his uncle. The car was never an overeager conveyance, and now, as he dodged the morning crush of vehicles and people, he imagined he could sense its reluctance to take him on this unpleasant journey. He puttered along as slowly as possible. When he entered the car park adjacent to the court building, a khaki-clad attendant waved to an empty spot and opened the door for him but ignored the women passengers.

They climbed the broad steps of the imposing red sandstone building. One of many relics built shortly before the turn of the century in the Indo-Saracenic style that had been the rage then, it had pointed arches and curlicue capitals, pierced openwork screens, bulbous domes on its roof, and beige brick accents surrounding the tall windows. Its intimidating grandeur moved Narin not at all.

A handwritten calendar tacked onto the door of their courtroom announced:

Learned Judge R. K. Karthikan:
Janappan vs. Janappan, 10 a.m.
Silence in Court.

They walked inside and found their assigned seats. Narin's counsel, R. Mutthuswamy, arrived minutes later and greeted them. Shorter than Narin, his body carrying a slight paunch, and wearing prominent black-rimmed glasses, he wore his trademark rumpled suit with tie askew. Narin wondered if he pulled his tie awry before appearing in public, for it seemed impossible that he could never get it right. He reminded Narin of an amiable owl.

Narin had not dealt with the legal system or lawyers before, and he was still not at ease with his attorney whose propensity to ruminate before answering any question made Narin impatient. Mutthuswamy also had a habit of throwing out "worst-case scenarios" as responses to issues Narin raised. With his scientific bent, Narin demanded a probability for each of these scenarios, which in turn exasperated the lawyer. They'd acquired a grudging mutual respect out of necessity over the last few weeks.

As the courtroom filled with officials, stenographers, and a few spectators, Narin watched others milling around the room. A florid British man stood out. He was late middle-aged, tall and bulky, wearing an impeccable beige suit and bright blue tie, and carrying a large leather briefcase. He picked his way slowly through the human traffic around him, a man on a serious mission.

Noticing Narin staring at him, Mutthuswamy said, "That's Mrs. Minalakshmi's counsel, Mr. James Castle."

"What? Isn't he that well-known lawyer who ..." Narin tried to remember cases in which Castle had been involved.

"Yes, you may have heard of his famous cases in the past. It's been a while, though. He's been in a decline, drinks like a fish at the Boat Club. I should know. I've seen him there often enough. No doubt, that's why your wife's ... first wife's family can afford him. Still sharp, though. It would be dangerous to underestimate him."

Narin watched James Castle, apparently sober, sit down at the counselor's table on his right, collect his papers, and close his eyes. He ignored the assistant who laid out documents, positioned a legal pad, and set pens just so on the table. The proceedings began.

JAMES CASTLE SOON focused on the *ritu kala.*

"So, Dr. Narinder, I must ask you if you did, indeed, consummate the occasion."

"I did not."

"Perhaps you could enlighten the court as to the reason for this failure? Was there a physical impediment?"

Narin wondered why he didn't simply tell the truth. He clearly remembered thinking of Neeta as he lay unresponsive beside his first wife. And the thought of "sexual congress" with Mina was abhorrent to him. "No," he said.

"No? Perhaps I can characterize you as being torn between ideal and duty, the latter of which seemed too irksome?"

Narin dropped his voice. "If you say so."

Castle continued, and when he had completed his interrogation, he wore a self-satisfied smirk.

"Yes," he said, "I would like to summarize, if I may, with the learned justice's permission. Defendant was invited to an elaborate holy ceremony by my client's family with the express purpose of sanctifying his marriage to the plaintiff, a marriage, which I emphasize, had taken place four years earlier and was duly blessed by the families of both parties, including the transfer of a substantial dowry from her family to his. Despite this outpouring of familial kinship, affection, and good faith, the defendant thought only of his illicit connection with another woman at a crucial time. A connection that resulted in his subsequent second marriage, which has brought disappointment, hurt, and maleficence to my client.

Have you anything further to add before my learned friend Mr. Mutthuswamy questions you, Dr. Narinder?"

Narin did not answer.

"Thank you, sir. I yield to Counselor Mutthuswamy."

As The Court recessed for the weekend, and Narin left the courtroom with Sheela, Neeta, and Mutthuswamy, he asked his counsel, "Why was Castle focusing so much on my reasons for … not consummating?"

Mutthuswamy adjusted his tie once again, tugging on it just so, an exercise in futility that he performed often. "I think I know where this is going. Castle is trying to make you out to be an unfeeling husband and an ungrateful son."

"Does that matter?" asked Narin in a resigned tone. "That's not exactly illegal, is it?"

Mutthuswamy sighed. He slowed his speech as if speaking to a recalcitrant child. "You have to think of the effect on the court. Judge Karthikan is human. In fact, he's known to slant his decisions based on how *he* thinks the case should be going."

"Surely that's not what the legal system is supposed to do— decide at an emotional level?"

"There's theory and there's practice, Narin. He is not going to do anything unethical that may get him in trouble, but he is quite susceptible to being swayed. The system gives him leeway, and he can take advantage of it. That will affect the most important issue here: the amount of your maintenance, present and past."

"Past?" Neeta asked, frowning.

This was not a surprise to Narin, who had paid closer attention to his counsel than she had.

"Yes, the years between Narin's first and second marriages. Castle can claim, reasonably, that his client is owed maintenance for that period."

"My god. How can we afford it?"

"Maybe my father will pitch in," Narin said sarcastically. "Let's put it to him tomorrow at the Grand Inquisition."

Narin had reopened communication with his father a few months before when the issue of the divorce had become concrete, as his father might be affected by the divorce and dowry settlements. Narin had little knowledge if anything had transpired between his family and his first in-laws regarding the matter, and his father supporting him might influence Subbu in his demands. He knew, through Sheela, that his father and Subbu were distant, but that any lingering animosity between them had evidently died down.

When Narin had informed his father of the scheduled date of the hearing, Mohan wrote back that he and Jyothi would come to Madras to see how they could help. That his mother was coming was a surprise to Narin, who hadn't seen her since his second marriage, and he was elated that she might be willing to accept him and Neeta. He was sure she wasn't coming to Madras to weigh in on the divorce trial.

Unfortunately, a major train derailment the previous day had led to the cancellation of most service on the southern branch of the railway, so the family had been detained. Their momentous meeting would not take place until Saturday, after the start of the trial.

SATURDAY MORNING DAWNED, bright and hot. Narin lay in restless sleep, his face dappled with sweat. He'd dreamt it was the final day of term at college, and he was walking unconcernedly into the examination hall where he was confronted by the redoubtable Chief Examiner Raja, a gash of a smile across his face, his outstretched hand holding a weighty ream of yellow foolscap quiz papers. Narin took the bundle from him, looked at the first question, and harsh reality descended as he realized he had forgotten to study for this test. He awoke in a blind panic, reached for his handkerchief, and mopped his face.

Narin dreaded the thought of his family meeting Neeta. His father would be polite, of course. The anger he had expressed in those long-ago letters had diminished, and he'd surely exhibit his controlled public persona, calm and unrevealing. He was unsure about his mother, whom he knew could be cold and distant with relatives she disliked. Then of course his twin aunts—how direct and overt would their disapproval be? At thirty-six, he wasn't intimidated by them anymore and could stand up to their double-barreled antagonism. Sheela would at least be supportive of him. But his concern was how he could intervene if their wrath were directed at Neeta.

They were all due to meet at his flat around lunchtime. He'd chosen the meeting place himself, but now wondered if the neutral ground of his Aunt Kala's house might have been better. But he wanted them to meet Neeta for the first time on her territory. He thought it would give her a small advantage. Not yet fully awake, he turned and reached for his beloved Neeta, but didn't find her. She must have already woken and was no doubt busy supervising the lunch arrangements. He spent the next half-hour reflecting on the decisions he'd made over the years, from the passive acquiescence to his first marriage to his deliberate entry into his second. He'd never regretted his second decision, but he now wished he'd initiated the divorce six years ago himself.

NEETA WOKE EARLY. Her sleep had been more restful than Narin's, though he'd thrashed around enough to wake her. She looked at him beside her, his dark, handsome face now relaxed in peaceful sleep. Which of them was more apprehensive of this meeting? She knew his concern was divided between the divorce proceedings and how his family would treat her. She had forced herself to be calm, to treat this event as a painful but rewarding passage.

Meeting his parents—how like him would they be? From what he'd told her about his family, she surmised he was unlike his brother, Gopal, eight years his senior in years but "fifty older in spirit," as he'd put it. She'd tried to extract information on his two elder sisters, but Narin seldom spoke of them, and characterized them as "typical subservient wives of solid middle-class burghers." She thought this harsh, but he merely muttered with a tight look, "You'll understand when you meet them. On the other hand, maybe you never will. It's probably better that way."

Her thoughts came round to Sheela. Why were the two youngest children of this traditional family so different? So free of convention? She hoped to gain an insight into this mystery by meeting their parents.

Her friendship with Sheela had deepened over the years, and now that they lived so close to each other, she enjoyed their frequent visits. Due to Sheela's nagging, she had started working at the Swami Jayaraman Clinic. Her patients were from the poorer working classes, women who might not have availed themselves of the state-run medical system. She was providing a valuable service to the community and often told Sheela how rewarding she found it.

She left the bedroom and stopped to glance in at Vishram, who was curled into a semi-fetal bundle of twitchy sleep. His grandparents would be meeting him for the first time, and she hoped that would assuage their animosity toward her and Narin. She had mentioned the upcoming visit to Vishram several times over the last few weeks and wondered now whether she should have warned him of any possible unfriendliness. Or should she have told him to curb his natural ebullience and talkativeness? Would that offend their traditional mores? Would it be one more fault stacked against her and Narin? Studying his untroubled, unlined face of youth, she decided it was best for Vish to be Vish.

She was determined to make a good first impression. Smile a lot, she told herself. And don't react to his aunts' jibes. Secretly, she was eager to meet—maybe confront—Narin's twin aunts, who, in her view, had been responsible for this whole mess. Enough, she thought; back to the practical. Food lubricates the social wheels. She had instructed their part-time cook to make a typical Tamilian meal instead of the mélange of North-South cuisine she and Narin enjoyed.

"It will give your family one less thing to complain about if there are no Konkan dishes," she'd said to Narin, who nodded but said nothing. She added with a wink, "And I'll make sure it's hot enough."

"If it's hot enough for them, you won't be able to touch it."

"Won't be much of a nuisance if I don't eat one meal."

"I can just see that now—you not eating in the presence of the entire family. They might think you're serving them poison." He chuckled. "I know. I'll make a big deal by starting to eat first—I'll act as their 'royal taster.'"

Neeta had suppressed her irritation. This was serious to her, and she was in no mood for Narin's levity. She'd forced a smile, nodded, and touched his hand. He'd grasped it eagerly and tried to draw her to him, but she resisted, patting him with her other hand. "I have lots of things to do."

As she left the room, she heard Narin say, trying to suppress his laughter, "And I hope you've kept the liquor out of sight."

SHEELA TENDED TO sleep late on weekends, but her Aunt Kala woke her at eight a.m. She looked at her aunt's smiling face with a surge of affection, remembering how welcoming Kala had been when she'd been sent to Madras to "straighten out" her problems. She was grateful that Aunt Kala had continued to encourage her in her studies and her work. Now, Sheela had reached the point of wanting her independence complete. Life was stabilizing. She had come to terms with the ending of her pregnancy, the psychological scars of which far outlived the physical. After giving her lover various excuses, she had recently begun to meet him again. After the first, extremely fraught meeting, she'd learned to relax again and enjoy his company. Even her guilt had softened considerably.

She wondered when she would summon the courage to tell her aunt she was going to get her own flat. Would Aunt Kala see this as abandonment? Sad that only boys, and not even all of them, were allowed to exercise this desire. Girls like her were complete outliers.

"Ready for the grand meeting?" Kala said.

"As much as I can be. Tell me again why you and Uncle aren't going?"

"I told you, we discussed it with Narin. There'll be quite a crowd there, and we thought having us would be too much. Too many cooks and all that."

"Narin would like your support."

"Yes, that's true. But it's complicated. We don't know all the details. Besides, your uncle doesn't enjoy conflict."

"But he's a lawyer."

"Doesn't like family conflict, I should've said. It's different, he claims, from a court presentation, which is impersonal, you know, and well regulated."

"Which is more than we can say for Aunties Sara and Saran."

"Now you remember to be polite to them."

"And when am I not polite?"

"Well, the way you talk about them is scandalous. You're lucky I don't tell half of it to your uncle. Or your parents. If you don't watch out, that language will come across when you see them next time."

Sheela shook her head. It had been a long time since she'd met her twin aunts. She no longer felt the dread of their presence as she had when she lived in Venpuri, because she was a different person now, no longer the odd-girl-out in her late teens. She felt confident that no mere aunts could threaten her self-assuredness. And yet their overpowering aura was not to be dismissed lightly.

The hairs on her arms stood up, and she shivered even in the warmth of the sun-filled room.

NARIN HAPPENED TO be standing on the balcony when he heard the squeal of ill-maintained brakes from a taxi below as it came to a bouncy halt. With a knot in his stomach, he first saw his aunts emerge, then his mother, none of whom he had seen for several years. He waved, though they weren't looking up at him. When he hurried downstairs, he found the others standing around, but his father was still in the taxi, haggling with the driver. Narin helped him out, and he noticed his father was moving slowly and appeared more tired than the trials of the extended journey might warrant. Mohan jerked back as the taxi rushed by inches away from him. He smiled austerely at his son, and they shook hands. Narin turned to his mother and was glad when she opened her arms to give him a hug. He nodded to his aunts, giving them the barest of *namaskaars*, and they reciprocated in kind. They looked unaged, as if by some quirk of stasis.

"Here, I'll get our servant to get the luggage," Narin said, taking a small suitcase himself. "Let's go up." He waved them toward the lobby of the apartment building, which had an ornate, fake marble staircase leading to the upstairs flats.

"How far up is it?" asked Sara, panting after a few dozen stairs.

"Third floor, I believe," answered her sister.

"No one in Venpuri lives above the second floor. It's not natural."

"You'd think they'd have a lift, grand as they are," Saran said, heedless of whether Narin, behind them, could overhear.

Neeta stood at the wide open door of the apartment. She had decided not to come down to greet the group, sending Narin instead, delaying the inevitable for a few moments. An awkward pause ensued as everybody stopped. Narin's mother, Jyothi, broke the impasse, moved forward, and greeted Neeta.

"How are you?" Her tone exuded genuineness, and she took Neeta's hands in hers. "I'm so glad to meet you at last. Thank you for having us."

Sara and Saran were perplexed by the sincerity of Jyothi's greeting. With a glance at each other, they made the best of it while reverting to their current quibble.

"All these stairs, they're so tiring, no?" said one.

"It must be so much hotter up here," said the other.

Neeta was polite but noncommittal as she greeted them, and they muttered their greetings in return. Narin, in passing, gave her arm a reassuring squeeze and shooed the group into the living room.

Narin had borrowed some furniture from a neighbor to add to the sparsely furnished room. Saraswathi and Saranmathi headed for the only couch present to sit together as they always did. Narin steered his parents to other comfortable chairs. As they all settled in, Sheela, who had arrived before her parents and aunts, entered with a tray of drinks.

Narin noticed his aunts staring fixedly at the many drawings on the walls.

"What on earth is that thing?" inquired Sara, pointing at an abstract drawing in many hues, punctuated with an angry diagonal slash of black.

"It's a representation of the Goddess Seeta's agony at her consort doubting her loyalty," Narin said, parroting the description he had extracted from Neeta months ago.

"Really? Where is Seeta anyway?" Saran got up for a closer look. "I don't see her at all. Who painted it?"

"It's a drawing. By Neeta."

Sara and Saran glanced at each other, considering how to proceed.

Jyothi jumped in. "Neeta, I didn't know you were an artist. Narin never wrote to me about that."

"Yes, I do a lot of drawings," Neeta replied softly.

"Well, I'm sure it's nice to have them where you and Narin can enjoy them."

"You should see some of her work from before," Sheela said, a twinkle in her eye. "They're called caricatures. Amusing drawings of people that are quite telling. But she's getting staid in her old age and only does these types of things, called abstracts."

"It's not good to make fun of people," Saraswathi said, or maybe it was Saranmathi.

"Auntie, that's not quite what a caricature is. It exaggerates the strange or odd side of people. It's meant to show their hidden characteristics instead of the outward ones."

Saran was still focused on the Seeta portrait. "This is much too hidden for me. I don't like it at all," she declared.

Jyothi played the peacemaker again. "Where's your son, Narin?"

Narin and Neeta both rose and moved toward the door, almost bumping into each other. Neeta stopped him with a gesture, saying as she left the room, "I was sure Vish was here. Maybe he's playing outside. I'll find him."

"He must've heard us come. We were making all this noise," Saran said.

"Surprising he wouldn't want to see his grandparents as soon as possible," her sister added.

Narin let out an irritated sigh. He turned to his parents. "Appa, I'm sorry your journey was so bad. Where did you stay last night? Did you manage to get a decent dinner?"

"Terrible, both terrible," Mohan said. "We were in Ozhukarai, at the Grand Lakeside something Hotel. Lake, my foot! No water anywhere nearby. Maybe that was better, as I can imagine how much worse the mosquitoes would've been."

"Terrible," concurred his wife.

"I told you we should've sent a telegram to Cousin Bharat to pick us up and drive us here. You know he had nothing better to do," said Sara as her sister nodded in vigorous agreement.

Mohan sighed. "And I told you it would've taken much longer with the state of the road between Ozhukarai and here. How could all five of us fit in his tiny Morris Minor with our things?" He paused a moment. "And the accident—the railways have such incompetents working for them now."

"Yes, all that rubbish about promoting the scheduled castes," interjected Saran. "I'm sure it was one of them who caused the accident. And it's all because of that Ambedkar fellow."

Narin rolled his eyes at the term "scheduled castes," which referred to historically disadvantaged groups, designated as discrete entities in the recently enacted Constitution of India. Dr. Ambedkar, a framer of the constitution, belonged to one of these castes. He had created a system of reserving places in schools, colleges, and workplaces for those of such castes, which only increased prejudice against them. Narin was thankful for the absence of his brother-in-law, Jaggie, who would no doubt have delivered a treatise on the inequities of the quota system.

His father backpedaled. "I'm not saying that at all, Cousin Saran. Just that the standards have fallen. People just don't want to work like we used to in our day." This earned a vigorous nod from his cousins, who appeared poised to continue the topic but were interrupted as Neeta returned with Vishram in tow.

The boy was dressed in his best khaki short-pants and a white shirt, not his usual disheveled outfit, and his hair showed signs of a hasty brushing. Voices quieted as he entered the room. Narin waved for him to come over, but Vishram, seeing Sheela, started his usual boisterous greeting, which he stopped on seeing Narin frown at him.

His grandmother Jyothi came over to embrace him. "What a beautiful boy," she exclaimed. She turned behind her to retrieve a small package, which she handed him.

"What is it?" asked Vish.

"Just say, 'Thank you, Grandma,'" Neeta admonished, and Vish mouthed a hasty thanks as he began to rip away the newspaper wrapping.

"He looks very much like you, Narin," Mohan said.

"I'm not like Appa. My skin is much lighter," Vish said, looking up at his mother as he untied a last knot, "like a North Indian." The twins let out a gasp.

He opened the package and extracted a carved wooden statuette of Ganesh, the elephant god, looked at it in puzzlement for a moment, then flashed a smile at his grandmother. "Thank you again, Amm-amma."

Though yet to hear from his formidable aunts, who were uncharacteristically silent, Narin was thankful that his parents accepted his son. Five years ago, when he'd written to them the terrible news of Vikrant's death, it had been gut-wrenching that they had not ventured beyond politeness. He realized how tense he had been when they'd asked about Vish, and now he relaxed, noting the genuine pleasure on his mother's face as she followed Vish with her eyes.

"Don't mention it, dear. You should keep it carefully. Ganesh brings luck. And you are going to school where?"

"Saint Stephens."

"Saint … what? Is that a Christian school?" barked Saran.

"Why on earth are you sending him there?" Sara asked.

"Auntie, it's not like that," Sheela said. "The convents run the best nursery schools in Madras. In fact, many of the good higher schools, too. They're very disciplined and give a good education. He's not going to start worshiping Jesus or anything."

"Well, I may," said Vish, twirling Ganesh around his head like a toy airplane. "Sister Catherine is always saying that Jesus will save us all."

There was a collective gasp. Narin glared at his son, willing him to be quiet, but didn't say anything as he was sure it would worsen the situation.

"Vish, you know we've discussed this, and it's how religious people talk," Neeta said before any of the others could speak. "You know we must respect their opinions, but we have our own, don't we?"

"Okay, Amma. I know we're Hindus, and Shiva is the best of all the gods."

This curious recommendation did not appear to satisfy anyone but Jyothi. "Well said, Vish. Let's talk about something else. You should say *namaskaar* to your grand-aunties here. This is Auntie Saranmathi, and this is Auntie Saraswathi. They have come a long way to see you."

Vish greeted them using the grand-aunt honorific and added, "I don't know any other twins. You do look alike." His smile disarmed them, and they held their fire. He sat back down and raised the Ganesh figure again. "Oh, have you read the *Two Brothers* by Grimm? There are twins in there. Also monste—"

"*Stop*," Neeta interrupted in a shaky voice. "I'm sure your grand-aunts know all about … that story, Vish. Now let your grandparents look at you."

"But they are," protested Vish. "I'm not hiding, am I?"

Neeta gave him another frown. He accepted a glass of lemonade from her and put on a demure expression. Narin, who thought he could've monitored his rapidly fluctuating blood pressure without any instruments, tried to relax.

"AND WHERE DO you get your *sambhar* powder?" Jyothi asked Neeta.

Lunch had been served, and the four hungry travelers were tucking in, Sara and Saran satisfied that the fare was not too tainted by Konkan culinary influences.

"Oh, my mother sends it to me."

"All the way from Konkan? How interesting—"

"I didn't know they even ate *sambhar* up north," said Saran, "but this is quite good."

Sara shot her a look of displeasure for praising a foreign ingredient and for once was ignored.

"Thank you. Amma will be pleased."

"You're not eating much at all," said Jyothi, noting Neeta's half-hearted attempts to eat food that tasted like red-hot needles to her.

"Oh, I tasted all the food as it was being cooked," Neeta said with a disarming smile, "and I must've filled myself up."

"Amma, this food is hotter than Auntie Kala's," Vish chimed in. "No wonder—"

"*Yes*, Vish," Neeta said through clenched teeth. "Please finish your lunch, and you can go play with your friend next door."

Lunch had been cleared away, and the family sat back in their chairs, sipping water and *mohhr*. Narin longed for his trademark whiskey, or maybe two. Sheela, reading his mind, winked at him.

Vish asked his mother if he could leave.

Narin exclaimed, "Yes," relieved that there'd be no more outbursts of candor from his son.

Vish jumped up with Ganesh aloft, threw a cheery *namaskaar* to the adults, and dashed out, knocking over a glass of water on the way.

"Now that the boy has left, Narin, maybe we should get down to business," Mohan said. "We missed the first day of court. How did it proceed?"

Narin gave them a brief summary, omitting the contretemps about the consummation ceremony. He thought it best to go right to the most difficult point. "The main problem for me is how the court will calculate the amount of maintenance. Mutthuswamy says that Castle can claim, legitimately per law, that I 'abandoned' Mina six years ago, and therefore must pay her the money from that time. He, of course, will argue that no abandonment followed and that maintenance should only start at the point of the divorce."

"Castle?" asked Saraswathi.

"James Castle, Mina's counsel."

"A Britisher? How on earth do they afford him?"

"Let's not go into all that, cousin," Mohan said in a placating manner. "It only matters if he is a capable lawyer."

"More," said Narin. "A shark, I think they call him."

"Mr. Mutthuswamy is also quite good, Appa," Sheela said. "He knows Mr. Castle well, so recognizes his tactics. They've done plenty of 'jousting,' as I think he called it."

"And how would you know, young as you are?" asked Saran.

Sheela sighed. "I'm not that young. And Narin has been discussing these matters a lot with me in the last few weeks. And I've been in meetings with Mutthuswamy."

This evidence of autonomy on Sheela's part did not please Sara and Saran, and they exchanged a meaningful look. Saran said, "What if the judge—what's his name—Karthikan—is he a Brahmin by the way?—says you have to pay from the beginning, Narin? How will you manage that?"

"Not all at once, I hope. There will probably be some kind of payment program."

"Perhaps I can help," his father offered. "If it's a monthly amount, it will be easier."

Jyothi murmured her assent.

Narin started, surprised and pleased at his father's unexpected offer.

"Oh, that would be wonderful, Appa," Sheela said. "Can you afford it, though?"

"Don't insult your father. Of course he can," Sara snapped. "Do you think he's a pauper?"

"Well, thank you for the offer, Appa," Narin said, "but it's my responsibility, and I will manage somehow if that's the decision."

"What about the dowry?" Saran asked.

"What about it? I don't think the court will care."

Sheela said, "No, Narin, remember this could be considered a nullified contract—I think that's what Uncle Maruti called it—so it may have to be returned."

"They didn't give us much anyway," said Saran, arbitrarily placing herself in the group that had benefited from the long-ago settlement. "And you didn't listen to us, Mohan, or we would've got more."

"It's not the amount that matters now, cousin," Mohan said. "If it comes to that, we can find all the things they gave us, or others the same, and return them." Ignoring her shocked look, he turned to Narin. "What other issues are there?"

"Counselor Mutthuswamy says the other side will claim that I did not respond to Mina's—actually her father's—repeated requests that she wanted to live with me." He noted his father's puzzled face, and his aunts gathering steam for a rebuttal, and forestalled them. "If they can show that, it would indicate bad faith about the marriage on my part, so might be grounds for a bigger settlement for them."

His father's face was drawn. "Did you ignore these repeated requests?"

"Of course not," said Neeta.

"And how would you know for sure?" asked Sara with a dismissive sneer. "Were you watching Narin every time he wrote back to the Vasans?"

"Don't be ridiculous, Auntie," Sheela said. "Of course Neeta would've read Narin's letters to his *Mamanaar.* And I know from talking with both of them that they had many discussions regarding the matter."

The twins clearly didn't approve of this show of support from Sheela, and Sara was about to respond when Mohan took charge again. "It must be a technical legal issue, yes? Not so much a matter of Narin replying to each of the actual letters."

"Well, we got so many for a while," said Narin, "I'm sure I skipped a few. Neeta and I used to say they just mimeographed different sections of the letters to create a new one." He smiled, but no one responded to this attempt at humor.

Neeta pursed her lips, wishing Narin wouldn't make light of the matter.

Sheela leaned toward her brother and whispered, "I wouldn't say that in court."

A chorus of simultaneous questions and comments arose, much of it from Saraswathi and Saranmathi, with no one listening to any of the others. Mohan finally held up his hand for silence. He waited a moment for the babble around him to subside. "We should try to stay with the subject. I doubt Mina said she wanted to live with Narin. That's her father speaking, but the court can still use it against him. Mutthuswamy will have to rebut it. We cannot change facts."

"So the final result is that Narin has to pay a lot of money." Sara said, "Did I not say this would happen?"

"And we may end up paying, as well," said her sister.

Narin chuckled inwardly at the thought of his redoubtable aunts paying any of his debt. Pity he couldn't tune them out as he used to do as a teenager.

"Narin should have tried to settle this years ago," said Sara.

"He could have been less stubborn about it," said her sister.

Mohan strained on the arms of his chair as he got to his feet. "I'm stiff with all this sitting. And getting a headache. I'm going outside to get some air and walk around for a few minutes. Good for the digestion, they say. See if you can find any ideas while I'm away." He left the room with heavy steps, and Jyothi rose to follow him out.

SHEELA REFILLED THE visitors' glasses as an uneasy silence fell, then fixated on the outside world's intrusions—the sound of heavy traffic on the main road, horns blaring intermittently, the squawks of sparrows peeping inquisitively through the open windows, prevented from entering not by the widely spaced bars, but by their instinct of self-preservation. She looked side-eyed at the Aunties S, who were breathing noisily as they gazed ahead, no doubt gathering momentum for some storm ahead, and wondered how long they'd stay so belligerent. She envied the birds outside and wished she could flutter away with equal ease.

Saran reverted to her favorite preoccupation. "Divorce. And now we will have this blot on our family. I'm sure it will affect the marriage chances of all our children. And our grandchildren."

"Our neighbor Sekhar was commiserating with us just yesterday," her sister added. "I don't think he was being sympathetic. Cousin Mohan isn't the only one to have to bear the burden of this disaster."

"Nor do you, really, Aunties," Sheela said. "Think how much worse it is for Narin, Neeta, and Mina."

The sisters turned as one toward her.

"You're a fine one to talk."

"Fat lot of help you've been here."

"What on earth do you mean, Auntie? I told you I've been meeting with Narin, Neeta, and Mutthuswamy for months. Of course I've been helping them."

"That's a fine thing. But you were always egging Narin on. Do you think we don't know what the two of you used to talk about while cavorting around on that swing in the back?"

This unexpected attack threw Sheela. The venom in their words staggered Narin.

"In Venpuri, Auntie? We were young … children, really. We just liked to be away from all the adults in the house. What do you think we were doing wrong?"

"Plotting, that's what. Always discussing how boring life was in our nice town. Always wanting something fresh. Always looking for excitement."

"That's simply not true," said Sheela, close to tears. "I was happy in Venpuri."

"Not happy enough to listen to us, though, were you?"

"What? About my getting married? Auntie, I've heard enough about that over the last ten years. Both boys you selected were … strange."

"Strange? Easy for you to say. It's the best you could expect, anyway. If you hadn't been so high and mighty, those boys would've been fine for you."

"That's quite unfair of you, Auntie," Narin said. "Sheela was always an obedient girl."

"Look at her now."

"Even the way she dresses. It's different. Not modest at all."

Sheela looked down at the folds of her light-green sari. Was it too tight? Was her blouse too short? She'd always considered her attire tasteful. She was confused and beginning to panic. She wished someone would comfort her—Narin? Neeta? "Auntie, what can you be talking about? This is the way all of us my age dress in Madras."

"Exactly!"

She could think of little to say to this definitive statement.

"Auntie, Sheela is happy living in Madras," Narin said. "Which, I might add, was your idea in the first place. She worked hard to get her degree, which isn't easy after you haven't been studying for a while. And she has a good job that she loves. Can't you see she is better off now than if she were living alone in Venpuri? Or married to some boy who wouldn't fulfill her?"

Sheela flashed him a grateful look.

"Fulfill? You talk about being fulfilled, but are you, Sheela?" Saran said, turning the full power of her displeasure on her niece. "I know you think you're happy now, but what about all you missed? What about children?" She paused for effect. "I see how you look at Vishram and long for a child. And a husband? Can you walk around freely when people know you are not married?"

The world was collapsing around Sheela. Her newfound confidence was evaporating under the pressure of her aunts' diatribes.

They'd hit on the one element of her life that she'd kept out of her thoughts. She thought back to four years before, when she'd talked with Narin of her acceptance at not being married and the joy of "not having a nasty mother-in-law." If only it were that simple. Her ambivalence, protectively bottled, safely unexamined, boiled up inside her as she considered her feelings for her nephew. Had Auntie Saran seen her feelings for what they were when Vish had run toward her with his usual effusive welcome? Was she so transparent? Was the presence of husband and children the sole indicator of happiness? Was she fooling herself?

She looked at her Aunt Saranmathi, then at Aunt Saraswathi, and was repelled by their censoriousness. She had to say something. She took a deep breath to collect herself. Narin seemed poised to jump in again on her behalf, but she held up a hand to stop him.

"You know, I *am* quite happy where I am. I know you think that being married and having children is the only way to be, but it's not. If I could redo my life and have it the way I wanted it, maybe being married would be good, but as it is, I've known for a long time that I will never be married, so I have accepted that. And I've talked about this over and over with Auntie Kala. She agrees with me and is very supportive. You don't know me anymore. I'm not the child I was ten years ago."

Jyothi, who had overheard as she came back into the room, said, "Sheela, you mustn't be rude to your aunties."

"Rude? I'm sorry if you think that's rude, Amma, but I must be clear about myself." She turned to her brother. "Narin, do you think I was rude?"

Narin had the look of a deer caught in headlights. "Sheel, I'm sure Aunties didn't mean it the way you took it. You have changed a lot in your manner of speaking, and Aunties aren't used to it."

Sheela looked at her brother in disbelief. They had talked about this confrontation for weeks, and he'd always been the one to prop her up, to support her, to suggest she should take no more guff from their aunts. Now he was backing away. Didn't mean it that way? No, that's *exactly* the way they'd meant it. To hurt. To show she was wrong, wrong all along in the path she'd chosen. The betrayal turned into a painful knot in her stomach. She felt conflicted in a way she never had before. She dropped her eyes while she collected herself, then raised them to look at her aunts, whose stern gaze had not left her.

Jyothi put her knitting down with a shaking hand, rose awkwardly, and said, "I thought my husband was coming right behind me. I should go find him."

Saraswathi watched Jyothi disappear into the outside corridor. Then she swiveled toward Sheela. "And we know what happened to you."

"What ... happened? When? What are you talking about?"

"Don't be thinking you can keep your secret to yourself, Sheela. We know, but we never told your parents, our favorite cousins, because we know it would have killed them. Their youngest daughter."

Sheela was staring at her aunts, who had never appeared friendly to her, but now appeared like menacing *naga* serpents. She looked at them, and they looked at her, and the stunning realization came upon her that they were not joking. They actually knew. They could not, she tried to persuade herself, they could not. It wasn't possible. How? When? Who had told them? She had to know.

"What are you talking about?" she asked in as calm a tone as she could muster.

"You know what. Your child. And what happened to it."

The world collapsed to rubble, grinding Sheela to dust. The impossible had happened, up had turned down. Tears swelled in her eyes as she moaned, "No. No. You cannot know. How? Who told you?"

Sheela heard an inarticulate sound from Neeta, who had frozen, her pretty face turned almost ugly. It took Sheela a second to realize it was not disgust but shock, shock tinged with the deepest concern.

She turned to look at her brother, who looked equally stunned, shaking his head as he mouthed, "Impossible. Impossible."

Saraswathi waited a few moments before continuing. "Yes, Sheela, we've known for over a year. And we know whom you were gallivanting with as well. A married man, too. Of the Vaishya caste. Mr. Nirathnan told Jaggie, who, of course, told his father."

Saranmathi added, "Cousin Subbu had the good sense not to tell your father, but he told us, as he thought someone else in the family should know of this terrible event." She looked at her sister, and in a tone that suggested she was talking about nothing more weighty than his giving them the time of day, continued. "I never thought Subbu could be so sensible."

Narin, stuttering, said, "Nirath … nan? Who the hell is that?"

"The man who's been keeping track of you, Narin," said Saran, "employed by Jaggie. And in watching you, he sometimes gathered information on your sister as well. She was at your house a lot, so he must have followed her many times. You've met him, apparently. He was at the station six years ago when you and Neeta were going off to Bangalore and your brother-in-law, Jaggie, and Subbu were at the platform with Mina."

Sheela, Neeta, and Narin turned toward each other as they shared an awful realization. This was the man whom they'd wondered about at the station, a stranger at a family meeting, one who didn't look "middle class" enough to be a friend and, tellingly, had not been introduced by Jaggie. Remembering that he'd seemed more than interested in studying the family members who were present to see Narin and Neeta off.

"And you, Narin, to have done such a thing—your own sister. Just because you're a doctor."

It took Narin a moment to realize what his aunt was accusing him of.

"How dare you!" Sheela yelled. "How dare you bring this up?"

"It's against the law, that's why. Narin could be thrown in jail. And all for you."

Sheela stood up slowly, as if in a dream, crying freely. She stumbled as she negotiated the low table in front of her. Neeta, unfrozen, rose to her side and attempted to take her arm, but Sheela pushed her away. She began to run as she reached the door, arms swinging as she prevented Narin from stopping her as well.

She ran through the outer room of the flat, through the open front door, slamming it behind her, and clattered down the steps. Vish was running up the steps as he returned from his play session. She did not register his look of dismay at her ignoring him as she swung past or hear his cry of "Auntie Sheela, what—?"

Sheela ran.

Sheela ran down the stairs, heedless of the detritus digging painfully into her bare soles.

She ran, almost tripping on every uneven, unforgiving tread, her toes curled for purchase, her body swaying as she careened. She righted herself and paused at the foot of the stairs in the marble lobby, blinking at the sharp points of light reflected from the merciless afternoon sun streaming through the open front windows, mottling sparkles of reflected light on the yellow walls.

She leaned against the banister and took deep gulping breaths, willing herself to be calm, but failing. Her mind was dying, it must be; how else to explain this agony, this pain?

She heard her name being called, footsteps behind her. Who was following her and why? She wanted to be alone; she had to be alone in some dark and welcoming corner to soothe her bruises. She looked up and behind her, her vision blurry, not recognizing who was there—saviors or tormentors?

She needed to get away.

Sheela pushed herself away from her support and ran out of the building into the street.

The noisy, dirty street. The crowded, traffic-filled, unforgiving street.

Sheela ran, turning to the left to escape her imagined pursuers. Her bare feet stung on the uneven, hot black macadam. Her foot dropped into a pothole, and her body swiveled grotesquely to the right, full square into the path of the speeding red garland-adorned Bedford Motors RL lorry.

295

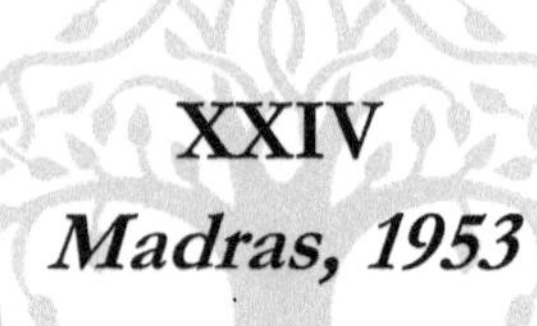

XXIV
Madras, 1953

Thirty-two hours later, Laxman took Narin's arm in his, a consoling gesture much appreciated by Narin. Laxman had flown in immediately from Bangalore on receiving an anguished telegram from Narin. If Ambika had not been nine months pregnant, she would have joined him.

"It's not your fault, Narin," Laxman said as they walked from the funeral pyre. "It's not."

Narin stared into the distance. Pain tore at his gut. "It doesn't matter if it wasn't. She's gone."

They had watched saffron-clad priests stack the wood pyre, ceremoniously lit by Narin's father and other male relatives.

They had watched as Sheela's white-shrouded remains were licked by the consuming flames, her body reflexively jerking and writhing as a last gasp of protest against death.

They had watched the fire's burning fingers climb higher and higher until the flames and smoke mercifully blotted the final indignities from their somber view.

Narin looked back at the pyre a moment before turning away, choking back his tears. "I can't believe my aunts. I can't believe they brought it up to her like that. We should've found another way."

"We could never have thought of this, Narin, none of us. We did the best for her."

"And the best was not good enough."

"Narin, stop, please."

Narin opened his half-closed eyes to look at Laxman, his co-conspirator in this dreadful debacle. His friend, who had twice arrived from Bangalore at his time of need, first to help his sister and now to help him. How could he ever repay this debt of gratitude? He thought of his other trial, the other death, his first-born, when Laxman had also been present and had stood by him.

Death. The antithesis of life, of all that he stood for, all that he had studied, and all that he strived for in his work.

"It's fate, isn't it?"

"What do you mean?"

"We can't escape it, Lax. Karma. It's like a spiteful onlooker, waiting for you to make a mistake so it can punish you."

"Narin, it's hardly that—"

"Yes, it is. I know my abandoning Mina must've led to my son being taken from me."

Laxman was shocked but stayed silent.

"And fate killed Sheela, too. She too had done wrong. It's inevitable. Inescapable."

The head priest was approaching them, an older man clad in saffron robes, face and bare arms bedecked with ashes. Narin's voice had carried enough for him to overhear. His face was troubled, and he extended a comforting hand to Narin.

"No, my son. Remember our holy text, the *Bhagwath Gita*, extols us to be wary of the influence of the false self. The ignorant think that they themselves are the doers of activities, but in reality, the material nature does those activities. It is a result of the interaction of the three *gunas* and material nature. All actions are performed as a matter of duty."

Narin was in no mood for metaphysical digression. "Duty? The ignorant? I'm sorry, *Shri puccari*, you have no idea of my sister and her gentle and happy spirit. If you are implying that she deserved this, you are wrong."

"No, Narin," Laxman said, "that's not what the honorable priest is saying. He means that, according to our *Gitas*, our natures control our actions."

The priest nodded in agreement, his features still concerned. He was about to continue, but Narin forestalled him. "Nature? So we don't have to admit responsibility for what we do? It's just some primal forces making our choices? So can I deny what I do? Or what someone else does? Karma. I cannot excuse the repercussions of karma, but I have to accept them."

The priest scowled at Narin but said nothing, and after a moment, he plodded away, shaking his head. Narin imagined his back radiating displeasure at this youngster daring to question ageless Hindu wisdom. No matter. His grief burdened him, and he'd have to cope with it in his own manner.

A sudden shift of wind sent a cloud of acrid black smoke floating low over the area, turning, swirling, its leading edge sporting tendrils like an angry hand blindly searching for earthbound victims. Laxman put his arm around Narin's shoulders and led him out of the crematorium, both coughing copiously.

NARIN PICKED UP the pile of unanswered letters lying on his desk. As he riffled through them, he noticed one without a return address. A Madras postmark. He opened it and read in Tamil:

> Dear Husband Narinder,
>
> I write to express my deepest condolences on the tragic passing of Elder-Sister Sheela. Words cannot express my sorrow. She was a wonderful friend to me even though I only saw her occasionally. We wrote to each other over the years, and she was very supportive of me. I will miss her deeply, as I am sure you and your

family will also. I am so very sorry for your loss. God's ways are difficult and not always comprehensible. I hope you will find solace in prayer.

Your Wife Minalakshmi

With further surprise, Narin saw a postscript in English, some words struck out and rewritten:

I stay with Elder-Brother Jaggie in Madras now. He has me working with a teacher for three months now. It is much to enjoy. If you want help on anything, please tell me. Maybe one day matters will be better by you and me. God bless.

Narin was shocked to find tears had clouded his eyes.

A SOMBER NARIN and Neeta met his lawyer Mutthuswamy outside the courthouse two months later, his divorce case having been adjourned due to his sister's death. They entered the dark-paneled courtroom with its whirring fans, its dismal lighting, and its ominous hushed tones, waiting for the rituals of the law to begin again.

Soon plaintiff's counsel, James Castle, was questioning Narin again. "Let me return to the issue of Mrs. Minalakshmi's desire to live with you, Dr. Narinder. You agree that that was her desire?"

"Yes," Narin said in a low voice.

"Did you at any time entertain her request?"

"It was quite impossible for her to live with us—with me—after the birth of my first child."

"And before that? I would like to point out that there was a period of …" He looked down at his papers, picked one up and brandished it. "… more than four years between your full acceptance of my client as your wife, and the birth of your first son."

"Yes—"

"And during that time, Mrs. Minalakshmi wrote you several letters on this issue? Which you treated in a cavalier fashion."

"Not cavalier, sir. It was simply not possible for me to comply."

"So ultimately, you admit that you had no intention of allowing the plaintiff to stay with you?"

"Yes. Yes."

"That would be considered abandonment under the law." Castle looked at him placidly.

Narin was silent.

Castle tried to conceal a smirk. "Dr. Janappan, you realize the import of what you are saying?"

"Yes, I suppose so."

"It implies your acceptance of the premise of abandonment."

Narin looked around a moment as if unsure whether he should agree or not and what that might mean to his case. Did it matter? Yes, he knew what his counsel might advise and what Neeta might say. His breath caught as he realized he'd almost added "and what Sheela might say." He tried to put the pain behind him. She was no longer there to be his rock of support. Tears came to his eyes, and he blinked hard to clear them. He made up his mind.

"I don't really care, Counselor. However much I can blame my father-in-law for not heeding my words and making alternate arrangements for my first wife—he should've had his daughter's happiness at heart—but however much I blame others, the main blame devolves on me. It cannot be denied. This is one of those mistakes you commit and for which there is no remedy."

"I have no further questions, Your Learned Honor."

"Your witness, Counselor Mutthuswamy."

NARIN PAID LITTLE attention to further proceedings, to the opposing counselors as they delivered their closing statements, to the somnolent observers, to Learned Justice Karthikan as he delivered the terms of the settlement in his sonorous voice, which concentrated the attention of those in the courtroom.

"In justice to him and in fairness to his second wife, so that no aspersion should be cast against her, he should have started sending a monthly allowance to the plaintiff from the date of his second marriage. It is not as though he was not in a position to do so. He was in active medical service, drawing a decent salary. Admittedly with the savings effected at that time, he and his second wife were living in a comfortable house in Madras. For a young girl rotting away here in misery, that must have been a tremendous heartache ..."

Narin thought about Vikrant. And Sheela. He looked at Neeta at his side, sitting stone-faced, watching the judge.

Irrelevant, he wants to scream. All this is irrelevant. Two of the beings most precious to me have been whisked away, and I must stand unresponsive. My aunts soldier on, trailing destruction in their wake, and sleep soundly every night on their overstuffed silk-cotton *metthais*.

Karthikan concluded, "The actions taken by Mrs. Minalakshmi's brother and father toward the plaintiff were surely predicated by their desire for her happiness ..."

Happiness? Narin reflected on the ephemeral nature of happiness, the unpredictable and unexpected turns of fate. What must he do to protect himself from reliving this agonizing pain? Must he stay distanced from life, must he be less involved, so as to better weather its inevitable punches? And how would that affect his relationship with his beloved Neeta and with his son, Vishram?

XXV
Chennai (formerly Madras), 2001

Vishram left the Vivanta by Taj Hotel and turned onto the wide, crowded sidewalk of Bharathi Salai, strolling past the pleasures of the Jam Bazaar—rated by Lonely Planet as a must-see—with its mountains of fruit, vegetables, and pungent spices. He dripped with sweat and paused to drink the refreshing milk of a green coconut, freshly sliced by the vendor's deadly looking machete.

He was heading to a complex of buildings twenty minutes away. He had determined that the Durga Flats was the last address of Mrs. Minalakshmi Janappan, who'd lived there from 1958 until her death in 1990. The irony of the complex's name was not lost on him. Durga, also known as Parvati, is the fierce Hindu Goddess of love, power, and devotion, often depicted with weapons of war. Love and power were notably absent in Mina's constricted life.

Devotion? Yes, she had that, an emotion abundantly misdirected toward his unwilling father. The last of her letters he'd found, written in 1973, still betrayed an undercurrent of longing to live with Narin. With a man who had ignored her for thirty-three years. With a man who had saluted her in letters as "Dear

Madam." Who'd haggled with her at every turn about the level of maintenance he owed her. Maybe hope does spring eternal.

The Durga had more than twenty three-story buildings of massive proportions set in a large compound. Cars and two-wheelers were parked helter-skelter on the dirt. A few attempts at greenery had been cordoned off by low rock walls, protected by "No Spitting" signs. Coconut and neem trees abounded. Children, seemingly hundreds of them, were running and playing without a care, dodging the occasional fast-moving vehicle that made scant effort to accommodate them. No mothers were present, testifying either to the area's safety or to their indifference.

No one paid any attention to him as he wandered through the yard. He found a faded sign indicating "Office" and followed its direction to one of the buildings, where he glimpsed several desks through open windows. He nodded to the khaki-clad guard, walked into the office, and waited in front of the first occupied desk he saw. The clerk wore a stained white shirt and white pants and sported a fat black pair of incongruous Ray-Ban sunglasses. He raised his half-balding head.

"Yes?"

"I'm trying to get some information about a Mrs. Janappan who lived here until a few years ago."

"Mrs. Minalakshmi Janappan?"

"Yes."

"What do you wish to know? You are where from?"

"Ah, from abroad." To convey a sense of urgency, Vishram added, "I'm here for a few days only. She is—was—known to my father, Dr. Narinder Janappan of Victoria ... Varasavakkam Hospital." He stumbled over the name that had replaced the Colonial Era one. It was important to drop connections. Everyone knew of this major hospital down the road, even if they might not know the person.

"Of course. Son of the ex-director? Good. I knew Mrs. Minalakshmi quite well. She lived here a long time, very long, yes, yes. She talked about your father a lot. Very good things."

No surprise. "Was she working? Did she have a job?"

"Yes, Kilpathy Plastics for a long time. Hard work, she said, but it was better than staying at home. She was finally doing well there. She was in charge of some small group of workers by the time she left in 1978 or so."

"What did she do after that? After she retired?"

"She was getting old, you know. I suppose she stayed at home lots."

"Did she have many friends here? Or many visitors?"

"Of course, yes, her brother … Mr. Jaggannath? The big lawyer, you know? He was coming to see her often. I think she was going to his house quite a lot, too. She told him all the time that Mrs. Jaggannath was such a good cook. And she had many friends here, too. You know, it's a very big place here, but very friendly too. A lot of people were finding Mrs. Minalakshmi very nice. And she was always joining in with things here. She was heading the tenants' group for a long time, too."

Vishram was thrilled to hear the clerk's account of Mina's accomplishments, a far cry from his previous impression of her.

"Do you think you can remember any of her particular friend's names?"

But too much time had passed. The clerk informed Vishram that the several people whose names he could have come up with had either died or moved to be with their families. Another dead end.

"This might seem strange, but do you know how I can find—or do you have—a picture of her?"

A wary mask dropped over his face as if he'd noticed something odd about this foreign visitor. "Why, *saar*?" he asked with a previously missing formality.

"She was really a good friend of my father, and I'm collecting photos of all his connections. I'm writing a memoir … a book about my father. Since I never met her, I don't know what she looked like."

He looked relieved. "Sorry, *saar*. I don't have any photographs of Mrs. Minalakshmi. Let me think. Maybe you can be contacting the son of her good friend, Mrs. Parthasarathy, now also passed, but who lives in Trichy."

"Do you happen to have his address? Or telephone number?"

"No, but he is living in Cantonment District there."

"Can you describe her? What did she look like?"

The wariness returned to his face as he seemed to be deciding exactly how strange his visitor was. "Look?" Confusion replaced wariness. "She was a woman, you know. Like many other women. What can I say how she looked like?"

He had been writing on a scrap of paper that he now handed to Vishram. It was the name of Mina's friend's son in Trichy. Vishram tucked it in his pocket. Further questions appeared hopeless. "Thank you very much. You have been of much help—"

The clerk held up a hand to stop Vishram and bent to rummage in a desk drawer. Moments later he emerged with a yellowed newspaper clipping in hand. "*Saar*, you may like this. I do not want it anymore."

Vishram glanced at, then pocketed the clipping. "Thank you again. *Po-ittu vuhrén*."

"*Suh-ree, saar.*"

Vishram walked out and rounded the corner, wending his way between a car and three scooters supporting each other like a surreal metal trinity. He glanced back and saw that the clerk had gotten up from his desk and was watching him from the office window. He waved to the man, but he did not respond.

Trichy was a city two hundred miles away. It didn't seem worth visiting on the off chance of finding a person of uncertain address who might have a photograph of Mina.

BACK IN HIS hotel room, Vishram reorganized the legal documents, letters, and miscellaneous remnants he'd found at his mother's house. He was thirsty. He pulled open the refrigerator to see a bottle of Indian Scotch—no mini-bottles here. It tempted him for some moments, but he'd been drinking much. He ordered superstrong Madras decoction coffee. Room service delivered it, and he emptied one cup and sat back in thought.

He had neglected the faded clipping in his pocket, and he now examined it. It was from *The India Times* dated December 20, 1984. The headline read, "Tenant Action at Durga Yields Results." The story, barely decipherable, detailed the success of a Mrs. Minalakshmi Janappan against the "rapacious" landlord of the Durga. She had initiated a rent strike in response to "atrocious conditions" and "abounding vermin" within many flats and had garnered widespread support. The reporter noted in discreet terms that there were rumors that Mrs. Janappan had been threatened, but she had persisted. There was a photograph of three people taken in front of the sign designating the Durga I building, but the caption was illegible. The outer two figures were men.

The central figure was a middle-aged woman with a wide smile on her face, her right hand clenched in a celebratory fist.

Vishram sat in reverie, troubled by the negative attitude his father had about Mina and Dr. Hansa's dismissal of her as "not industrious." Sad that they had not followed her later life.

Hansa—a particular incident from the '70s stormed into his memory. He'd graduated from college in Madras and would soon be on his way to America. His mother had gone downstairs a half-hour before as a visitor had been announced. She came back with a smile, looking exhilarated. She sat across from him and stared.

"What?" Vishram asked.

"It is the strangest thing. That was Dr. Hansa, you know, my bridge partner."

"I know Dr. Hansa, Ma. I'm surprised you didn't call me down to say hello to him."

"Well, he was in a hurry. But he had something particular to say. You'll never guess what it is."

His mother was never so coy. And she still looked, if not excited exactly, as if she had a surprising revelation to impart. "I have no idea, Ma. What?"

"He came to suggest that we should think about marrying you to his niece."

"What?"

"Yes, can you imagine? He must know your father and I have never even considered such a thing, and the whole idea of arranging a marriage for you … seems bizarre, no?"

"Yes. I wonder where he got the idea. Who is this anyway?"

"Preeta. You met years ago. She's in the U.S., New York, I think."

"Preeta Hansa?" he said, his eyes opening wide.

"Yes, why?"

"Oh, my god. She's been there for a year now, right? At NYU? I don't believe this. You remember my friend, my schoolmate Rajan, who went abroad after high school? He's at NYU, too, and he knows her well and …" He wondered whether to continue. His mother looked at him questioningly, so he plunged ahead. "And now she's living with someone. An older Jewish man, her professor, I think Rajan said."

His mother looked mystified. "Living with?" It took her a moment to realize the implications of that phrase, "living with a man" being unheard of in 1970s Madras. Puzzlement turned to shock. "No. You must be mistaken."

"Well, that's what Rajan said. More than once. I suppose her family knows nothing of it."

"No. Of course not. How terrible. Her mother would die if she knew."

"I don't think it's all that terrible, Ma."

"And Hansa thinks he can get her married? To you?"

"Well, I don't think they've consulted her." He smiled. "And she isn't married to this man. There's still hope for me." His mother did not smile. "Incidentally, why did this whole thing come up? What made him think of it?"

Neeta's shock wore away, and a half-smile appeared. "He said it might be best for a young boy like you, to keep you out of temptation. His words. Temptation. Vish, that's funny."

Funny was a curious word for it. He looked at his mother whose light olive face was glowing. He continued watching her, confused, as different emotions played on her countenance until she burst into laughter. After a moment or two, he joined in, not knowing why, but enjoying this moment of unrestrained hilarity on his mother's part, so unlike her and so exhilarating to participate in. After they had calmed down, he asked her what had been so risible.

She gave him no specific answer, repeating, "It's just too funny."

He had let it go then.

Now it made sense. The echo of the reason his father was given for his disastrous first marriage more than thirty years before had resonated with his mother. The same dubious impetus for an arranged marriage without consulting the compatibility or desires of the two parties. His mother's laughter had been a cover for her secret burden. Why hadn't she told him the truth then? Or ever?

Vishram gazed out the hotel window at the street below. A group of children floated by, dressed in khaki and black school uniforms, swinging their satchels, their voices audible even at this height. They were in pairs, boys with other boys, arms over shoulders, and girls with girls, some holding hands. He watched their laughing faces and childish jousting until they disappeared around the corner of the hotel.

Focusing on the children brought Elena's desire for adoption back to his mind. He rummaged around and found the faded photograph of him as an infant with Vikrant. He examined it closely, idly outlining his brother's image with his fingernail. He thought again of the shortcomings of his own only-child upbringing. How would a sibling for Neel play out? Shouldn't he want something more for Neel? Neel didn't seem as isolated as he'd been in his youth—only children being not uncommon these days, but still. He recalled pleasant memories of his aunts' and uncles' families, all with multiple children, the noise of siblings quarreling and making up, their obvious bonding, the mothers refereeing when things got out of hand.

He picked up the phone and punched Carla's number. Her machine answered. He took a deep breath. "Carla, it's me. I need the contact information of your friend Devi who runs that adoption agency. Thanks, and see you tomorrow."

Elena would be ecstatic.

He picked up some scattered documents and began stuffing them back into the folder. He was drawn again to Mina's letters to his father, easily recognizable as the paper was thinner and cheaper than others. He took note of her improving English in the later letters. One caught his eye; he hadn't noticed it before, but oddly, he found it was addressed to him. He smoothed out several pages to read the letter.

> May 13, 1988
> Dear Vishram,
> You may have never heard of me, so this may come as a complete shock. You may know me as Auntie Mina. I am old now, and the urgent need to send you this overrides any reticence I might have had before.
> I was young once. And insipid. And callow. And— here it is—I was married to your father in May 1936. I was thirteen years old. We divorced in 1953.

I was controlled by so many others when young. By my mother, whose decision it was to take me out of school, as there was no good reason for a girl to be educated. By my father, who concurred. By my Elder-Brother Jaggie, who saw everything through his narrow vision of how the world should be. And how sure they were of their vision, never doubting it, never altering it. Would it be better to feel that way? I often wondered. Fewer worries.

I remained in their control for years—no, decades—my supposed desires transmitted by my brother to your father without ever really consulting me, though in looking back, would I have said anything different? When your world is so constricted, do you not take the easiest path?

Your father, Narin (how tricky it is for me to say that name), for all his faults on the issue of our marriage, did want the best for me. He did try to persuade my parents to continue my education after he married again (to your mother) to ensure that I might have some independence. My mother did not see it that way, and my father concurred again.

Funny, isn't it, that my divorce, a legal proceeding to free me of a marriage I had never enjoyed, also freed me from the control of my parents and my brother. Why? Because they were ashamed of my status as a divorcee, a sullied woman who would forever be a shame to their family. I was no longer welcome in my Chettapur home.

It was a revelation to me. It gave me the strength to leave there and do something by myself. Of course, I chose Madras because Elder-Brother Jaggie was there. I had to be practical until I attained full independence.

And truth to tell, I liked being in the same city as your father.

My independence grew. I got a job. Believe me, it was scut work for years, but I stayed with it until I became a manager after twenty years. I learned to read and write English (as this letter shows). It was strangely fulfilling, especially when I got a flat on my own in Durga Complex (with the reluctant help of Elder-Brother Jaggie) where I made friends for the first time, real friends, and took part in local activities. You should look up the full account of the tenant strike in *The India Times*. Maybe even your father would've been proud of the changed me.

Of course, I stopped writing to him when I was fifty. Fifty! The cusp of my independence.

So I felt complete.

I met you once.

You were there when I came to your father's house. Your mother wasn't. Convenient, and fateful, as I had not written to your father about my impending visit. Knowing his open visiting hours reserved for his patients, I arrived without warning, as I thought it not presumptuous, being almost one of that ilk myself.

But you were there. A twelve-year-old child, who looked up inquiringly (oh, that look, so like your father's) as you came out from behind a green-and-white curtain covering your nook under the stairs as I walked in, and stopped, staring at me (oh, not rudely, Vishram, not at all, just childishly). I flattered myself that you had an intuition of who I was. And coincidentally, as we looked at each other for a very long moment, your father escorted his previous patient out of the house, talking in a low voice, that voice I had not heard for so many years, if not decades; that voice I had never heard be so kind, so solicitous, so engaged. Engaged to the point he almost missed my presence as he saw the patient out, who was effusively thanking "Doc" for taking such good care of him.

And then he saw me, and he started, shocked, as he belatedly recognized my changed self after not having seen me for almost seventeen years.

What did he see then? Not the simpering and shy thirteen-year-old he had married. Not the still shy but somewhat more assertive sixteen-year-old he rejected from his bed and his embrace. Not the quiet eighteen-year-old woman at Madras Central Station who appended a "Write to me, husband," to her father's importunities. But an almost middle-aged woman of a certain girth, a certain repressed style, a certain bearing that spoke volumes about her life.

Still in shock, he realized you were also there, his twelve-year-old second child, the protectorate of his life, the one who knew nothing of this story. He perforce introduced me as your "Aunt Mina" and asked you to go upstairs because, I remember, the evening pop music program was about to begin on Radio Ceylon, and would you want to miss that?

You would not. You smiled. That smile, so like your father in his younger days, brought a pain to my heart. You left with no further thought of this mysterious Aunt M., whom you had never heard of before and never would see again. Without any knowledge of what I was to your father.

And why was I there?

I had asked myself that every step of the way from my tiny but comfortable flat in the Durga Complex to St. Peter's Road, many steps in the blissful heat, which I didn't resent. After all those years, after all those letters he wrote me, addressed to "Dear Madam," why was I on my way to visit the man I still felt for, the man I never knew? I couldn't answer that. Something drew me there, something that could not be brooked, could not be denied.

We sat in the entranceway, Dr. Narin Janappan and I, that sparse area with two doors, three wooden chairs, the intruding stairs, and the flapping privacy curtain. He didn't invite me into the living room—a telling point, wouldn't you agree, Vishram?

And what, after all this setup, did we talk about?

What was there to talk about?

He assumed, of course, that I was there to badger him once again about increasing my allowance.

As if it could have been that specific.

As if my feelings were only bound up in that paltry sum of money I noted in my bank every month.

No, I just wanted to see him. Narin. My husband, though not legally anymore, of course. The boy I had married and the man he had become. To see him once as he was, in his environment, with his child. To see him and imagine how it would have been if life could be re-written, if the wheels of time could be turned back, and I was the one who had been allowed to continue school, encouraged to do well, and enrolled in a prestigious college.

If I hadn't been relegated for years to a menial job connecting meaningless plastic components together day after endless day at Kilpathy Works Limited.

If we had been together.

If we'd had the child, the man-boy you'd become.

If we'd had the life I never could have.

I think of the line in John Greenleaf Whittier's poem:

For all sad words of tongue or pen,
The saddest are these: "It might have been."

Yours in affection,
Minalakshmi Janappan

P.S. There are many more details of my life you should know, but it's hard for me to continue. I have attached a chronology of events from June 1936 to now with notes. I hope you find it illuminating.

As Vishram shakily put the letter back, a wave of resentment washed over him at his father having withheld it. He searched for the attachment but couldn't find it. He wondered why his father (or mother?) had apparently thrown it away but kept the letter itself. The manila folder lay there in its fat and silent serenity, holding pages that told a story he could never have imagined, reproaching him for having failed to ferret out more details. It was a story of love and pain and redemption, which he'd grown up in complete ignorance of, an overprotected boy with a nagging sense of loss, an inadequacy of love, and detachment from his outwardly normal parents. The story made sense now, incomplete as it was, with one of the principals remaining forever a faint presence, a partial being, a woman profoundly mistreated.

There was a knock at the door as he was reconsidering the tempting bottle of scotch nestled in the refrigerator. He called out to ask who it was. There was no reply. He ignored it. Probably housekeeping. A second, more impatient knock forced his hand, and he went over to fling the door open.

Elena.

She released her Rollaboard, whose handle fell to the floor with a clunk, flashed a smile, and embraced the surprised Vishram.

She brushed his ear with her lips and whispered, "Now let's get this show on the road."

Author's Note on Names

Readers familiar with South Indian Brahmin names will note that the names here do not follow convention, which is, in order: family (or place-of-origin) name, father's name, "your" name.

Narin's father, therefore, is correctly named Venpuri Kanthikar Janappan (typically V. K. Janappan); Narin would be Venpuri Janappan Narinder (or V. J. Narinder); and his son, Vish, would be Venpuri Narinder Vishram.

A phrase such as "Saraswathi and Saranmathi married into the Janappan family" would be correct, but confusing, since the sisters married cousins of Narinder's father, who would have different "last" names.

Rather than risk confusing readers, I have chosen to convert the names to the first-name last-name form used in other parts of India, and, of course, in much of the world.

Acknowledgments

Many people have helped me with this book. Inspired by newly discovered facts about my family, I wrote a first draft with much invention, which might have been laughable to my first readers, but I received only positive responses. I thank Elizabeth Reagh, Susan Spencer, Ken Carlton, Maxine Reagh, Raza Mir, Deb Victoroff and my gen-Z son Dylan Reagh despite his acerbic comments.

An edit and a workshop with Heather Aimee O'Neill helped tighten up loose ends and improved things immensely. Again, I thank many of the above for rereading and commenting. Dr. Nergesh Tejani, also an early reader, helped me with the medical details in the book.

My interaction with my publisher (and editor), Bill Burleson, and Vicki Adang, has been nothing if not positive, and I thank them for making this part of a potentially fraught journey a smooth one.

About the Author

Chandru Murthi was born in India and has spent most of his life in the United States. He is an engineer and sustainability consultant by training. This left-brain activity has been counterbalanced by working in theatre for many years, maintaining a difficult-to-categorize blog, and writing this, his first novel.

This story is a highly fictionalized version of dysfunctional family history, which saved him from having to invent many major plot points.

A longtime resident of San Francisco, he has also lived in Brooklyn for almost two decades.

He is the author of the article, *The Poet, the Physicist, and the Immigrant*, a true story of the colorful characters involved in the creation of the first commercial database in the United States. He has just completed his second novel, an eco-thriller, *The Trouble With Waste*, set in New York City.